To Dream Again

Irene Northan was born on Tyneside, NE England and raised in Devon. Phyllida, published in 1976, was the first of 20 fiction titles and 1 non-fiction title written before her death in June 1993. Irene was a founding member of Brixham Writers' Circle, a member of the Romantic Novelists' Association, Librarian of Brixham Museum, and Reader for the South West Arts.

Also by Irene Northan

The Devon Sagas

To Dream Again
A Safe Haven
Daughter of the River

Irene
NORTHAN
To Dream Again

CANELO

First published in the United Kingdom in 1991 by Headline Book Publishing

This edition published in the United Kingdom in 2021 by

Canelo
Unit 9, 5th Floor
Cargo Works, 1-2 Hatfields
London, SE1 9PG
United Kingdom

Print ISBN 978 1 80032 493 0
Ebook ISBN 978 1 78863 321 5

This book is a work of fiction. Names, characters, businesses, organizations, places and events are either the product of the author's imagination or are used fictitiously. Any resemblance to actual persons, living or dead, events or locales is entirely coincidental.

Look for more great books at www.canelo.co

Printed and bound in Great Britain by Clays Ltd, Elcograf S.p.A.

Chapter One

Mercy Seaton ran down the lane, her skirts flying, her dusty boots slithering on half-hidden stones. Above her on top of the hedge-bank, small green sloes were already forming on the blackthorn bushes, and the spiny branches were a tangle of old man's beard and late honeysuckle. Mercy had no time to notice them. She had looked forward to this evening for weeks, to spending a few hours at the Regatta, the golden crown of summer, with its fair, its fireworks, its excitement; but today of all days she had had to work late. Her hand still felt hot and sore from wielding flat-irons, and her body, beneath her stays, was clammy with perspiration, but she did not slacken her pace.

It was the noise which brought her to a halt – raised voices, cat-calling, taunting. One voice sounding angrily above the rest was painfully recognizable.

Old Daddy Widecombe leaned over his gate curiously.

'Sounds like they'm on at your grandma again,' he said. 'You'd best get down there quick, Mercy, chile.'

She scarcely heard him, for she was already on her way, her heart pounding with dread at the thought of what she should find when she turned the corner. The scene which greeted her was distressingly familiar. Half a dozen village boys, their faces sharp with mischief, were surrounding their victim, teasing her relentlessly.

'A lady or a duchess, too drunk to know which – old Blanche Seaton piddled in a ditch,' they chanted as they circled her, their words accompanied by a steady shower of stones and dried cow-pats.

In their midst stood Mercy's grandmother. Her hair was in disarray, her feet planted apart as she tried desperately to retain her balance while with one hand she hit out wildly at her tormentors. Her other hand grasped a gin bottle as though her life depended on it.

'Yokels! That is what you are!' she yelled. 'You ought to be ashamed of yourselves!' The words were a little slurred but each one was enunciated carefully in the most well-bred of accents. Even when very drunk Blanche Seaton never forgot that she was a lady.

'We ought to be ashamed of ourselves! My! My!' one of the boys mimicked her. Then he ran forward and attempted to take the bottle from her. Blanche's fist caught him squarely on the nose, and at once blood gushed out, cascading down his face.

''Er 'it me!' he bellowed tearfully. 'The mean old cow's broke me nose!'

'Serves you right if she has, Georgie Hannaford!' cried Mercy, rushing up. 'It's no more than you deserve, attacking a poor old woman like that. Off you go, the lot of you, or I'll make your ears smart, and that's a promise!'

At the sound of Mercy's voice the boys retreated, but only enough to be out of reach.

'Oh look, 'tis Mercy! 'Ave mercy, Mercy!' they taunted, dancing round.

'Come to fetch your Gran, 'ave you?' demanded one. 'Where's yer carriage, then? What's the matter, did yer coachman fall asleep?'

'The King's coming to tea, is 'e?' demanded another. 'Your Lizzie'll know 'ow to keep un 'appy. I'll bet.' And he wiggled his hips suggestively while the others roared with laughter.

These were old jibes. Mercy had heard them often enough before, yet they still stung her. She fought to keep her expression calm.

'That's about your level, Billy Dawe,' she retorted. 'Attacking old women and making coarse jokes. Your Ma must be really proud of you.'

Billy responded by pelting her with mud. His action encouraged his companions and soon Mercy and her grandmother were ducking under a hail of missiles.

'Stop it! Stop it!' Mercy rushed at Billy.

He ducked under her arm. As he did so one of the other boys ran behind her back and kicked Blanche in the shins. At her grandmother's cry of pain Mercy spun round and caught the culprit by his hair.

'Ow! Let go!' the boy yelled, his face screwed up with pain. He tried to kick her too. Mercy held him at arm's length and tightened her grip.

'Go on, go away, all of you!' she cried.

The boys hesitated and one made a move towards her. She clenched her fist tighter and her prisoner gave a yell.

'I'm warning you, I'll pull harder,' she declared.

'Oh go, blast 'ee!' shrieked the boy. 'She'm pulling my hair out by the roots!'

Reluctantly the others moved away. Only when they were out of sight did Mercy loose her hold, and the snivelling boy shuffled away rubbing his head. Just before he turned the corner, however, he bent down swiftly and picked up a stone. It caught Mercy a glancing blow on the arm.

Wincing with pain, she was annoyed to find she was shaking. It was silly to let a few stupid louts unnerve her so, they were a pretty cowardly bunch, but it was not fear which distressed her. It was the fact that her grandmother had been the butt of the scum of the village yet again. Oh why did she do it? It was bad enough that she made herself so unpopular with her high and mighty ways, but why did she have to invite ridicule too by getting so hopelessly drunk?

Blanche was sitting on the ground now, her legs sticking out stiffly in front of her, her arms clasped around the bottle.

Mercy went over to her. 'Are you all right, Gran?' she asked.

Slowly Blanche looked up. Her dark eyes, glassy with drink, were disapproving.

'If you are addressing me you will refer to me as Grandmother,' she said haughtily. Then she added condescendingly, 'Though I have no objections to being called Grandmamma at times.'

Mercy sighed. It was too much to expect Blanche to thank her for her concern.

'Are you all right, Grandmother?' she repeated. 'Here, let me help you up.'

'I think I prefer to remain where I am,' said Blanche with ponderous dignity. She hugged the bottle more tightly to her bony bosom. It was full. In spite of having no stopper she had not let one drop of gin spill during the scuffle.

Mercy wondered where she had got the money from for drink. It was always a mystery where she got the money, but then, quite a few things about Blanche were a mystery.

'You can't sit here in the dirt,' coaxed Mercy. 'Come on, let me help you up and we'll go home.'

'I shall sit wherever I choose.' An obstinate note had entered Blanche's voice.

Oh no, please don't let her be awkward, not now, Mercy silently pleaded.

She knew all too well how difficult Blanche could be when the mood took her, and it was always she, Mercy, who had to cope, for Ma and Lizzie were afraid of Blanche's sharp tongue and domineering ways. Joey was too young, and as for Pa... Well, when did he care about anything other than his own pleasure? He preferred to spend all his time in the Oak. His mother could sit in the lane until eternity, he would never lift a finger to help.

'Please, Gran – Grandmother,' begged Mercy.

But there was no response. In desperation she tried to lift the old woman. Blanche simply went rigid, making any attempt to remove her impossible. Mercy knew better than to go for assistance; no one in the village would be over-eager to help Blanche. Instead, she pulled and heaved strenuously without result, until exhaustion and frustration forced her to stop.

'You're an obstinate old fool!' she cried. 'I've half a mind to leave you here.'

She knew she would not. Her grandmother was a difficult woman at the best of times, at worst she was drunken, dirty and argumentative; yet Mercy had a sneaking regard for her. No, more than that, she was fond of the old harridan. She had such spirit; and when she was sober and in a good mood – rare events both – she would tell wonderful stories about her girlhood. Many people in the village reckoned that her claims to be of good birth were the result of too much alcohol on a fertile imagination. Mercy was inclined to agree. She had the doubtful privilege of being Blanche's favourite grandchild. She shared a bed with her, and she knew there was a consistency about her stories which rang true - stories of elegant living and servants, but these were details any housemaid would know. The idea that Blanche was of high birth was too ludicrous to contemplate.

There were some things which Blanche never mentioned, however, no matter how confiding she was or how drunk. She never told who her family were, nor what catastrophe had driven her to eke out an existence in a mouldering overcrowded cottage in Devon; and no one, not even Mercy, dare ask her.

Mercy eased her aching back ready for one more attempt to move her grandmother. As she did so she heard the sound of booted feet hurrying down the lane. She straightened defensively, thinking that her tormentors had returned. When she saw the familiar figure she could have wept with relief.

'Joey! Thank goodness!'

Her youngest brother came hobbling towards her, his clumsy hobnailed boots seeming too heavy for his thin legs.

'What's been happening?' he demanded.

'Nothing unusual,' she replied bitterly. 'Some of the lads have been on at Gran and now she's gone all difficult. I can't move her.'

'Don't worry, I'll lend a hand. Mr Miracle himself is here! I'll take this arm, you take the other. Now, come on, Gran, ups-a-daisy. Sam Prout's cows'll be along any minute and you don't want them wiping their feet on you, do you? Goodness knows, you smell as though they've been through here already.'

'Joey!'

Mercy tried to sound reproving, but it was no use, she could never be stern with him. From the day he was born Joey had been able to twist her round his little finger. For all he was so thin he had surprising strength, and together they were able to get Blanche to her feet and half carry, half drag her back to the cottage that was home to them all.

'Idn't 'ee ready yet? Where'm you bin?'

The questions came from a girl who was sitting on the garden gate, idly swinging to and fro. She was dressed with some pretension to fashion; the plum-coloured dress, as it strained to keep her generous curves in check, was adorned with too many bows and flounces to be stylish; and her straw hat, decorated with a spectacular bunch of crimson feathers, could have been considered vulgar. For all that, though, her pretty face was good-humoured as she addressed Mercy.

'The Regatta... ! Oh, I'm sorry, Dolly, I'd forgotten. We've had a bit of trouble.'

'So I sees!' Dolly eyed the dung-bespattered Blanche warily.

'Look, I'll be a while yet... In fact, I'm not sure I can come. You go on without me.'

'I'll wait. Twouldn't be no fun without 'ee. Us'll catch the next omnibus, that's all.'

'Are you sure? I'll be as quick as I can.'

Mercy flashed a harassed smile at her friend as she and Joey dragged Blanche up the garden path. As they passed Dolly, however, the old lady raised her head.

'You are a trollop!' she declared loudly. 'You dress like one. You act like one.'

Dolly jumped back off the gate. 'There idn't no call for you to say that, Mrs Seaton,' she protested.

'Take no notice. She's had a bit of a shock. She doesn't mean it,' said Mercy hastily, although both she and Dolly knew better. A more waspish soul would have pointed out that Blanche's shock was probably connected more with the gin bottle she still firmly clasped, but Dolly was too kind-hearted.

''Tis all the same to me. I don't pay no 'eed,' she said cheerfully and climbed placidly back on the gate to continue her wait.

A familiar musty, foetid smell greeted Mercy and Joey as they entered the cottage. Damp had been seeping into the cob walls for generations, covering everything with a greeny-black mould, and one sun-drenched August day was not enough to dry it out. Mercy did blench, however, at the cloud of flies which droned its way from the slop-bucket to the table where the remains of the dinner lay congealing on dirty plates. Her mother and her sister, Lizzie, sat drinking tea, oblivious to the squalor. Although they looked up as the trio shuffled in, neither rose nor made any effort to help.

''Er be all right?' asked Ma apprehensively, more because she was afraid of her mother-in-law than through any concern for her.

'She will be when we get her to bed,' replied Mercy.

There was still no offer of help.

Somehow she and Joey pushed and pulled the old woman up the narrow staircase and laid her on the bed. Then with a dexterity born of long practice Mercy pulled off Blanche's boots, eased the stained dress over her head and undid her stays. Her grandmother fell back on to the pillow and began to snore. Her skin was sallow and wrinkled, like that of a plucked chicken, and the spirit and vigour which made her so formidable when she was awake had gone. Lying there in her soiled flannel petticoat and equally grubby chemise she looked what she was – a dirty, drunken old woman. Mercy looked down at her with irritation tinged with pity. For the hundredth time she wondered what had brought her grandmother to such a state. She longed to peel off those filthy undergarments and give them a good wash, but she knew better than to try. Blanche was none too fond of soap and water, and she could show her disapproval most violently and when least expected.

The tiny attic was already like an oven, and now the room was filled with the stench of gin, cow-dung, and unwashed flesh. A sudden wave of fatigue swept over Mercy. Everything about her seemed so squalid and sordid. Surely life was not meant to be like this? Surely it had something better to offer? She felt she was too weary to go out now; only the thought of Dolly waiting patiently goaded her into getting ready.

She had hoped for a longer, more elaborate toilette – incongruously, toilette was one of her grandmother's words – thankfully she had already laid out her best serge skirt and clean white blouse that morning. Cold water on her skin revived her, and putting on fresh clothes made her feel better. She had little time to do more than scoop her dark hair on to the top of her head and anchor it with hairpins and put on her hat. She was pleased with the hat. It was far from new. She had taken ages retrimming it with swirls of cheap pink veiling, and – a great extravagance – a huge pink artificial rose. Looking at herself in the broken fragment of mirror she felt satisfied. Every minute spent on the hat had been worth it; it made her look soft, almost ethereal, and emphasized her brown eyes. Excitement began to stir in her. She felt pretty and it was Regatta time. For a couple of hours she could forget about home, perhaps pretend that she was someone quite different, more elegant, more genteel.

Gingerly carrying Blanche's soiled dress she hurried downstairs to find Ma and Lizzie still sitting, the tea grown cold and grey in their unwashed cups. They got on well together those two, happy to accept their lot and unwilling to make any effort to improve things. Indolent and sluttish, their lives revolved around tea and gossip, interspersed with brief periods of activity when jobs got started but seldom finished.

'Goin' out?' Ma asked unnecessarily. 'It'll be time to come back afore 'ee gets there.'

'We'll be in time for the fireworks and the fair. They are the main things. Can you give Gran's dress a wash; it's all messed up?'

Mercy held out the garment, but Lizzie turned her head away.

'I don't want un,' she said vehemently. 'The smell turns my stomach, I've been that bad all day.'

Mercy did not ask what was wrong with her. She did not need to, not with the way Lizzie had been vomiting into the chamber-pot every morning lately.

'Well, how about you, Ma?'

Ma looked vaguely over her shoulder in the direction of an insanitary collection of bowls and pails. 'Oh, put un to soak over there. I'll do un later,' she said.

Mercy knew what that meant. The dress would stay soaking until the smell became too much, the bucket was needed for something else, or until she tackled it herself.

'Idn't you going to' 'ave no tea? There's a bit of cold bacon 'ere.'

Ma meant well, but Mercy took one look at the greasy meat with its attendant bluebottles and suppressed a shudder.

'Thanks. I'll just take a bit of bread and cheese with me,' she said.

Dolly was still waiting.

'At last!' she exclaimed as Mercy hurried from the cottage. 'Yer, I like your 'at! Is that the veiling you got from the market?'

'Yes, that's where the smart people shop, all the carriage trade.'

Dolly gave a chuckle then said admiringly, 'Well, no one'd know 'ee didn't buy it at Williams and Cox's, unless you tell un. But then, you allus turns 'eads.'

'And you mean you don't? You have to fight the men off with a stick.'

'Oo said anything about fighting?' asked Dolly roguishly.

And they both laughed. Dolly could always make Mercy laugh. For all she was brash and not overparticular where she bestowed her favours, she hadn't a mean bone in her body. It was impossible to be miserable for long in her company.

Together the girls trudged up the lane towards the main road, their skirts hitched up to keep them out of the red dust. Mercy ate the bread and cheese as she walked, and the nourishment added to her feeling of well-being.

Torquay was drawing the crowds like a glittering magnet. On the Newton road horse-drawn traffic mingled with the new-fangled motorized transport, causing much tossing of heads and nervous shying from the animals. The omnibus, when it came, was already full, though both girls managed to squeeze on board for the couple of miles to Torquay. For Mercy the ride alone was part of the excitement of the evening. Buses were an extravagance she could rarely afford. Tonight, however, was special and among the pennies hoarded for her evening's entertainment she had carefully laid aside some for her fare.

The crowds were such that the bus had slowed to a walking pace long before they reached the Strand.

'Oh, let's get off 'ere. Us'll do better on foot.' Dolly's face was bright with anticipation.

'Very well.'

'Yer, let me catch 'old of your arm, else us'll be parted!' exclaimed Dolly, gripping Mercy as the crowd swirled round them. 'Lor', did you ever see such folk? The world 'n' 'is wife be 'ere, seemingly. Oh, Mercy, look 'tis there! The fair!' Her fingers tightened their grip in her excitement, making Mercy wince.

'Mind what you're doing,' she protested, laughing. 'I'll be black and blue.'

'Sorry… Oh, come on, let's get over there quick.' The brilliant lights and the breathy discord of steam-organs attracted Dolly, but Mercy firmly pulled her in the opposite direction.

'Later,' she said. 'The fair will be there for a while, never fear. Let's find somewhere to stand for the fireworks first.'

'Us idn't going to see much among this lot,' complained Dolly, still drawn to the excitement of the fair yet appreciating the sense of her friend's words.

Mercy was forced to agree with her, and she raised her head to look for a vantage point. Together the girls drifted with the current of bodies towards the pier, then Mercy exclaimed, 'Look up there! We'd have a marvellous view from there.' She pointed to the solid mass of the Rock Walk above them, facing the sea.

'Gawd, I idn't going up there! I idn't no bloody fly!' protested Dolly, who disliked unnecessary exercise.

'Come on, there are steps we can go up.'

''Tis too steep. There idn't no room, either; do you see all they folk up there?'

Dolly kept on raising objections as Mercy steered her relentlessly towards the Walk.

They made their way upward in the gathering dusk, taking the narrow paths and steep steps with Dolly protesting and puffing all the way. Many people had chosen this particular viewpoint, but somehow the girls managed to squeeze themselves into a space on a rustic bridge which clung to the cliff face. From the bridge they could see everything – the fair, the great sweep of Torbay and, best of all, the pier, from which at any moment the firework display would begin.

'There, isn't this worth the climb?' demanded Mercy.

''Ee do 'ave good ideas sometimes,' agreed Dolly grudgingly. 'But I idn't 'alf in a muck sweat.'

Mercy laughed. Clinging to the handrail she looked down to the road below, where there was such a press of bodies that a tram trying to clank its way along the sea front had given up the unequal struggle and remained stranded, like some antediluvian monster, in a sea of summer hats. Everyone was good-humoured, even the besieged tram driver, who was placidly lighting his pipe. It was as though the Regatta had spread a special sort of magic over everything.

In the darkness Mercy savoured the beauty of the night. How she wished she could keep it for ever, captured behind a picture frame or beneath one of the glass domes that covered waxed fruit. While others fidgeted, impatient for the fireworks to start, she gazed about her, taking in each detail to hoard like a miser's treasure for the future. Out beyond the bay the Channel stretched black and infinite; closer to shore there were so many lights from the yachts riding at anchor that it was hard to tell where the land stopped and the sea began.

Although winter was the usual time for the gentry to come to Torquay, for two days in August they returned for the sailing. Mercy loved to see these wealthy people – the smart gentlemen in brass-buttoned blazers and cheese-cutter caps, and the elegant ladies in huge hats like overblown flowers. Beautiful beings who led beautiful lives, who did not have to break their backs every day wielding flat-irons.

Mercy gazed towards where the grand yachts danced at anchor. Just supposing Blanche's stories were true, she thought. Someone from my family could be on board one of those, someone important and wealthy. And what if they discovered who I am and invited me to visit them? It was an impossible dream, but pleasant enough to blur the reality of the crowds and the darkening night sky...

'They'm still lookin' at us!' Dolly's voice broke in.

Mercy started at this rude interruption of her thoughts.

'Who are?' she asked.

'Lor', 'ee don't take notice of nothin', do 'ee? They two swells down there. They keep lookin' at us.'

'Ignore them. We don't want strange men pestering us,' said Mercy firmly.

Then curiosity got the better of her and she looked down. The steep slope was newly clothed with palms, magnolias, ilexes, and flowering cherries, which were still immature. On the crowded terrace below everyone was looking towards the sea, waiting for the first sign of the fireworks. Only two faces gazed upwards. Even in the gloom she could see that they were both male and young. At the sight of Mercy leaning over they waved their straw boaters with exaggerated gallantry.

'How impertinent!' exclaimed Mercy, drawing back abruptly.

''Ee don't 'alf sound like your Gran sometimes,' chuckled Dolly. ''Ow impertinent!' she mimicked. 'That's 'er ladyship to a T.'

'You wouldn't talk like that if she could hear you,' grinned Mercy.

'You'm right there, I've no fancy for a slice of 'er tongue, thanks. Oh my gawd!'

Dolly finished with a shrill squawk as a rocket shot skywards and exploded with an ear-splitting bang which reverberated round the cliffs, setting up the seagulls for miles. A spontaneous groan of approval burst from thousands of throats as golden stars cascaded into the bay. Mercy was so entranced she forgot the impudent young men. She was transported to a different world, filled with light, colour, and beauty. All too soon the set piece at the end of the pier exploded into life.

'Can 'ee make it out?' demanded Dolly. 'I can't see what 'tis. Yes I can! Tis the King and Queen. Idn't that 'andsome? Good old Teddy and Alex!'

Dolly's triumphant shout was drowned by the welter of cheers which broke from the crowd; then the foghorns and hooters of every craft in the bay sounded, adding to the pandemonium. At last the cacophony died down and the people began to move.

'Ah…Tis the end. What a shame!' said Dolly. 'Which way do us go down?'

'I'm not sure,' replied Mercy. 'There seems to be a slope over there, but it will take us out of our way.'

'Us don't want that,' said Dolly firmly. 'Us wants to get to the fair as quick as possible.'

'Then, we'll go down the steps.'

'Not they steps us come up?' wailed Dolly. 'I'll never manage they in the dark.'

'We appear to have arrived in the nick of time,' said a masculine voice. 'May we be of assistance to you ladies?'

Two young men confronted them, the very two from the terrace below. They had somehow managed to push their way against the human tide on the narrow path. In their brightly coloured blazers and white flannels and with their straw boaters set at identically jaunty angles, they were a typical pair of mashers, young toffs out for some fun.

Mercy felt shy of them, and a little wary. 'Thank you, we do not need any assistance,' she said politely.

Dolly had other ideas. 'Yes, us do!' she declared. 'Us wants to get off this danged cliff but us don't fancy the steps in the dark.'

There was such an open invitation in her tone that Mercy squirmed inwardly. 'Oh, Dolly,' she breathed reprovingly. 'We don't know them.'

'And us never will if 'tis left to 'ee,' replied Dolly in a whisper that was all too audible.

'In that case may I be permitted to help one of you young ladies down?' The first young man held out his hand.

Mercy backed away. He was darkly good-looking and there was something a little too bold and self-assured about his manner for her taste.

Dolly had no such qualms, she accepted his hand and the pair of them began to descend.

'If you won't let me help you at least let me lead the way.' It was the second young man who spoke. He was quieter than his friend and his voice was good-humoured. 'Otherwise you'll have to stay here until morning, which sounds jolly uncomfortable. You had better follow me. Don't worry, there aren't many steps, mainly sloping paths.'

Mercy was still unsure. Dolly and her escort were almost out of sight, however, so she had no alternative but to accept the young man's help. Although the descent was really quite easy, as they reached the bottom Dolly was determined to make the most of it.

'I don't know what us'd 'ave done if 'ee 'adn't come along,' she declared dramatically.

'We were only too delighted to help, weren't we, Lisburne, old man?' replied the dark young man. 'Surely you'll give us the pleasure of your company for a little longer? Can't we escort you somewhere?'

'Don't 'ee talk 'andsome?' Dolly beamed. Then she added winsomely, 'Us was goin' to the fair, supposin' us ever gets through the crush.'

'To the fair it is, then,' said the darker of the two.

Mercy was in an agony of embarrassment. They could not go off with two young men they had just met! Gentlemen they might claim

12

to be but the bold eyes of the dark one were flickering rather too appreciatively over Dolly, taking in every voluptuous curve.

'I'm afraid we can't let perfect strangers escort us anywhere,' she said, surprised at her own firmness.

'I assure you we aren't perfect,' replied the dark young man, his eyes still devouring Dolly, who let out a delighted shriek and thumped him amiably.

Mercy gave a resigned sigh, not at all happy at the way things were going.

'Perhaps if we introduced ourselves?' suggested the other young man. 'Then, at least, we won't be complete strangers. I'm Peter Lisburne. And this reprobate is Frederick Parkham.'

'Freddie to my friends,' added his companion.

''Ow d'ye do?' Dolly said formally. 'I be Dolly Dyer – *Miss* Dolly Dyer.'

'No, not really?' Freddie Parkham looked at her in delight. 'Jolly Dolly Dyer, eh?'

'Yer! What be wrong with my name?' demanded Dolly defensively.

'Absolutely nothing. It is delightful,' Freddie assured her.

'That be all right, then,' said Dolly mollified somewhat. 'Be us goin' to that fair or baint us?'

The pair of them moved away, never bothering to see if the other two were following. Soon they were swallowed up by the crowd and only the scarlet feathers of Dolly's hat marked their progress.

Peter Lisburne looked down at Mercy. 'It seems we're going to the fair,' he said. 'Would you object if I escorted you?'

The scarlet feathers were bobbing further and further away, soon they would be out of sight completely.

'Oh, very well,' replied Mercy. Then she realized she had sounded ungracious. It was not that she disliked the company of young men, far from it; and Peter Lisburne was certainly attractive with his fair hair and athletic build; but he and his friend came from a different world – the world Blanche talked about. Her grandmother's stories, fanciful though they were, had made Mercy all too aware of the difference between their way of life and her own. And now she was overcome with awkwardness, not certain what to say or do.

'Thank you, you are very kind,' she added, speaking carefully in imitation of Blanche's well-bred tones. 'Please, Mr Lisburne, can we hurry or we'll lose Dolly and your friend?'

It was no easy matter moving through the sea of bodies. At last Peter said, 'I'm afraid we have lost Freddie and Miss Dyer for the moment. We'll soon find them at the fair.'

Mercy felt less optimistic. She knew Dolly of old, and she suspected that her friend was quite happy to be lost if she were in the company of a presentable man.

For some reason the crowd came to a standstill, solid and impenetrable.

'Look, it's useless trying to get through this. Let's make for the Princess Gardens,' suggested Peter.

Mercy allowed herself to be guided across the road to the gardens which skirted the outer harbour. It was quieter here, though many people were strolling along the gravel paths. Fairy lights had been lit, so that glowing pinpoints of flickering colour edged each lawn and flower-bed. Mercy was enchanted.

'Oh, this is lovely!' she exclaimed. 'It's— it's like something out of a fairy story...' She stopped, fearing that she had said something foolish.

But her companion replied, 'It is, isn't it? You'd think we could come across the Sleeping Beauty, or maybe find the Princess looking for her Frog Prince in the fountain over there.'

Mercy laughed at his nonsense. Peter smiled back. It was a nice smile that gleamed beneath his blond moustache – in fact, his whole face was pleasing. Not as dashing as Freddie Parkham's perhaps, nevertheless, it was one where laughter was never far away. She noted with approval that it also lacked his friend's over-bold, almost predatory expression.

'I'm glad you laughed,' he said. 'I was afraid you weren't enjoying being in my company.'

'I'm sorry if I've seemed rude!' exclaimed Mercy in distress. 'It's simply— well, we've only just met, and I don't want you to get the wrong impression of me.'

'Let me assure you that you haven't been at all rude. And as for getting the wrong impression, never for one moment did I think you were... were...'

'A flighty piece?' supplied Mercy.

'Exactly!' Peter laughed, delighted at the description. 'You know, I'm the one who is at a disadvantage.'

'How?'

'You know my name – I don't think you have told me yours.'

'Oh, it's Mercy Seaton.'

'Mercy! That's a lovely name.'

'Do you think so?' She looked at him sharply, suspecting he was laughing at her. To her surprise she saw that he meant it. 'I don't like it. People make so many jokes about it. And besides, I don't know anyone else called Mercy. It was my grandmother who chose my name, and no one dared to argue because she is rather formidable...' Formidable was a word she had read in a book, and she decided that it suited Blanche perfectly. Now when she spoke she pronounced it with great care.

'Well, good for formidable grandmothers,' declared Peter. 'Ah, we're nearly there.'

'At last!' breathed Mercy. 'I've been so looking forward to the fair.' She did not mean him to hear her exclamation, but he did.

'This is your first visit? You didn't come last night?'

'No, I couldn't get away,' said Mercy with dignity, though the truth was that she could not afford to come for two nights.

'I suppose you work.' Peter said the words with surprise, as if such a thought had just occurred to him.

'Yes, I work in a shop, a high-class dress shop.'

Now why had she said that? What difference did it make if Peter Lisburne knew she worked in a laundry? She felt angry with herself for being so silly – and thankful that her cheap cotton gloves prevented her workraw hands from betraying the truth.

It had taken them quite a time to make their way from the Rock Walk to the Strand; then with a suddenness that was breath-taking they were at the fair. Their eyes were assaulted by myriad lights from the harsh naphtha flares and their ears were stunned by the music from the steam-organs. To Mercy it was all wonderful, and she gazed about, her eyes bright, her cheeks flushed.

'Where shall we start, Miss Seaton?' asked Peter, who had been watching her evident pleasure.

'The roundabout! The Golden Gallopers! I always start on they—' she cried, then stopped. It was not her lapse from well-bred speech which had caused her concern. 'I'll pay for myself, of course. I'd prefer it,' she said hastily.

'And I would prefer it if you didn't.' Peter turned and faced her. 'You are doing me a great favour just being with me; it would be no fun alone, I assure you.'

'But you came with your friend.'

'If he hadn't met jolly Miss Dolly, he would have met someone else. He always does.'

'Then why did you come to the fair if you expected to be by yourself?' Mercy was determined not to be swayed by his arguments.

'If you want the truth, to avoid an appallingly tedious dinner party at home. Being here with you is infinitely better than that. I am greatly in your debt, so you must let me do something to redress the balance.'

His face was unexpectedly serious, so serious that she hadn't the heart to refuse him.

'If you are sure…' she said, and saw his expression relax.

'Absolutely sure! You wish to try the Golden Gallopers, you say? Right, let's find them.'

How long she had waited for this evening, but even in her most ambitious imaginings she had never dreamed of such an escort! She had never met anyone like him before. Although she addressed him as Mr Lisburne, already she thought of him as Peter. The well-bred, nameless gentlemen who peopled Blanche's stories she had pictured as cool and haughty, but Peter wasn't a bit like that. Once her initial shyness had worn off she found him easy to talk to. She liked his manners, too; he was always so proper, calling her 'Miss Seaton', and being concerned that she was enjoying herself. He treated her like a fragile being, and Mercy felt cosseted – a rare and very pleasurable experience for her.

His self-assurance impressed her. So this was what wealth and position gave you, confidence and a knowledge of your own worth! Mercy had never realized it before; she had only considered riches to be a means of keeping warm and nicely dressed and having plenty to eat. She was surprised to discover that there was more to it.

Together they sampled everything the fair had to offer. Mercy grew concerned at the amount of money Peter was spending on her. When she protested he was quite astonished.

'But I'm spending nothing,' he declared. 'Just a few pennies here and there. What's the point of coming if we don't try things?'

He was so enthusiastic, and clearly enjoying himself so much, she didn't like to raise the subject again. At the hoopla stall he declared he would win her a prize, and to his delight he did indeed win a tin of butterscotch. The fact that it had cost him far more in hoopla rings than it would have done in a shop did not worry him.

'Look, it's got roses on, to match your hat,' he observed as he presented it to her.

Peter's confident manner wavered only once, when he had met some people whom he knew. Mercy was conscious of hard, disapproving stares in her direction, and would have tried to melt into the background, but Peter firmly took her arm. Raising his boater with a flourish he said, 'I don't think you know Miss Seaton, do you?' There was an air of bravado about him when he spoke which reminded her of her brother, Joey, who always put a bold face on it when he was caught doing something wrong. And I suppose I'm the something wrong in this case, thought Mercy. His family are going to have something to say when they hear that he's been out with a common working girl.

At last the haughty woman and her party swept away, muttering something about it getting late.

'Is it?' asked Mercy in alarm after they had gone. 'Late, I mean? The omnibus goes at half past eleven.'

'You needn't bother about the omnibus. I'll take you home in a cab—'

'No thank you,' she cried, horrified. The thought of Peter seeing where she lived was too terrible to contemplate. Then she added more calmly, 'You've been so kind already. I must catch the omnibus. Dolly might be there and without me she wouldn't have anyone to walk home with.'

To her relief he did not argue, instead he consulted his gold pocket-watch.

'If that is what you really want then I won't insist. But it is only a quarter to; we've time to have something to eat before you disappear like Cinderella. Where would you like to go?'

'Somewhere quiet, please,' said Mercy, remembering the encounter with the haughty woman, 'if you're sure…'

'I am quite sure. I have not the slightest intention of parting from you one second earlier than I must. Besides, I'm starving.'

'Me too,' agreed Mercy.

'Good, that's what I like to hear.'

They found a small restaurant in Torwood Street, well away from the crowds at the fair. Mercy had read somewhere that in London these days it was considered very smart for ladies to dine out late in the evening. Now she was doing just that. She tried hard to behave as though entering a restaurant was an everyday occurrence for her, but it was difficult. The cutlery, in particular, impressed her, laid out as it was with gleaming precision. And it all matched! So unlike the motley collection of implements which she was used to. The table-linen, too, was of such a snowy whiteness she had to restrain herself from showing a professional interest in how it had been laundered. Thoughts of the laundry reminded her of the lie she had told Peter. A small lie, it was true, but it cast a disproportionately large cloud over her enjoyment.

A waiter shook out her napkin for her and handed them both menus. Mercy thought he looked alarmingly dignified, but Peter was clearly quite undaunted. He scanned the list of dishes and said, 'We're in rather a hurry. What do you recommend?'

'The lamb cutlets are extremely good, sir.'

'Would you like the cutlets?' Peter asked her. She nodded her head. 'Very well, we'll have the lamb, please, and hurry. Oh, and bring a bottle of the Bordeaux—' Peter suddenly looked at her quizzically, then said, 'On second thoughts, bring a bottle of Muscadel... Have you ever had wine before?' he asked when the waiter hurried away.

'No, never.'

'Then I think you will like this one I've chosen. It's sweet.'

Mercy was struck by his thoughtfulness, choosing a wine to appeal to her taste sooner than his own. Such consideration prompted her to confide, 'I've never had lamb cutlets, either.'

His brows rose in astonishment. 'Haven't you?' His expression turned into a beam of pleasure. 'Then I'm happy I'm the one to introduce you to two new experiences – wine and lamb cutlets...You really are an extraordinary young lady, you know. Not many girls would have been so honest. But I'm glad you are. I shall watch you eat your supper with all the more pleasure.'

As he mentioned her honesty Mercy hurriedly put her gloved hands out of sight in her lap, as if to hide away her lie.

When the meal arrived it was not the decision of which knife and fork to use which prompted near-panic inside her, she knew she had only to follow Peter's example – it was the fact that if she took off her gloves to eat she would reveal the coarseness of her hands. In the end she attempted to eat with her gloves on, though her fingers slipped on the polished cutlery.

'Wouldn't you be more comfortable if you took your gloves off?' asked Peter gently.

For a moment she wondered what to do – suddenly her deceit seemed so silly. She liked him very much; he was amusing and good-humoured, above all, he was kind; it didn't seem right to tell him even the smallest of lies. Putting down her knife and fork Mercy pulled off her gloves.

'I haven't been truthful with you,' she said.

'Haven't you?' Peter looked at her warily.

'No. I don't work in a shop. It was a stupid lie. I suppose I wanted to impress you. I work in a laundry. I do ironing...'

She waited, tense in case he was angry.

All he said was, 'Do you really? That must be awfully hard work,' in a tone which combined sympathy with curiosity. For the first time it occurred to Mercy that this evening was as much a novelty for Peter as it was for her.

'I don't suppose you've had supper with a laundress before?' she asked. And was gratified when he grinned at her.

'No, I haven't. What an evening this is for firsts! It won't be the last, will it? If you would not object...'

It was there again, the youthful uncertainty masked by pretty speeches. Mercy caught her breath, not quite believing what she had heard.

'You would like to see me again?' she asked.

'Yes, very much. Would tomorrow...?'

'I must work tomorrow.'

'Ah, yes, I had forgotten.'

He stroked the rough skin on her hand with cool fingers. Mercy had never seen a man with such hands, long and slim, with clean manicured nails. She sat very still in case any action others should spoil the beauty of the moment.

'I'm off this Saturday, in the afternoon,' she said at last.

'Then, Saturday it is! At about two-thirty? Shall I come to fetch you or would you prefer us to meet somewhere else, the Strand, for example?'

So he had noticed her reluctance for him to come to her home. Grateful for this consideration Mercy replied thankfully, 'The Strand would be best, I think.'

'Good.' Peter smiled at her and released her hand with obvious reluctance. 'Perhaps we had better finish our supper, unless you want to miss your omnibus.'

The wine should have tasted like nectar, the lamb cutlet like ambrosia from the gods, but Mercy hardly noticed them. Her attention was all for Peter. At that moment nothing else existed. She must have eaten the meal, however, and drunk the wine, for Peter rose. He dropped a pile of coins on the table in a casual manner, which would have made Mercy gasp at any other time, but on this occasion she was completely absorbed by her companion and by bewilderment that anything like this should be happening to her. It was the sort of situation she had dreamed of. It didn't, it couldn't be happening in real life, could it?

Together they left the restaurant; hand in hand they hurried back through the thinning crowds to the fair. The omnibus, already full, was waiting for the last stragglers in the queue to squeeze themselves on board. Mercy caught sight of Dolly peering from the upper, looking to see where she had got to.

'Until Saturday,' said Peter as they reached the omnibus. Swiftly he raised her hand to his lips and kissed it. It was such a romantic gesture, and to Mercy it was the perfect climax to her evening.

The omnibus was already moving away as willing hands pulled her on to the platform. Looking back she saw Peter waving, then they turned the corner into Fleet Street and he was lost from sight.

It was the last omnibus, put on specially for the Regatta, and so packed with home-going revellers that Mercy had no chance of a seat. She did not mind; she was happy to stand, clutching her precious tin of butterscotch, reliving every moment of the evening as they chugged their way back up the Newton Road. When they reached the stop nearest to the village she got off and waited for Dolly to join her.

Dolly jumped down, more rosy and considerably more crumpled than when she had set out.

'Where'd 'ee get to, then?' she demanded jovially.

'We went to the fair and then had supper.' Mercy struggled to keep her voice casual, as if the evening had been nothing out of the ordinary. 'We didn't see much of you.'

'That's not what Freddie said,' giggled Dolly. She had been drinking, but she was not drunk.

'Well, at least, you should do your buttons up properly again after-wards,' said Mercy.

Dolly looked down at her plump bosom and gave a shriek of laughter. 'My, I'm at sixes and sevens, baint I?' she said, quite uncon-cernedly arranging her dress as they began to walk down the lane to the village. 'That Freddie, 'e was a real scream. Laugh! Us didn't stop all evenin'…! What was 'is friend like?'

'Very nice. I'm seeing him again on Saturday.'

'You baint!' Dolly stopped in astonishment. 'You sly maid! Well, don't do anythin' I wouldn't do. Mind, that'll give 'ee plenty of rope…' And she shrieked with laughter.

Mercy was glad her friend did not question her further. She was fond of Dolly but the beauty of the evening was too new and precious to be shared.

'Wait for me, you two!' a familiar voice called out behind them.

'Joey, where've you come from?' Mercy asked in surprise.

'I was on the omnibus. I went to the Regatta too!'

'Oh, Joey, me 'andsome, I forgot about 'ee,' said Dolly contritely. ''E was upstairs, with me.'

'Dolly paid my fare.'

''Twere nothin'. I 'aven't lashed out much this evenin'. I've bin treated all of the time – No, there aint no call for that,' demurred Dolly as Mercy took out her purse to repay her. 'Save it for a time when I be desperate – like Friday…' and she broke into fresh chuckles.

'Did you see 'em? Weren't they splendid?' demanded Joey.

'What? The fireworks?' asked Mercy.

'Oh, they were good, but I'm talking about the yachts. *The* yachts, the *Shamrock* and the *White Heather.* They were all lit up. Oh, I wish I could have seen 'em race! It would've been a lot more exciting than picking tiddies, I'm sure.'

'Picking potatoes,' Mercy corrected him automatically.

Joey ignored her. 'The *Shamrock* won, you know. Good old Tommy came out on top.'

'Tommy, eh? I didn't know you knew Sir Thomas Lipton personal,' teased Dolly. 'Fancy, King Edward's friend, Sir Thomas, being a friend of yorn, too.'

'We're great mates, didn't you know? He invited me in for a glass of champagne, but I said sorry, I've got to get 'ome…'

The final word disappeared in a huge yawn, and Joey suddenly leaned against Mercy, overcome with fatigue. She slipped her arm about his bony frame, and Dolly did likewise saying, 'There, boy, we'm cuddled up like pigs in a sty.'

The three of them stumbled their drowsy way down the dark lane, their mouths full of Mercy's butterscotch. The air was filled with the scents of honeysuckle and meadowsweet, and invisible creatures scuttled about in the hedgerows as they passed. It was all so far removed from the glittering activity of Torquay that Mercy thought she had imagined the whole evening. Only the cold surface of the butterscotch tin clasped in her hand proved to her that it had been real.

Dolly left them, taking the lane which led to the cottage she shared with her mother. Mercy and Joey continued on until they came to the familiar garden gate. Everything was in darkness. Once inside the kitchen Mercy groped for the lamp. The surge of its glow lit the squalor of the room and at the same time the musty stench assailed her nostrils.

Joey blinked sleepily in the light. 'I saw the fellow who set you to the omnibus,' he said. ''E was a real toff. You aren't seeing 'im again, are you?'

'Yes,' said Mercy, 'I am.'

'Oh…' was all Joey said, the one syllable expressing his disapproval.

Suddenly the difference between Peter's world and her own seemed to yawn like a black chasm, and for Mercy the enchantment of the evening disappeared. It had been a wonderful experience – but it wasn't meant to last. She would meet Peter again on Saturday, as she had promised, and that would have to be the end.

'Cab, sir?' asked a voice hopefully.

Peter shook his head. It was a beautiful night. He had not far to go so he decided to walk, not because he wanted the exercise but because he was reluctant to go home. It was the dread of having to play host at yet another of his mother's claustrophobic dinner parties that had driven him from the house. The thought of being charming to people he did not particularly like, of laughing at unfunny jokes, and, above all, of being under his mother's unwavering scrutiny for hours on end had been more than he could stand. However, having made his escape he must now return to face the consequences.

All the same, he had no regrets. He always enjoyed the unexpected, and the meeting with Mercy had been just that. She intrigued him, this lithe girl with hands like nutmeg graters and eyes as huge and dark as wet pansies. He had enjoyed being with her, to see her face light up with delight at the simplest things and to listen to her voice with its carefully corrected diction. Did laundresses usually speak like that? He thought not.

Peter walked away from the crowds, along roads lined with Italianate villas discreetly bounded by trees and stone walls. He was not aware of his pace slackening as he topped the rise and began the sharp descent towards his home. A carriage with its lights ablaze rumbled past him and turned into Hesketh Road. Laughter came from one house, the strains of a piano duet from another. The Regatta was exerting its lighthearted influence even here, among the most genteel and respectable of dwellings. Only the Villa Dorata remained silent and almost in darkness.

The Villa Dorata had been built by a cotton manufacturer with a passion for things Italian, whose fortune had been one of the casualties of the American Civil War. It had been at a time when Torquay was staking a vigorous claim to outshine the Mediterranean resorts, and Peter's grandfather, who had bought the property, had been quite content to live with the exuberantly Latin embellishments. The same could not be said for Peter's mother. When she took over, she had insisted upon the more suggestive statuary being removed. The external walls of rich gold that gave the villa its name she had had painted a more discreet cream. In doing so she had crushed the joyous soul of the house, or so it had seemed to Peter.

He trudged up the gravel drive, his ears filled with the sound of the sea on the beach below and the wind rustling the stiff leaves of the palms which lined his path. The porch lanterns were still lit, a silent rebuke to him for deserting his post. His feeling of contentment drained away.

'Good evening, sir.' Rogers, the butler, took Peter's boater. 'Mrs Lisburne would like to see you in her boudoir.'

'Surely not at this hour? Can't it wait until morning?'

'Madam said as soon as you came in, sir.'

With a terse nod Peter crossed the marble-tiled hall to the staircase. From behind the closed dining-room door he could hear the muffled sounds of the maids clearing away. He toyed with the idea of having a whisky before he went up, he had had very little to drink this evening, then decided against it. His mother would smell the alcohol on his breath and it would give her one more cause for disapproval.

He went upstairs and knocked at his mother's door. At once her maid opened it. Peter wished the servants were not quite so prompt, their efficiency always gave him the notion that the whole household was watching for him, waiting, checking up. It was silly, he knew; the truth was that his mother trained her staff well; nevertheless, he could not rid himself of the feeling. Shadowlike, the maid withdrew.

Mrs Lisburne looked up as he entered. She was sitting at her writing-table, her hair, once as golden as Peter's but now streaked with silver, was loose, lying in waves on the pink silk of her peignoir-clad shoulders. It occurred to Peter that dressed so informally she should have looked soft and feminine. Instead she seemed forbidding.

'Good evening, Mama,' he greeted her.

She made no immediate reply. At last she said, 'Haven't you forgotten something?'

Obediently he bent and pecked at her cheek. She accepted the kiss without emotion.

'It is a pity you did not stay home for dinner. We had a delightful evening,' she said. 'Without you we would have been thirteen at table. Fortunately Mrs Foster sent to say she was indisposed, so we were twelve after all.' Her voice was even, her tone reasonable, yet somehow her displeasure was evident. Peter wished she would fly into a rage with him, just once in a while. However, such was not Agnes Lisburne's way.

She went on, 'Of course, it was a little awkward not having a host, so Major Gifford, as your father's oldest friend, stepped into the breach admirably. "We must not blame Peter too much for not wanting to dine at home," he said. "After all, we're only young once." Wasn't that kind of him?'

Peter felt it was just the sort of unoriginal thing the major would say: he was a man who thought in cliches. Aloud he said, 'Yes, Mother, it was.' He knew the anecdote had been repeated not to make him feel more at ease; it was to remind him that yet again he had failed to do his duty. In spite of himself he felt the familiar sense of shame, which had dogged him since childhood, begin to settle in the pit of his stomach.

'Rose was looking particularly charming. She had on a new dress, I think. At least, I had never seen it before. Blue satin trimmed with bugle beads, very pretty. She seemed disappointed that you weren't at home. I rathershe had been looking forward to seeing you again.'

His mother hoped he would one day marry Major Gifford's only daughter, the heiress to a tidy fortune. She was a nice enough girl, though too pale and insipid for Peter's taste.

'I saw Rose yesterday evening at the Regatta Ball. I danced with her three times. Wasn't that enough?'

His mother refused to give him a reprieve. 'After showing her such marked attention one evening don't you think it was unkind to neglect her the next?'

'Marked attention? They were duty dances! We aren't living in the days of Queen Victoria now, Mother! Three dances can't be regarded as a declaration of undying love any more!'

'Not in your eyes, perhaps, but did you stop to think of how Rose considered it? Young men can be very thoughtless, I am afraid. I cannot expect you to be any different. I would be grateful if in future you would let me know if you will not be in to dinner, especially when we have guests. However, you obviously had an agreeable evening and that is all that matters.'

'But, Mother—'

'I do not think we need to talk about it any more, do you? Although it is very late, you know, I did not want to go to bed before you returned home.' Even when dismissing him there was reproof in her voice.

Peter left his mother's room submerged in the guilt she always instilled into him. He had never managed to come up to his mother's expectations, at least, certainly not since the death of his father.

To be honest Peter could recall his father only as a vague distant figure who had impinged rarely on his childhood, though he remembered clearly the day his father had died. He had been taken into his mother, sobbing bitterly, affected more by the sudden climate of grief among the servants than by any sorrow of his own. His mother had made no attempt to comfort him. Instead she had looked down at her son, a boy of seven years old, and said, 'Now that Papa has gone you are the man of the house. It is a great responsibility, I know, but you must always be aware of the duty you owe to Papa's memory and to me. I shall need your comfort, your support, and your love.' It had not been a plea nor a request but a demand. Peter's small shoulders had bowed beneath an unfair burden which had not lessened with the years.

For some time Peter sat cast down with gloom; then his misery became charged with resentment. It was ridiculous being so miserable. He had gone out and enjoyed himself instead of staying at home! He wasn't a child, he was twenty-two, a man who could do as he pleased.

His thoughts went back to Mercy, and he was surprised how quickly the memory of her face with its dark eyes came back to him, lifting his spirits.

His mother would not approve of Mercy, that was certain, and she was bound to find out soon enough that he had been seen in her company. In a strange way Peter both dreaded this discovery and looked forward to it. It would bring about the inevitable well-modulated recriminations, but it would also present a challenge. His choice of friends was something which his mother could not control; he was of age and able to go out with whom he wished, whatever his mother thought, a fact which garnished Mercy's attractions with all the desirability of forbidden fruit. He hadn't really meant to see her again, the words had seemed to come of their own volition, but once spoken he had not regretted them. He found her quite fascinating, this ordinary working girl who ironed other people's linen for a living.

Upon consideration he was very glad he was going to see her again on Saturday, it should prove a new experience for him, something to look forward to in a life which was, at times, deadly dull.

Chapter Two

Joey knew that it was raining even before he opened his eyes. The kitchen was filling with smoke as Ma tried to encourage a reluctant fire, a sure sign the weather had taken a turn for the worse.

From his bed in the dark cubby-hole beneath the stairs Joey got the benefit of all the household's early morning activities. From outside in the yard came the regular squeak-splash, squeak-splash of the pump, followed by the rattle of pails as someone – probably Mercy – fetched the water. Upstairs Lizzie's child, William, was raising his voice in protest at something, and Joey wished his sister could keep her babe quiet when other folks were trying to sleep. He groaned and snuggled further into his bed, ignoring the prickling of straw through the mattress-ticking. He never liked getting up; this morning was going to be worse than usual.

'Come on, lazybones. Some folks sleep their lives away,' Mercy chided him gently.

'It's not time to get up yet,' he protested drowsily.

'Yes it is, long past. Pa's gone already.'

Joey reluctantly swung his legs out of bed and groped for his trousers, then pushed his bare feet into his boots. The big question now was whether to make a dash across the yard in the rain to the privy and relieve himself, or wait. It was no use, he'd have to go, he was bursting.

The combined effects of the drizzle and the pungency of the midden revived him a little, enough to make him realize that his stomach was rattling with hunger. He would have sat straight down to eat but Mercy intervened. 'Soap,' she said firmly, 'and water.'

'But I'm starving.'

'You're always starving. Five minutes spent washing won't make any difference.'

'Nor will washing after I've been out in the tiddy field. Honestly, Mercy, what's the point in washing when I'll be covered in mud in no time?'

'Well, at least, the mud won't get a chance to soak in, will it? And how many times do I have to tell you that it's a potato field not a tiddy field?'

'Stop botherin' the boy! Leave 'im be,' protested Ma, who always adopted the line of least effort.

'Encouraging him to wash isn't exactly bothering him. It's something he should learn,' stated Mercy in exasperation. 'How is he going to get anywhere in the world if he can't keep himself decent?'

''E's only tiddy pickin', when all's said and done,' retorted Ma.

'Now he is, but who's to say what he'll be doing in ten or fifteen years' time, given the chance...?' Mercy stopped. Joey was already slopping water into the chipped enamel bowl and liberally soaping himself.

Mercy could go on a bit when she chose, but she was the only person who cared about him. She knew how much he hated the tedium and back-breaking grind of farmwork, and she encouraged him to think ahead. After he had finished with schooling he might never have opened another book without Mercy's intervention. She would borrow books from the village school teacher for him, and sometimes, if she had any money to spare she would buy others second-hand from Torquay Market, and together they would read them. Ma could not understand why they bothered, and Lizzie was openly scornful. But Joey didn't care; Mercy had faith in him and wanted him to get on, and if that meant having to wash then so be it.

The smell of carbolic wafted through the kitchen, and he had to admit it was an improvement on what had been there before. He balked, however, when she handed him a comb.

'Take it,' insisted Mercy firmly, seeing his expression. 'You don't want to get nits like Georgie Hannaford, do you?'

Joey pulled an even longer face but complied. 'You don't happen to have a bit of cologne or hair-oil about you, do you?' he asked.

'Saucy!' Mercy smiled as she aimed a mock blow at his head.

He thought how pretty she was. He didn't know of anyone who was half as pretty; and his heart swelled with pride because she was his sister, an emotion he never felt when he looked at Lizzie. He was glad to see Mercy smile because he thought she'd seemed rather miserable this morning. Perhaps, like him, she was just overtired after the Regatta.

He settled down to his bread and cocoa, closing his ears as the noise upstairs intensified. William was screaming at full pitch and Lizzie had now joined in, yelling persistently, 'Stop your racket, you little varmint!'

Suddenly the kitchen door opened and there stood Blanche. She was wearing an old coat over her flannel petticoat, and her legs, scrawny as a fowl's, ended in boots that had long since had the toes kicked out of them. For all that, she was an impressive sight, for she was angry, and anger made her awe-inspiring.

'Silence that child!' she commanded, glaring round with eyes still red from yesterday's drink.

There was no question that she should be obeyed. Mercy hurried upstairs, to return almost at once carrying the child, quieter now, with his face crimson and his lower lip trembling pathetically. Lizzie followed after, and at the sight of his mother William remembered all his grievances and opened his mouth to bawl again. Hurriedly Joey cut the corner crust from the loaf and spread one end with plum jam.

'Here you are, young Bill. Get your teeth into that,' he said.

William paused, his mouth open, then decided that eating was better than making a noise. He accepted the proffered crust and settled on Mercy's lap to reduce the bread to a messy pulp.

'There,' said Joey, 'the poor lad was just hungry. You don't look after him proper.'

'Properly!' Blanche and Mercy corrected him in unison.

'Properly,' amended Joey. 'Well, she doesn't, does she, Ma?'

'Yer, I don't want no more lip from 'ee.' Lizzie moved towards him, her hand raised menacingly.

Mercy intervened swiftly. 'The babe's quiet enough now. Let that be an end of it,' she said. 'Do you want some cocoa, Lizzie? The water's still hot.'

Lizzie shot her a glare of dislike which suddenly changed to near alarm as she clapped a hand over her mouth and dashed outside.

Blanche watched her go with scorn.

'Why don't you go back to bed, Grandmother? You'll get some peace now,' suggested Mercy.

Joey could feel the tension in the room as they waited for Blanche's reply.

His grandmother was in no mood to be obliging. She looked round her with venom, bleary about the eyes and unsteady on her feet, otherwise none the worse for yesterday's drinking bout.

'I cannot find my dress,' she declared, ignoring Mercy's suggestion.

They all looked towards where the dress still soaked in the bucket, oozing dye inkily into the water.

'I'm afraid I forgot it,' said Mercy.

'Never mind, I'll give un a rinse through in a minute,' put in Ma.

Blanche focused on her daughter-in-law. 'You will leave my dress alone,' she commanded, in a tone which betrayed only too clearly what she thought of her capabilities.

Ma shrank visibly.

Lizzie returned then, green of face, her hair lank from the drizzling rain, and Blanche transferred her animosity.

'Is it too much to hope that this time the man can be persuaded to marry you?' she said.

Lizzie sank into a chair by the fire and glared at her without speaking.

Blanche was not deterred. 'I suppose anyone can be a fool once, but twice is sheer stupidity. Do you never learn? That child' – she indicated William – 'grows more like Harry Dawe every day. It is a miracle his wife has not seen the resemblance already. She must be as blind as she is stupid. Are we to be treated to a change of visage this time, or are we to have to put up with the fact that Harry Dawe has once more reproduced himself in our midst?'

Blanche was certainly on form this morning. Out of the corner of his eye Joey saw Lizzie gathering herself for the fight. She was afraid of her grandmother, but she shared the old woman's vindictive streak and her vicious tongue. She always came off worse; she lacked Blanche's intelligence and her vocabulary, yet it never prevented her from responding.

'What do 'ee know of it, you stinkin' old slummick?' Lizzie demanded.

Joey drained his cocoa-mug with haste and got up from the table. The fur was going to fly any minute and he didn't want to be around when it did. Mercy also rose and handed William to Ma, who looked as if she, too, would like to escape.

'We'd best be off before we're late,' Mercy said, steering Joey out before her.

Picking up the bread and cheese she had already prepared for him, Joey noticed that she had also placed two pieces of butterscotch on the top. One he popped into his mouth, the other into the fibrous darkness of his pocket for later. An old sack, one side torn open, hung from a nail on the back of the door, and this he put over his head, his only protection against the rain. Together they turned out of the gate.

'Blanche is in fine fettle this morning,' Joey observed.

'She certainly is... Oh dear, I still didn't do her dress – though it never would have dried today.'

'Perhaps it'll keep her off the drink for a bit. She can't go down to the Oak in her shimmy, can she?'

'I wouldn't put it past her to try,' Mercy smiled. She had the collar of her coat turned up against the elements, and the hem of her skirt was already wet. Her fleeting smile had gone and now she looked tired again, the penalty of a late night.

One other aftermath of the Regatta was troubling Joey. 'That toff of yours, what's his name?' he asked.

'He's a gentleman, not a toff. And he isn't mine,' replied Mercy with more than usual sharpness.

'If you say so, but what's his name?'

'Mr Lisburne – Peter.'

Joey wished she hadn't known his Christian name. The Mr Lisburne part was all right, formal and anonymous; if she knew he was called Peter it implied a certain closeness, and Joey was never happy at the thought of her being close to any man.

'When are you seeing him again?'

'On Saturday afternoon.'

'Oh... !'

'But that's to be the end of it. I won't see him again after that, you'll be pleased to know.'

'Why'll I be pleased to know?' demanded Joey, even though it was true. 'I never said anything against the fellow.'

'No, but you looked it. You are right, of course. It would never do.'

She looked so sad when she spoke Joey was sorely tempted to protest that of course it would do, she was good enough for anyone. Then he had second thoughts; he didn't want to lose her, particularly not to a toff called Mr Peter Lisburne.

Their paths divided. Mercy carried on towards the Newton road, while Joey took the lane to Prout's farm. He had another mile to trudge although he knew he wasn't certain of any work when he got there. Of all the jobs he had ever done on the farm he hated potato picking the most; it was back-breaking and at the end of the day he finished with hands so raw and painful he couldn't bear to touch anything – and for ninepence a day! At some places you could get a bit extra for casual work, but you'd never catch Sam Prout paying out a ha'penny more than he needed to.

Usually Joey got to the farm early, not because he was keen but because if he were first sometimes Farmer Prout set him to help with the stock instead of sending him out to the fields, and this meant he would get breakfast. It had only happened a couple of times yet Joey still dreamed about them. Sam Prout was tight-fisted over his money but his missus was lavish with the food, probably because she realized she got more work out of their labourers if they weren't half-starved. Today, however, he was out of luck. There were quite a few people waiting hopefully in the farmyard when he got there. He'd be fortunate just to get potato-picking.

'Be 'ee comin', boy, or baint 'ee?' demanded a gruff voice. Sam Prout was regarding him irritably. 'I wants they tiddies today, 'ee knows, afore this weather sets, not some time next week.'

'Sorry, maister.' Joey looked about and realized that the others had left the yard.

'Stone Acre,' Sam Prout directed, 'I'll be along meself presently. Don't 'ee be dawdlin' none, do 'ee 'ear?'

'Yes, maister.' Joey was already hurrying after the others. He caught them up further along the lane, a silent and morose bunch, shrouded like himself in sacking against the rain. The wet weather had depressed everyone's spirits, there was none of the lively chatter that usually made the tedious work more bearable.

'Rotten old morning,' remarked Joey conversationally to his neighbour.

The only response was a discouraging grunt. Joey sighed. Ahead of him stretched the long dismal hours. He tried to think back to the previous evening, to the crowds and the excitement of the Regatta – he had liked that, being among so many people with so much going on – but the Regatta was over, gone until next year. He thrust his hands into his pockets and encountered the piece of butterscotch Mercy had given him. Already it was growing sticky with the humidity and warmth of his body. To save it from further deterioration he put it into his mouth and began sucking appreciatively. It looked as though the toffee was going to be the only bright spot in his whole day.

—

The Orchard Hygienic Laundry was situated on one of the roads leading out of Torquay, in a flat expanse which had once been a quarry. If there had ever been any orchards in the vicinity no one could remember them; high cliffs now towered above the grey building, giving it a forbidding air.

Mercy and Dolly went into the staff entrance together. In the subterranean corridor which served as a cloakroom Mercy took off her coat and gave it a shake, spraying droplets of water everywhere.

'Yer, watch out! I be wet enough as 'tis,' protested Dolly.

'Sorry.'

Mercy hung up her coat then followed her friend into the long ironing-room, tying on her apron as she went. They were early, but the stove was already lit to heat the flat-irons, and the girls hurried towards it, eager to snatch an opportunity to dry off. For once they were grateful that the management were way behind the times and had not gone in for gas-heated irons.

'Move yer girt bum out of the way, Annie Efford, and let's see the fire,' Dolly said cheerfully to a woman who was already there, her skirts held out like sombre butterfly wings to the heat.

'Girt bum? Look who's talking!' grinned Annie, good-naturedly making room for them.

'That's better. Us've a few minutes yet afore old Ma 'Oskins gets after us,' said Dolly.

For a while they were enveloped in the acrid smell of wet wool as their skirts steamed in the heat. Then Dolly turned to Mercy.

'You'm quiet, maid. You'm all right?' she asked.

'Yes, thanks. I've just got the miseries.'

''Tis the weather. That, and the end of Regatta. Nothin' but the winter to look forward to.'

It was true, an air of anticlimax hung over the whole of Torquay, and everyone seemed conscious that the days of revelry were gone for another year. No wonder Mercy felt dispirited.

'Was 'ee serious last night, about goin' out with that fellow again?' asked Dolly.

'Yes, I'm seeing him on Saturday.'

'Nice, was 'e? Did 'e treat 'ee well?'

'Yes, very well. He was a real gentleman.'

'They be the worst sort; watch your Ps and Qs come Saturday,' cautioned Dolly. 'And make sure 'e takes 'ee somewhere flashy. If 'e wants the pleasure of your company make un pay for it!'

'But I don't want to go somewhere flashy.'

'Why not? 'E can afford it.'

Mercy wasn't sure why not. She simply felt that her time with Peter should be spent somewhere quiet, so they could talk. At the fair there had been little chance of proper conversation, she had learnt only the sketchiest of details about him – he was an only child, for example, and his mother was a widow. There was so much more she wanted to find out; she didn't know where he lived— Then she remembered! After Saturday she would not be seeing him again. For some reason the thought made the gloom of the day close about her a little more.

'Watch out! Yer comes Missus!' warned Dolly.

Reluctantly they moved away from the fire to their ironing-tables as footsteps approached.

Mrs Hoskins entered briskly, the keys hanging from her belt rattled 'like a ruddy gaoler's', as Dolly had remarked once. Her eyes were never still, darting about the room, checking that every employee was in place, the stove was well stoked, the tables were prepared. When her gaze reached Mercy her expression grew stony and her lips pressed together as she scrutinized her closely as if searching for faults. Finding none she gave a snorted 'Hm!' and moved on.

''Er knows!' breathed Dolly when she was out of earshot. 'And what 'er don't know 'er've guessed!'

'Oh dear! Well, there's nothing I can do about it except keep out of his way,' sighed Mercy, cleaning her iron with Bath brick then wiping it on a cloth, ready for the first shirt.

'Not much else 'ee can do, maid,' agreed Dolly.

Unfortunately Mercy had attracted the attention of Mr Hoskins. He was notorious for letting his hands wander where they shouldn't and for lying in wait for some unsuspecting girl in the store-room or in one of the darker corners of the vast building. It was Mercy's bad luck to be his current favourite. Mrs Hoskins knew about her husband's tendencies yet never reproached him. The blame was heaped upon the hapless girl, and therefore her disapproving 'Hm!' boded ill for Mercy.

If the truth be known, Mercy quite liked her job. It was hard on the feet and back, and Mr Hoskins was an extra hazard; nevertheless, she got great satisfaction from seeing the crumpled linen being transformed into a smooth, immaculate shirt beneath the weight of her iron. She was good at it, too, which was why she was given the things which needed skill. She liked the fresh clean smell of the clothes and the glossiness of the highly starched collars and cuffs and shirt fronts after she had ironed them.

They were a friendly bunch of girls in the ironing-room – though girls was something of a misnomer for they included a couple of grandmothers, and if the banter which went to and fro among the tables was somewhat earthy at times it was no worse than she heard at home. All the same, it was disagreeable to have more personal matters discussed in public.

'That was a fine gentleman 'ee was with last night, Mercy girl,' remarked Annie Efford. 'I seed 'ee with un down at the fair.'

'Oh…' replied Mercy discouragingly.

'Where'd 'ee get to meet the likes of 'e, then?'

'At the Regatta.'

'I guessed as much meself. Where at the Regatta?' persisted the ever curious Annie.

Mercy would not be drawn. She did not want to talk about Peter and to have him made the butt of the girls' jokes. It did not seem right somehow. 'Oh, just at the Regatta,' she said.

'Lor', 'ee don't give much away, do 'ee? I only 'ope 'ee was more generous with the poor fellow.'

'We don't all have your giving nature, Annie,' replied Mercy calmly.

When the laughter had died down the conversation returned to the Regatta in general, much to her relief, but now that Peter was in her thoughts once more he was difficult to dislodge. In fact, he crept into her consciousness more often than she liked during the next few days.

Mercy awoke on Saturday morning determined that this was the last time she would see Peter Lisburne, yet trying to ignore the knot of happy anticipation which had settled somewhere in her stomach. She noted with relief that the day was warm, she would not have to wear her coat which was shabby and splitting under the arms. Not for anything would she have considered putting on a shawl like the village wives. Thoughts of what she would wear had given her much anguish; why, she wasn't sure, for the matter was cut and dried. She would have to wear the same blouse and skirt she had worn at the Regatta, for the very good reason she had nothing else. Her hat posed a problem; to wear her newly trimmed one with the pink rose would excite comments from the girls at work; in the end she decided to wear her workaday one, a far from new black straw, and to carry her best hat in a paper bag.

For once Dolly's sense of curiosity was dimmed by her own affairs. She, also, had an assignation that afternoon, with a fellow from the Electric Company, and she was so involved in telling how she had met him and how quickly the friendship had flourished that she made no mention of Mercy's paper bag.

At the laundry, in the dark hole where the girls left their hats and coats, there was a cupboard which was recognized by everyone as the resting place of anything fragile. Mercy placed her precious hat on top of it, then hung her black straw on a hook close by.

For Mercy the morning held a strange quality, she could hardly believe that in a few short hours she would be seeing Peter again. As the day progressed her qualms about meeting him seemed to fade, leaving only happy anticipation. It was unfortunate that Mercy's sense of wariness was also dulled, for Mr Hoskins wandered in and out of the ironing-room several times during the morning, something which would normally have put her on her guard.

She was coming back from the privy when he pounced. Her route led down a passageway behind the boilers, where the roaring of the furnace and the hissing of water deadened all sound. The first she knew of his presence was a pair of arms encircling her from behind, imprisoning her, and a hand groping up the front of her blouse trying to find her breasts. It had to be Mr Hoskins, she knew, by the mingled odours of strong tobacco and cheap violet hair-oil.

The yell of protest she gave was scarcely audible above the rumble of the boilers, and only caused Mr Hoskins to tighten his grip, his fingers probing her flesh.

'You don't want to be difficult,' he breathed in her ear. 'Why can't you be nice to me? A pretty girl like you?'

Mercy struggled harder, trying to kick her way free. Albert Hoskins was a veteran of innumerable such encounters and managed to avoid her flailing feet. His grip was hurting and, frustrated by Mercy's blouse fastening at the back, his free hand was now pulling at her skirt. His breath came in loud, excited gasps. Panic surged through Mercy, combined with growing anger. Hoskins was stronger than he looked and she knew she would never break his grip by force. Then she realized the more she struggled the more excited he became. Albert Hoskins liked his victims to be unwilling.

At once she ceased fighting and went supine in his grip. For a second surprise and disappointment made him ease his hold. As soon as Mercy felt his clutching hands loosen she took her chance. Ramming her elbow forcibly into the pit of his stomach she broke free and ran for all she was worth back towards the ironing-room.

Mrs Hoskins was in there, she could hear her voice. Mercy hurriedly pushed her blouse back into her skirt and re-pinned the strands of hair that had come down in the struggle. As she entered she hoped her employer would not notice her distress, she was only too well aware her cheeks were scarlet with anger and humiliation and she was having difficulty blinking back the tears. The older woman glared at her with eyes so searching and hostile that Mercy's heart sank.

'Where have you been?' demanded Mrs Hoskins.

'To the privy, Mrs Hoskins.'

'For all this time?'

'Yes…'

'You aren't ill, are you?'

Mercy shook her head, conscious of the silence which had fallen over the room as the other girls listened to the exchange with interest.

Pointedly Mrs Hoskins looked up at the clock on the wall.

'Thirty minutes you've been gone,' she said, her voice cold with venom. 'That is thirty you will make up at the end of the morning.'

Half an hour of the scant time before she met Peter!

Mercy wanted to protest she hadn't been gone so long, but she knew it was useless, just as it was useless to protest about the behaviour of Albert Hoskins – it would simply result in the loss of the job she so sorely needed.

When Mrs Hoskins swept from the room an angry buzz of conversation rose from the other girls.

'Lyin' in wait for 'ee, was 'e, maid?'

''E needs seeing to, that 'Oskins. I'd soon doctor 'im if 'e set about me.'

37

'It's not fair for 'er to take it out on 'ee. 'Er should keep 'er old man in better order.'

For some reason sympathy from the others was hard to bear. Mercy was forced to bend her head swiftly so her friends would not see her tears. Dolly noticed them, however, and slid a comforting arm around her shoulders.

'Us'll look out for 'ee, never fear. The old goat won't get to 'ee again,' she promised.

Mercy managed a grateful smile. She knew the offer was genuine, where Albert Hoskins was concerned the girls in the ironing-room invariably closed ranks for protection.

The morning's work drew to a close, the baskets of unironed linen were emptied, the flat-irons cleaned and stacked away. But Mrs Hoskins did not return.

'Per'aps 'er's letting 'ee off,' suggested Dolly hopefully.

Mercy was less optimistic. She had seen the vindictiveness in Ma Hoskins's eyes, just as she had seen the dog-like devotion with which they followed Albert.

Left to herself Maud Hoskins was a reasonable woman, hard-working and fair. It was her tragedy that she had fallen in love with an incorrigible lecher. She could neither leave him nor accept him for what he was, with the result she was torn apart by jealousy for most of the time. It was this jealousy which prompted her to wait until exactly one-thirty, finishing time, before she swept back into the ironing-room, followed by a porter pushing a basket filled with freshly washed sheets.

'This should occupy you for a good half-hour,' she informed Mercy.

Mercy looked at the linen in dismay. 'There's more than half an hour's work there,' she protested. 'And the fire's nearly out.'

'Then I suggest you stoke it up again quickly,' replied Mrs Hoskins, making for the door.

''Tis a danged shame!' declared Dolly. 'Yer, look, I'll 'ang on for a bit and give 'ee an 'and.'

Mercy was about to say she couldn't spoil her friend's day off, but her protestations were not necessary. Mrs Hoskins heard Dolly's generous offer.

'If you do that you'll be looking for another job on Monday morning,' she said tersely.

Mercy could see Dolly shaping up to make some sharp reply. She gently pushed her friend towards the door. 'Please go,' she urged. 'Thanks for offering, but it's not worth losing your job over it.'

Reluctantly Dolly and the others left. Mercy set to on the extra work, with one eye on the clock. She was also alert to any noise outside, she dreaded that Albert Hoskins might appear. She had never worked so swiftly in her life, determined not to be late for Peter. It was way past two o'clock by the time she had finished. She was clearing up when she heard footsteps approaching and she tensed up, but it was only Annie Efford; her husband also worked in the laundry, as a maintenance man.

'I just brought a pasty and a jug of tea to my old man,' she said. ''E's working late on one of they boilers. I saw old Ma 'Oskins go into 'er office. There weren't no sign of that dirty old devil. I thought I'd best come and see if 'ee were all right.'

'That was kind,' said Mercy. 'I've just finished.' Together they hurried to where Mercy's black straw hat hung on its peg in solitary splendour.

'Put your 'at on and let's be going,' said Annie. Seeing Mercy take the paper bag from the cupboard she demanded good-naturedly, 'What've 'ee there, maid?'

'I'm going out this afternoon...' she began.

The paper bag didn't look right. It was too flat. With a sinking heart she opened it and drew out the battered remains of her best hat. It had been stamped on, the veiling ripped into strands, petals stripped from the rose.

'Oh my!' gasped Annie. 'That's got to be deliberate! It weren't no accident! But who...?'

Mercy was too stunned to do more than stare at the ruin. She had few enough pretty things, and she had been so pleased with her hat. And now it was crumpled and filthy. Vaguely she was aware of Annie speaking.

'The old cat!' she was saying. 'The mean, jealous old cat!'

'Who?' asked Mercy.

'Why, old Ma 'Oskins, of course! I saw her come from this direction, and I thought 'er looked a bit peculiar. What'll 'ee do now?'

'What can I do?' said Mercy dully. 'Accuse her and lose my job, or tell her that her husband's no better than a mean old tom-cat and still lose my job?'

'You'm right, maid. There idn't no justice for 'ee if you'm poor,' sighed Annie. 'Let's get away from this place. Us see enough of un as 'tis.'

Mercy parted company with Annie at the laundry gate and then began to hurry down the hill towards the Strand where Peter was waiting.

If he's still there, she thought desperately. More than likely he's given up and gone home. What will he think of me letting him down like this?

Where anything pleasurable was concerned it seemed she was destined to be late. She had quite a walk ahead of her, and as she caught sight of her reflection in shop windows her steps became increasingly leaden. She looked so bedraggled – and as for her hat! She could hardly bear to look at her old black straw.

Perhaps it will be just as well if Peter isn't there, she decided, at least he won't see me in this state.

But Peter was there. It was much to his surprise; he was usually too impatient to wait for anything or anyone. As the minutes ticked away and Mercy still did not arrive he felt an acute sense of disappointment creep through him. Somehow he had not expected to be left standing like this, something about Mercy led him to believe she would keep her word.

Then suddenly there she was, dodging and weaving her way through the Saturday shoppers, one hand clasping a funny little black hat to her head, her pretty face rosy with exertion.

'I'm sorry – I'm so late—' she panted, hardly able to get the words out.

'Steady on! Get your breath back,' he laughed, absurdly happy because his faith in her had not been misplaced. Gently he drew her out of the stream of people into the shelter of a doorway. Mercy leaned against the wall and closed her eyes as she took in great gasps of air. Peter was quite alarmed.

'You shouldn't have rushed so,' he said with concern. 'You look quite done in.'

Mercy opened her eyes and managed a smile, although she felt hot and sticky and her face was wet with perspiration. Oh, this wasn't how she had intended things to be at all! She searched for her handkerchief to wipe her brow but could not find it. It was one more precious possession she had lost that day. Peter handed her an immaculate linen square.

'You shouldn't have hurried,' he repeated. 'I would have still waited.'

'Would you?' asked Mercy.

'Of course,' he replied with conviction, knowing it was true.

'I was afraid you wouldn't. I didn't mean to be late. I had extra work to do...'

'You should have explained that you had an appointment,' said Peter gravely.

Mercy could not help smiling at his innocence. 'I don't think Mrs Hoskins, my employer, would consider it much of an excuse. She doesn't like me as it is. That's why she brought me a whole pile of things to do just when we were finishing.'

'How unfair!' Peter was incensed. 'Couldn't you have refused point-blank?'

'Only if I'd wanted to be sacked on the spot.'

'You should have complained to...' Peter's, voice tailed away as he realized that there was no one to whom she could complain. 'It's unfair! You've done more than enough for one day so from now on you must take your ease. Cabby! Cabby!'

'Where are we going?' asked Mercy in bewilderment.

'Let's see if we can find somewhere pleasant where we can have some tea.'

Mercy sank back against the scuffed leather seats, and sniffed the aroma of horse and straw pervading the interior of the cab.

'Is something wrong?' asked Peter.

Mercy shook her head. 'It's just that I've never ridden in a cab before.'

It occurred to her that perhaps she should not be riding in this one; it wasn't quite respectable for a – a girl and a young man to be unchaperoned. However, it was too late; they were already clip-clopping into Torwood Street.

'You really are wonderful company, Mercy.' Peter was beaming by now. 'There's none of this blasé I've-seen-it-all-before nonsense with you. If something is new you admit it. You've no idea how refreshing it is.'

'I'm glad you think so.' Mercy was flattered that he considered her to be different; in her own eyes she seemed very ordinary.

The cabby, appreciating that they were in no hurry, took the journey at a leisurely pace, and when he finally deposited them on the Babbacombe Downs he pocketed a handsome tip.

The way to the beach was too steep for a cab horse to tackle, and Peter insisted upon hiring a donkey to take Mercy down.

With much laughing and argument she allowed herself to be lifted on to the side-saddle.

'Ready?' asked Peter mischievously. 'Then away we go!'

Seizing the donkey's bridle he led it off at a brisk trot which gathered momentum as they slipped and slithered down the increasingly steep incline which led to the cove, causing Mercy to cling on for dear life. By the time they reached the bottom they were going full pelt, until they finally collapsed on to the beach, donkey and all.

'You mazed fools!' The stout owner of the beast came puffing down behind them, her petticoats flying. ''Tis a wonder 'ee didn't break your necks!'

'There's no harm done, madam, I assure you,' said Peter with grave gallantry. 'And let me congratulate you on having such a superior animal, a truly splendid steed.' He slipped a coin into her apron pocket, then suddenly planted a kiss on her cheek.

The donkey-owner, who could recognize the chink of a half-crown when she heard it, gave a smile of surprising coyness.

'Mazed fool,' she said again in a very different tone.

Peter helped Mercy up.

'The woman is right – "you'm a mazed fool",' she said.

To hear her lapse into broad Devonshire made Peter roar with laughter.

'That cottage looks as though it might provide us with some tea to restore our nerves,' he suggested.

Mercy, who was brushing the sand off her skirt, felt in definite need of a restorative. For this meeting with Peter she had made up her mind to appear elegant and worldly, at the very least to look her best, but circumstances were certainly against her. This final tumble on to the sand had spelt doom to her dreams of elegance, and she hoped fervently the fall had not revealed her bloomers.

'Tea would be nice, thank you,' she said.

Peter looked at her sharply. 'Are you all right? You didn't hurt yourself in the fall?'

'No, why?'

'You suddenly sounded different – subdued.'

'It's just I feel so... so untidy.' Mercy held out her sand-covered hands to indicate her equally sand-covered skirt.

'Untidy?' Peter's astonishment was sincere. 'But you look delightful. I confess I'm as proud as Punch to be seen with the prettiest girl in Torquay, even if she is sprinkled with sand.'

'Oh!' said Mercy, her breath quite taken away.

'And I feel honoured that you agreed to come out with me this afternoon. When I asked you I didn't appreciate the difficulties you would experience. Here I am, I rose late, ate a leisurely breakfast, strolled into town and had an equally leisurely lunch at the Yacht Club, while all the time you were working. I suppose you hardly had any time to eat your lunch or have a rest, did you?'

Mercy, who had had neither rest nor lunch, felt the gulf between their worlds widen alarmingly.

Peter looked at her, with that sharp perceptive look she was beginning to recognize.

'You did have lunch, didn't you?'

'Well...' Mercy was never a comfortable liar.

'You haven't! How thoughtless of me! We'll go to one of the hotels on the Downs immediately—'

'I'm not hungry, honestly. Tea at the cottage will be fine!'

Mercy was panic-stricken at the thought of entering a smart hotel dining-room in her present dishevelled state. She could also have added that missing a meal was no novelty to someone from a household where money was perpetually short.

'If you're sure... We'll see what the cottage has to offer?'

Fronting on to the beach, below a steep wooded cliff, was a row of cob and thatch dwellings, and set outside one of these was a table. Although it looked rather rickety, it was spread invitingly with a fresh white cloth and laid with cups and saucers.

'Is it possible to obtain anything to eat here?' Peter asked the neat little woman who came to open the door.

'Indeed 'tis, sir. Strawberry jam and cream and cut rounds fresh-made, as much as you wish.'

'Splendid! And a very large pot of tea also, if it isn't too much trouble.'

Beneath the warmth of Peter's smile the woman positively glowed in her eagerness to please. Her friendliness prompted Mercy to ask if there was somewhere she might wash and tidy herself, something she would never have dared to do in a large hotel. As she splashed cold water on her face in the back scullery of the cottage she reflected that Peter had quite a way with women. At first it had not been so obvious, overshadowed as he was by the more aggressive charms of Freddie Parkham, but she was growing more and more aware that his boyishness was very appealing – and that he had no qualms about using it.

Refreshed and feeling more self-assured Mercy went out to join him.

'Just in time. I'm afraid these looked so tempting I've already started.' Peter waved a half-eaten bun in the air as proof.

Mercy persuaded herself she was not hungry, because her grandmother had told her that to eat too much was indelicate. She took one of the small soft bread-buns, slowly spread it with home-made jam and crusty yellow cream, then ate it with deliberately slow nibbles. Peter ate with gusto. For a man who had had both a hearty breakfast and lunch he managed to make great inroads into the fare provided. He ordered more; and gradually Mercy's stomach turned traitor and she, too, tucked in. Far from being shocked Peter regarded her with approval, and soon they were arguing happily about whether it was correct to put on the jam before the cream or the cream before the jam.

It was a pretty beach, with pink-tinted sand and shingle reaching from the green wooded cliffs to the clear aquamarine sea. With its cluster of cottages and small stone jetty curving into the bay it was a fishing port in miniature, alive and bustling. Several old men and women sat among the upturned boats mending nets, and children scampered about the shore, while every now and then neat-hoofed donkeys would be driven along the steep tracks leading to the cliff top, their twin panniers swaying as they picked their way through the trees.

On the jetty a handful of onlookers watched a crabber unload the last catch of the day. A young boy, who was supposed to be helping with the unloading, had picked up a spider-crab; its spindly legs and elongated claws waved frantically in the air, and holding it at arm's length he was chasing a small girl. His antics made Mercy laugh.

'He's so like Joey,' she said. 'That's just the sort of mischief he would get up to.'

'Joey? Is he your brother?'

'Yes.'

'The only one?'

'No, I have three, but Tom and Eddie, they're older and they are both married and live up-country.'

'Joey is your favourite.'

'Why do you say that?'

'Because of the way you look when you speak of him. He is a lucky boy, having you as a sister.'

Mercy felt her cheeks flush, not so much because of his words as the appreciative way in which Peter had said them.

'I don't think he would always agree with you,' she smiled. 'I'm afraid I'm often a great trial to him. He's always in trouble with me for playing tricks.'

Soon she was telling Peter of the time when Joey painted the eggs in a neighbour's henhouse green and the poor woman thought her precious birds had caught a dreadful disease.

Peter listened with rapt attention, demanding more of her family's adventures whenever she stopped.

'I want to hear about you,' she pleaded.

'There's nothing to tell. It's all very dull,' was his reply.

There was nothing for it but to carry on relating incidents at home and in the village, though she was careful to be selective in what she told him; her tales bore no whiff of the squalor in which she lived nor of the heartache caused by Blanche's drinking or Lizzie's wantonness.

Peter seemed particularly fascinated by the idea of so many people occupying such a small house.

'Seven of you! How do you do it?'

'Nine of us when the boys were home. We managed somehow. There are many people far more overcrowded than we are.'

'No!' Peter was astonished.

Mercy found his fascination puzzling until he said, 'You all have such fun,' in a voice of great wistfulness.

'Don't you have fun too?'

'Not at home. It's so empty and quiet. Just great rooms with no one in them but Mother and me.'

'Haven't you got servants?'

'Oh yes, but they're not… not…' He struggled to find the right words. 'They're not family. They're not close,' he concluded.

45

Mercy, who had never thought of her life as enviable, had to do some rapid reconsidering. She tried to imagine life without Joey and Baby William, without Blanche. Her family were often a trial, and yet the idea of being without them invoked a strange emptiness. She began to understand some of Peter's interest in a way of life so divorced from his own.

The shadows cast across the beach were beginning to lengthen as they left the cottage and started the slow climb up the hill. The going was steep; it was natural for Peter to take Mercy's hand, and even more natural that he did not release it when they reached the top.

'You don't have to go home for a while, do you?' he asked.

'No.'

'Good, because I don't want this afternoon to end yet.' Peter's hold tightened on her hand and though his fingers were smooth they were strong.

They walked along the cliff top in the sunshine, gazing out to sea, identifying the places just visible round the long hazy curve of Lyme Bay – Teignmouth, Dawlish, Exmouth – Mercy had never felt happier. She found it hard to believe her day had started so disastrously. The incident with Mr Hoskins and his wife's spiteful revenge might have been no more than part of an unpleasant dream. Even the loss of her precious hat no longer stung.

If Mercy had tried to imagine her ideal man he would have resembled Peter pretty closely – tall, good-looking, amusing, courteous and considerate. And there were things about Peter which far exceeded her imagination. He was interesting to talk to, and shared her love of books, though he was better read. He enjoyed the theatre – an unknown territory as far as she was concerned. He had travelled widely. He was fond of sailing; and she listened entranced as he told her about the yacht racing at the Regatta and the people involved. She was more puzzled than ever how he could find stories of her home life intriguing when he knew such interesting people. It seemed that everything he did added to the golden aura she was building around him.

The shadows lengthened further and the time to part could be put off no longer.

'When do you have your next free day?' asked Peter. 'Don't say next Saturday; it means waiting a whole week to see you.'

Mercy shook her head reluctantly. 'It's worse than that. I only get one Saturday off in four. I don't work Sundays, though.'

'Only Sunday? That's terrible! How about in the evenings? No – I'm being thoughtless, aren't I? You'll be tired then, won't you? I'm beginning to learn enough about that dreadful laundry to know they keep you working there until all hours.'

'We do often have to work late,' admitted Mercy. Then she added shyly, 'But I would like to see you again on Sunday.'

'Sunday it is, then. Waiting so long won't be easy!' Peter's smile faded as he looked at Mercy, his expression softening. 'No, it won't be easy at all,' he whispered. Then slipping his hands about her waist he drew her to him and kissed her. They were on a secluded part of the cliff top, shielded from the public gaze by a thicket of hawthorn. Mercy would not have cared if the whole world had been watching. Her response to the warmth and sweetness of his lips was startling, a sudden flaring of emotions she had scarcely been aware she possessed.

At last Peter released her, letting her go as if she were a delicate piece of porcelain.

'I should apologize for that,' he said, 'but if I did I'd be telling a lie, because I'm not sorry.'

Mercy was having difficulty collecting her thoughts.

'Nor am I,' she said eventually.

Peter smiled, and taking her hand once more pressed it to his lips.

'Until Sunday,' he said softly.

Chapter Three

'Who is he?'

At the sound of Blanche's voice Mercy started guiltily. For some weeks now she had been meeting Peter regularly, whenever she could steal the time. She had parted from him not half an hour since, and crept stealthily into the bedroom so as not wake her grandmother. She saw that the old woman was propped up on one elbow, looking at her with dark eyes that glittered in the wavering candlelight.

'Who's who?' she asked unconvincingly.

Blanche gave a snort. 'Do not play games with me, girl! These days you are always mooning about the place, in a dream half the time. What other explanation could there be? Who is the man? One of our country bumpkins?'

'Certainly not!'

'Then who? Must I go through the rhyme? – Tinker, tailor, soldier—'

'He's none of those!' cried Mercy, unwilling to put up with Blanche's taunting. 'He's a gentleman.'

'A gentleman? You fool!' Blanche sat bolt upright. 'I thought you had more sense than to follow Lizzie's road.'

'I'm not following Lizzie's road, as you call it. He treats me with the greatest courtesy and respect.'

'Ha!'

'He does!' Mercy was stung by her grandmother's scornful disbelief. 'He's a perfect gentleman.'

'And what does a perfect gentleman want with a laundry-maid, eh, if it is not to get her behind the nearest bush with her skirts around her neck?'

'Grandmother!'

'There is no need to blush. You know nothing of gentlemen or you would never call them perfect. If he has not got what he wants from you yet it is only a matter of time.'

'But he's not like that!'

'No, of course not. He is completely honourable. You have no doubt spent an evening with his family. Tell me, how did his father greet you – and his sisters, are they agreeable girls? And what of his brothers— ?'

'He has no brothers or sisters and his father is dead,' Mercy cut in.

'The only son of a widowed mother! You are a greater fool than I took you for. I had always credited you as the one person in this family with some sense. But I was wrong! Totally, totally wrong!'

Before Mercy could protest Blanche blew out the candle, leaving the girl in darkness. There was a rustle of bedclothes as the old woman pulled the blankets over her head, cutting short any further conversation on the subject.

Undressing in the dark presented no problems for Mercy, she had had to do it often enough when her grandmother was in a bad mood. As she prepared for bed she had to admit Blanche had a point. What future was there for her with Peter? Over the weeks since she had known him she had tried to school herself to look no further forward than their next meeting, but sometimes she could not help looking beyond; next month, next year, where would her relationship with Peter have taken her? She knew the greatest agony she could suffer would be never to see him again. She had fallen in love with him; no amount of telling herself she was the biggest fool on earth could alter that.

At work even the ever-optimistic Dolly viewed the situation with misgiving.

'I suppose 'ee know what you'm doing,' she said cautiously. 'I mean to say, where's it going to get 'ee? This gallivantin' is all very fine. But it won't lead nowhere, will it? 'Cepting trouble. Can't 'ee settle for someone a bit more suitable? Shall I ask Tom if he's got a decent friend?'

Contrary to expectations Dolly was still seeing Tom, the young man from the Electric Company, a good-natured soul who adored her.

Mercy declined the offer politely but firmly.

'You'm sure?' Dolly was not easily deterred. 'Us could 'ave a rare old time, the four of us.'

'Thank you, no,' repeated Mercy.

Undismayed Dolly was content to continue with Tom as her main topic of conversation.

'Did I tell 'ee I went to tea with 'is folks on Sunday? I was scared, I don't mind admitting, but there was no need. They were as nice as ninepence. Do 'ee know what 'is mother did? 'Cos it was such a raw day, Tom and me couldn't go for a walk to be on our own, like, so 'er banked up the fire in their front room and let us go in there. Made everyone else shift to the kitchen. There's not many as would've done that, not first time of meeting, is there?'

She went on to sing the praises of her Tom, the kindness of his family, the splendour of their tea. Mercy wished she would stop. She envied Dolly her comfortable courtship, warm by the fireside, surrounded by loving kindness. She knew such pleasures were not for her. It was unlikely she would ever meet Peter's mother, never mind being welcomed into the bosom of the household. Black despair weighed her down.

'If the irons moved as fast as the tongues in this room we'd all make our fortunes,' snapped Mrs Hoskins from the doorway. She strode purposefully down the aisle between the rows of tables, her footsteps heavy, her keys clanking menacingly at her waist.

Without turning her head Mercy knew she was heading in her direction. Sure enough, the woman stopped beside her table. An ominous silence followed.

'These are required urgently, Seaton,' she said at last. 'Have them finished before you leave. And none of your sloppy workmanship, mind, or you'll do them again.'

Mercy looked as the fresh consignment of clothes was tipped into her basket and she groaned inwardly. Every garment was a difficult one, heavily adorned with frills which would need hours of careful work with a small goffering iron to bring them up properly.

Aloud she simply said, 'Very good, Mrs Hoskins,' for she knew her employer was just waiting for her to utter one word of complaint.

I almost wish the old harridan would dismiss me, Mercy thought angrily, as she set the goffering irons to heat and damped down the clothes. But she knew Mrs Hoskins gained far too much pleasure from tormenting her ever to do such a thing.

Má Hoskins was becoming adept at finding subtle ways to make Mercy's life difficult – keeping her quota of work until last, so that she was always struggling to catch up, or making sure her load consisted of intricate items which needed extra work, such as today's frilled garments. Often Mrs Hoskins simply insisted on the work being done again, on the pretext it was unsatisfactory though they both knew it was not. Infuriating though she was she paled into insignificance compared with the problem presented by her husband.

Albert Hoskins had not given up his pursuit of Mercy, far from it. He would come into the ironing-room upon any pretext and, standing so close to her that the cloying scent of his hair-oil enveloped her, he would find some excuse to try to paw her. She did her best to avoid him but it was not easy. He had a way of creeping up to her on feet as silent as a cat's. The first she would know of his presence would be an arm about her waist or a clammy hand caressing her arm.

She knew that before long she would be forced to leave the laundry. She had begun to look for alternative employment but it was not easy to find; she was not naive enough to expect Mrs Hoskins to give her a decent reference. She wished she could afford the luxury of just walking out, but hers was the only money coming into the house. Joey's earnings were too small and irregular, and as for Pa's wages they seldom got past the Oak intact. There was nothing for it except to hope a new job would come up before something happened. It proved a vain hope.

It was a damp and chilly November day, already the sky through the laundry windows was beginning to darken. By contrast the ironing-room seemed warm and cosy, so the girls had started to sing at their work. Perhaps that was why Mercy did not know of Albert Hoskins's approach until two hands slid over her breasts.

'Stop it!' she cried, dodging aside.

'Oh come on, it's only a bit of fun. I like a bit of fun.'

His face was flushed, his eyes were bright. He reeked of cheap spirits. Hoskins sober was unpleasant, Hoskins drunk was repulsive. Mercy struggled to move away, but his arms still imprisoned her.

'Come here! Come here! I've got a message for you, that's what I've got!' he leered. Nuzzling his slack mouth close to her ear he began whispering obscenities while at the same time his fingers dug deeper into her flesh. It was horrible and disgusting and she could not free herself. Then, incensed beyond endurance, she struck out blindly at his head. She was hardly aware that she did so with a flat-iron.

Albert Hoskins dropped like a stone to the floor and lay there. The last notes of the singing faded away and an awed hush fell upon the ironing-room.

''E'm daid,' remarked Annie laconically. 'Dirty old devil! Tis no more than 'e deserved.'

Attracted by the unaccustomed silence Mrs Hoskins hurried in and saw her husband lying prone on the floor.

'Albert!' Her scream was piercing. 'Albert!' She flung herself on her knees beside him.

''E'm daid,' repeated Annie with relish.

Dolly stepped forward. 'No, e'm not. Look, e'm stirring. Move back, Missus, do! 'E needs a bit of fresh air, that's all.'

Albert Hoskins groaned, then groaned again and opened his eyes. 'She hit me,' he said in tones of wonderment.

All eyes turned towards Mercy who was standing frozen with shock, the iron still in her hand.

'You hit him? With that?' Mrs Hoskins looked from the girl to the flat-iron. There was a silence as she contemplated the enormity of what had happened. 'You might have killed him,' she began, then with mounting hysteria she went on, 'It's what you wanted to do, wasn't it? To kill him! Murderer! You deserve to hang! To hang, do you hear me?'

She made a lunge for Mercy but the girls held her back.

'Mr 'Oskins idn't too bad,' Dolly tried to calm things down. 'Look, 'e's only got a cut and a bit of a burn on 'is face. The doctor'll fix 'im up in two shakes.'

Strangely, Mrs Hoskins seemed more involved with her animosity towards Mercy than in caring for her husband. 'The police!' she shrieked. 'Why hasn't anyone called the police? I want this creature arrested at once.'

At last Mercy broke out of her shocked trance and faced the woman. Suddenly she was angry.

'Yes, call the police!' she declared. 'And when my case comes to court I shall tell how your husband is nothing more than a dirty old tom-cat who pesters girls until they can't take any more. If I hadn't hit him someone else would!'

'Who would believe lies like that?' demanded Mrs Hoskins.

'The whole of Torquay! Everyone knows what he is like – a dirty, disgusting animal – and you know, so why haven't you done anything about it?'

'Lies! Dreadful lies!' countered Mrs Hoskins, but her voice was beginning to lack conviction.

'It's the truth and you know it!' Mercy confronted her. 'Otherwise, why haven't you asked me *why* I did it? Well, he went too far. Call the police if you wish but don't complain if the *Torquay Directory* splashes the story across its pages. Yes, and other papers too, so the whole country knows what sort of man you married.'

Mrs Hoskins swallowed hard, her face taking on a pinched look.

'Get out!' she said in a low voice. 'Collect your things and go! And think yourself lucky you haven't finished up in prison!'

Mercy knew she was lucky: but for the fact that Albert Hoskins had approached her from behind and therefore had not received the full impact of the blow, she might indeed have been facing a murder charge.

Ice-cold and shaking with delayed shock she fled from the room. Snatching up her coat from its peg she ran from the laundry without bothering to put it on. People turned to stare as she dashed past but she did not care. All she wanted was to get as far away as possible. A stitch in her side seized her with agonizing cramp and her breathless lungs became a fiery torment, only then did she slow down. She was at the outskirts of the town by now, where the houses were interspersed with fields and orchards, and quite suddenly she collapsed against a farm gate and sobbed bitterly.

Gradually she grew conscious of the persistent drizzle which was soaking her and of her coat still clutched in her hands. Slowly she pulled it on, the wet sleeves of her blouse sticking to the lining. Then wiping her face inadequately with the back of her hand she began the dismal trudge home.

Her family greeted her unexpected arrival with surprise. Her account of her dismissal silenced them with disbelief. Ma was the first to recover.

''It 'im with an iron? Never!' she said at last. 'Oh, 'ee shouldn't have done that, maid! 'Ee really shouldn't! Not to your maister! Tidn't right!'

She seemed more distressed by her daughter's attack on authority than anything else. But support for Mercy came from an unexpected quarter. Lizzie's pregnancy was proving uncomfortable and so, out of sorts and clumsy with her swollen stomach, she was delighted to hear her sister had struck a blow at the sex who was the cause of so much discomfort.

'Yes 'twas!' she declared. 'I 'opes 'ee thumped the old goat real hard, that I do! Men! They care for nothing but their own pleasures. We're the ones as suffer. 'Ee did fine, Mercy, my maidie. 'Ee did fine!'

'How will we manage for money?' asked Mercy anxiously.

'A splendid time to be wondering that!' rasped Blanche. 'You should have thought of it before.' Then she added, almost gently for her, 'Still, what is done is done. And matters will not be improved if you catch your death of cold. You are soaked through. Here, drink this then put on some dry clothes.'

From the bottle she held in her arms she poured some gin into a cup. It was not a drink Mercy liked; even the smell turned her stomach; but she was so touched by her grandmother's unexpected gesture that she swallowed the gin in one gulp. As it coursed through her veins it warmed her. Soon she found it blurring the edges of the nightmare events of her day.

'We'll manage somehow,' she said optimistically. 'I'll get work again soon, you'll see.'

It did not prove to be so easy. There was no shortage of work, but as she had no reference and she was unwilling to state why she had left her last place of employment Mercy stood little chance. All that was open to her was occasional farmwork and two mornings a week scrubbing out the bar parlour at the Oak – a task of which Lizzie was no longer capable.

'Ask your toff for some money,' suggested Joey. 'You're still seeing him regular, aren't you?'

'Regularly!' Mercy corrected him automatically. 'Anyway, don't be silly!'

'What's silly about it? It's time you got something out of him. What do you go out with him for, otherwise?'

'Joey!' At the tone of Mercy's reproof the boy began to head for the door. 'Where are you going now?' she asked.

'None of your business!' he retorted, and left, slamming the door behind him.

Mercy sighed. She was growing concerned about him; he was so cross and moody these days.

''E'm growing up; tasting 'is oats,' said Ma. 'Leave un be.'

Mercy could not help being anxious. She did not like him being constantly in the company of boys such as Billy Dawe and Georgie Hannaford. Most of all she was distressed by his surliness towards herself. They had always been so close; she sensed her little brother was growing away from her and it hurt. His suggestion that she should ask Peter for help stung her. Didn't he know she would never do such a thing?

She had not told Peter of the change in her circumstances; it would have meant telling him about the trouble with Albert Hoskins. No, she would have died of shame having to recount such things to Peter. Her love for him was the only beautiful thing she had and she refused to let the sordid details of her life intrude.

–

Peter had his own problems at that moment. His mother, having decided upon Rose Gifford as the most suitable wife for her son, was using her considerable powers of coercion to get the matter settled. At first she had been quite subtle, but Peter began to notice how often he and Rose appeared at the same functions. It seemed that everywhere he went he found himself escorting her in to supper, or partnering her at bridge. Only when people began to refer to them as 'the young couple' or speak of them in the same breath did he realize how firmly his feet were being guided towards matrimony.

Eventually he was goaded into declaring, 'Mother, I must tell you, I have no intention of marrying Rose.'

Agnes Lisburne opened her eyes wide in amazement and said, 'What an extraordinary statement! Who suggested that you should?'

The solid grounds of his complaint shifted from beneath his feet.

'Well, didn't you— wouldn't you— ?' he stammered.

'I confess, I think she would be an excellent choice, but so would several others. Maud Blandford, for example, she's a charming girl. Or Alice Dixon. Why you should bring up poor Rose's name in such a way I cannot imagine. Has her father been speaking to you?'

'No,' admitted Peter uncomfortably, 'but it seems that everywhere I go, there she is too, an—'

'I do not see why you consider it to be peculiar. Our families have known each other for years; we move in the same circles; our friends are their friends. Of course you meet frequently! What an extraordinary boy you are!' No hint of fondness softened her final statement.

Peter withdrew feeling foolish; so often in an interview with his mother he left feeling foolish, or guilty, or both! Had he imagined it?

He almost persuaded himself it was possible, and felt relieved at his own idiocy.

His relief was short-lived. That very Sunday, after church, the vicar patted him on the shoulder and said in a confidential tone, 'From what I hear it will not be long before I have the pleasure of putting up the banns for you, eh, Mr Lisburne?' He did not name the prospective bride, but he looked towards Rose, who was getting into a carriage with her father, and gave a very un-clerical wink.

Peter made some mild reply. He felt annoyed and trapped, and his mood was not improved by the way Rose gazed at him adoringly out of her pallid eyes. Now, to see Mercy looking at him in such a way – that would be a different matter...

Thinking of Mercy made him uneasy. She had seemed different lately, more withdrawn and quiet, not a bit like the affectionate care-free girl of the summer. The idea that she might be falling out of love with him troubled him. He was not a vain man, nor was he stupid; he knew he could offer Mercy so much, and the thought she might be rejecting him was an uncomfortable one. Yet it would be typical of her; she was so fastidious about not accepting gifts that a simple posy of flowers or box of chocolates provoked a protest. Why, then, should he be surprised if she abandoned him, one of the wealthiest young men in Torquay?

Abandoned! It was a strange choice of word, even in thought. Peter tried to imagine what existence would be like without Mercy and her unstinting adulation and warm bright smile. With a shock he realized he would indeed feel bereft, and yes, abandoned. How far their relationship had moved on from the carefree flirtation at the Regatta. That was in the past, what of the future? Peter's brow knotted with anxiety as he tried to work out a solution.

'This has just arrived for you, sir. It was delivered by hand.' Rogers held out the letter on a silver salver.

Recognizing Freddie Parkham's scrawl Peter opened it.

'Not bad news, I hope?' asked his mother, looking up from her embroidery.

'Not really. Freddie and I had arranged to go to the theatre this evening, but he has to go to Plymouth on urgent business and won't be back in time.'

'So you will be home for dinner?'

'Yes, I suppose so.'

'Splendid! Now numbers at my table will be just right.'

'At table?'

'A few old friends. Being certain that you will be dining with us makes the round dozen, a very satisfactory number.'

Peter could have groaned aloud. He had walked straight into a trap he should have seen opening before him; it was too late now to think of an excuse. Silently he cursed Freddie, the more so as he was certain his 'urgent business' was a raven-haired little actress from the Theatre Royal.

'Who is coming?' he asked, though he could guess.

'Sir John and Lady Thorpe, the Blandfords—'

'And the Giffords?' cut in Peter.

'Certainly. Did I not say old friends? Naturally that includes the Major and Rose.'

Now Peter did groan aloud.

His mother looked at him sharply. 'I trust you will be nice to Rose. I will not have you being discourteous to any of my guests.'

'Of course, Mother,' he replied, irritated at being addressed like an erring schoolboy.

How much easier it would be if he could tell Rose openly and frankly he had no wish to marry her. But polite society did not work in such a way. He would have to spend the evening involved in a game of matrimonial cat-and-mouse; and he was not looking forward to it.

The Giffords were early, and Peter found himself constantly paired with Rose. No matter how many times he excused himself to greet new arrivals, within minutes she would be at his side again, whether by accident or design he could not tell, he suspected the latter.

'Isn't Rose's dress charming?' his mother asked him. 'Such a delightful shade of pink.'

Peter had no option but to agree. 'Yes, very pretty,' he said.

It was true, the dress was pretty and he knew enough about female fashion to guess it had cost a small fortune. But pink velvet did not flatter Rose, it made her look scrawny. He had a sudden vision of how Mercy would look in that dress, the skirt flaring out from her small waist, the soft colour glowing against her creamy skin. He longed to be able to give her such clothes. How proud he would be to be seen with her…

His mother was addressing Rose and her words broke into his thoughts.

'…such a clever choice for a young girl, so suitable. Did you know that pink is Peter's favourite colour – or perhaps you guessed, you sly boots?'

Peter felt himself go crimson. To witness his mother in this arch mood was embarrassing enough, but her words had alarmed him. They were far too pointed for comfort.

Bright colour suffused Rose's face and she glanced up at Peter half shyly, half encouragingly.

Peter was completely tongue-tied. Frantically he sought for a non-committal reply. Nothing came. To his intense relief Rogers announced that dinner was served. Peter was the host, so as protocol demanded he offered his arm to Lady Thorpe. Unfortunately there was no salvation to be found with her.

'Such formality amongst friends,' she declared with a little pout. 'Let's dispense with anything so stuffy. Major Gifford, dear, can I beg you to oblige and take me in to? And as for you, Peter, I am sure there is a young lady not a million miles away who will make you a far more suitable dinner partner than an old married lady like myself.'

Lady Thorpe, who was in fact young and very elegant, slid her arm through the major's, leaving Peter no alternative but to offer his to a beaming Rose.

At table he found he had Lady Thorpe to his right and Rose to his left. Desperately he tried to engage Lady Thorpe in conversation. Every time he tried she said, 'My dear boy, there is no need to be polite with me! I understand these things, I promise you. I will be perfectly happy chatting away to the major about my garden.' She spoke in a stage whisper, so that her words were distinctly heard by everyone, and Peter's discomfort increased as ten pairs of eyes regarded Rose and him with fond indulgence.

From then on everything he said or did was regarded as having undertones of love. When he helped Rose to more wine he was being attentive; when he fetched her wrap he was being a true Romeo; when he suggested that the gentlemen should join the ladies his words were greeted with cries of, 'Been apart long enough, have you? Don't worry, my boy, we've all been through it. We understand.'

There was no mistaking it, he was steadily and relentlessly being pressured into proposing to Rose. That his mother had engaged the support of her friends he did not doubt, for every now and again one or other would look towards her and catch her eye with a conspiratorial glance.

The whole evening was assuming a nightmarish quality as far as Peter was concerned, and leaving the dining room for the drawing room did not alleviate matters. He felt the atmosphere charged with a subdued excitement which he did not fully understand but which he found irritating. His mother was plotting to marry him to Rose, but how he was not sure. He was totally unprepared, however, for her next manoeuvre.

The coffee-cups were circulating, along with the trivial conversation, when Lady Thorpe suddenly said, 'Agnes, dear, those are remarkably fine pearls you are wearing this evening.' She spoke in artificial tones, as though she had rehearsed the speech. All other conversation ceased as everyone's eyes turned towards her. Only Peter's mother seemed unaffected. She twisted the rope of pearls she was wearing round her fingers and held it up to the light.

'Surely you have seen these before, Margaret?' she said. 'I was given them on my wedding-day by my poor husband. They hold such happy memories!'

She dabbed at her eyes with a handkerchief in a gesture so false that Peter felt embarrassed – and uneasy.

'Such a gift must, of course, have a tremendous sentimental value. I'm sure you would never part with them,' said Lady Thorpe in the same artificial voice.

'Oh, I must part with them one day, but only to a very special person.' Agnes Lisburne lowered her eyes demurely. 'They are family heirlooms. They will be given to Peter's bride on her wedding-day – if he ever chooses a wife!'

All eyes now turned towards Peter.

'Of course Peter will choose a wife, won't you, dear boy?' Lady Thorpe laid a gloved hand on his arm. 'And you will choose well, I am sure. How pretty your bride will look wearing those pearls. I think they are such flattering jewels for a bride, or indeed any young girl. I think it is something in the way that a delicate youthful complexion is complimented by the smooth exterior of the pearls.'

'Do you think so?' Agnes Lisburne examined her necklace as if seeing it anew. 'Shall we try it and see, Rose, my dear? Let us see how these look on you.'

She took off the pearls and slipped them round Rose's neck.

Peter struggled to calm his rising panic; he could see his mother's strategy now.

'There, doesn't she look delightful,' Agnes beamed at the blushing Rose.

Her smile assumed a steely quality when she looked towards her son. 'Don't you agree that Rose looks charming, Peter?' she demanded. 'Would not she look delightful wearing them as a bride?'

The whole room waited expectantly for his answer.

Peter felt his hands go moist with apprehension. What was he to answer? If he said no, then he would be insulting a guest. If he said yes he would be, in effect, declaring his intention to marry the girl. Desperately he searched for a diplomatic answer – but in vain. If only Rose would stop gazing at him with such hope and adoration.

'You look first-class, Rose,' he blustered at last. 'When you eventually get some fellow to the altar make sure you get him to buy you a set of pearls, eh?'

The silence in the room became almost tangible, the atmosphere heavy with sudden embarrassment.

Peter cursed himself for his clumsiness. Surely he could have phrased it better? Rose's already crimson complexion turned an even deeper hue, then her face crumpled. Peter realized with alarm that she was crying. Wrenching off the necklace she flung it down, then fled from the room.

Major Gifford leapt to his feet and followed her, pausing at the door to glare at him and declare, 'You— you—' but his vocabulary proved inadequate, and he contented himself with an inarticulate snarl before hurrying in pursuit of Rose.

The other guests shuffled awkwardly, uncertain of what to say or do, except Lady Thorpe who sat twisting her hands in anguish.

'Oh dear, Agnes, perhaps we should not have—' she began in a voice which trembled on the edge of tears.

Mrs Lisburne silenced her with a look.

Peter swallowed hard, hoping the sudden nausea that had assailed him would fade; he was in trouble enough without disgracing himself further. Once more he was conscious of eyes looking at him, this time they were hostile. He had no alternative but to leave the room.

His mother came to his room as Poole, his manservant, was packing his valise.

'You are going away?' she asked, as Poole dutifully melted from sight. 'Yes, I suppose you have no alternative, having behaved so abominably.' Her voice was calm and even, in a way which struck icily at Peter's insides.

'I didn't mean to behave badly. I'm sorry I upset Rose—'

'What's the point in saying such things to me? It is Rose who should be hearing them,' his mother cut in. 'I suggest you go to the Giffords' house first thing tomorrow and offer your humblest apologies and beg her forgiveness.' It was not a suggestion, it was an order.

Peter took a deep breath. 'No, Mother,' he said.

Agnes gave no sign of having heard him. 'There are our other friends, too, of course,' she continued. 'Quite how I am going to face them in the future I do not know. I just hope they are kinder and more considerate of my feelings than my own son. How someone I nurtured could have behaved so disgracefully! To raise the expectations of that poor girl! She was so sure— Everyone was sure you intended to marry her and then—'

'No, Mother!' Peter broke in again, suddenly forceful. 'I will not accept responsibility for everyone's expectations. That was your doing. I have never shown any preference for Rose. She is a girl I have known all my life, nothing more. I am deeply sorry I hurt her. But it was your doing.'

'How can you say that?' Agnes demanded.

'I can say it because it is true. You have been conniving for ages to manoeuvre me into a corner so I would have to marry Rose, dragging in all your friends to assist you in your plotting. Do you think I didn't know?'

'Conniving? Plotting? What kind of words are these for a son to fling at his mother?' From anyone else the speech would have sounded hurt or disappointed. Agnes Lisburne's tone was harshly reproving.

'Oh, I can see you'll never admit anything! Very well, I will apologize to Rose – by letter. I don't suppose she wants to see me again. And I certainly don't want to see her!'

'And after that? You appear to be preparing to leave.'

'I don't know. I'll go to my club for tonight. After that... I've no definite plans.'

Agnes regarded her only child with near-contempt.

'No doubt in your own good time you will inform me where you are hiding,' she said.

All at once Peter was tired of being on the defensive.

'Mother, I am not going into hiding,' he stated harshly. 'Nor am I going to marry Rose, and that is final!'

'Indeed, and—'

'The subject is closed, Mother! If you have nothing else to discuss with me I will bid you good night.'

Agnes was clearly taken aback.

'Really—!' she began again.

'Good night, Mother!' Slowly and deliberately Peter began to undo his tie.

Finally Agnes was forced to face the unpalatable truth. Her son was defying her.

'Pah!' she exclaimed angrily. 'Pah!' And with that she swept from the room.

He wanted to leave Torquay. Only one thing kept him – his meeting with Mercy the next day.

'I'm going away!' He said the words bluntly and without warning.

'Away? Where?' asked Mercy.

'I'm not sure yet. London at first, I think, then probably abroad, somewhere where the sun shines. I'm so tired of this cold and wet.'

Mercy felt her world crumble about her.

'And tired of me?' she asked in a small voice.

'Tired of you? Good heavens, no!' Peter was appalled. 'I adore you, you know that. You are the one bright thing in my whole world.'

'Then how can you leave me?'

This was the problem which had been gnawing at Peter all night long.

'It's not that I want to leave you,' he said. 'It's just I feel I can't live here any longer. Not in Torquay, where everyone knows me.'

'Why, what have you done?' demanded Mercy, alarmed yet determined to stand by him long before she knew his crime.

'It was all so frightful…' Peter told her of the events at the dinner party. '…So you see, I shall probably be shunned by everyone from now on. That is, if Major Gifford doesn't take a horsewhip to me first,' he finished.

Mercy had a sudden urge to smile. Compared with her own situation it seemed so trivial. Then the disconsolate droop of his shoulders touched her.

'It will blow over soon, you'll see,' she said gently. 'As soon as some other young man comes along for Rose this will all be forgotten.'

'Yes, but what do I do until then? Can't you see, I have to get away?'

'Yes, I suppose so. When will you come back? You will come back, won't you?'

There was such appeal in her expression that Peter felt himself torn. He longed to break free from his present narrow existence. But to be without Mercy...

'Come with me,' he said suddenly. Then with mounting conviction, 'Yes! Come with me! It's the perfect solution!'

Mercy did not answer. She sat very still.

'What's the matter? Don't you like the idea?' asked Peter.

'That depends.'

'On what?'

Again Mercy did not answer immediately. She wanted to go with him. Oh, how she wanted it! But she knew too many girls who had taken that path, and where had it led them? Without exception they finished up alone, fending for themselves, usually with a child or two in tow. That prospect did not worry her, she knew she could cope. What she would not be able to bear would be the agony of seeing love disintegrating to be replaced by distrust and disillusion, even hatred. She was not sure she could risk that. But Peter was talking to her.

'We'll go to London, get a special licence.'

'What do we want a special licence for?'

'To get married of course! You don't think I was suggesting anything else, I hope.' Peter looked both hurt and indignant at the idea.

Mercy loved him when he was like that, half tender man, half ruffled schoolboy.

'Well, did you?' he demanded. 'How could you think such a thing? I love you far too much to consider any other sort of relationship.'

She drew in her breath sharply.

'You love me?' she asked, her voice unsteady. These were the words she had most wanted to hear him say. She had heard them in all her dreams, and now she was hearing them in reality.

'Yes, I love you,' he repeated. 'I wish I could think of some more original way to express how I feel. I've never known anyone like you before nor experienced any emotion as powerful as this. When we are apart you are all I can think about. You are the most important thing in my entire existence, and I can't bear to imagine the rest of my life without you. It would be empty and desolate beyond all bearing.' He reached out and took her hands in his, drawing her close to him. 'That's why I'm pleading with you. Please marry me.'

Mercy took in every word he spoke and treasured it. Peter's love was something she would always hold to be very precious. Just for a moment she allowed herself to indulge in a dream of being Peter's wife. The idea was so beautiful it hurt…

'We cannot do it,' she said suddenly.

'Why not?'

'It would cost a fortune!'

Peter laughed and put his arms around her.

'I promise I can afford a licence – and a little over. You do want to marry me, don't you?'

Mercy wished that he would not hold her so close. It was hard to be determined when she could feel his heart beating against hers, but she knew she had to try.

'We're too far apart. You should marry a lady,' she protested.

'In my eyes you are a lady. That's sufficient for me. Why are you making all these objections? Don't you love me?'

'Of course I do!' The admission tore out of her before she could stop it. 'But I can't marry you because I did something awful – really awful, not like you upsetting Rose. I nearly killed someone.'

'I don't believe it!'

'I did. It was Mr Hoskins at the laundry. He – well, he got rather forward so – so I hit him with a flat-iron. It was a miracle he wasn't killed.'

Even as she spoke she knew that her attack on Albert Hoskins was not the real reason for her refusal. She was afraid to marry Peter, and that was the truth of it. The gulf between their worlds was too great. It could not be crossed.

'You hit him with what?' Peter stared at her.

'A flat-iron.' It occurred to her that he might not know what it was, that he had probably never seen one in his life, so she mimed the action, ironing invisible garments.

Peter let out a yell of laughter and clasped her even tighter to him.

'Mercy, you're wonderful, do you know that? This Hoskins person, he deserved what he got. I refuse to let a flat-iron come between us ever! Now will you say yes to my proposal of marriage and have done with it?'

How could she continue to deny him? She loved him too much.

'Yes! Oh yes!' she cried. And deliberately closed her mind to the difficulties she knew lay ahead.

Chapter Four

The rumble of a cart woke Mercy. There were footsteps, too, and the clank of a milkman's churn, and she wondered if she would ever get used to the constant activity of city life. The winter's morning was still dark; she could scarcely make out Peter's outline, but she could feel his warmth as he lay beside her. Beneath the comfort of the counterpane she twisted her wedding-ring round and round, finding reassurance in its presence; even after being married for a whole month she was sometimes afraid that this was all a dream and at any moment she would wake up and find Blanche beside her instead of her husband.

It had been harder than she had expected, saying goodbye to her family. Lizzie had been openly envious, Blanche contemptuous, and Joey had feigned total indifference, but beneath their varied reactions she had sensed a tide of family affection that had taken her unawares. Then Ma had cried and Dolly, who had come to see her off, had joined in so lustily that, before she knew it, she was making a tearful third.

She had never travelled by train before so the journey to Paddington enthralled her with its speed and comfort. Nestling in the cushions of a first-class compartment, from time to time she allowed her gaze to creep up to the luggage rack to her brand new suitcases. Peter's manservant, Poole, had wanted to take them to the luggage van, but Mercy had refused to allow them out of her sight. For once Peter had put his foot down about her accepting gifts from him and insisted upon giving her the money to buy what she needed.

'Circumstances are different now we are to be married. Surely you would like something nice for your wedding, wouldn't you?' he had pointed out.

It was an argument against which Mercy had little defence. It was obvious she could not accompany Peter to London wearing her old black skirt and the jacket with the much-mended seams.

'Just get enough to tide you over for a few days,' Peter had advised. 'The rest you can buy in London, where you'll have far greater choice.'

Looking at the case she knew to be packed with cambrics, silks, and cashmeres, she could not imagine what else she could possibly want.

Their wedding had taken place early one frosty December morning in a chilly London church, with the verger as one witness, and a postman, dragged in none too reluctantly from his rounds, as the other. From there Mercy began her new life as Mrs Peter Lisburne, in a furnished apartment off Sloane Street.

Pale edges of light were beginning to steal round the curtains; Mercy judged it was getting late. Carefully, so as not to disturb Peter, she began to worm her way to the edge of the bed.

In spite of her precautions he stirred. 'Getting up already?' he mumbled. 'It's still dark.'

'Not quite. It's late.'

'Why, what time is it?'

'Seven o'clock.'

Peter gave a groan. 'It's the middle of the night.'

'Not to me. Normally I would have been up a couple of hours by now.'

'Quite uncivilized. Only sparrows get up at this hour.' He turned towards her, putting his arm about her, pulling her gently back into bed.

Unresisting Mercy moved towards him until her body was shaped against his and her lips rested against his cheek, brushing the unshaven stubble on his chin. His free hand moved to her breast and she could feel the warmth of his fingers caressing her through the thin fabric of her nightgown.

'There, isn't this better than getting up on a dark morning,' he whispered.

In reply she moved even closer to him, arousing his body with hers. This side of marriage had come as a pleasant surprise. Country born and bred, she had come to her marriage-bed more well-informed than most of her town-dwelling contemporaries – at home it had been well drilled into her that 'men get the pleasure, the women get the pain'. Doubtless the pain would come later, but in the meantime she was experiencing much more of the pleasure than she had expected. Sometimes her reaction to Peter's love-making troubled her: she had been quite unprepared for its passion and its energy, but she could not help herself.

Peter slowly undid the tiny pearl buttons of her nightgown and drew the garment over her head, almost making a ceremony of the act in a way which aroused her. His silk pyjamas had been discarded and now he moved over her. Eagerly Mercy drew him in, her senses burning from the feel of his caressing touch, from the sensuality of his skin on hers.

'I've married such a wanton,' murmured Peter later, as they lay content and drowsy in each other's arms.

Mercy looked at him sharply, suddenly afraid that he found her response to him too forthright. She relaxed when he merely smiled and brushed a stray lock of dark hair from her forehead.

Secretly he was very pleased to find he could bring his bride to such emotion. It had been her frank adoration and gentle beauty which had first drawn him to love her, the depths of her unrestrained passion had been quite unexpected. He felt a sudden surge of pride that such a lovely and warmly responsive creature was his and his alone. In this blissful torpor, with her soft body still moulded to his, Peter's eyelids began to droop and he fell asleep.

Mercy, also, succumbed to drowsiness for a while, then the unaccustomed lateness of the hour prevented her from sleeping properly. After a while she gently disentangled herself from Peter's sleeping embrace and tiptoed to her dressing-room. At first it had astonished her to have a room entirely devoted to getting dressed, until she found what she considered adequate in the way of clothes and what Peter thought of as minimum requirements were very far apart.

Now she selected what clothes she would need, picking out a morning-gown in soft blue merino wool trimmed with a collar of white muslin; then she ran her bath. Apart from her time spent with Peter, this was her favourite part of the day. She still marvelled at the gleaming whiteness of the tiled bathroom, and the shining brass taps which not only gushed water but warm water into the bargain! No standing out in the yard in all weathers, having to work a pump-handle which liked nothing better than seizing up when you least expected it. Having lived all her life in a household where every drop of water had to be carried Mercy revelled in the luxury of warm scented suds.

As she lay there she wondered what Ma and Lizzie would think of having just to turn on a tap. She suddenly found herself assailed by a sharp attack of homesickness. She missed them all! Quarrelsome, slovenly, and difficult they might be but they were her flesh and blood and she loved them. Surely it would not be too long before she saw them again? Brushing away the tears she reached out for a bath towel. It was time to begin another day in her new life.

The dining-room was empty when she entered, and the meagre flames of the newly lit fire had not gathered strength enough to give out any warmth. Mercy shivered. What she needed was some break-fast. The sideboard was devoid of all signs of food and she decided to go in search of some. When she pushed open the baize door which led to the domestic quarters she found herself in a dark corridor. Ahead of her the smell of cooking and the sound of voices indicated the kitchen. Her only previous foray into this region had been on the day when Peter and she had moved in; there had never seemed to be the need to visit it again, for Poole had the knack of anticipating her needs. Invariably he had ushered the cook in to her for the day's menus even before she had chance to ring the bell. She felt that now would be an excellent opportunity to look at the kitchen properly.

She opened the kitchen door and at once a stunned silence fell on the room. Three pairs of eyes glared at her indignantly.

'Madam!' Poole put down the mug of tea he had been drinking and leapt to his feet, putting on his jacket as he did so. 'Madam, is there anything wrong?'

'No,' Mercy assured him. 'I would just like some breakfast, if you please.'

'Madam has only to ring.' Poole's expression was reproving. 'Cook will get it immediately.'

The cook, a solid surly woman, had also leapt to her feet.

'I'm sure I didn't know you were up, Madam. I'm not accustomed to such early rising. Your breakfast will be ready soon. I'm sure I do my best, but it's not easy being single-handed. I'm used to having a kitchen-maid on hand.' Her voice carried as much whining insolence as she dared.

'Perhaps Nelly could help you,' suggested Mercy, because she felt something was expected of her. The look of outrage on the house-maid's face convinced her she had made a blunder.

'Nelly has her own duties, Madam,' put in Poole. 'If I might escort Madam back to the diningroom I will ensure that breakfast is served as soon as possible. There was really no need for Madam to come to the kitchen. It would have been sufficient for Madam to ring.'

He shepherded Mercy along the corridor and back through the baize door, disapproval in every line of his stick-thin figure. Like an errant child Mercy returned to the dining-room, thoroughly chastened.

From the start she had not liked Poole. He seemed to be constantly hovering behind doors. It was because of Poole she steadfastly refused to have a lady's maid. She reckoned there were enough servants in the house already without adding more appendages to her marriage.

While she waited in the dining-room Poole brought in a selection of silver chafing-dishes and placed them on the sideboard, his silence a further reproof to her. She felt quite relieved when Peter arrived.

'How you can get up so early and look so lovely I really don't know,' he greeted her, planting a kiss on her cheek.

'Sh! What will Poole think?' she whispered, flushing.

'What does it matter what Poole thinks?' Peter demanded, cheerily examining the contents of one dish after another. 'Ah, kippers! And scrambled eggs, too, I think.' Piling his plate he came and sat opposite to her at the table. 'And talking of Poole, what's this I hear about you exploring the kitchen this morning?'

'Has he been complaining?' demanded Mercy.

'Certainly not!' Peter looked aghast at the idea. 'He simply mentioned it as he was laying out my clothes. I'm glad he did because I don't think it was a wise thing for you to do.'

'Why ever not?'

'Well, Cook might not like it. The kitchen is very much her domain, you know. I can't recall my mother ever going into the kitchen.'

Mercy looked at him in utter astonishment. 'Are you telling me I mustn't go into the kitchen of my own home?'

'I wouldn't put it as strongly as that. But Cook might take offence or think that you are checking-up on her.'

'But surely you pay her wages so I'm entitled to check up on her? Otherwise how do I make sure she is doing her work properly? It might be filthy in there, or full of thieves and vagabonds for all we know.'

This thought had clearly never struck Peter before and for a moment he looked puzzled, then said, with the air of one who has just had an inspiration, 'You can safely leave it to Poole. He'll know how to keep an eye on things. Above all, though, we don't want to upset Cook, do we? Whatever would we do if she gave notice?'

It seemed to Mercy that cooks were a very sensitive breed, and she wondered how any employee of Mrs Hoskins would get on if they attempted such airs and graces. It was on the tip of her tongue to point out they didn't *need* a cook, that she was quite capable of seeing to their meals, but just then Poole entered with the post.

Mercy watched as Peter flicked through the envelopes. Rather a lot of them were bills, and she felt a pang of conscience as she thought of all the money she had spent recently.

'Why, there's one for you!' declared Peter.

'For me?' Although she had written several this was the first letter she had received since coming to London. She took the cheap blue envelope from him and looked at it. 'To Mrs Peter Lisburne' it said, and she felt incredibly proud when she saw the words.

'Aren't you going to open it, or are you content to admire the outside?' teased Peter. 'It's got a Torquay postmark; maybe it's from your family.'

It wasn't. When Mercy opened it she found it was from Dolly. Dolly, who was no great hand with the pen, had written exactly as they had been taught in the village school. 'Dear Mercy,' it began, 'I hope you are well, I am in good health. Thank you for your letter. London must be an interesting place...'

As she read the stilted phrases Mercy was suddenly transported back to the dark little classroom that smelled of chalk dust and other less pleasant things. She and Dolly had sat together under the eagle eye of Miss Bowden, whose tight white curls and huge bosom had bounced energetically with every movement...

'Not bad news, I hope. You look quite sad,' said Peter.

'No, it's just from Dolly,' replied Mercy, conscious that for a brief moment she had been perilously close to homesickness again. In truth, there had been precious little news in it, for Dolly had been too overawed by the act of putting pen to paper, but Mercy cherished it none the less.

Her letter read and re-read she looked up to see that Peter had cast his mail to one side and was helping himself to more toast and marmalade.

'Are there no more letters from Torquay?' she asked.

'No. Were you expecting one?'

'Well, I thought that perhaps your mother…'

Peter's face darkened a little. 'There'll be no letter from my mother for quite a while: for one thing, she doesn't know my address, and for another she doesn't know about our marriage.'

'You don't think you should let her know? You are her only son.'

'A fact she has never let me forget.' Peter's expression softened, and he stretched across the table to cover Mercy's hand with his own. 'Don't worry, my love. I'll let her know all in good time. As I have tried to explain to you, she is not an easy woman, especially when I do something of which she disapproves. All I'm asking for is for us to have a few blissful weeks together undisturbed, just you and I.'

'Do you think she will disapprove very much?'

'I'm afraid she will.'

Mercy gave a sigh. 'I don't like the idea of causing trouble between you and your mother,' she said.

Peter just laughed. 'Once you have met her you'll realize there has always been trouble between us. Though you are the most adorable, most beautiful cause of contention there's ever been.'

He leaned forward towards her and Mercy half closed her eyes in blissful anticipation of a kiss. At that moment Poole entered with fresh coffee, and the pair of them sat bolt upright.

'What are we going to do today?' Mercy asked to cover her confusion.

'How about a stroll in Hyde Park? It promises to be a nice bright day. Then a little luncheon at home?'

The trees in Hyde Park were stripped bare of their leaves and the grass had been seared by the icy winds. Nevertheless, it was one of Mercy's favourite parts of London. Peter had taken her on innumerable sightseeing trips round the city which she had enjoyed enormously: there was so much to interest and impress her. Sometimes, though, she found the ceaseless hustle and bustle overwhelming and she longed for the sight of a familiar face or something peaceful. The park was the closest thing she could find to the woods and fields she was used to, and she and Peter walked there frequently.

It seemed inevitable that any outing with Peter would eventually turn into a shopping expedition. Somehow, she did not quite know how, their stroll had taken them out of the park and along Piccadilly. The shops of the Burlington Arcade drew Peter like a magnet.

Already she had noticed how adept her husband was at spending money. It was an occupation still new to her, one which made her uneasy. With difficulty she managed to dissuade Peter from buying her a very expensive fan. Instead she steered him towards a bookshop, and they spent an enjoyable half-hour browsing among the shelves. Of all the things which Peter wanted to buy for her it was for books that she was greedy. There was so much she didn't know, so many subjects of which she was ignorant... A small publication caught her eye.

'This is the one I would like you to buy for me, please,' she said, handing it to Peter straight-faced.

'*Etiquette for Ladies.* Are you sure?' he asked in mock horror.

'Yes, very sure. Even though I'm not a lady I would like to learn to behave like one, for your sake.'

'Well, I suppose I would be a cad not to buy it for you, despite its exorbitant price of sixpence. I trust you have no objections if I choose some other books on more flippant subjects? A decadent novel or two, perhaps, and some frivolous poetry?'

Smiling, Mercy shook her head; she knew that he would choose titles he thought she would enjoy. Watching him make his selection from the packed shelves she wondered at his unceasing kindness and generosity to her, and decided that she must be the luckiest woman alive.

That afternoon Peter went to spend an hour or two at his club. Mercy felt lost without him. She was reluctant to ask him not to go, knowing how much pleasure meeting his friends gave him. She regretted that she had no such acquaintances of her own, and she wondered how you got to know people in London. True, they did occasionally meet people known to Peter during their expeditions, but the outcome of these encounters was distressingly similar: the men would eye her appreciatively while at the same time throwing knowing glances in Peter's direction, and the women would treat the pair of them with icy politeness and frosty stares.

'Is it that they don't believe we are married?' Mercy had cried in desperation. 'Does everyone take me for your fancy woman?'

'Of course not! The trouble is you are too pretty, and no other woman dare let her husband near you. They can't stand the competition,' Peter had consoled her.

As time passed she began to realize the truth: no matter how bright and shiny her wedding-ring, nor how elegant her clothes, she still could not be taken for a lady. It was something she was determined to rectify, so she settled herself in front of the drawing room fire with *Etiquette for Ladies* and addressed herself to the knotty problems involved in receiving calls and leaving visiting cards until it was time to dress for dinner and then the theatre.

Mercy never expected a chance meeting with Freddie Parkham to mark the depth of the gulf between her old life and her new. They were leaving the theatre when they encountered him in the crush. He was accompanied by a young woman whose incredible blonde hair could not possibly have been real but whose equally incredible bosom undoubtedly was.

'Lisburne! Of all people,' he cried, clapping Peter on the back heartily.

'Freddie Parkham! I'd no idea you were in town!'

'Just come up to visit my tailor. But what about you? You're certainly keeping good company, you old dog!' Freddie's bold searching eyes swept over Mercy.

At that moment his companion piped up stridently, 'When do we eat, Freddie? Me belly thinks me throat's cut.'

'Presently, Vi my sweet,' he replied calmly. 'Why don't the four of us go on somewhere for a bite of supper? Just as soon as we've finished the introductions – though we've met before, haven't we, my dear?' His over-bold eyes rested on Mercy once more. 'I confess I can't remember your name. Millie, is it? Or May?'

'It is Mercy,' said Peter. 'Mercy Lisburne.'

'Lisburne?' Freddie stared at them.

'We were married last month. Aren't you going to congratulate us?'

The expression on Freddie's face changed immediately. His once appreciative eyes glittered coldly.

'My best wishes, Mrs Lisburne,' he said in a haughty voice. 'Normally one congratulates the husband on these occasions. However, I think in this case it would be more appropriate to offer my congratulations to you. Now, if you will excuse us...'

''Ere, aint we 'avin' supper wiv yer friends?' demanded Vi.

'Unfortunately I had forgotten we have a prior engagement. Perhaps another time.'

With a last contemptuous look in Mercy's direction Freddie turned and strode away through the thinning crowd.

His insolence had completely taken Mercy's breath away. It was a reaction she had seen in women but not one she would expect from a man, especially one who claimed to be a friend.

Peter, too, seemed stunned. 'How dare he! Talking to you like that!' he declared at last. 'He'll take back every word if I have to give him the thrashing of his life!'

He would have followed his erstwhile friend if Mercy had not clung to him. She had never seen him so angry.

'No, don't!' she cried urgently. 'He's not worth it. Let's just go home and forget him.'

Peter was reluctant to give up so easily. Then he caught sight of the distress on his wife's face. 'You're right, he isn't worth thinking about. Look, there's our cab.'

At first it was sheer anger which kept Mercy awake that night. The duplicity of Freddie Parkham! It was all right while he thought she was Peter's mistress, his floosie. According to him it was quite acceptable for a gentleman to bed a working-class girl – but to marry one, that was a very different matter! The injustice of it tormented Mercy hour after hour. Gradually she reached a different, more painful, conclusion. Freddie Parkham's double standards were hard and unjust – but they were the standards of society. It was the Freddie Parkhams of this world who made the rules, not the Peter Lisburnes, nor the Mercy Seatons. Now she and Peter were going to have to suffer for having flouted the rules. For herself, she knew she could stand it, but the thought that she might have ruined Peter's life distressed her terribly.

By dawn her pillow was soaked with tears, and she was convinced that Blanche had been right. She should never have married Peter.

–

'That's it! I dun't want no more!' Sam Prout shut the farmyard gate with a resounding thud as if to emphasize the finality of his words.

Joey gave a sigh and turned back the way he had come, his hands tucked under his armpits for warmth. One day's employment in the last three weeks, that's all he had managed to get! Much as he hated farmwork at least it provided *some* money.

'I reckon I'll go over to the quarry, there might be summat there. Are 'ee cornin'?' asked his companion, Georgie Hannaford.

Joey shook his head. 'It would only be a waste of good boot leather, there's nothing going there. Things are so slack Pa was sent home this morning. I'm going back indoors, in the warm.'

He knew he was being optimistic, seeking any warmth in the cottage; when he had left the fire had been a poor, miserable affair that could only send out the most meagre thread of smoke. Still, he'd be out of the wind and the rain, that had to be some improvement.

He heard raised voices long before he reached the door.

'You'm a thieving old hag, that's what 'ee be! Twasn't meant just for 'ee! 'Twas for all of us!'

It was rare to hear his timorous mother so incensed, so he hurried in to find out what had upset her. One glance at the scene in the kitchen and he needed no further explanation. A letter bearing Mercy's handwriting lay on the table. It was open, and standing over it, her arms clasping no fewer than three bottles of gin, stood a triumphant Blanche.

'Where does it say so?' she was demanding. 'Point to the exact phrase in the letter where it says that the money was intended for everyone.'

For a moment Ma looked confused; whatever learning that had been thrust her way had long since been forgotten, and she knew she would be doing well to pick out the occasional word in Mercy's letter, let alone a whole phrase.

''Cos it always is!' she declared eventually. 'My Mercy 'er'm a good li'le maid! 'Er knows 'ow 'ard things be. 'Er sends summat reglar to 'elp us out! 'Er don't need to put it in fancy writin'.'

Blanche glared at her contemptuously. 'Your Mercy? When have you ever done anything for the girl, other than to bring her into the world? Without me behind her she would never have married so well! That is why she sent me the money.' She cradled the bottles in her arms like babies.

Joey groaned. Not for the first time he wished that Mercy had never left. She would have found some way of keeping the peace, one way or another; and he tried to think what she might have done.

'So there's a letter from Mercy?' he said.

His mother looked up, registering his presence for the first time.

'Yes, there be. And that old slummick got to un first and took all the money, 'er did!' she exclaimed, close to tears.

'You should get up earlier in the morning, then you would meet the postman first!' Blanche gave a toss of her head and stalked up to her room.

Ma made to follow her but Joey held her back.

'Let her go,' he said. 'She'll be asleep by the time she's finished one bottle, and when she is I'll nip in and take the rest from her. Harry Dawe'll give me the money back for them, never fear. Once she's well and truly off we'll see if she's got any cash left. Only, you'll have to do that bit. Mercy always said she kept her money up her bloomer-leg; it wouldn't be proper for me to go rummaging about there, would it?'

A smile flickered across Ma's face. 'You'm goin' to get your ears boxed, bein' so saucy,' she chuckled. 'But 'ow you'm come 'ome so soon? No work?'

'None at all.'

'Oh well, never mind, us'll 'ave to manage. Shall I make us a cup o' tea? And 'ee can read Mercy's letter to un.'

Sipping the tepid, grey tea Joey read out Mercy's account of life in London, to the accompaniment of Ma's exclamations of: 'Well, I never!' and 'My dear days!'

Mercy's letter served to stir up Joey's smouldering discontent; he spent the rest of the day trying to work out what sort of future lay ahead of him. As far as he could see it was a permanent place on Sam Prout's payroll if he were lucky or else breaking his back in the stone quarry, and these prospects held no attraction for him at all. To get away from the village seemed the only solution to his problem. Mercy had done it, why shouldn't he?

Next morning he rose unusually early and packed his few belongings into a canvas bag.

'My, you'm sure to be 'ead o' the line this mornin',' his mother remarked, pushing the bread and dripping in his direction. 'Sam Prout'll die o' shock, most likely.'

'I'm not going to Prout's farm, Ma. I've made my mind up, I'm going to try and get something better. I'm going to start in Torquay. If I don't find anything there I'll move on. But I've got to try.' Joey spoke defiantly, bracing himself for the protests he felt sure were to come.

His mother just looked at him sadly. 'Reckon, you'm right, boy,' she said at last. 'You'm like our Mercy. You'm got too much about 'ee to spend your life clearin' stones from Sam Prout's fields. You'm be sure to let us know 'ow you'm getting on, though, won't 'ee?'

'Of course I will. And if I find anything close to home I'll be back to see you soon.'

'Then you go, boy, an' good luck to 'ee.'

Joey was glad to leave the house before Blanche or Lizzie were awake. Saying goodbye to Ma was bad enough. He wiped his eyes vigorously on the sleeve of his jacket as he went up the lane. True, he was only going to Torquay, at least, for now, but it wasn't the distance that counted, it was the fact he was leaving home which gave him such a lump in the throat.

By the time he had reached the Newton road excitement was beginning to overcome his sadness. Ma had insisted upon him taking some bread and cheese with him, as well as a couple of the precious shillings salvaged from Mercy's money. As he strode towards the town Joey's spirits rose with every step.

The morning was not fruitful. He had decided to start his search in the harbour area, perhaps helping with the fishing boats or unloading the larger craft which moored at Haldon Pier, but his luck was out. He tried again at every building site he came across, and on the railway, where the line between Torquay and Paignton was being widened. There were no jobs available for an unskilled boy of fourteen. Shop-keepers took one look at his country boots and shabby appearance and chased him away. The coal merchants pronounced him too puny to be of use to them. He trailed back and forth across the town, trying everything he could think of without finding a job.

It was as he was leaving yet another building site that a little cafe caught his eye. It was a modest place, no more than the front room of one of the terraced houses, but on that chilly, dark afternoon it looked warm and inviting. It had a notice in the window: 'Tea and a slice of bread 2d.'

Joey went in. The tea was strong and the bread spread with margarine, but to him it was very welcome. The woman who poured his tea observed him curiously.

'You'm not from round 'ere?' she said conversationally.

He curled his fingers round the thick pottery mug, luxuriating in the warmth.

'No,' he said. 'I've come to look for work. I suppose you haven't anything?'

The woman shook her head. 'Sorry, my lover,' she said kindly. 'I'd take 'ee on and welcome if I could, but I scarce makes enough to keep me! You knows what 'ee should do? Try they 'otels! They takes on plenty of casual folk this time of year.'

'Hotels?' Joey looked at her incredulously. 'I'd never be taken on there!'

'Don't 'ee be too sure! 'Tis only some 'otel workers who 'as to be done up like a dog's dinner. There's plenty more who works out the back, in the kitchens and such. 'Im next door' – with a jerk of her head she indicated her neighbour's house – ''e's a kitchen-porter down the Grand,' and 'e idn't nothin' fancy, I can tell 'ee. Give it a try, boy. They can't 'ang 'ee for askin'.'

Thanking the woman Joey left. Working in an hotel had never entered his mind, but it was worth a try. At least, that was what he thought until he saw the imposing facades of some of them, then his courage almost failed him. It was desperation that drove him on, along with the discovery that no matter how impressive the edifice somewhere or another it had a more humble entrance labelled 'Tradesmen'. In the darkness it was not always easy to find his way to the back door; once there the response was heartening. The 'Sorry, not at the moment' and 'I've just taken on a new lad this morning' were considerably more cheering than any other comments he had received that day.

Then, at his fourth attempt, success!

'Washing-up! Live in! Start now!'

The man who answered his request seemed so harassed by his responsibilities that Joey was convinced he must be the owner of the Devonshire Hall Hotel.

'And the wages...?' he asked hesitantly.

The man glared at him. 'Wages? When you're all found?' Then he relented. 'We'll give you a week's trial, then we'll see. Go down those steps and tell Arthur I sent you. Quick boy, I haven't got time to hang about.' Joey did as he was told, and found himself in a steamy subterranean chamber lined with plain, wooden tables and racks. Along one side was ranged a row of huge stone sinks at which an old man and a boy were washing-up. The old man had the most remarkable feet Joey had ever seen. Splayed out at ten-to-two they were encased in laceless boots which had been cut into an incredible lattice-work to make room for innumerable corns and bunions. He saw him staring and gave a grin, showing large yellow teeth.

'It's the standing on these stone floors. It plays merry hell with my feet,' he said cheerfully. 'And who might you be?'

'Joey Seaton. Please, are you Arthur? 'Cos if so, I've come to do the washing-up.'

'The washing-up, eh? So Mafeking's relieved at last! Yes, I'm Arthur.'

'The owner said I was to tell you he sent me.'

'The owner?' For a moment Arthur looked nonplussed, then he grinned again. 'Fussy little blighter with a red nose, fidgets a lot? He's not the owner, though he's so full of his own importance. No, he's just the undermanager, Mr Matthew A. Bell.' Arthur dropped his voice conspiratorially so that the boy at the sink could not hear. 'Otherwise known as Mabel for more reasons than one!'

Joey chuckled.

'Right then, young 'un. Stow your bag in that corner out of the wet, get yourself an apron out of the cupboard, take a drying-cloth off the line, and you're in business. Oh, I nearly forgot our companion in crime here! Come and say hello to Barty.'

The boy at the sink turned a cherubic face towards them. He seemed to be about Joey's age but was so small he had to stand on a box to reach the sink.

'My name is Bartholomew,' he said primly, and turned back to his work.

'That's put me in my place,' chuckled Arthur, giving Joey a friendly nudge. 'Well, come on, my friend, let's get to work.'

Compared to potato-picking his new job seemed like a holiday to Joey. Dirty cups, saucers, and plates were sent down from above in a creaky lift, stacked on the tables, then when they were clean they were put into another lift and sent upwards. He quite enjoyed the novelty of working the pulleys, and said so.

'It's a good job, this. Nice and warm and not too hard.'

Arthur gave a snort. 'Nice and warm and not too hard? Just you wait until later, my lad! These are only the tea things, a pleasant little occupation to keep us out of mischief. When they start serving dinner upstairs then life gets really hectic.'

Joey didn't quite believe him, only he was too polite to say so. He soon found out Arthur had not exaggerated. As dinner-time approached the tempo in both the kitchens above and the scullery below quickened. Pots, pans, and bowls came down in increasing numbers, then came plates and glasses, cutlery and serving dishes, all needing sorting and scraping before washing; as Arthur said: 'The glasses can't go with the cutlery, and the cutlery can't go with the china.' He was astonished that anyone should use so much stuff just to eat; more than that he was astounded by the amount of food which was wasted.

'There's nothing wrong with it!' he protested, watching bread being tipped into the slop-bins.

'It's beneath some folks' dignity to eat bread; it's just put out for show,' said Arthur. He looked keenly at Joey. 'Are you hungry?'

Joey had to admit that he was.

Arthur surveyed the latest delivery of washing-up.

'There's a roll there which hasn't been touched, you have it,' he said. 'Let's see what there is to go with it. Ah yes, a slice of fresh beef, just the way the customers get it.'

'That's not allowed!' said Bartholomew.

'You shut your mouth! If you go telling tales I'll shut it for you!' said Arthur with surprising savagery. Then he added in an undertone, 'Not that he isn't right, mind. You can throw food away but not take it away...'

'Unless you can do it without being found out,' supplemented Joey, eyeing the beef roll with eager anticipation.

'That's right. I can see we're going to get on a treat.' Arthur beamed delightedly.

'We have supper at eight,' Bartholomew put in, determined to spoil things. 'You won't want it after eating all that.'

Joey gave him a scornful look. 'Just you watch me,' he said with his mouth full.

It was late when they finished work. Joey could not work out why the gentry wanted to go on eating so late at night, it seemed against the rules of nature to him; but while they ate the washing-up continued. There was no finishing until the last item had been washed, wiped and put away, the sinks and draining-boards scrubbed and the cloths washed out. Only then was he allowed to limp, bone weary to bed. As he lay in his narrow bed in the male staffs dormitory above what had once been the stables and was now grandly rechristened the motor garage Joey was utterly content. He might be aching in every limb, with hands stinging from immersion in hot water and soda, but his stomach was full, something he had rarely experienced.

More than that, he had broken away from the drudgery of farmwork and now a new life stretched before him. For the first time since he could remember Joey fell asleep thinking of the future with happy anticipation.

Chapter Five

Mercy rubbed her forehead to dispel a slight ache, and laid aside her book with a sigh. Not so long ago she would never have believed that she could grow tired of reading; not so long ago she could never have imagined that she would have little else to do. It was incredible the way her life had changed so dramatically. Sometimes she still had doubts, wondering if she had ruined Peter's future by marrying him. Doubts he always kissed away when she expressed them. To him the differences in their backgrounds were completely unimportant, and this made her love him all the more. She felt extremely lucky to have married a man who was so indifferent to the divisions of class.

Outside, the street slumbered under the oppressive heat of a city June, making her long for the freshness of a sea-breeze, for not even the lightest of gusts disturbed the dust and straw which had accumulated in the gutters. It seemed an age since she had last breathed sweet Devon air. Suddenly she longed to go back just to see Ma and Joey and Blanche. She wondered how they were getting on without her.

Feeling restless, Mercy leapt to her feet and strode about the room, pausing to run a critical finger over the furniture. Nelly's dusting left much to be desired, and there was a gritty rim round each of the ornaments. Almost gleefully she opened a drawer and took out a cloth. Keeping an ear open for the unexpected arrival of Nelly or Poole, she began dusting, chuckling at her own furtiveness. She had heard of secret drinkers but never secret cleaners. All the same, the simple activity gave her satisfaction.

She had just finished and returned the duster to the drawer when the sound of a cab in the street below announced the return of Peter. Running to the window she was in time to see him striding across the pavement. She watched him, cherishing the neat elegance of his movements; so much love welled up inside her that for a moment she felt quite breathless. No matter how much boredom and loneliness she had to endure she knew it was worth it to be married to Peter. As she watched, a small man in a crumpled alpaca jacket detached himself from the shadow of the area steps. He headed directly towards Peter who side-stepped him with agility and hurried indoors, leaving the man to retreat into the shadows once more. Mercy found the scene disturbing. When Peter entered the drawing-room, after he had given her his customary long lingering kiss, she asked, 'Who is that man?'

'What man?' Peter pressed his face against her hair, smelling her fragrance.

Mercy was determined not to be diverted. 'You know very well what man! I know enough to recognize a tallyman when I see one.'

'A tallyman?' His surprise was genuine.

'A debt-collector, then. We've got money troubles, haven't we?'

'If you knew, why didn't you say so?' He looked almost sulky.

The discovery did not come as a complete surprise; she had begun to suspect something was wrong from the way Peter frowned at his mail each morning then discarded half the letters unread. There had been a daunting similarity about the handwriting on those – angular, decisive, official – as if all accounts clerks had attended the same calligraphy class.

'Oh sweetheart!' she said. 'You should have told me!'

'What, and have you worry? Besides, it would have spoiled your fun getting new things – and mine in buying them for you.'

His generosity was so overwhelming that at first she could do nothing but cling to him.

Then she asked, 'Are things very bad? How much do we owe?'

'Not much – just a few thousand.'

'A few thousand!' Mercy pulled away from him aghast. 'How many is a few?'

'Three, four... I'm not sure.'

She felt sick, too anxious even to be angry; things were far worse than she had suspected.

'Don't you think you should find out?' she demanded. 'So that we know how much we owe.'

'That would be very depressing.'

'Even so, it must be done, otherwise how are we ever to start repaying? What had you planned to do?'

'I don't know,' confessed Peter. 'Just avoid the dunners, I suppose.'

'For the rest of our lives?' exclaimed Mercy in horror. 'That's no sort of an existence! No, we must see what we can raise on my jewels and clothes; we can move to somewhere small and dismiss the servants—'

'Hold on a minute!' protested Peter laughing. 'Things aren't too good at the moment but they aren't so bad we need to live like paupers, you know. There's no necessity for you to go out scrubbing floors for a while.'

'There isn't?' She could not understand how he could admit to thousands of pounds worth of debts and still smile. She was also realizing how little she knew about his financial affairs. Until now it had seemed unimportant, he had always spent money so confidently, it had never occurred to her to query if it were there to spend.

'No, of course not. This embarrassment is purely temporary. Everything will be paid off in a couple of years.'

'Then why wait?'

'Because I can't get my money till then – not until I'm twenty-five. That is a condition of my father's will.'

'Oh!' Mercy was so relieved that her knees gave way, and she sat down suddenly. 'Who has control of your money – your mother?'

'Yes. I have a regular allowance in the meantime, a mere pittance of £500 a year.'

Once she would have thought such a sum to be a king's ransom. Now, although she only had a vague idea of their living expenses, she knew they were far in excess of £500.

'What do we live on?'

'Tick,' said Peter frankly. 'And you don't need to worry about the rent; I paid the first quarter which will keep the landlord quiet for a while. As for the servants, I don't suppose they expect to be paid regularly.'

'You don't suppose the servants expect to be paid regularly?' she demanded. 'Why not? They have to live – like anyone else!'

'They have their bed and board provided,' said Peter, as though that explained everything.

'That's not enough…' A sudden dread thought seized her. 'When did you last pay them? This quarter-day? Last? You have *paid* them something?'

'Well…' Peter looked uncomfortable.

For the first time anger took hold of Mercy. How could he have let their affairs get into such a mess? Anger was not her only emotion, however. She also felt hurt and disappointed: hurt because he had not seen fit to confide in her and disappointed at finding such a major flaw in the man she loved, for the inability to manage their finances was a major flaw. She had been too poor for too long to think otherwise. Owing money to anonymous traders was bad enough, but not paying their servants was going too far.

'You haven't paid them, have you?' she cried furiously. 'We owe them their wages, don't we? Well, it won't do! I refuse to face Poole and his airs and graces knowing we owe him money. Something must be done!'

'But what?' Peter was startled by this outburst.

'Firstly we'll raise money for the wages. I've got more than enough stuff that can be sold. Then you are going to write to your mother to tell her of our marriage and explain that as a married man you have greater responsibilities and therefore need a larger allowance.'

'I'll write soon,' promised Peter.

'Now!' declared Mercy firmly. 'Or else I will write it myself!'

'Oh, I don't think that would be a good thing.' He looked alarmed at the idea. 'Very well, if you think I should.'

'I *know* you should!' came the emphatic reply.

Agnes Lisburne read her son's letter with a sense of mounting triumph but no surprise. There was little about her son's domestic affairs she did not know, thanks to information regularly received from his manservant, Poole; information for which she was at pains to pay promptly and well. Never for one minute had she considered interfering. If there was one thing which Agnes understood it was the value of impeccable timing; after waiting patiently, she had received the letter from Peter, with its undertones of urgency, right on cue, just as she had known she would.

Agnes was forced to admit to herself that Peter's marriage had come as a shock. But then it was so like Peter to marry a girl he could have had for a few pretty dresses and some cheap jewellery! Agnes allowed herself a moment of satisfaction, like a general who sees his carefully laid plans gradually come to fruition, then she meticulously refolded the letter, put it in her writing-desk – and deliberately ignored it for the next two months.

-

If London had been warm in June it was stifling by August. Even the most impressive buildings had acquired a dusty look, and there was an airlessness about the streets which Mercy found enervating. Peter, also, was feeling uncomfortable.

'Let's go up to Scotland for a while,' he suggested. 'The best shoots will be taken, but I dare say we'll find something. Fresh air, wonderful scenery, and I'll teach you to shoot grouse! It'll do us both good.'

Mercy did not think this a good idea. Much to Peter's horror she had pawned a lot of her jewellery, an act which had caused some dissension between them. The money raised had paid the servants and cleared one or two of the more pressing debts. Having made a step in the right direction she was determined there would be no backsliding.

'Perhaps when we get a reply from your mother—'

'*If* we get a reply!' Peter broke in. 'She's deliberately tormenting us, playing cat-and-mouse.'

'Surely not?'

'It's obvious you don't know her. She's a woman who likes to have her own way at all costs. Believe me, if she ever does agree to help us financially it will be at a price.'

'What can she do to us now we are married?'

'I don't know. But my mother will think of something, if only to prove she can still manipulate me.'

Mercy thought that Peter was exaggerating, though she said nothing. As the weeks went by, however, and their repeated pleas to Mrs Lisburne went unanswered, she did begin to wonder if his words had contained more than a grain of truth.

Summer slipped by into a crisp autumn as their finances grew steadily worse, in spite of Mercy keeping a tighter control on the household spending. It was becoming increasingly obvious to her they could not keep on the house; they would have to move somewhere smaller in a less fashionable area. She determined to speak to Peter about it that afternoon, when they took tea together. But before she got the opportunity the unthinkable happened. They had a visitor.

'Mrs Lisburne, Madam!' For once Poole's imperturbability cracked a little as he made the announcement.

Peter and Mercy were too astonished to do more than stare at each other in bewilderment.

Then Agnes entered, pausing in the doorway to regard the pair of them, self-possession personified.

'Mother!' Peter leapt to his feet.

'I'm afraid I may have come at an inconvenient moment,' said Agnes coldly.

'Not at all – we weren't – this is such a surprise,' Peter stammered. 'We're having tea. Won't you join us?'

'Don't you think that introductions are in order, first?'

'Yes, of course. I was forgetting that you two have not met. Mother, this is Mercy, my wife.'

If Mercy was expecting to see a hint of kindness in Peter's mother she was disappointed. Instead she saw a well-dressed woman with Peter's colouring and his same neat air of elegance; a woman who would have been considered beautiful if only there had been one spark of warmth in her being. Mercy looked into blue eyes that were like Peter's, but so much colder, and she began to fear her husband's assessment of his mother's character might be right. Those eyes continued to glare, assessing her icily.

'You forgot we had not met? What a strange lapse of memory, not to realize your mother and your w— the woman to whom you are married are not acquainted!'

Agnes recovered from her slip masterfully, refusing to refer to Mercy as her son's wife. She did not bother to address one word to her.

Peter had recovered from his surprise sufficiently to fetch his mother a chair.

'You will join us for tea, Mother?' he asked.

'Very well.' Agnes stared pointedly at the table which was laid for two. 'But if it is too much trouble...'

Mercy realized with a start that both Peter and his mother were looking in her direction. Of course, it was up to her to ring for another setting and more hot water, wasn't it? Flustered, she reached for the bell. In doing so she caught her plate with the sleeve of her tea-gown and knocked a scone on to the floor. It lay, butter-side down, on the green carpet, thrusting her into an agony of indecision as to whether to pick it up or not. At that moment Poole entered in answer to the bell and she opened her mouth to give him his orders; there was no need – he already had more crockery, hot water, and fresh scones on a tray. She closed her mouth, feeling foolish and also irritated at having her wishes anticipated yet again.

As the manservant began to withdraw Agnes regarded Mercy steadily, as if expecting some action; when Mercy did nothing she said, 'Poole, there appears to be a mess on the floor. Clear it away, if you please.'

'Certainly, Madam.' Poole dealt deftly with the scone and withdrew. Mercy wished that the floor would open and swallow her up.

Sitting bolt upright on the edge of her chair Agnes took one sip of tea before discarding it. Then, without any undue preliminaries she spoke of the purpose of her visit.

'As soon as I heard of this marriage I made inquiries about having it annulled,' she said bluntly. 'This was impossible, as no doubt you intended it to be.' Turning to Mercy she addressed a remark directly to her for thetime. 'Since legally and irrevocably you two are married we must make the best of it. After all, I have but one son, the hope of the whole Lisburne family.' Her voice could hardly restrain her scorn. 'Well, if I must have you, whatever your name is, as my daughter-in-law then I must. And here is how we will go about things. I will see to it your allowance is doubled, and any debts – there are debts, I assume? - cleared up. There are some conditions pertaining to my generosity: you—' She fixed Mercy with her cold blue eyes – 'you will never again have communication with your family in any form whatsoever; I will not have it known that we are allied with a bunch of hobbledehoys. To ensure your abstinence I am willing to send that rabble the lavish sum of two pounds per week, a donation which will stop immediately if you contravene my wishes.'

'No!' cried Mercy, appalled at the idea. 'You can't ask such a thing! It's inhuman!'

'Inhuman?' Agnes regarded her coldly. 'I presume you have been sending money home ever since your marriage? How much longer would you be able to continue subsidizing your worthless relations without my help, eh? Have you considered that?'

Mercy was struck dumb by the thought.

The other woman nodded triumphantly. 'If you want my assistance you must abide by my conditions,' she said with satisfaction. 'In addition, I insist that you are educated to fit your new station in life. I have already engaged an excellent governess who will go with you and give you regular tutelage.'

'Go with us? Where?' demanded Peter.

'Did I not say...? You are to go abroad for a spell. I have already taken a house for you in Brittany, at a quiet resort where you are unlikely to meet any English people. After a suitable period has elapsed I will permit you to return to the Villa Dorata. I will openly accept this woman into my home, though we may have to devise some story about you having met and married abroad.' Mercy was too stunned by these bewildering terms to reply but Peter asked quietly, 'And if we refuse?'

'You are in no position to refuse – unless you wish to go on living in obscurity on £500 a year until you are thirty.'

'No, twenty-five,' said Mercy, stirring from her stupor. 'You only have control of Peter's money until he is twenty-five—'

'I might have expected you to have a good grasp of his financial affairs,' retorted Agnes. 'I fear you have been misinformed. Under normal circumstances I do have control until he reaches twenty-five, but in the event of his marrying someone of whom I disapprove my control remains for another five years.'

'Is this true?' asked Mercy, horrified. She could not believe that yet again Peter had been less than open with her where money was concerned.

He would not meet her eyes. Instead he faced his mother. 'I congratulate you on a thorough piece of work,' he said. 'I can see now why it took you so long to reply to my letters. But you have wasted your efforts. We'll have nothing to do with your conditions, even if it means having financial problems until I'm fifty, let alone thirty!'

'You use very brave words now. You will sing another tune in a year or two,' said Agnes. 'You have scarcely been bred to poverty, have you? Doubtless this woman could manage, but not you.'

'I can learn!' Peter retorted. 'And I could get a job!'

As Agnes burst into humourless laughter, Mercy gently took Peter's hand in hers. Her anger with him had melted. She was proud of him for standing up to his mother in such a way; but she had been doing some serious thinking of her own. It was a bitter decision to make: she must either renounce her family or condemn her husband to a life of poverty and exclusion. The choice tore her in half with a pain which made her gasp, but she knew that there was only one possible solution.

'Perhaps we should do what your mother wants,' she said.

'How can you say that?' Peter stared at her aghast.

Mercy glanced over to where Agnes sat, imperturbable. She would have preferred to discuss this in private with Peter but her formidable mother-in-law showed no signs of withdrawing.

'When you think of it, it's the only solution to our problems,' she said at last. 'We can't go on as we have been doing. I'm not talking just about money, though goodness knows we're finding it impossible to manage on your present allowance. No, I mean about you missing your friends and the busy social life you have been used to. By marrying me you lost all that.'

'None of that is important!' declared Peter.

'But it is, my darling! I hate to see you becoming more and more isolated because of me. Now, if we agree to your mother's terms you would be accepted by society again and I would be better fitted to be your wife – which is something I want very much indeed.'

'Even though it means giving up your own family?'

She drew in her breath at the enormity of what she would lose. Joey and the rest would be hurt. No matter how she might try to explain they would think that she had abandoned them, grown too grand to acknowledge them. But at least they would be secure financially. A steady income of two pounds a week would seem like a fortune to them.

'You've made sacrifices, so must I,' she said quietly.

'I still won't agree!'

'Can you think of an alternative? What work could you do to bring in the sort of income you are used to or give you back your old place in society? I only want you to be happy. Can't we at least try it?'

'No!' Peter, his face flushed with emotion, thrust her hand away from him. 'You don't know what you are asking. It will be giving up our freedom...'

'Freedom to sail straight into the bankruptcy court?' Agnes broke her silence.

Two pairs of eyes stared in Peter's direction, one pleading, one mocking.

'Oh, very well!' he cried, and stormed out of the room.

Mercy faced her mother-in-law. She had had enough of retreating. It was time to take a stand.

'You think I am agreeing to your terms because of the money, don't you?' she said. 'Well, I am not! I am doing it to help my family financially, certainly, but that is not my only reason. I love your son very much. No one knows better than me that I'm not a fit wife for him. And I am determined to change all that! He'll never have cause to be ashamed of me. Never!'

'Indeed?' Agnes raised a supercilious eyebrow but her words lacked their customary sting. For a fleeting moment she wondered if she had made a mistake and that this little nobody might prove to be more intractable than she had expected. Then she dismissed the thought; she had been manipulating people all of her adult life, she was certain she would never be defeated by a tuppenny-ha'penny laundress!

—

That night as they lay in bed, Mercy slid her arms about Peter. For once he did not respond. Instead he turned an unyielding back to her and pretended to go to sleep. Ever since his mother's departure he had been silent and remote. Undismayed Mercy snuggled closer and gently kissed the back of his neck, only to have Peter move away sharply with an exclamation.

She rolled back to her side of the bed and curled herself up into a miserable ball. Peter had never rejected her like this before and she did not know what to do about it. They had had disagreements in the past, so minor they had never survived the first loving overture. Now, though, Peter was so hurt and angry he wanted nothing to do with her. How she wished that Agnes had never come. Even their financial worries were preferable to this. Then totally without warning her distress evaporated, to be replaced by a burning resentment. What right had Peter to be so surly? This was all his fault. It was because of his incompetence that they were in debt, yet it was she who was making all the concessions and the sacrifices. She was the one who would never see her family again. A picture came to her of Joey growing up to be a complete stranger, of Blanche growing older and becoming more dependent upon alcohol now that there was no one to dissuade her, and as for Ma… Poor Ma had never been very capable, how was she to cope with Lizzie and Pa and Blanche all alone? The tears began to flow down Mercy's cheeks, and being unable to find a handkerchief she sniffed quietly to herself. But not quietly enough. Peter heard her.

'Mercy?' His tone was concerned and distressed.

And the next moment she was in his arms.

'Please don't cry,' he begged, brushing away the tears with his lips.

'I tried to do what was best for us. A–and you are b–behaving as if it were all my fault!' she sobbed.

'It was just that you seemed to be siding with my mother against me.' Even now he could not suppress his hurt.

'Oh no, never that!' Mercy was so startled she stopped crying. 'I'd never do that, ever! But it seemed the only solution. True, we'll be living our lives to suit your mother, only for a while, though. And won't we be suiting ourselves in the long run, with all of our problems solved? Besides, she *is* your mother. It's bad enough to have to give up my family, I don't want to make things worse between you two!'

'My mother was the cause of the rift not you, so don't worry on that score. And as for making things worse…' Peter began to kiss her ear. 'Since the day I married you things have been getting steadily better.'

He pulled her closer and gently began to undo the tiny buttons of her nightgown.

–

With daunting speed the servants were dismissed, the lease on the house surrendered, and they were on their way to Brittany.

At first Mercy regarded setting up home in Brittany with some misgivings. She had always wanted to travel, but to live in a foreign country upon Agnes Lisburne's instructions smacked too much of enforced exile. She had agreed to it, but she did not have to like it.

Peter was particularly loving towards her these days. He was almost too eager to please. It was as if, having failed her so badly, he was determined to make amends. Mercy knew that her love for him was as strong as ever; it was her faith in him that had been damaged. Then she came to see that her view of him in the early heady days of their marriage had been unrealistic. He was a man, with faults and weaknesses. How much better it was to love the real Peter, frailties and all, rather than some imagined perfect creature.

Poole accompanied them to Brittany, and there was one new member in the entourage, Miss Herriot, who was to take change of Mercy's education.

Emily Herriot came with impeccable references, having been governess to the children of Agnes's cousin for twenty years. She was a small-framed woman who seemed to be made of sprung steel, so brisk were her movements. She also had a habit of taking charge.

'I expect her to ask if I've washed the back of my neck at any moment,' protested Peter in a low voice.

Mercy smothered her laughter. She found the starchy governess rather alarming, although they shared a dislike of Poole, which was a good point of mutual sympathy.

Their new home was a solid, stone-built house, furnished in the traditional Breton manner with large, splendidly carved pieces. It may have been because she was living by the sea once again, or perhaps it was because the slower pace of life suited her but whatever the reason, once her initial qualms at living abroad had died down, she felt more at home in Trevignac then she had ever done in London. Only the absence of her family prevented life from being ideal. There were her lessons, too, to give her days a sense of purpose. The curriculum was a narrow one, drawn up by Agnes and strictly adhered to by Miss Herriot; but Mercy never complained. She was conscious of how much leeway she had to make up and therefore worked hard.

To find that none of the servants spoke English had been something of a shock at first.

'Nonsense! What better way to learn a language than by speaking it!' Miss Herriot briefly dismissed her misgivings. 'I'll teach you each phrase you need to know and then you can repeat it to the appropriate person.'

This learning parrot-fashion was not an unqualified success.

'You had the right words, my sweet,' Peter assured her, controlling his merriment with difficulty after listening to one of her attempted conversations with the cook. 'Miss Herriot has taught you well in that respect, but I'm afraid you are being defeated by her accent. Poor Cook couldn't understand a word.'

'Do you mean that Miss Herriot can't speak French?' asked Mercy incredulously.

'I'm sure she can *write* it very well. It's her accent – it isn't one you would hear in France.'

The knowledge that the governess was not infallible reduced her to more human proportions in Mercy's eyes and made her less awe-inspiring. 'I think I'd better rely on you for help with my French,' she smiled.

'That's a good idea if you want to be understood,' he grinned, squeezing her affectionately.

She was pleased to see that he, too, was enjoying his stay in Brittany. She had been afraid that, because they were his mother's instructions, he would be resentful and unhappy. But he was obviously content. He had the ability to make the best of things with a good will, a quality doubtless perfected during a lifetime spent with Agnes. Sometimes he would go sailing when the weather allowed, and he had made friends with the local doctor with whom he played chess. Most of all he seemed happiest when talking to the country people. Unlike Miss Herriot, his French was fluent, and Mercy could soon determine the difference in accents. One aspect of their lives which did not please her, however, was the appointment of a lady's maid. For months she had held out against employing someone simply to help her dress and look after her clothes, but Miss Herriot was adamant.

'Every lady *must* have her own maid,' she said in tones which implied any other arrangement was not proper. 'Mrs Lisburne was quite definite on that point.'

'Does the girl you've chosen speak English?' asked Mercy.

'No,' admitted Miss Herriot. 'All the more opportunity to practise your French.'

'Very well, I'll see her,' sighed Mercy.

Peter was all in favour of the new addition to the household. 'Marie-Jeanne seems a jolly sort of girl,' he said, soon after she had arrived. 'I was talking to her this morning and I was quite impressed. Miss Herriot did well to find someone so capable. I think she'll make my beautiful wife even more lovely and desirable, so that everyone will say how lucky I am!'

Even when cosseted in Peter's embrace and comforted by his words Mercy was still not sure about the girl. There was something about her she could not like, despite her careful manners. There was a voluptuous, almost carnal air about her which reminded Mercy vaguely of Dolly, but a Dolly minus the good nature and generous heart. At times Mercy thought she caught her new maid looking at her with an expression which bordered on contempt. She wished she had a command of French, and the nerve, to reprimand her for the disdain in those haughty brown eyes.

By contrast the lessons with Miss Herriot were proving far less of an ordeal than she had feared. She worked hard at the studies, appreciating the patient instruction given to her by the governess. In turn Miss Herriot was clearly delighted to have so willing and able a pupil, so much so that, in time, she ignored the narrow timetable laid down by Mrs Lisburne and included such subjects as politics and international affairs.

'I think you will find this interesting,' the governess said one day, taking a copy of a magazine from a leather attaché case. 'This is *Votes for Women*. I hope you will find it a thought-provoking publication. I would be most grateful if you would read it discreetly. I would not like it known by Mrs Lisburne that I subscribe to such a periodical; she would not approve.'

'You mean I should keep it from my husband?' said Mercy doubtfully.

'Goodness, I was not thinking of Mr Lisburne! I meant that manservant of his.'

'Poole? What has he got to do with it?'

'You don't know? How do you think Mrs Lisburne is so well informed of all that goes on here? Take my advice, dear. If there is anything you do not wish to get back to the Villa Dorata then keep it well away from that Poole fellow.'

This news stunned Mercy, even more than the discovery that Miss Herriot was a covert suffragette. She was heartened to find she had such a staunch ally in the governess though it served to increase her dislike of the manservant. When she told Peter, however, he took the news philosophically.

'I suppose we should have suspected something of the sort,' he said. 'It's extremely annoying.'

'Aren't you going to dismiss him, or at least speak to him about it?'

'I think not. He has served me very well all the time he has been with me. And he has been honest in other respects. Besides, you know the way my mother works – the poor fellow probably had no choice in the matter.'

Mercy looked at him for a moment, irritated by his calm acceptance of the situation. He still did not seem to take her disapproval of Poole seriously, despite Miss Herriot's disclosure. Then she realized that she could expect no other reaction from Peter, it was the generous side of his nature that made her love him so much. She flung her arms about him.

'I can think of no other man who would behave so charitably!' she exclaimed. 'You are wonderful!'

'I know,' said Peter complacently, 'but I like hearing it from your lips.'

Mercy laughed and kissed him. Then she kissed him again.

'Now I feel I am truly appreciated,' smiled Peter. 'I was beginning to wonder when I saw you reading *Votes for Women*.'

'You don't mind, do you?'

'Not at all. I think I would rather like being married to a New Woman. It might prove exciting. All I ask is that you don't chain yourself to railings too frequently, or throw bricks through the windows of 10 Downing Street more than once a week. I wouldn't like you to get talked about.'

'I promise to restrain myself,' Mercy assured him gravely.

She marvelled again at her good fortune in being married to a man like Peter. On her wedding-day, nearly two years ago, she had been convinced that she could not love him more; but she knew that this was not true – that love seemed a very poor thing compared to what she now felt for him.

The golden days of autumn clung for a long time on the Breton coast, then made way for the cold sea mists of winter. Mercy found her studies very absorbing; Miss Herriot introduced her to subjects the existence of which she had barely been aware, though even the liberal governess looked askance when Mercy insisted upon taking lessons in cookery.

'It seems such a waste not to learn about French cuisine now I've got the chance,' Mercy pointed out. 'Madame Le Clos is a renowned cook, and she only takes a few pupils, so I was lucky to be chosen. Besides, as she doesn't speak any English it will be good for my French.'

'Ah, if it benefits your French then I'm sure there can be no objections,' Miss Herriot replied, her eyes twinkling.

Mercy's studies did not always go well. One grey morning, although she applied herself to her lessons she found it hard to settle. She felt slightly off colour, due, she suspected, to shellfish at dinner the previous evening. Miss Herriot watched her struggle with her first exercise in French grammar and then a rather knotty essay on political theory before she remarked, 'The rain seems to have stopped. Shall we take a stroll for half an hour, just to get a breath of fresh air before lunch? You are looking peaky.'

Mercy closed her book with relief and ten minutes later they set out, well wrapped up against the chill wind. They had not gone far when Mercy realized she did not have a handkerchief.

'It's no use. I must go back and get one,' she said. 'This cold wind is making my nose run.'

'That is not a remark I would recommend using when you return to the Villa Dorata,' chided Miss Herriot.

'I know,' laughed Mercy. 'And no doubt I should stand in the hall and ring for Marie-Jeanne to fetch one for me, when it is far quicker for me to go up and get it myself. Wait here, I won't be long.'

Mercy hurried back up to the house and went up to her room to get the handkerchief. Of Marie-Jeanne there was no sign but as she walked swiftly along the corridor she thought she heard the maid laughing. The small door leading to the servants' quarters was open and as she passed it she was sure she heard Marie-Jeanne's voice followed by that of a man. So Marie-Jeanne was entertaining an admirer in her room, was she? The sheer audacity of it almost took Mercy's breath away.

'Mademoiselle Marie-Jeanne is in for a surprise,' she muttered grimly.

As Mercy hurried upstairs her rubber-soled outdoor shoes made no sound on the wooden treads. The maid's door was ajar, and it swung open silently at her touch. She had given no thought as to what she might find, though remembering Marie-Jeanne's air of latent promiscuity she should have anticipated the scene which met her eyes.

Two naked figures moved together on the bed, the faded coverlet pushed aside by their writhing. Marie-Jeanne, her eyes closed, had twined her legs about the man's body.

Mercy stood, unable to move, her attention no longer on Marie-Jeanne. Her eyes were taking in the man's bare back – the scattering of freckles so golden across his shoulders, the blond hair tapering so perfectly into the nape of his neck, the curve of the vertebrae beneath his white skin sweeping into the arc of his narrow waist. She gazed in mute fascination, unwilling to admit to herself that they were so familiar, so beloved.

She must have made a noise for suddenly they both turned and looked at her, their expressions ludicrous in their horror. The hysterical urge to laugh that welled up within her faded at once, and she rushed forward.

'Out!' she screamed at the maid, advancing towards her. 'Get out!'

What she meant to do to the girl she did not know. All she wanted was to make her hurt, to give her some of the anguish she was feeling now.

Marie-Jeanne saw the expression on her face. Rolling out of bed, naked as she was she ran out of the room, screaming in terror. Mercy snatched at her hair, but the maid evaded her, leaving a few dark strands twined in her fingers.

'Mercy!' Peter disentangled himself from the bedclothes and came towards her.

'No!' She put out a hand to push him away. 'No!' she repeated, her voice low with anguish and disgust. 'You smell of her!'

Then she turned and stumbled down the stairs. She was vaguely aware of a figure coming along the corridor and Miss Herriot's voice saying, 'Wherever did you get to, my dear? I found your handkerchief. You had dropped it…' But Mercy took no notice. She ran into her bedroom and slammed the door.

Once inside she did not know what to do. She sat on the bed, then got up again, walked back and forth, then flung herself into the big carved chair, rocking herself frantically back and forth. Time and again, like something from a ghastly bioscope picture, the scene she had just witnessed passed before her eyes. Peter lying with another woman, pleasuring himself with someone else's body. Nothing she did could ease the pain.

When he came in, fully dressed now, Peter found her sitting on the bed, her knees crooked up in front of her, her arms wrapped tightly around her body, as if such pinioning was the only way to stop herself from disintegrating. He came and sat beside her, but she gave no sign that she was aware of his presence.

'I'm sorry…' he said.

Still she did not move.

'I'm sorry,' he said again. 'I thought you had gone out.'

That stung a response from her.

'You thought I'd gone out! Is that the only excuse you can give?'

'I didn't want to upset you.' He looked uncomfortable but his face registered remarkably little guilt. 'It was nothing serious.'

'Nothing serious! You call rolling about naked with my maid nothing serious?' She could not believe what she was hearing.

'Oh really, Mercy! You're reading far too much into this.'

'I'm reading into it exactly what I saw. How long has this affair been going on?'

'It isn't an affair – don't exaggerate its importance.'

'Then what is it?'

'An interlude… a dalliance…' He searched for a suitable word. 'The sort of thing which goes on all the time.'

She stared at him. 'Not in my home!' she cried. 'Not with my husband!'

Peter reached out to comfort her but angrily she resisted. Suddenly tears were streaming down her cheeks. 'Why?' she sobbed. 'That's all I want to know. Do you love her very much?'

'Good Lord, no!' Peter seemed startled at the idea.

'Then, why? What have I done wrong?'

'You've done nothing wrong, darling. You're my wife and I love you desperately.'

'Yet you go to another woman!' Mercy's sobs were shaking her whole frame.

'That has nothing to do with love.'

'What is it, then?'

'It's hard to explain – a sort of need, I suppose.'

'A need I can't fulfil?'

'You could call it a different sort of need. Oh, sweetheart, I wish you wouldn't distress yourself over this. It isn't important. I keep telling you that but you won't believe me.'

Mercy looked at him through her tears and saw that he was remarkably calm about the whole thing.

'How did you expect me to behave?' she asked.

'Well, just ignore it. That's the usual thing wives do.'

'Whose wives?' Her astonishment at his attitude was even beginning to break through her pain.

'Wives in general, I suppose. The done thing is to turn a blind eye.'

She stared at him in disbelief and saw he was being quite serious.

'You are unfaithful to me, you break my heart – and you expect me to turn a blind eye?'

'But I wasn't unfaithful.'

'Then what do you call going to bed with my maid?'

'That was something else entirely, nothing which affects you and me!'

He believed it! That was the incredible thing! He was clearly sorry to have distressed her but he genuinely could not see why she was so upset! Is this how it is in high society? Mercy wondered. Are husbands allowed to satisfy themselves where they please and their wives pretend not to notice? If so, she wanted none of it.

'Go away!' she cried. 'I want to be by myself!'

'But I don't like leaving you when you are so upset.'

'Please!' It was a cry of anguish that Peter could not ignore. Reluctantly he left the room.

Still fully dressed Mercy sat on the bed and wept. Then, when the tears would come no more she stared dryeyed at the ceiling until she knew every crack and blemish in its surface. Time meant nothing to her; neither did hunger nor thirst. How long she would have remained in such a state there was no knowing if Miss Herriot had not appointed herself guardian. It was the governess who helped her to undress and get into bed, who brought her hot water-bottles and tea, who spoke to her in soothing whispers. Mercy had no idea how much the older woman knew or guessed, but she was grateful to her.

Peter did not share her bed that night; he slept on the narrow cot-bed in his dressing-room. He could not have slept much, though, for more than once, during the long wakeful hours, Mercy heard his footsteps approach the adjoining door into the bedroom; then he seemed to think better of it and go away.

It took every ounce of Mercy's willpower to get out of bed the next morning. It would have been so much easier to cower under the bedclothes trying to pretend yesterday had never happened. Then common sense prevailed; she accepted she would have found out about Peter and Marie-Jeanne sooner or later. It was the housemaid, Amelie, who brought her tea and hot water. Mercy did not ask the whereabouts of Marie-Jeanne.

Peter was eating breakfast when she entered the dining-room. He jumped to his feet.

'Are you feeling better?' he asked anxiously.

'I feel perfectly all right,' she replied.

She might have been talking to a perfect stranger, and he flinched at the coldness of her tone. Although she had no appetite Mercy took a small portion of breakfast from the serving-dish: anything to try and recapture normality. But the first bite of toast turned to dust in her mouth and she occupied her time cutting her bacon into smaller and smaller pieces.

The meal finished and the day begun, she found no relief from her misery. It hung about her like a painful aura. Studying was out of the question. Peter suggested they drive out along the coast, but none of it registered with Mercy. That night, when he tried to enter her bedroom, she just stood there and looked at him. No words were needed, the expression in her eyes was enough. Peter turned back into his dressing-room.

It went on like this for days, then a week, then two, then a whole month, with Peter trying every way he knew to reach her, without success.

'What do you want?' he cried in eventual desperation.

But she couldn't answer him. That was the trouble – she did not know.

Deep down, she still loved him but had lost her trust in him, and that hurt. Peter's notion that his dalliance, as he called it, did not involve her was bewildering and distressing. She missed him, though. She missed his physical presence in the large feather-bed, his warmth, the comfortable contact with his body as he lay beside her. Gradually her loneliness for him grew harder to bear than her pain, so that one night, when Peter entered the bedroom as usual, she did not turn away from him as she had done so often of late. Instead she moved over to her side of the bed.

Instantly Peter was beside her, his arms pulling her closer, and whispering almost incoherently, 'Oh, my darling! Oh, my darling!' over and over again.

To her surprise Mercy saw there were tears in his eyes: proof, if she needed it, that the last few weeks had been as hellish for him as they had for her. There was no withstanding this evidence of his love for her and she melted against him, crying a little, too, and whispering her love for him between urgent kisses.

Their marriage had teetered on its foundations, and recovered. They were happy once again, and both of them tried to put their trauma behind them. Life was not quite as blissful as it had been before, perhaps – the spectre of Marie-Jeanne still hung over them – but it was happy none the less.

The incident seemed to mark the end of a phase in their lives. Next morning a letter arrived from Agnes. In her narrow, authoritative copperplate she told them it was time they came home. Anyone else might have suggested such a move, or asked if it were convenient. Agnes merely ordered them. Mercy did not mind, they would have had to return to England soon, anyway, for her suspicions had been confirmed. She was pregnant.

Chapter Six

'That should have been you, you danged fool!' snapped Arthur indignantly, as the under-housekeeper bore off a smug Barty to serve in the hotel workers' dining room.

'Why?' demanded Joey. 'I'm happy as I am.'

'Happy are you? You enjoy standing here, day in, day out, up to your elbows in God knows what?'

'There are worse jobs.'

'Yes, and there are lots a jolly sight better. You don't want to stay down here too long, otherwise you'll never get away. You should be upstairs where the paying customers are – where the money's to be made.'

'What, serving suet pud to the commis and the housemaids?'

'That's only the beginning, you idiot. From there you can go anywhere – the coffee room, the ladies' dining room, the banqueting room – they're the places where you get the tips, not down here sloshing about in dishwater.'

'Well, it's Barty on the ladder of success this time. He was here before me, after all.'

'Maybe, but you've got twice as much about you. You could really get on, if you'd only bother. You take a leaf out of that oily little squirt's book. Didn't you hear him? "Yes, ma'am. No, ma'am. I'll do anything you say, ma'am." You're bright. You could look quite spry if you'd smarten yourself up. And you can talk posh when you want. I've heard you! You'd be just the sort they'd like to serve the rich old biddies their tea and toasted muffins.'

'You sound just like my sister,' laughed Joey. 'She was always on at me to improve myself.'

'She was right, make no mistake about it. Otherwise you'll end up like me, washing up after other people for a living, nothing to look forward to but the workhouse when I can't manage that.'

'How come you didn't do better for yourself, then?' asked Joey. 'You must have been a likely lad in your day.'

'I was. Like a fool I threw away every opportunity I had.' For a moment there was genuine regret in Arthur's voice, tinged with bitterness. Then he swiftly returned to his normal bantering tone and said, 'Besides, my feet weren't up to it. Always let me down, have my feet.'

Arthur had given Joey something to think about. Did he want to go on washing up for the rest of his days? At the moment he didn't mind it, but he realized that it was because of Arthur's company. If it had been Arthur who had left for upstairs instead of Barty the job would swiftly have deteriorated into drudgery.

'All right,' he said at last.

'All right what?'

'I'll do as you say. I'll follow the example of my wise old professor and make an effort to rise as high in the hotel industry as he didn't.'

'We'll have less of the cheek, unless you want a swipe round the earhole,' said Arthur. Then he grinned. 'But I'm glad you listened to what I said. Take anything that comes along, son, just so's you get out of here.'

Joey grinned back. It was strange how Arthur's advice was so close to Mercy's, both of them urging him to get on. It made him think that maybe he did have prospects. All it needed was some effort from him and a bit of luck.

Thoughts of Mercy set him wondering about her. When he had first come to the Devonshire Hall he had asked Arthur if he had heard of a well-to-do family called the Lisburnes.

'No, they aren't on my visiting list,' he had said. 'But you can always look them up in the *Torquay Directory*. It regularly publishes lists of all the nobs and where they live. Why d'you want to know, anyway?'

'They're relations,' replied Joey. 'I'm thinking of calling.'

'Oh, my, lucky them!' Arthur had raised an eyebrow and not believed a word.

It had been easy enough to find an old copy of the *Torquay Directory*. 'Mr Peter Lisburne, Mrs Agnes Lisburne – the Villa Dorata, Meadfoot', it had said. There was no mention of Mercy. Nevertheless, when he had a free hour Joey would often take the cliff path and look down on the villa. He could never get over its size and its opulence. In her last letter, Mercy had explained that she was severing all ties with them.

He had felt indignant at first, and hurt, thinking she had abandoned them. But when the postal orders started coming regularly from a local solicitor he guessed she had not had any option. She had mentioned going abroad for a while, even so, he was quite convinced that she would return to Torquay. When she did Joey wanted to make sure she would be proud of him. It was not a sudden decision on his part, merely a growing feeling that one day he would really be worthy of visiting a sister who lived in a house like the Villa Dorata.

In the meantime his first chance of self-improvement arrived. It was not much of an upward step, just being a porter, but at least he had a glimpse of the glittering life above stairs. As he lifted expensive pieces of luggage in and out of the gleaming limousines, under the zealous gaze of menservants and uniformed chauffeurs, he knew that Arthur had been right; if he wanted to make his fortune he had to get among the wealthy clientele – and soon!

–

The baby in the lace-trimmed basinet was crimson-faced with anger. His small fists beat the air, his pink-gummed mouth formed an O of outrage as he yelled his fury.

'Goodness me, what a noise!' Laughing, Mercy picked him up and held him close. He smelled warm, of milk and wet and good baby-soap. He was soaking, as she had expected; she knew it was not the discomfort which caused his outcry but boredom, for the noise stopped immediately. In his scant three months of existence John Peter Francis Lisburne had learned how to get his own way.

'Such a wicked boy, you are,' she whispered, her lips close to his plump cheek. 'The wickedest boy from here to Plymouth, and the noisiest. I don't know what we are going to do with you.'

The baby, lolling his head against her shoulder, seemed remarkably unmoved by her pronouncement. Secure in the knowledge of his mother's true sentiments – that he was the most perfect baby ever created – he merely gave a satisfying burp and proceeded to dribble over her velvet-clad shoulder.

Mercy laughed with delight.

Behind her the nursery door opened. She did not need to turn round to know who had entered; the brisk step and rustle of starched linen told it all.

'Mrs Peter! Is something wrong?' Nanny's voice indicated that she knew full well it was not.

'He was crying, so I came in. He's very wet…' To her ears her voice sounded nervous and apologetic.

'There's really no need for you to attend to him. He'd have taken no harm for a minute or two.' Already Nanny had somehow inserted herself between Mercy and the baby and was unpinning his napkin with rather more energy than was necessary.

'He was crying.'

'Babies do! He was only exercising his little lungs, you know. I left him for just a moment. I was fully aware of what he was doing.'

'I wasn't suggesting—'

'In my experience it's not a good idea to pick up Baby the moment he makes a sound. We mustn't make a rod for our own backs, must we?' Nanny turned and cooed down at the child. 'We're becoming quite the little tyrant, aren't we? We think we've got everyone at our beck and call like poor Mama. But Nanny knows better!'

Mercy gritted her teeth at the blatant smugness of the woman. 'I merely came into the nursery to see him,' she said.

'Of course, Mrs Peter. But we must think of what's best for Baby, mustn't we? It will do him no good to get over-excited by being picked up and played with too often.'

'Are you suggesting I should not come in to see my own son?'

'Good gracious, no, Mrs Peter! I wouldn't presume to say such a thing! You are always welcome in the nursery, you know that. Perhaps you would like to come and see Baby have his bath this evening. He does enjoy it so.'

To see him have his bath! Not to bath him herself! Not to play with him! Not to fondle her own baby!

Mercy took a deep breath to calm her rising temper. She had already had several altercations with Nanny, who was of the old school – starched through to the soul. It had done no good. Nanny had been hired by Agnes and answered only to her. Mercy knew better than to appeal to her mother-in-law. Agnes Lisburne regarded the baby as one more being to be dominated – and one more weapon to use against her.

Nanny West was certainly conscientious and efficient. In her care the baby would be well looked after. The trouble was it was a job Mercy wanted to do herself, she had had plenty of experience caring for Joey and for William. But the combined forces of Agnes and Nanny fought against her.

Just as Mercy was about to make one more bid to gain control of her baby Nanny remarked, 'If you'll pardon me for asking, Mrs Peter – isn't today Mrs Lisburne's at-home?'

Taken by surprise Mercy replied, 'Yes, why?'

'It's just that, if you'll excuse the liberty, ma'am, there is rather a nasty stain on your left shoulder, and with company coming in half an hour…'

Mercy twisted her head and saw that the blue velvet of her gown was indeed badly marked where the baby had dribbled. She was in no fit state to receive visitors.

'Thank you, Nanny. I'd better go and change.' She sighed with resignation, knowing the battle for the nursery would have to wait.

Every Thursday afternoon Agnes Lisburne was at home between the hours of 3 and 5 pm, a fact that she had printed neatly across the corners of her visiting cards. How Mercy hated those two hours! To be compelled to sit under the scrutiny of her mother-in-law's friends and acquaintances was agony to her. She submitted to it simply because it was part of the price of being accepted by Society. She knew that for her to be absent, or even late, would give Agnes ample scope for vicious comment. Not that she minded for herself, it was always Peter who got the backlash.

Hurrying into her dressing-room Mercy found her maid there, putting away clean lingerie.

'Oh, Stafford, look what's happened! I'll have to change!'

'Of course, Madam. Will your cream cashmere do? I've just pressed it.'

Already the maid was nimbly unhooking her dress.

'It will do splendidly. It's such a nuisance! I never remember to put something over myself when I pick up the baby.'

'Never mind, madam. I'll soon sponge it out.'

'It's extra work for you.'

'Five minutes, no more. I know if I had a baby as lovely as Master John I'd get nothing done all day for playing with him.'

Stafford allowed herself the ghost of a sigh for what might have been. Gaunt, sallow of skin and middle-aged, she bore no resemblance to Marie-Jeanne other than in her skill. Her previous situation had been with an octogenarian; and, if in choosing her, Agnes had hoped to buy another ally among the servants she had failed. Stafford was delighted to have someone young and beautiful to dress, after a lifetime spent encasing aged bodies in out-dated bombasine. A heart overflowing with love was locked in her bony chest and it had had no outlet until she entered Mercy's service. Now she poured adoration indiscriminately upon Mercy, Peter, and the baby – though not on Agnes. Stafford had been in service too long not to recognize a dictator when she saw one. She helped Mercy into the afternoon gown of fine creamy cashmere, and redressed her hair, with an air of unquenchable goodwill.

'And the amber earrings, perhaps, Madam? There, perfection!'

'You don't think I look too young in this?' Even now Mercy was never quite confident about her appearance.

'Not a bit of it. The dress couldn't be better, it's just right for your colouring.' Stafford held the door open for her and added in a confidential tone, 'You'll put every other lady in the shade, Madam. You mark my words.'

Mercy gave her a grateful smile as she passed. Stafford watched her go along the corridor. To look as beautiful as Mrs Peter and still be so unsure of herself... but then, with her background... Here Stafford stopped.

She was so loyal to Mercy that she would not even *think* gossip.

Agnes was already in the drawing-room when Mercy entered and she looked pointedly at the small French clock upon the mantelpiece. Although there was still five minutes to go before the most punctual of her guests would arrive her face registered disapproval.

'I suppose one must not expect young people to be prompt these days,' remarked Agnes. 'They do not show the consideration for others that was prevalent when I was a girl.'

'I was detained at the last moment,' said Mercy calmly.

'What could have been more important than showing courtesy to one's guests?' Then Agnes added, 'I am surprised that you have changed out of your blue velvet, especially after I commented upon how suitable it was for the occasion.'

'A slight mishap,' muttered Mercy. No doubt Nanny would supply full details of the incident to Agnes.

Agnes, with her talent for spotting other people's weaknesses, had long ago discovered that to attack her daughter-in-law personally was ineffectual, for Mercy had been reared in a far harder school than most of her victims. The best method to discomfort her was to threaten other, weaker vessels.

Miss Herriot had been her most recent pawn. The promise of Agnes's influence to gain a good post for the faithful governess had been the price of Mercy's continued obedience.

'I hope the mishap was not on account of your maid's deficiencies?' Agnes demanded.

Mercy had barely time to declare, 'Certainly not!' before the first guests were announced.

As she helped the guests to tea and chatted to them politely, like a diligent daughter of the house, Mercy longed for the at-home to be over. True, there were fewer callers now than when she had first arrived at the Villa Dorata, when as Peter's new wife she had been a nine days' wonder. It had been hinted, at Agnes's instigation, that Peter and she had been married abroad. But it had taken Torquay society no time at all to smell a mystery. Suddenly, finding out the truth about the new Mrs Lisburne was adding piquancy to tea-tables all over the town, and the drawing-room at the Villa Dorata had held twice its usual number every Thursday.

The birth of John had given Mercy a welcome respite from wagging tongues, and by the time she had returned to the social round people had found some other topic upon which to focus their attention. Nevertheless, she never lost her dislike of the at-homes.

The hum of voices and the discreet clatter of Crown Derby china filled the drawing room. Then the door opened and Rogers announced, 'The Honourable Charlotte Dawson-Pring.'

An immediate stir greeted the announcement, and Agnes hurried forward to welcome the newcomer with unusual effusiveness.

'She's the granddaughter of the Earl of Hembury,' Mercy's neighbour, Tilly Hewson, whispered in her ear. 'Quite an individual.'

The new arrival certainly was distinctive. A little older than Mercy she was striking rather than beautiful with the sort of strongly chiselled bone structure that would ensure she would be as handsome at sixty as she was at thirty. She wore a long black satin tunic patterned vividly in orange, gold and scarlet and belted with crimson leather. A black and gold scarf was twisted round her auburn hair in lieu of a hat or headdress. Most women would have looked bizarre in the costume, inspired by the Russian ballet, which had taken London by storm, but Charlotte Dawson-Pring had all the self-assurance of a person of consequence and carried herself accordingly. She looked magnificent.

After being welcomed by Agnes and ushered to a chair, she leaned back and reclined in a careless manner that would have sent Miss Herriot into palpitations.

'Oh, it's so good to be back,' she said, embracing the entire assembly with one wave of a much beringed hand. 'Sometimes I think I only go abroad for the pleasure of coming home again.'

'Where have you been this time, Miss Dawson-Pring?' asked Agnes.

'To Egypt. It was incredible! Along the Nile are areas where the way of life cannot have changed for hundreds – no, thousands of years.'

The whole room was hushed, everyone, including Mercy, waiting to hear more from the distinguished guest. All except Tilly Hewson. She was so eager to let it be known that she was on Christian name terms with an Honourable that she blurted out, 'And did you see a camel, Charlotte?'

Miss Dawson-Pring's eyes narrowed. 'I saw quite a few, Tilly,' she said. 'Were you inquiring after one in particular?'

If Tilly Hewson was conscious of having been made to look foolish she gave no sign. 'Oh, Charlotte, you are such a tease,' she twittered, trilling her little-girl laugh. 'Please, do tell us more about your adventures.'

Miss Dawson-Pring, however, was no longer in the mood to recount stories of her journey; her attention had been caught elsewhere.

'Hello,' she said, looking directly at Mercy. 'What's this I see? A new face and no one thought to introduce us.'

'How remiss of me. Of course you have not met, have you? Miss Dawson-Pring, may I present my daughter-in-law?' Agnes did the honours with a hint of unease. Introducing such a nobody to the granddaughter of an earl was a formidable responsibility.

Charlotte Dawson-Pring seemed quite unaware of any undercurrents as she scrutinized Mercy in a manner that in a less illustrious person would have been considered impertinent.

'So this is the mysterious beauty the whole town is talking about,' she declared loudly. 'Well, I can quite understand how you came to steal our most desirable bachelor from under our noses. Every eligible female for miles must hate you.'

'If they do they are keeping their enmity very secret,' laughed Mercy.

'What a pity! There's nothing like a little dissension and malice to add spice to a dull season. Come over here and sit by me. I want to know more about you.' Mercy's heart sank. There was no ignoring the imperious way the other woman was patting the seat next to her.

'I am afraid you are in for a sad disappointment,' she said. 'There is little to tell.'

'Nonsense! You appear out of nowhere, looking absolutely delightful, and carry off the prime hope of every scheming mother from Exeter to Plymouth. There must be a story here and I am determined to hear it.'

'Where do you want me to begin?' asked Mercy, hoping that her anxiety did not show too blatantly. 'Where do you come from? What are your people?'

'I'm a true Devonian; as for my family, they are country people.'

'What was your maiden name?'

'Seaton.'

'A Devon family, you say, yet I've never heard of you. Why?'

'I expect it is because my family live so quietly. They don't go out into society.' Mercy parried the questions carefully, giving the answers that had been drummed into her by Agnes. She was conscious of the tension building round her, of everyone waiting for her to give something away.

'Live quietly!' exploded Miss Dawson-Pring. 'They must have buried themselves in some bog on Dartmoor for me not to have heard of them. Where did you say you lived?'

'I don't think I did.'

'Well?' Clearly Miss Dawson-Pring was not used to receiving evasive answers.

The earlier panic which Mercy had felt was beginning to give way to an icy calm, tinged with indignation at being questioned like a criminal.

'But what of the mystery, Miss Dawson-Pring?' she said. 'Here you are, wanting me to give the whole game away. Where would be the fun in that?'

For a moment Charlotte stared at her, indignant at being thwarted. Then a spark of admiration appeared in her pale green eyes.

'Bless me, you may be right! At least give us a clue to work on, as they do in all the best mysteries. Let me see, what shall it be? I know! The name of your father's house!'

'Fernicombe!' said Mercy promptly, her own eyes glinting with mischief, for the Seaton home really was No 1 Fernicombe Cottages.

'Never heard of it!' declared Miss Dawson-Pring, 'it sounds fishy to me, very fishy indeed! What are you hiding, eh? Tell me that?'

Suddenly the humour went out of the situation. A hush fell upon the room as everyone waited to hear Mercy's reply.

She drew in her breath to make a sharp retort. She was tired of being baited; if these silly women wanted something to prattle about she would certainly provide it! Agnes's face froze into severe lines, silently commanding her to hold her tongue, but Mercy was past caring.

Then the door opened and in walked Peter.

'I thought I would return home in time to join you, ladies,' he said smiling. 'That is, if you will permit me.'

Any woman interrupting such a tense moment would have been greeted with silent indignation – but not a man – and certainly not Peter. His appearance was a signal for a chorus of cooing pleasure and chirrups of welcome. The only dissenting voice came from Charlotte Dawson-Pring, and even she was making only a token objection.

'Shall we let him stay, ladies? Or shall we turn him out?' she demanded.

'I promise I'll be good,' said Peter.

'In that case we'll definitely turn you out!' she retorted.

This prompted an outbreak of laughter from the others – all except Agnes, who maintained a stiff silence, and Mercy, who suddenly felt limp from the realization that she had nearly ruined everything.

Peter's eyes met Mercy's across the room, sending silent messages of love, and she smiled back at him. Aloud he said, 'I see you have already met my wife, Miss Dawson-Pring.'

'Indeed I have, and find her both charming and intriguing. You are not thinking of sitting here, are you? Because there's no room and I flatly refuse to move. I disapprove of married people sitting together.'

'Then if I can't sit by my own wife I must sit beside someone else's.'

'There's room here!' Tilly Hewson's languid air disappeared as if by magic, and she prettily gathered her skirts to one side to make room for him. 'There!' she said coquettishly, slipping her arm through his. 'Now we can flirt with each other.'

'Very well – if you are sure no one will tell my wife,' hissed Peter in a stage whisper.

Everyone laughed. The tension in the room had now dissipated and general conversation broke out once more.

Mercy was afraid that Miss Dawson-Pring might resume her close questioning so she said, 'I'm sure you must have seen the Sphinx while you were in Egypt. Is it as imposing as it always seems in pictures?'

'More so!' Miss Dawson-Pring took the bait and started to talk about her exploits in Egypt, much to Mercy's relief.

The afternoon came to an end eventually, and as the last visitor departed Agnes turned to Mercy, her eyes glittering coldly.

'It was a particular honour having Miss Dawson-Pring here today,' she said. 'She mixes in the very highest circles.' Agnes paused to add emphasis. 'A wrong word to her could have the direst result, do you realize that? Social ruin with no chance of ever being accepted back into polite society again. I hope I make myself clear?'

Mercy nodded. Lack of clarity had never been one of her mother-in-law's failings. In view of the warning, and the cross-examination she had already suffered at the hands of Charlotte Dawson-Pring, Mercy hoped fervently that it would be a long time before she met that aristocratic lady again.

She found Agnes's control of every aspect of her life oppressive. She knew now why Peter had objected so strongly to giving way to his mother's terms. In her heart she knew they had had no alternative, but sometimes, when Agnes was even more dictatorial than usual, she wished some other solution could have been found. It was too late now, though.

Since returning to Torquay Mercy had not made any friends of her own. There was no one, Peter apart, with whom she could share confidences or jokes, as once she had done with Dolly. At times the temptation to go and see her family was almost unbearable, but she had given her word and would keep to it. There was another reason why she never travelled the short distance back to her old home – she feared she might not be welcome. When she had first been forced to abandon Ma, Joey, and the others she had written a letter of explanation but had received no reply. Perhaps they thought the steady two pounds a week well worth her loss. Dolly had been sympathetic at first and had seemed to understand, now even she no longer wrote. Whether this was because she was too busy or because she was hurt that she, Mercy, made no attempt to visit her there was no knowing.

Being in a well-remembered landscape yet having to play the stranger gave Mercy a feeling of unreality and increased her sense of isolation. It was all the more extraordinary, therefore, when one afternoon Rogers entered the drawing-room and announced a visitor for Mercy.

Agnes looked at the butler in surprise. 'What sort of visitor? Have they no card? No name? Surely, Rogers, you are capable of announcing visitors correctly.'

The back of the butler's neck went red at the reprimand. 'There is a card, ma'am, but it is, er, rather unorthodox.'

'What are you talking about, man? How can a visiting-card be unorthodox? Give it to me at once.'

Rogers presented the silver salver. Agnes gingerly picked up the grubby piece of pasteboard. She turned it over once or twice then snapped, 'I cannot make head nor tail of it. You must try!'

Mercy gazed at the card thrust at her. It bore the name of a local manufacturer of mineral waters, along with the statement 'Purveyors of Best Quality Non-Alcoholic Beverages to the Gentry and to the Premier Hotels of Torquay' – all of which had been scratched out in ink. Turning it over Mercy saw a familiar shaky hand.

'"Mrs Blanche Seaton",' she said in astonishment. 'My grandmother! She's here!'

Agnes's response was immediate. 'Mrs Peter is not at home,' she rapped out at the butler.

'Not at home to her own grandmother?' demanded a haughty voice. 'Stuff and nonsense!'

Blanche stood in the doorway, an almost unrecognizably tidy Blanche, clad in a grey flannel two-piece which was a little too large but otherwise quite presentable and a grey hat adorned with black and white feathers. She stood there, completely sober, exuding dignity.

'Is it customary for a lady of my advanced years to be kept standing in the hall?' she asked acidly. 'If so, manners have certainly deteriorated since my day. Mercy, come and kiss me, child!'

Mercy needed no second bidding. 'Grandmother, this is such a surprise!' she declared, flinging her arms about the frail figure. 'How is everyone? Is Joey getting on well? Is Ma all right and—'

'All in good time, my dear.' Blanche responded to her grand-daughter's greeting with unexpected warmth, then patted her gently on the shoulder. 'Perhaps we should have introductions first, do you think?'

Laughing and crying at the same time Mercy declared, 'Of course! What am I thinking of! Grandmother, I would like to present my mother-in-law, Mrs Lisburne.'

Blanche extended a hand encased in a much-darned cotton glove. 'Pray do not disturb yourself, Mrs Lisburne,' she said. 'I am glad to see that such an absurd custom has fallen out of favour.'

'What absurd custom?' asked Agnes, caught unawares.

'That of a lady rising to greet one who is senior to her.'

Agnes, who had previously made no attempt to move, shot to her feet. Before she had time to say anything or take the proffered hand, however, Blanche withdrew it and turned to Peter.

'And this, I presume, is my grandson-in-law. Hm! He's a fine-looking fellow, I'll say that for him!'

'Delighted to meet you at last,' replied Peter, bending to kiss Blanche's hand.

Blanche nodded approvingly, a sudden gleam in her eye. 'By the look of you you can do better than that,' she said, and proffered a wrinkled cheek. 'I like him,' she announced after Peter had obliged. 'Mind, you will need to watch him with other women.'

Her words hit too near the mark. But Blanche was apparently too busy examining a portrait over the fireplace to notice Mercy's and Peter's reactions.

'Your husband?' she inquired of Agnes.

Agnes was still struggling to regain her composure. It was unheard of for her to come off second-best in anything, and to be worsted by this scrawny old woman was unthinkable. She took a deep breath to calm herself.

'My *late* husband,' she said at last.

'I see where your boy gets his good looks.'

'It was painted to celebrate his appointment as Chairman of the Torbay and South Devon Bank,' retorted Agnes, returning to the fray.

'Hm! As I thought. Trade!'

'Your family is a distinguished one, of course,' said Agnes with ominous sweetness, scenting a chance to gain the upper hand.

'And a long established one,' agreed Blanche calmly. 'Our ancestor came to this country in the thirteenth century, you know. He was a kinsman of the Count of Provence and so was entrusted to accompany the Count's daughter, Eleanor, to England for her marriage.' There was a pause. 'Her marriage to Henry III, of course,' she added, as though talking to a backward child.

Agnes's first reaction was to be furious with such a blatant piece of effrontery. A kinsman of the Count of Provence indeed! She opened her mouth to say what she thought of a mad woman who claimed to be related to a queen of England, albeit in the distant past, then she stopped herself. There had been such a tone of authority in Blanche's voice that it made her think twice. But it was preposterous!

While Agnes grappled with her uncharacteristic indecision the moment for a cutting response passed, and sheaware Peter was offering their uninvited guest some refreshment.

Mercy held her breath as her grandmother's eyes rested covetously on the array of crystal decanters on the side-table.

To her relief Blanche replied, 'Thank you, no. My visit must be a brief one. My purpose is to see my greatgrandchild, since I understand I have one, and to inquire about the health of my granddaughter since she no longer communicates with her family.'

'As you can see, she is in excellent health,' retorted Agnes.

'A fact which she would no doubt tell me herself, if given the chance.'

Agnes faced her squarely. 'You are to have no communication with my son's wife. The conditions were explained to you fully.'

'Conditions! What conditions? That we accept payment in lieu of Mercy's company?' Blanche suddenly delved into her purse and threw two sovereigns on to the table with a contemptuous gesture. 'That is what I think of your conditions, Madam. I am surprised someone with your pretensions to gentility could devise such a plan.'

Agnes winced. 'Your granddaughter agreed...' she cried angrily.

'But I did not! I do not know what duress you placed upon the girl – it must have been severe for her to cut all ties with us. I say to you now that it will stop. Immediately!'

'And your weekly allowance? What of the money?' demanded Agnes.

'You think I would consider money before my granddaughter? Such an accusation does not even deserve the dignity of a reply!'

A tense silence fell upon the room. Mercy gazed at her grand-mother with dumb admiration. She had long known that there were few who could get the better of Blanche in any argument – but to conduct herself with such control and authority! She suppressed a sudden chuckle as she observed that while Blanche had returned one week's allowance so dramatically, she had made no mention of the other money that had been paid to her family during the preceding months. She also realized that her grandmother must be missing her very much to have gone to such lengths to come and see her. She was touched and very moved.

'And now, if it is not too much trouble, I would like to see my great-grandson.' Having dealt with one matter to her satisfaction Blanche was ready to move, imperturbably, to the next.

'He is asleep. He always sleeps at this hour. He cannot be brought down!' declared Agnes, making one last attempt to exert her authority.

'Then, perhaps if we are very quiet, a visit to the nursery?'

Agnes was about to refuse this request too when she realized that there was no point – Blanche had not even been addressing her. She had been talking to the girl, and now the three of them, Mercy, Peter, and the appalling Mrs Seaton, were leaving the room and heading for the stairs. Agnes felt as though she was living through a nightmare; time and again she had felt the ground shift from beneath her feet, cut away by a gaunt scarecrow of an old woman dressed in someone's cheap hand-me-downs. Worst of all was the knowledge that she herself had been made to lose her temper. She, whose iron will and rigid control were a by-word in Torquay society! This was the final blow, and she longed to plead the onset of a migraine and retire to her room. Only the desperate need to score at least once over this Seaton woman drove her to follow in the wake of the others, up to the nursery.

The baby was not asleep. In fact, he was more than ready for a diver-sion after enduring a tedious afternoon, and he greeted the visitors with beaming smiles and chuckles, making it evident he wished to be picked up and admired. Nanny West was less delighted with this invasion of her domain. Heartened by the presence of Agnes she dared to give a disapproving sniff at the way in which her charge's routine was being disturbed.

At the sound of that sniff Blanche looked up. 'You have a cold, nurse?' she demanded. 'Surely you know better than to remain in charge of my great-grandson when you have a cold?'

Nanny West bridled and said that it was nothing.

Blanche glared at her. 'One more sniff and I strongly advise that you and your attack of "nothing" are sent packing until you have recovered!' she snapped.

Nanny West looked at Agnes for moral support. Finding none she suddenly wilted into a corner. Contrary to her silent forebodings over-excitement did not trouble the baby. After being duly admired and played with, he was settled back in his cradle by Mercy. He was asleep before the visitors had tiptoed to the door.

Once outside Blanche took charge. 'I am sure you want to hear all the family news, so I suggest that we withdraw to your sitting room,' she said, adding ominously, 'You do have your own sitting room, I presume?'

Mercy had not. Agnes was far too eager to keep her under constant surveillance.

'We can go into the morning room, can't we?' Mercy looked at her mother-in-law for approval.

'I suppose so. There is no fire there, and there's scarcely time to have one lit.' Agnes felt duty-bound to put forward as much objection as she could.

'The cold will not bother us,' Blanche assured her. As Agnes made to follow them into the morning room she added, 'My dear Mrs Lisburne, I am sure we have taken up more than enough of your valuable time. We do not want to bore you with our family talk.'

Faced with such a rebuff Agnes had no option but to withdraw, though not before she heard Blanche remark loudly, 'A house this size and you have no sitting room of your own? What an extraordinary arrangement!' Once inside the morning room grandmother and granddaughter faced each other in silence for a few seconds, then Mercy flung her arms around Blanche's neck, saying tearfully, 'You've no idea how glad I am to see you. I've missed you terribly.'

All sentimentality had long ago been knocked out of Blanche – or so she had thought – now, though, she found her arms eagerly embracing Mercy and she heard herself saying, 'There, there, child, did you not think that I was concerned about you?'

Mercy looked at her inquiringly.

'You forget, I know just how cruel the gentry can be,' she continued. 'Not that she is true gentry, that woman.'

'You can't mean Mrs Lisburne!'

'Who else? She is certainly not out of the top drawer. A governess who did very well for herself, I would guess, or maybe the daughter of one of the lesser clergy.'

'Surely not?' Mercy had so come to regard her mother-in-law as the epitome of high society that she could not accept that she might be anything other than high-born.

'Believe me, an upstart! I can always tell! Certainly no one to strike *you* with awe. Your lineage is far more illustrious than hers, never fear.'

Mercy thought back to Blanche's comments earlier in the afternoon. She had heard the story about an ancestor coming over with Eleanor of Provence many times before, and had never considered it to be more than a romantic tale. Now, though, she began to wonder. Not only had Blanche spoken with complete conviction, her behaviour had been most impressive. Incredibly, she had reminded Mercy of Charlotte Dawson-Pring. They both had the same air of innate authority and confidence. Before Mercy could ask any questions, however, her grandmother firmly changed the subject. As far as Blanche was concerned the matter of their ancestry was closed.

'Now, I want the full truth of what has been going on here!' she demanded. 'You need not tell me it was that female who forced you to stop communicating with us; I know you too well to think otherwise. But there has to be more. She still holds the purse strings?'

Mercy nodded.

'Tightly?'

Again Mercy nodded.

'That husband of yours must have an allowance of some sort, so what possessed you both to return here, right into her web? Debt?'

Mercy kept silent, and Blanche sighed. 'You may as well tell me,' she said.

'We had very little money when we first married,' said Mercy loyally.

'And Mama would not help out without conditions. Oh, I know her sort; she will give nothing away if she can avoid it. So your Peter has not come into his full inheritance yet? How long have you to wait?'

'It should have been this year, but because Mrs Lisburne does not approve of our marriage she is forcing us to wait until he is thirty, in five years' time.'

'I knew I was right. I could tell at a glance she would not relinquish control one second before she must. Nevertheless, that does not mean you have no say in your own lives.'

'How can we, when she calls every tune?'

'Those methods can work both ways. Five years may seem a long time to you now; they will pass. Agnes Lisburne knows that, even if you do not. What are her financial arrangements afterwards?'

'I have no idea, though I have no doubt she will be well provided for.'

'And this house?'

'It is Peter's now. Mrs Lisburne was left a dower house of her own out at Chelston, I believe.'

'Which she declines to occupy, even though her son is married and with a family, I suppose? That is something you can use to your advantage.'

'You aren't suggesting that Mrs Lisburne will be in straitened circumstances once Peter comes into his money?'

'No, but Mrs Lisburne of some modest residence in Chelston is not going to have the same place in society as Mrs Lisburne of the Villa Dorata, is she? There is no reason why she cannot move to her own property. You should tell her so.'

'But the unkeep of the villa?'

'It seems unlikely Peter inherited a house of this size without the wherewithal to run it; even if it were so I am convinced that any competent lawyer could ensure suitable arrangements were made. Get that woman out of this house! You are mistress here, Mercy.'

Mercy had a heady vision of life in the Villa Dorata without Agnes. To be able to organize life just to suit herself and Peter and the baby. It was a lovely dream though not very realistic.

'I must admit I am tempted,' she smiled. 'Only, poor Peter would be the one to suffer, he always is. His mother sees to that.'

Blanche nodded. 'From what I have seen I do not doubt she is capable of spreading the story round that he had turned his widowed mother out of the house, or some such tale. Well, if you will not go to extremes remember that you are not some poor relation without a voice, you are the true mistress here. Above all, you are my grand-daughter, and as such need not kow-tow to anyone. Stand up to her! Do you promise?'

Mercy nodded, heartened and delighted by Blanche's support and by her unexpected burst of family pride. Perhaps her background was not such a cause for shame after all. The sense of isolation that had had her in its grip ever since her return to Torquay began to lessen in the face of her new optimism.

'Enough of my problems!' she exclaimed. 'Tell me, how is everyone? Is Lizzie's baby a boy or a girl?'

'A boy. Harry Dawe to the life, I fear. What is it about that man which stamps itself so indelibly upon his offspring? As for the rest of the family, your brothers never bother to come home now, your father remains the insensitive lump he always has been, and your mother and Lizzie are as stupid as ever.'

Her family pride had not lasted long and these last remarks were so typical of the old, vitriolic Blanche that Mercy burst out laughing. 'And what of Joey?' she asked.

'Apart from you he is the only one of the bunch who might amount to something. He has a steady job at the Devonshire Hall Hotel, and is earning well, if the fancy clothes he wears these days are anything to go by.'

'I would love to see him again.'

'Then why not? I think you are well and truly released from any stupid promise that woman forced upon you, and he is the only member of the family who would not disgrace you by his appearance.'

'What about you?' asked Mercy mischievously. Blanche brushed a hand over her flannel skirt. 'Borrowed plumes,' she said, 'and pretty tawdry ones at that. No, take my advice; write to us as often as you like, but stay far away from Fernicombe Cottages. Remain in contact with Joey by all means. Forget about seeing the rest of us. We would only be ammunition for that woman!'

Mercy protested at this but Blanche shook her head.

'Think about it, child, and you will realize that I speak sense. Now I have to go. I think I have disrupted life at the Villa Dorata enough for one afternoon.'

In truth, she was beginning to think with desperate longing of the bottle of gin she had hidden behind the wood-stack. All day she had been sober and she could feel a driving need for alcohol taking over her body.

If Mercy guessed the reason for her grandmother's prompt departure she gave no sign. She hugged the old lady.

'It has been a wonderful, wonderful disruption,' she said. 'Thank you for being such a help. You've no idea what a difference your visit has made!' She kissed her grandmother again and again, then had a sudden thought. 'How will you get home? By cab? Have you enough money?'

'By cab? To Fernicombe Cottages? How short your memory is!' Blanche raised a sardonic eyebrow. 'No, I will go as I came, by omnibus. I have my fare, thank you.'

'If you are quite sure?' Mercy was still doubtful. 'If the regular payments to you cease I'll find some way of sending money home, I promise.'

Blanche smiled, showing yellow, uneven teeth. 'That was what I was banking on,' she said.

As soon as Blanche had left, ushered out by a dignified, disapproving Rogers, Mercy hurried to the window to watch the scrawny grey-clad figure make its way along the drive. The notion that perhaps she would never see her grandmother again made her eyes mist with tears. When they had cleared there was no sign of Blanche. Indoors and out, there was no clue she had ever been there, not even a tea-cup or a wineglass, yet, as Mercy wiped her wet cheeks with a wisp of a handkerchief, she knew that life at the Villa Dorata would be different.

Agnes, however, sought to paper over the cracks in her authority immediately.

'Are we to expect any more visits from your family?' she asked sarcastically. 'If so, I will tell Rogers to get out the best Worcester tea-service.'

'There's no need for that,' Mercy replied. 'Whatever is suitable for your guests will be suitable for mine.'

She saw the steely light of battle spark in Agnes's eyes, but she refused to flinch. She had allowed her mother-in-law to take far too great a control of their lives, she saw that now. Those days were over.

'Mrs Lisburne,' she said calmly, 'I have no wish to quarrel with you. For over a year and a half we have lived exactly by the rules you laid down, and that is quite long enough. It's time my wishes were taken into consideration. I intend to give notice to John's nurse and appoint someone more in sympathy with my own ideas.'

'Oh, you do, do you? What makes you imagine that I will stand by and let you re-order my household?'

'Whose household?' asked Mercy.

Agnes gasped, considered her words, then took a deep breath.

'On the matter of your sitting room,' she said, 'if you are determined to go to all the bother when there is a perfectly adequate drawing room I suppose you could have the old chintz room.'

Not a muscle on Mercy's face flickered. The chintz room was cold and gloomy, and had once been delegated to the housekeeper.

'I prefer the yellow boudoir on the first floor,' she said. As Agnes began to protest she added ominously, 'I've always thought Chelston to be a very nice area in which to live, haven't you?'

Agnes stared at her, for once struck dumb. Then she stalked from the room.

Mercy allowed herself a sigh of relief, her first major confrontation with her mother-in-law over. She had been right – after Blanche's visit life at the Villa Dorata would never be the same again.

Chapter Seven

Joey whistled silently to himself as he strode jauntily along the corridor. At the last door, the one which bore not a number but the title 'The Moorland Suite', he stopped and picked up a Pekinese dog which snuffled at his ankles.

'Time to hand you back to your missus, Ming, my boy,' he said. At his knock the door was opened by a stout figure lavishly adorned with diamonds that glittered incongruously against a shabby flannel houserobe. Mrs Haddon always greeted the return of her beloved Ming herself and never entrusted the task to her maid. She held out her arms for the animal, gathering it with words of love and endearment, as if they had been apart for years instead of half an hour. Joey waited patiently until the ecstasy of greeting was over.

'Was he a good boy, Joseph?' she inquired with a hint of coyness.

'Very good indeed, Madam. He should be comfortable for the night now,' replied Joey, who understood the unspoken questions in that one delicate inquiry. He added, 'We had a good run on the beach. And on the way back, you'll never guess, Madam! He nearly caught a rabbit.'

'No! Oh, my clever darling!' Mrs Haddon clutched the animal to her and buried her face in the dog's hair. 'What exciting times you do have with Joseph! But then dear Joseph is your special friend, isn't he? He looks after you so very, very well. And now he is going to get you something delicious for your supper, aren't you, Joseph?'

'Indeed, Madam. I saved some roast chicken specially for him.'

'Oh Joseph! Chicken! Are you sure? I mean, the bones...' For a moment Mrs Haddon looked stricken.

'You have no need to worry, Madam. I examined every piece thoroughly.'

Mrs Haddon's raddled face relaxed into a smile. 'Of course we've no need to worry. Silly me! I know what good care you take of my darling Ming.'

As if to confirm her knowledge she slipped two coins into Joey's palm.

'Thank you very much, Madam.' Joey pocketed the coins without a glance. Usually Mrs Haddon only gave him one half-crown. He reckoned it was the story of the rabbit that earned him his bonus. Admittedly his version of the encounter had been something of an exaggeration; it was doubtful if the myopic Ming had been able to see the rabbit which leisurely crossed their path let alone recognized what it was.

Still, Mrs Haddon is tickled pink, Joey told himself as he hurried down the staff stairs. Old Ming's being treated like a hero and I'm an extra half a crown better off, so everyone's happy.

Below stairs, in a side-pantry, Barty regarded the care with which Joey was setting the tray.

'A clean cloth, silver dishes and covers! You'd think it was for old Ma Haddon herself instead of that fleabag of hers,' he said peevishly.

'Barty, my boy, serving in the staff dining room is doing you no good at all. I have never heard such disrespectful talk.' Joey paused in his task of arranging dog biscuits on a silver bonbon dish to regard the boy with mock severity. '*Mrs* Haddon to you. And as for her dog, far from being a fleabag he has such distinguished and ancient pedigree that if he could talk he wouldn't even give a "Good day" to the likes of you; though he happens to be a particular friend of mine.'

'Is that so? Well, animals are not allowed in this hotel, and you are aiding and abetting. Someone should report it, they really should.'

Joey gave a sigh. 'Stop and think before you go running off to have a word in Mabel's ear,' he said. 'Do you imagine no one knows there's a dog in the Moorland Suite? Has it never crossed your feeble mind the management of this hotel might be turning a blind eye, because if they throw out Ming Mrs Haddon will certainly go too? And Mrs Haddon is a very rich lady.'

'That shouldn't make any difference.'

'It shouldn't, but it does!' Joey gave a chuckle and patted Barty on his smooth pink cheek. 'If you're a good boy and don't go snitching to the management you might find a friend like Ming too, one day.'

He knew what was ailing the other boy right enough. Jealousy! Barty's rise on the ladder of success had stopped at the staff dining room, while, through the workings of chance and an epidemic of measles, Joey had been promoted to floor waiter. Temporarily at first, but once there he had taken Arthur's advice and made himself so indispensable to the guests on his floor that he had stayed. He was now with the paying customers and he learned quickly. Late night snacks which never appeared on the bill, subversive errands to one of Torquay's illicit though prosperous bookmakers, pandering to the whims of a Pekinese dog whose very presence was against the rules – these and similar activities ensured a steady flow of tips into the pockets of Joey's trim green and gold uniform. Tips which far exceeded his meagre wages.

The tray completed to his satisfaction he covered it with an immaculate damask napkin and took it upstairs.

This time it was Mrs Haddon's maid who answered the knock. He handed over the tray, then thankfully made his way to the staff quarters, his duties for the night complete.

In the narrow corridor he almost bumped into the night porter going on duty, his head down as he fastened the buttons on his waistcoat.

'Taking up more than your fair share of room, aren't you?' the porter demanded amiably.

'Who, skinny little me? It's you who takes up all the room, other-wise, why do you have such a job doing up your buttons, eh?' Joey grinned back.

'For being so cheeky, young 'un, I won't tell you there's a letter for you. Expensive paper, lady's handwriting.'

'Don't tell me, then. I'll find out for myself. Probably just from one of my wealthy admirers.'

The porter's reply was lost in the air as he hurried across the yard to the staff entrance.

In spite of his blasé attitude Joey was surprised and excited to receive a letter. He recognized Mercy's handwriting immediately. He had heard about Blanche's visit to the Villa Dorata, of course, and he knew that Mercy was now free to communicate with the family again, but somehow he had never expected her to contact him. The message was short. It merely said that Mercy was very happy to be able to write to him; she hoped he was well and could they perhaps meet on his next day off? The text was neatly penned and formal; it was in the postscript his old familiar Mercy was revealed. She had written, 'Please say you will come, for I have far, far too much news to be packed into a silly old letter. I hear that you have grown up so much you are no longer my little brother. *Do come!*'

How could he resist such an appeal? Without further ado he hurried back into the hotel and, slipping unseen into the writing-room, he purloined some of the hotel's notepaper and an envelope for his reply.

—

At first Joey took no notice of the fashionably dressed young woman who entered the tea-rooms, until she spoke.

'Joey?' she said hesitantly. 'Joey, it is you, isn't it?'

'Mercy!' He leapt to his feet. His immediate reaction was not astonishment that she looked the complete lady but the fact that she seemed to have diminished in size, for he now towered over her.

The same thought must have occurred to her, for she exclaimed, 'Goodness, you really have stopped being my little brother!'

As they literally sized each other they burst out laughing.

'I don't believe it! Can this be the sister who used to give me a thump every time I dropped my aitches?' demanded Joey.

'Don't blame me. You're the one who has shot up like a weed,' Mercy beamed back at him. 'A very handsome weed, if I may say so.'

'You certainly may. Torquay's latest heart-breaker, that's me. Look, we don't have to take our tea standing up, do we? We are allowed to sit down. I hear it's the latest craze.'

'You haven't changed,' said Mercy. 'Never lost for a reply.'

'I get that from Blanche.' His face grew serious. 'From what she says you've had a bit of a rough time these last couple of years.'

'Only in patches. I knew when I married Peter it would not – could not be plain sailing. Things are easier now. Grandmother's visit helped a lot. I think one of the greatest reliefs is I'm no longer pretending to be something I'm not. I used to work in a laundry – if anyone asks I say so.'

'Good for you! And has anyone? Asked, I mean?'

'Yes, the Honourable Charlotte Dawson-Pring, no less, grand-daughter of the Earl of Somewhere or another. She said, "I hear you used to be a laundress," and I replied, "Yes, I was. A good one." My mother-in-law nearly had a fit. But the Honourable Charlotte was not a bit taken aback. In fact, we've become quite good friends.'

'And what about your husband?'

'Peter? He is the dearest, kindest man ever.'

'So you've no regrets?'

'About marrying Peter? None at all!' Mercy's reply was decisive. 'And there is the baby! Oh, Joey, you have the most adorable little nephew there ever was!'

'I was wondering when we'd get around to him,' chuckled Joey. 'Even Blanche was impressed; though her comments on his nurse would have made your Honourable Charlotte What's-her-name blench.'

'I doubt it, knowing Charlotte. The nurse was one of the things I put my foot down about. She's been replaced by someone who isn't a reincarnation of Napoleon. But that's enough of me and my affairs. What about you? Are you enjoying working in an hotel?'

'I am indeed!' Joey's face lit up with enthusiasm. 'You know, I think I can really get somewhere in this business. Oh, it's hard work at the moment. Come to think of it, it will always be hard work. But I love it, and I mean to get on. I want to become a manager of a really superior hotel like the Devonshire Hall – in the end.' He grinned mischievously. 'I've found I like to live in style.'

'You'll get there, I know it. Oh, I'm so glad, Joey! I really am!' Mercy beamed at him with delighted pride. 'As for the style, from that suit I can see you're learning quickly.'

Joey gazed down at the sharp grey pin-stripe which had cost him quite a few of his tips.

'Would you believe that a Pekinese dog bought most of it?' he said.

'You've filled out, too. The food must be good.'

'Marvellous, and lots of it. Some of the overflow I take home on my days off. It's against the rules, but everyone does it. You should see the waste even so!' This was one aspect of his work which still troubled Joey. 'It's a funny old world, isn't it? One half hasn't got enough to eat and the other half has too much.'

For a moment there was silence, as each reflected on the numerous times they had gone to bed hungry. Shame for her own affluence engulfed Mercy briefly, but those days of want were still too close for her pleasure in the luxuries of life to be dimmed for long.

'How's everyone at home?' she asked.

'Getting on fine,' Joey assured her. 'Pa still spends all his time in the Oak, but apart from that things are much better. I reckon Blanche must be slowing down because these days Ma usually beats her in the race for the money you send. That helps a lot. I can spare a bit, too. And Lizzie is working full time in the dairy at Prout's farm. So the Seatons are pretty comfortable at the moment.'

'I'd love to come and see you all!'

'Why not? It would be grand to have you back for a visit.' Despite his enthusiastic words Mercy sensed hesitation in his manner. He went on more cautiously, 'Better leave it for a bit, though. It's not that we don't want you, of course. You see, the Seatons may be better off, but when it comes to the social graces we're still lagging behind, especially when Lizzie and Blanche have a go at one another. You're somebody now, Mrs Lisburne of the Villa Dorata, and I bet it hasn't been easy for you. Don't do anything that would set you back, not now.'

Mercy was about to protest that she did not care about her social position, but she had second thoughts: she remembered only too well what her family could be like, and their behaviour could affect not only Peter but John too. She could not take that risk, not yet.

Eager to brush away those harsher memories she said, 'What did you mean when you said a Pekinese dog had bought your suit? Were you joking?'

'Certainly not! It was the honest truth!'

Joey launched into tales of the people he had met and the amusing things which occurred at the Devonshire Hall Hotel. In turn Mercy told him of her new life and the happenings at the Villa Dorata. Almost unconsciously they ordered tea, and mechanically they consumed toasted muffins and cream cakes, never letting the conversation falter for a moment.

Finally the waitress, eager to get home, was forced to break into their conversation to ask them if they would like the bill. Startled they looked round to see that the tea-rooms were in near darkness. They were the last customers.

'It can't be that late!' declared Joey in horror. 'I'm due on duty in ten minutes!'

'We'll share a taxi, then.' Mercy began to look in her bag for her purse.

Joey put out a restraining hand. 'Allow me,' he said.

Mercy bit her lip to hide a smile at the nonchalant way in which he glanced at the bill and then cast a handful of coins on to the table.

'In that case the transport is on me,' she said.

Joey's man-of-the-world air disappeared swiftly as they climbed into the taxi, to be replaced by a huge grin.

'This is what I call style,' he beamed, as the engine coughed into life and they set off, somewhat bumpily, toward the Devonshire Hall.

It took them some time to persuade the taxi-driver that it was the staff entrance of the hotel they wanted and not the Grand Foyer. As Joey explained, being late on duty was bad enough, but a mere waiter could not possibly be seen arriving through the guests' entrance.

'You've no idea how wonderful it has been seeing you again,' said Mercy, as they drew up in the narrow lane at the back of the hotel.

'And seeing you, too. We'll get together again soon, won't we?'

'Of course.' Mercy hugged him hurriedly. 'Give my love to everyone at home, along with this. It's a letter and a little something for them.'

Through the envelope Joey could feel the outline of sovereigns. 'Trust me,' he said. Then leaning back into the taxi window he planted a kiss on her cheek, whispering in her ear, 'That'll give the driver something to think about!'

Mercy was still laughing, her eyes bright with happiness as the taxi drove away.

By the time he had changed into uniform Joey was fifteen minutes late going on duty. He sped up the staff stairs hoping his absence had not been noticed. In his haste he ran into the under-manager, who was standing at the end of the corridor, every line of his short corpulent body expressing displeasure. At the sight of Joey he took out a watch from his waistcoat pocket and regarded it in a gesture of exaggerated surprise.

'It is only a quarter past, *Mr* Seaton!' he said. 'It is extremely kind of you to break into your social life long enough to honour us with your presence.'

'I'm sorry I'm late, Mr Bell,' gasped Joey breathlessly.

'Not nearly as sorry as you are going to be, I assure you. Fifteen minutes!'

'I've never been late before—'

'And you think that is an excuse for being late now? Such slipshod thinking will not do at the Devonshire Hall Hotel, Seaton, do not imagine that it will! Fortunately we found a replacement for you in good time. You can take his place in the staff dining room, a position that will be permanently yours if your conduct does not improve!'

Without waiting for further explanations or excuses Mr Bell turned on the heel of his patent leather boot and stalked away. As he did so a door opened and Barty emerged carrying a tray. He made no attempt to conceal his feeling of smug self-satisfaction at the sight of Joey.

'Mabel give you a good roasting, did he?' he inquired. 'Serves you right for being so late.'

Joey swallowed his annoyance. 'Mabel?' he said. 'Mabel? Is that any way to refer to the under-manager? If you want to remain up here permanently, Barty, my lad, you're going to have to learn better manners than that.'

'My name is Bartholomew!' protested Barty. Joey did not hear. He was already hurrying downstairs to his new and, he sincerely hoped, temporary situation in the staff dining-room.

It was thanks to the intervention of Mrs Haddon that he was reinstated. Under Barty's charge Ming had not enjoyed his evening exercise, which had been hasty to say the least, and his supper had been served in a most unsatisfactory manner. Mrs Haddon, who knew the hotel's rules about pets as well as anyone, was far too tactful to make her complaints specific. She merely let it be known that the new young floor waiter was nowhere near as satisfactory as the previous one and that she hoped to see Joseph back as soon as possible.

Next day Joey returned to his former duties, official and unofficial. He was particularly conscientious during the next few weeks; he already had one black mark against him, and with lads like Barty breathing down his neck eager for promotion he had to be careful.

The coming of spring emptied Torquay's hotels as the fashionable winter visitors sought pastures new. The Devonshire Hall was no exception, with only a handful of permanent guests remaining. Even Mrs Haddon had taken Ming for a change of scene. A tense air hung over the staff for this was a time when work was in the balance, and everyone took careful note of all arrivals and departures, hoping against hope to hold on to their jobs during the precarious weeks until the summer visitors came.

Joey, however, was in his usual cheery mood as he finished his breakfast.

'I'm glad someone's got something to sing about,' grumbled the bleary-eyed night-porter.

'It's my day off,' replied Joey. 'And I don't propose spending it nattering with you. Nothing personal, Rod, old fellow. It's just that I've got better things to do.'

He had his day planned to a nicety. First a visit home for a couple of hours to see how everyone was, then a meal out somewhere – the food at the Devonshire Hall had shown up all too clearly the deficiencies in Ma's cooking – then, if the weather did not improve he would go to the Picturedrome in Market Street. His head busy with the delight of having money jingling in his pocket and a whole day to spend it in, he returned to the long room above the hotel garage which he shared with a dozen others. He removed a package from his locker. In it were the slices of beef, half a dozen savoury pastries and some chocolate biscuits he had stored away the night before. Ma and the rest of them always looked forward to seeing what he had brought.

One quick glance at himself in the once ornate mirror, a casualty from the banqueting-room cloakroom, and with the parcel under his arm he set off. He got no further than the door.

It was strange how a man as small as Mabel could entirely fill a doorway. Puffed up with his own importance under-manager stood there, his pig eyes glittering with something like triumph.

'Where are you going, Seaton?' he demanded.

'Why, home, Mr Bell. It's my day off.' Something in the man's expression made him feel uneasy.

'Indeed? What are you taking with you?'

Joey looked down at his parcel. Already the brown paper was stained with grease from the pastries.

'Just a few things, Mr Bell,' he said.

'Perhaps you'd better show me what sort of things.'

Mabel pointed to a scrubbed deal table. Joey had no alternative but to put down the parcel and undo the string.

Mabel looked down at the somewhat squashed contents, his face registering distaste. 'I suppose it is useless to ask if you have paid for these items?' he asked.

'No, of course not! They were going to be thrown away,' protested Joey, his unease increasing.

'Nevertheless, they are hotel property and you know the rules. Food is not to be taken away from the kitchens.'

'Everyone does it!'

'Then it is your misfortune to be the one caught stealing—'

'It's not stealing! It was going to the pigs, honestly!'

'...to be caught stealing,' repeated Mabel, 'and so there is only one course of action. Pack your things, be in my office in a quarter of an hour to collect any moneys due to you, then you will leave the hotel premises immediately. Under no circumstances can you expect a character reference.'

He leaned forward and gathered the parcel together, picking it up by the tips of his fingers as if to avoid contamination. He stalked out with it paying no heed to Joey's desperate protests.

After the under-manager had departed Joey sank down on to his bed. It was so unfair, though he had to admit not totally unexpected. He knew the hotel management frequently made an example of someone, just to keep the rest on their toes, especially at slack times.

The clank of a bucket made him look up. An elderly woman, mop in hand, stood in the doorway so recently occupied by Mabel.

'I suppose you heard all that, Kitty?' said Joey despondently.

'Couldn't 'elp it, boy. A cryin' shame, I calls it!' She leaned her weight on her mop. ''E sneaked on 'ee, that's what 'e did! Must 'ave done!'

'Who sneaked on me?' asked Joey in surprise.

'That little un, the one that looks like one of they cherrybums. I've never trusted un further than I could fling un.'

'Barty?'

'Dun't know 'is name. But 'e was standing' by your cubby-'ole there, just closin' un, and my, didn't 'e jump when 'e seed me. I thought then, You'm up to summat 'ee shouldn't be, boy. And now us knows what, dun't us?'

Fury rushed through Joey, and he sprang to his feet.

'I'll thrash the hide off him. I'll—'

'Fust you'd better parcel up them bits and bobs of yourn and get over to see Mabel,' advised Kitty. 'If you keeps un waitin' 'e's liable to start dockin' pennies off your money.'

She was right. Joey slipped her a shilling he could ill afford now, and speedily rolled his possessions into a bundle. His interview with Mabel was short and terse, and his back wages were handed to him in near silence.

As he left the hotel Joey made a profitable detour via the men's washroom, where he encountered Barty.

If Barty had hoped for immediate promotion to floor waiter he was out of luck. Mabel took one look at him and relegated him once more to the staff dining room. At the Devonshire Hall it was out of the question to have a floor waiter sporting a black eye and a split lip!

'So, you have been dismissed without a character. It is rapidly becoming a family tradition.' Blanche regarded Joey blearily across the kitchen table. Her brief excursion into sobriety at the Villa Dorata was now a memory, and she nursed her gin-bottle like a favoured child.

'What you'm goin' to do now, me 'ansome?' asked Ma, her face wrinkled with anxiety.

'I'll find something, never fear,' said Joey with a confidence he did not feel. He knew very well that it was the wrong time of the year for seeking employment, especially without a reference.

Work did prove very difficult to find. Joey lowered his sights from being a waiter to anything in the hotel industry, and then just to anything. Mercy would have helped him, he knew, if his pride had not prevented him from letting her know of his situation. A week after he lost his job a letter, redirected from the Devonshire Hall, came from her suggesting tea but he cried off, pleading a change of duty hours as his excuse.

Torquay offered him no prospects of work; he was forced to extend his search beyond its boundaries. He tramped the coast road past the gasworks into Paignton. He had done it all before! The neighbouring town was not as stylish as Torquay, perhaps, but it was modern and bustling. Above all, it was enjoying a modest boom; if all else failed he might get work on building the new terraces or smart villas that were springing up. Everywhere he went, however, he was out of luck.

He almost missed the little boarding-house – it was so insignificant and shabby it did not command attention.

Only the faded letters painted directly on to the brickwork announced 'Beds, Breakfasts, Dinners, Teas'.

Not hoping for much Joey went round to the back door. At his knock it opened, letting out a waft of stale air heavy with the odours of mildew, ancient cooking, and doubtful drains. There was no guessing the age of the man who held on to the door, he might have been anything from thirty to eighty, for the sallow pallor of desperate ill health had apparently permeated from his being into the very clothes he wore. Even the grubby apron tied round his meagre waist had never got any nearer to whiteness than putty-grey. His clinging to the doorpost was less to bar Joey's entry than support himself.

'Yes…?' The one word seemed to exhaust him.

'I'm looking for work,' said Joey. 'I'm strong and reliable, and I'll tackle anything.'

The man was silent for a long time as he looked Joey up and down with pale, shadowed eyes.

'Do anything, you say?'

'Yes.'

'Queenie does the cooking. You do the rest. Ten bob a week, all found.'

The man did not wait to see if Joey accepted. He crossed the room, supporting himself on the furniture at each step, and disappeared through a narrow doorway. Not certain whether he was supposed to follow him or not Joey stood hesitantly in the scullery.

The door opened again and in walked a girl. She was older than himself by about four or five years at a guess, a young woman really, but there was nothing youthful about her heavy tread nor the solid pastiness of her features. Everything about her was plain and gave the impression that she had stepped straight from childhood into middle age.

'Dad take you on?' she asked.

'I think so,' said Joey.

'Don't you know? I expect he did, we need someone, goodness knows! I'm Queenie Dixon.'

'Joseph Seaton.'

'Come on then Joseph. I'll show you where you'll sleep. We've thirty in here when we're full, twenty at the moment. Working men mostly, some from the building, some from the railway widening. They have their breakfasts here and a cooked tea. There's plenty to do, as Dad's not up to it any more. I'd be obliged if, as soon as you've settled in, you'd come down and start straight away.'

As she talked she led the way upstairs. Joey followed her, noting the cracked lino and the scuffed and torn wallpaper. Up another flight they went, and another, with Queenie becoming more and more puffed as they progressed.

'This is yours…' she wheezed, as they arrived at an attic room lit by a single skylight. 'It's not much… At least, you'll be on your own… unless we get a sudden rush.'

The tone of her voice told him that this was most unlikely.

'Thank you, Miss Dixon,' said Joey. 'It'll do fine.'

Queenie gave a giggle that was surprisingly girlish. 'You don't need to call me Miss Dixon,' she said, suddenly embarrassed. 'Queenie'll do for me. See you downstairs in a few minutes.'

As her heavy tread descended the stairs Joey looked about him despondently. He had a job right enough, and he was still in the hotel trade, of a sort – but this was a long, long way from the Devonshire Hall.

Chapter Eight

'Are you sure you're comfortable?' Peter looked at his wife with concern.

'I'm fine, darling, honestly I am,' laughed Mercy. She leaned back in her rattan chair, bracing herself slightly against the gentle swell of the waves. Below deck the engines kept up a steady throb. 'I'm only having a baby, you know. I'm not ill.'

'You're having my baby, and if that doesn't deserve a little extra care and attention I don't know what does.'

Mercy stretched out her hand to him, and he enfolded it in his. They sat together in happy silence, until the saloon door opened and the others emerged on deck, headed by Charlotte.

'Really, Tilly, that's the last time I partner you at whist,' she was complaining.

'I'm sorry, Charlotte dear. I get so confused.' Tilly made little fluttering gestures of contrition.

'All I can say is thank goodness there are only four suits. I hate to think of the mess you'd get into if there were more. Now what are you two doing?' Charlotte's gaze took in Mercy and Peter sitting together. 'You're flirting! If there's one thing I can't stand it's married couples flirting with each other. I won't have it on board my yacht. Stop it at once!'

'In that case I'll have to spoon with you,' grinned Peter.

'No, you won't! I'm not the spooney sort.' Charlotte pretended to fend him off.

'Then who can I flirt with?'

'There's always little me,' said Tilly, in her most winsome voice.

'Of course! Tilly! My thanks for taking pity on me. Let's leave these heartless females and take a turn about the deck.' Peter sprang to his feet and offered her his arm with a flourish. Giggling, Tilly accepted it, and they strolled away.

'You want to watch Tilly, she's got her eye on your husband,' Charlotte observed.

'You don't think she was being a bit too blatant to be taken seriously?' smiled Mercy.

'Don't be fooled by all that fluff and little-girl manner – beneath those frills Tilly has a will of iron. Her appetite for men could have earned her a fortune in another walk of life.'

Mercy laughed. 'Having failed to scare me you're now trying to shock me, eh? It's no use, you know. I'm unshockable.'

'I'm afraid you are, still, it was worth a try. Don't say you weren't warned. Tell me, are you enjoying yourself?'

'Enormously, thank you.'

'Good, because I've decided to make up a party for Cowes Week, and I'm hoping you and Peter will come.'

'How kind of you; but it's not possible. It's less than three weeks before the baby is due.'

'Ah, so it is, more's the pity,' Charlotte conceded.

'Are we allowed to know what is such a pity?' asked Peter, returning from his stroll, with Tilly still clasping his arm.

'The imminent arrival of your offspring is upsetting all my plans,' said Charlotte.

'What plans?'

'I'd fully intended to take a jolly lot of people to the Regatta at Cowes, staying on board the *Cleopatra*, of course. Now Mercy says she can't come.'

'I'm afraid she's right.' Peter smiled at his wife.

'There's no reason why you should not join the party,' said Mercy. 'You'd enjoy it so much.'

'You and George will be coming too, won't you, Tilly?' demanded Charlotte.

'Oh yes, please. Thank you, Charlotte, dear.'

'That's settled, then,' said Charlotte decisively. 'You'll have to come now, Peter, to keep George company. If you don't he'll have no one to talk to, since the rest of us don't know our stays from our sheets.'

'That isn't true, and you know it,' replied Peter, laughing. 'And I'm not going to get into an argument, because I can see where it will lead.'

'Does that mean you'll come?' Tilly squeezed his arm and looked at him like an eager child. 'Oh, good! George will be delighted!'

Mercy watched her display of enthusiasm with wry amusement. She found her childish behaviour absurd in a grown woman. Only later did she experience a niggling doubt that Tilly's excitement might be more on her own behalf than George's. Almost at once she brushed the doubt away, irritated with Charlotte for having put such an idea into her head.

As the summer dragged on the weather turned sultry, making the later stages of her pregnancy uncomfortable. She felt huge and ungainly, and she tired easily.

'I won't go to Cowes,' said Peter persistently. 'I'll send a note of apology to Charlotte.' He was still saying he'd stay on the morning the *Cleopatra* was due to sail.

'You will do no such thing!' Mercy kissed him, savouring his fresh smell of shaving soap and cologne. She knew how much he wanted to go. She had noted with fond amusement that his bag was already packed. 'You'll go and have a marvellous time, winning everything in sight, just to please me.'

The days passed more slowly than Mercy had anticipated, and she looked forward to Peter's return with increasing enthusiasm. Yet when he did return their reunion was vaguely unsatisfactory. She found that his talk of his stay aboard the *Cleopatra* - of events she had not shared and people she had not met – gave her a bleak feeling of exclusion. As for her own conversation, even to her ears the domestic trivia sounded incredibly boring. She blamed her lethargy and low spirits. Once the baby was born things would improve, she assured herself.

When William Christopher Lisburne did arrive he chose to do so at the height of the Torquay Regatta, so that instead of racing across the bay in his yacht, *Jasmine*, Peter was sitting by the bed, holding Mercy's hand.

'You should have gone. You had such a good chance of winning this year,' she protested weakly.

'I'll have a good chance of winning next year instead.'

'It doesn't seem right, having the *Jasmine* at her moorings throughout the Regatta. The crew have lost all chance of any prize money. They won't even get any starting money, and they rely on it…'

'Is there anyone else you want to worry about?' smiled Peter affectionately. 'I've only lost a couple of days' racing. As for the crew, I've made sure they've received something extra to celebrate the birth of this young man, here. Now are you satisfied?'

Although Peter told her time and again he was not disappointed Mercy was not convinced. It was as if a small dark cloud overshadowed the joy of William's birth. A larger cloud was to follow, for the new baby proved to be difficult over his feeds and a light sleeper. To make matters worse John was jealous of this intruder and demanded more of Mercy's attention for himself. She found herself spending longer and longer in the nursery.

'This is what you get for involving yourself too closely in your children's upbringing,' Agnes observed acidly one evening, as a pale and weary Mercy joined her for dinner. 'Employ a good dependable nanny and leave the job to her, that's my advice.'

'You don't think that bringing children into the world should involve a greater responsibility than just paying someone's wages?'

'I hope you are not presuming to instruct me in my responsibilities!' There was ominous edge to her voice.

Mercy sighed. 'I'm sorry, Mrs Lisburne. Of course I was doing no such thing. It is merely that our views on bringing up children are so different.'

'In which case there is no point in discussing them. Will you ring for Rogers to serve the dinner?' Agnes always made a great show of having relinquished the reins of the household.

'Should we not wait until Peter comes home?'

'He is dining with the Hewsons. Had you forgotten?'

Mercy had not forgotten. She had not been told. Somewhere inside her a small niggle of apprehension stirred; she managed to keep her expression impassive as she replied, 'Let's hope that he is enjoying himself.'

She lay awake for a long time that night, waiting for Peter's return. It was way past midnight before she heard him enter his dressing-room. Lying tensely in the big bed she listened to his movements, expecting the connecting door to open and Peter to climb in beside her... She waited in vain.

'Why didn't you come to bed last night?' she asked him next morning.

'I didn't want to disturb you, so I slept on the dressing-room couch.'

'It wouldn't have mattered if you had disturbed me.'

'Yes, it would. You need your rest. You're looking very tired these days.'

'Too tired to be amusing company for you?' She was tempted to retort. But there was a fidgety, downcast air about Peter this morning and some instinct warned her not to provoke any squabbles.

'Did you have an enjoyable evening at the Hewsons'?' she asked with well-controlled calm.

'Oh so-so.' Peter began to read the morning paper, hiding behind its fold.

Mercy wanted to know more, only, the paper proved to be an impenetrable barrier. She waited for him to lower it. When he did not she silently left the room. He did not appear to notice her departure.

During one of Agnes's interminable at-homes Charlotte gazed at her pointedly over the teacups and said, 'You're looking decidedly peaky. You need cheering up. Tear yourself away from your children for a few days and come with me to Upper Lee.'

'Upper Lee?'

'My place in Somerset. I have to go there next month to do my lady of the manor act. It'll be terribly dreary, which is why I'm relying upon some of my more interesting friends to come and help liven things up a little.'

'I'd love to come... Oh, but I can't. Peter will be away then.'

'What's that got to do with it? You aren't going, are you?'

'No, it's going to be an all male party.'

'Oh, one of those! All the more reason for you to come to Upper Lee.'

'I don't think I'd like to without Peter. One odd woman would make your party out of balance.'

'Stuff and nonsense! We aren't going in two by two, you know. It's to be a country house-party, not a trip in the Ark. Where's Peter off to, anyway?'

'To France. I think you know Colonel Boyer? Well, they are going in his yacht.'

'On the *Tango*? I thought the colonel was trying to sell her? I've heard he's in financial trouble.'

'I don't know about that. Perhaps he wants one last voyage in her before he loses her. As far as I know their official destination is Dinard.'

'If Peter is off to Dinard then I insist you come to Upper Lee. I know of lots of people who will love meeting you. My cousin, Alston, for one. He can't resist a beautiful woman – he'll be at your feet in a trice.'

'You make it sound as though you're organizing some sort of assignation for me,' laughed Mercy.

'What's sauce for the gander...' began Charlotte, then she seemed to reconsider her words. 'To put it plainly, your husband and his friends will be thoroughly enjoying themselves while you and the other wives stay demurely at home. It's not right! Strike a blow for female freedom!'

'That's not what you were going to say.'

'No, but it will have to do,' said Charlotte, her face inscrutable.

Mercy noted her expression and did not press her further. She was very well aware of her friend's fondness for intrigue. 'I'm afraid I'll have to strike a blow for freedom some other time,' she said, smiling firmly.

'There won't be a better time.' Charlotte gave a resigned sigh. 'I'll put you on my guest list, in case you change your mind at the last minute.'

'Is Colonel Boyer really in financial difficulties?' Mercy asked later, as she and Peter went down to dinner. 'Who told you that?'

'Charlotte. She said he was looking for a buyer for the *Tango*.'

Peter did not reply immediately. When they reached the foot of the stairs he said with forced casualness, 'That's not quite accurate. The *Tango* has already been sold... Oh, I suppose I may as well tell you sooner than later. I've bought her!'

'You've bought the *Tango*.' Mercy stood stock still. 'You've bought a steam yacht?'

'Yes. That's why we're going on this trip, so Boyer can show me the ropes and give me a chance to try her for myself. Decent of him, I'd call it.'

'You've bought a steam yacht!' Mercy could still not believe it. 'What did she cost? Whatever it was, can we afford it?'

'She was a bargain, truly she was. Poor old Boyer needs the money so desperately he let her go for far less than she's worth. Anyway, I've given Boyer my word, and I'll not go back on it.' Peter was adamant, then his tone softened suddenly. 'Just wait until you've seen her, darling! She's a beauty. Clyde built, best Burmese teak on a steel frame, and the interior – the carved mahogany is magnificent. Some

143

of the soft furnishings look a bit shabby, so I dare say you'll have a great time putting things to rights.'

'Oh, Peter!' Mercy shook her head, halfway between tears and laughter. It was absolutely crazy buying a yacht she feared they couldn't afford. Her knowledge of their income was not as clear as she would have liked. In spite of their earlier unfortunate experiences Peter still held the quixotic view that he alone should worry about their financial situation. She knew that they were considerably better off than they had been, but whether their finances could support a steam yacht she was not sure. But his enthusiasm was infectious, she couldn't bear to spoil things for him. 'When do I see our latest possession?' she asked.

'You mean you aren't furious with me?'

'I won't say I approve, but seeing that it is too late to argue we may as well enjoy her.'

'You're marvellous, do you know that?' In a burst of exuberance Peter flung his arms about her and swung her off her feet.

'Put me down, you fool!' gasped Mercy, laughing. 'I refuse to be side-tracked. When am I to be allowed to see the *Tango*.'

'Tomorrow! She's on the River Dart, having her engines over-hauled before the run to Dinard. We'll drive over there in the morning.'

They found the *Tango* easily enough, moored to a jetty and looking trim in the crisp autumn sunshine. To Mercy's relief the yacht was smaller than she had expected; she had feared something large and ostentatious, in the style of the *Cleopatra*. Instead, the *Tango* proved to be a single-funnelled vessel, with neat lines and a raked bow.

They explored her from bow to stern, with Peter extolling the virtues of every feature and fitting. Only the engine-room, still occupied by workmen, was omitted. Mercy was conscious of having to quell her enthusiasm which was mounting to match his.

'Where shall we go in her?' asked Peter later as, windblown and happy, they drove away from the shipyard.

'Isn't it getting a little late in the year for a voyage?'

'Not for the *Tango*. She's up to bad weather. Boyer's taken her out in all conditions. How about the South of France? Or Portugal?'

'I don't know! I can't choose!' laughed Mercy.

'Let's make our minds up after I've done this Dinard run. I'll know better how she handles then. We'll go somewhere nice, though, just the two of us!' Peter slid one arm about her, kissing her cheek and almost entangling himself in her veil.

'Perhaps we should complete this journey first,' smiled Mercy. 'With you driving one-handed travelling in this car is more dangerous than any transatlantic crossing.'

In the days which followed Peter was very busy with preparations for his trip, poring over charts with Colonel Boyer, and spending hours down at the Yacht Club discussing the intricacies of running a steam yacht with other owners.

'I can see we'll have to go on a long cruise. It's the only way I'll ever get to see you,' Mercy protested.

'Are you feeling neglected? Poor love! It's just until I get the hang of *Tango*, I promise you. I'll tell you what! I'll bring you something really pretty from Dinard, shall I?'

'Just bring yourself,' she assured him. 'You're all I want.'

–

It was a rainy day when he finally did set sail, accompanied by Colonel Boyer and a couple of other friends. Mercy wandered about the house, unable to settle. Finally she went upstairs to fetch a book.

The door to Peter's dressing-room was open so she glanced in. It was neat and well-ordered except for a piece of paper on the floor. Mercy went to pick it up. As she did so she could not help noticing that it was a bill from a local jeweller for a diamond pendant in the shape of a letter M, complete with gold chain. The price made her wince at first, then she smiled. So this was the 'pretty thing' that Peter had promised her. To make sure he did not forget he had bought it before he sailed. Well, she was quite content to go along with his little deception.

It was barely seven o'clock next evening when Charlotte called. She and Mercy had agreed to go to a concert together.

'There, we've just to collect George and Tilly,' she said, as the Rolls Royce purred its way up the hill.

'I hadn't realized the Hewsons were coming.'

'George is going to give us the benefit of his manly protection.'

'I hope poor George appreciates the honour,' chuckled Mercy.

'He will do, never fear, or I'll have a sharp word to say.'

True to Charlotte's prediction George Hewson seemed delighted to find himself escorting three ladies. Tilly, however, appeared oddly reticent.

'Oh, I hadn't realized… If only I'd known… Oh dear…' she twittered.

Charlotte gave a snort of exasperation and said, 'Do get into the car, Tilly, for pity's sake!'

At Charlotte's imperious tone Tilly gave a whimper and obediently climbed into the car, where she proceeded to sit huddled in her seat, her velvet wrap pulled tightly about her. From time to time she shot Mercy nervous baleful glances, and Mercy wondered what imagined slight or drama was bothering Tilly Hewson now. She really was an extraordinarily silly woman.

The Pavilion gleamed palely in the street lights, contrasting sharply with the profound darkness of the harbour beyond. Its pale walls and curving domes gave the sea front an almost oriental air.

After the concert Tilly seemed to recover her spirits, and as they stood up to leave she took in the elegant interior of the Pavilion with one excited wave of her gloved hand. 'Doesn't this place thrill you? Oh, the joy of having a smart venue for concerts and plays at last. How did we manage in the old days?' Her gesturing dislodged her wrap, allowing Mercy to see for the first time that she was wearing a pendant. It was in the shape of the letter M, picked out in diamonds, and suspended from a slender golden chain. Then Tilly caught her eye, and immediately covered the pendant with her hand, as if desperate to hide it from view.

The sudden guilty gesture drew Mercy's attention. Why should Tilly care whether she saw the pendant or not? It took several minutes for the significance of it to sink in. A letter M picked out in diamonds! That had been the description on the jeweller's receipt she had picked up in Peter's dressing-room, the 'pretty thing' she had thought was hers. Puzzled, she stared at Tilly. The other woman gazed back, a curious expression that was part nervousness, part triumph in her eyes. Mercy knew then that the pendant had never been intended for her. The M had been for Matilda. Peter had bought it for Tilly Hewson! Mercy stood very still. Everything about her seemed to recede.

No! she thought. No, this can't be happening again! He promised! Peter promised! The words swirled like a maelstrom inside her head, causing her to sway perilously.

'Mercy! Are you all right?' Suddenly Charlotte had taken charge of her, and made her sit down.

'I'm sorry,' said Mercy weakly. 'I – I just felt rather odd.'

'You're tired!' Charlotte had no doubts on the subject. 'I said you were looking peaky. Come along, we'll get you home immediately.'

'No!' exclaimed Mercy. Then more quietly she repeated, 'No, don't spoil things on my account. I've recovered now. It was just a momentary thing. It has passed.'

'Are you sure?'

'Yes, thank you. It was nothing important!' As she spoke the words Mercy's eyes settled on Tilly. The hostility of her gaze drove all triumph from the other woman's expression and Tilly stepped back, shocked.

'A momentary thing or not, you must take my arm,' insisted George kindly.

Does he know? wondered Mercy. My husband and his wife are having an affair! Does he know? She thought not. He was too calm, too devoted in the way he looked at Tilly.

For Mercy to remain equally calm during supper required a super-human effort. Only pride and a grim determination not to betray one iota of weakness beforeHewson woman kept her going. Her performance must have been superb for it was Tilly who excited their hostess's concern.

'Are you feeling all right, Tilly?' demanded Charlotte. 'You've not said two words together all during supper.'

'I'm… I'm just a little tired,' Tilly murmured.

'Not you too! There must be something going round.' Fortunately Charlotte was quite satisfied with her diagnosis and did not probe any further.

The seemingly interminable supper party came to an end eventually, allowing Mercy to go home. Her iron control held until Stafford had helped her to undress and tidy away every last item of clothing. Only when the door closed behind the maid did Mercy allow herself to give way to the pent-up tears which had been gathering all evening.

The unthinkable had happened. Peter had been unfaithful again, and she felt as if her world had come to an end. She thought back to the terrible days after the Marie-Jeanne affair, the way she had slowly and painfully struggled to pick up the threads of her relationship with Peter once more. It had cost her much in effort, in pride, and in determination. She had achieved it because she loved him and had wanted to believe in him. He had sworn it would never happen again. But it had! It had!

The next two weeks were a torment. Sometimes she longed for Peter to be home, so that she could fling her accusations at him and have things out in the open. At other times she was glad he was still away, for she felt the sight of him was more than she could bear. It was an agony, trying to maintain an outward everyday composure serene enough to deceive the sharp eyes of her mother-in-law. Somehow she managed it, only to spend her nights tossing restlessly, hour after hour.

'You are looking decidedly wan,' remarked Agnes one. 'If you will make a martyr of yourself to your children, can you wonder you look worn out?'

Day slipped painfully into day, while in her head anger fought with pain, indecision with resentment, doubt with distress.

Then one morning Rogers entered her sitting-room and announced, 'if you please, Mrs Peter, the *Tango* has been sighted. She's just off Thatcher Rock.'

The butler's words only emphasized her indecision. What was she to do? Confront Peter immediately? Try to ignore the whole affair – as he had once told her was the normal way to behave – or should she walk out and leave him? She had to make a decision and make it quickly.

Then all at once it was too late. The car was pulling up at the front door, Peter's light brisk steps were echoing across the marble floor, and his voice, bright with laughter was calling, 'Where is every one? Have I no wife, no children, no mother? I'm home!'

It was extraordinary! He looked and sounded exactly as usual. His features bore a healthy tan, thanks to the wind and weather, and he brought with him something of the fresh outdoors. Apart from that he was unchanged. Mercy looked down at him from the stairs, still unsure what to do. Then the hall became a scene of hectic activity as servants scurried back and forth bringing in Peter's luggage.

Before she could make up her mind Peter saw her. Striding up the stairs, he enfolded her in his arms.

'Oh I've missed you,' he whispered against her hair. 'I've missed you terribly. I must have been mad to go away for two whole weeks.'

Mercy knew she should not believe him. She knew she should push him away and cry 'Liar!' Yet the moment his arms were about her, and she felt him close to her again, something in her responded to him despite her pain. It was weakness, she knew, and she despised herself for it, but, for the moment, she was glad to have him back again.

'Rogers has served tea in the drawing-room.' Agnes's voice cut in, full of disapproval at such a public display of emotion.

'Very well, Mother. I'll go and wash my hands like a good boy,' replied Peter cheerily. 'And while we have tea I'll tell you all about my adventures. The *Tango* was superb, behaved like a perfect lady the whole time, even when we hit some very dirty weather. She's the best investment I've ever made.'

Mercy listened to him as he enthused about the yacht and about his trip. This was not the time. The recriminations would have to come later, when they were alone.

She found it unexpectedly difficult to broach the subject. The evening wore on without her finding a suitable moment to accuse him. It was getting late. Once they had gone to bed and he had taken her in his arms again to make love to her she knew the chance would be gone for ever. And she wanted desperately to accuse him! She wanted him to know the pain and humiliation he had caused her.

'I promised to bring you something from Dinard, didn't I?'

Peter's words returned her to reality with a jolt. She looked at the elegantly wrapped parcel that he placed on the bed.

'Go on, open it. It's not going to explode,' he encouraged her.

Mercy continued to regard it with misgiving. Then, conscious of Peter's eager gaze, she began to unwrap it. Slowly she removed the paper to reveal a dressing-case. It was of blue leather, trimmed with silver. Inside, the fitted bottles of cut glass and silver gleamed against the lining of blue watered silk. It was a beautiful gift, and an expensive one.

'You don't like it?' Peter sounded surprised and hurt. 'Why do you say that?'

'Because of the expression on your face.'

'It's a lovely dressing case.'

'Then what's wrong?'

Mercy took a long slow breath.

'It wasn't what I was expecting,' she said. 'Expecting? What do you mean?'

Again Mercy paused.

'I thought my present would be a diamond pendant in the shape of a letter M. I saw the bill from the jeweller's. I found it on the floor. I thought it was for me. M for Mercy. I'd forgotten that M stands for Matilda too.' She braced herself for his denial, for his remorse, for his apologies. None came.

'You have been going through my papers!' At the accusation in his voice she looked up to see that he was glaring at her, white with indignation.

'I did not!' she retorted. 'I picked it up off the floor. I couldn't help seeing—'

'You couldn't help seeing— ? Oh really, Mercy, I'm surprised at you! That was a despicable thing to have done. You must have known it was a private matter. I expected better of you than that.'

'You expected—' Mercy's voice choked in disbelief. 'You have been unfaithful, you have betrayed and humiliated me, and all that bothers you is that I read one of your bills? I can't believe it.'

'It's more than that, and you know it. You have broken my trust in you. No man likes his wife reading his correspondence behind his back. And I tell you straight, I won't tolerate it!'

'*You* won't tolerate it? My God! Are you denying that you've been unfaithful, and with Tilly Hewson, of all people?'

'Of course I am. It was only a mild flirtation.'

'A mild flirtation? So you weren't lovers?'

'For heaven's sake don't be so dramatic! Tilly and I had a bit of fun together, nothing more. You've been off-colour of late, ever since William was born, so I sought a little amusement elsewhere. It never was serious, and it's over and done with now.'

'Never serious! Yet you bought her a very expensive pendant!'

'Of course I did. It was a token gesture to a friend, that's all. It is nothing to concern you.'

'It does concern me,' Mercy exclaimed. 'I hate the idea of you going with another woman. It hurts me. It humiliates me.'

'It shouldn't. It doesn't affect our marriage in any way. I've told you that before!' He took a step towards her, but Mercy swung sharply away.

'You've also told me before that you would never do such a thing again. Remember? When we were in Brittany?'

'I broke my word, and I'm sorry, but really you expect too much. You are being completely unreasonable.' For Mercy the conversation was assuming a nightmarish quality. She could not believe what she was hearing.

'Suddenly this mess has become my fault!' she cried. 'Can you deny it? If you hadn't gone prying among my things none of this would have come to light.'

'So, because I found you out I am to blame? There's something very wrong with your logic!'

'Or is there something very wrong with our marriage?' Their voices had been rising to an angry crescendo. Now, at Peter's bitter statement, a deep silence fell between them.

'There seems little point in continuing this conversation,' he said, beginning to make for his dressing-room. 'But what are we do to?' Mercy cried.

'Do?' he seemed puzzled by the question. 'I suppose we'll do what other people do in the same circumstances – be polite in public and try to keep out of each other's way as much as possible.' With that he closed the dressing room door behind him, leaving Mercy alone and devastated.

She could not believe he meant it, that the rift in their marriage was too great to heal. But as day followed day with Peter being icily polite on the few occasions when their paths crossed, Mercy's distress hardened into resentment and anger. Never before had she been so conscious of the difference in their standards. The division yawned like a chasm. Back at Fernicombe Cottages morality had had a pretty tough fight against poverty, ignorance and deprivation, but at least standards there had been based on the essentials of life – relationships and the need to survive. No one would have set a trivial act like reading a private piece of paper above loyalty between husband and wife. This rupture had not been her fault and she refused to be made to feel guilty. Seeing Peter apparently so calm and unaffected, going to the Yacht Club and his other rendezvous just as usual, added fuel to her burning indignation. She knew she had to get away, if only for a few days. She reached for the telephone.

'Charlotte,' she said. 'Is your invitation to come to Somerset still open?'

There was a slight pause at the other end of the line.

'Certainly,' said Charlotte. 'So you've come to your senses at last, eh?' And there was a note of satisfaction in her voice.

Chapter Nine

As the Rolls Royce purred its way through the lush Somerset countryside Mercy wished she had not come.

'It is only a country house party you know, not an invitation to an execution,' remarked Charlotte, observing Mercy's glum face.

'I know, and it's awful of me to be such a misery,' said Mercy ruefully. 'It's just that I've never been anywhere without Peter before, and I won't know anyone—'

'You'll know me, which is more than enough to be going on with,' said Charlotte. 'And its high time you branched out on your own more.'

'Maybe, but I still feel uneasy. I mean, what will your other guests think of sitting at table with an ex-laundress?'

'So that's what's bothering you, eh?'

'Yes, partly.'

'If they don't like it they are at liberty to leave. Just be yourself. You aren't to spend the next few days feeling inferior, do you hear?'

'I didn't say I felt inferior. I'm merely being realistic. Some people hold peculiar views on the subject and I don't want to cause you any embarrassment.'

'Anyone with peculiar views will hear some even more peculiar comments from me, so let's hear no more on the subject. You'll be fine.'

Mercy steeled herself to live up to Charlotte's expectations, though it was not easy when the car swung into the long curving drive of Upper Lee. Feeling exceedingly nervous Mercy followed her hostess into the house, wondering what had possessed her to come, and wondering how on earth she was going to survive the next few days.

'If you please, ma'am, tea is being served in the library. There's a nice fire in there.' The trim little maid waited hopefully, clearly expecting Mercy to follow her downstairs. Mercy took one last look round. There was a nice fire burning in her bedroom. What a pity she could not spend her time here in snug privacy. She gave a sigh and surrendered herself to the inevitable.

It seemed as though a sea of faces greeted her when she entered the library, although she realized there must only be a dozen or so guests.

'There you are, Mercy,' Charlotte greeted her. 'I thought you had deserted us. Do have some tea before it becomes totally undrinkable, and I will introduce you to everyone gradually.'

Feeling decidedly awkward Mercy looked round for somewhere to sit.

'Please, take my chair.' A young man in Army uniform, tall and fresh-faced, leapt to his feet.

Almost before she could draw breath Mercy found herself seated at a low table in the company of several other people. With creditable speed her new acquaintance had supplied her with a cup of tea and a cress sandwich and had sat himself down beside her.

'I think we should introduce ourselves,' he said. 'Charlotte will get round to it eventually, of course, but why wait? Archie Nicholson, Captain in His Majesty's Coldstream Guards, at your service.' He rose and bowed briefly.

'Mrs Lisburne.' Then because it sounded so formal she added, 'Mrs Mercy Lisburne,' as she extended her hand.

'Lisburne? That name is familiar.' A tall young woman with an abundance of untidy red hair, who had been reclining next to her suddenly sat upright. 'Lisburne. You're the one who used to be—'

'Do wait your turn, Lilian,' admonished Captain Nicholson cheerfully. 'Mrs Lisburne, this fiery lady is Mrs Manning. The extremely elegant lady on her right is Mrs Zena Pritchard, and the languid gent is Mr Charles Wentworth. There, that's enough introductions to be going on with.'

'Where a lady as delightful as Mrs Lisburne is concerned I think it's more than enough. I suggest we keep her all to ourselves.' Charles Wentworth rose and bowed, his eyes roving over Mercy a little too appreciatively for her comfort.

'Trust you two to get excited at the advent of a pretty new face.' It was Mrs Pritchard, who spoke. 'You're right, Lilian,' she said, in a high, clear voice. 'We have heard of Mrs Lisburne. I never expected we would be fellow guests.' Her tone betrayed her disapproval all too blatantly.

Mercy's spirits, already low, sank a little lower. No matter what Charlotte said, her humble origins were going to make a very uncomfortable difference, if the disdainful expression on Zena Pritchard's face was anything to go by.

'This is my first visit to Upper Lee,' she said, in an attempt to steer the conversation into safer waters. 'It's a beautiful house, isn't it?'

'Quite delightful,' Zena Pritchard agreed. 'But then, with your background, I am sure you are an authority on fine houses. One must get to know them so very well when one has to scrub the floors.'

Lilian Manning smothered a giggle at her friend's comment, though both men had the grace to look uncomfortable.

Mercy swallowed her mortification with difficulty. If only she could flee to the secluded safety of her bedroom. Then suddenly, quite clearly, in her head she heard Blanche's voice snort derisively, 'Hoity-toity trollop!' All thought of flight left her.

'There you are mistaken, Mrs Pritchard,' she said evenly. 'I did not scrub floors for a living.'

A brittle silence fell, as Zena Pritchard glared angrily at her. Mercy steadfastly held her gaze, and at last the other woman gave a false little laugh.

'How foolish of me!' she said. 'Of course, you were a laundry-maid, weren't you? If you please, Mrs Lisburne, give us the benefit of your professional opinion. What do you think of the laundry-work on this tablecloth?'

Determined not to show that she was ruffled Mercy stretched out a hand and felt the white linen.

'Extremely well done,' she said. 'I would have given it less starch, but that is purely a matter of taste.' She leaned back, the smile on her face growing tighter by the minute. 'And now, what of you, Mrs Pritchard? I was going to ask you in which field you excel. But I fancy you have just demonstrated the sum total of your talents very clearly.'

From somewhere behind her Mercy heard a suppressed snort of laughter.

Zena Pritchard shot bolt upright in her chair, fury etched on her face. 'Let me say—'

She did not get the chance to complete her sentence, for she was interrupted by Charlotte.

'I'm going to break up this cosy *tete-a-tete*,' she said, with blatant disregard for the tense atmosphere. 'I'm going to steal Mercy away for a minute. Someone is dying to meet her.'

'If you will excuse me.' Mercy inclined her head politely in farewell and rose gratefully.

'I'm sorry you fell in with that crowd,' Charlotte said, guiding her across the room. 'The others aren't too bad, but Zena Pritchard is a bitch. I only invite her to give her poor husband a bit of respite. Now, Mercy, let me introduce you to my cousin, Lord Alston. Alston, this is the Mrs Lisburne you've been so eager to meet.'

'This is indeed a pleasure, Mrs Lisburne. I hope you will forgive my impertinence in having Charlotte bring you to me, instead of vice versa. To be honest, I thought you might be in need of rescuing.'

Lord Alston, despite his rank and ancient lineage, was middle-aged, middle height, and of medium colouring. There was nothing to mark him out as the cream of the aristocracy. Indeed, standing there in his country tweeds, he seemed like a prosperous farmer. But Mercy didn't care how he looked: she was grateful to him.

'You are absolutely right, my lord,' she said. 'My thanks for coming to my assistance so promptly.'

'I must confess I was sorely tempted to let well alone for a while. You seemed to be putting up a remarkably spirited defence. It was exceedingly impolite of me to eavesdrop, but I can't, in all honesty, say I am sorry. I haven't heard anything so amusing for ages.'

'I am glad you were so well entertained, my lord,' said Mercy, a little stiffly.

'There, I have annoyed you. Now that is something for which I do apologize without reservation. My only excuse is that I find your combination of beauty and spirit quite irresistible. They are a very potent force, you know, and rare.' The compliments should have sounded forced and extravagant, yet somehow they did not.

'I'm not annoyed, I promise you,' she said hastily. 'I think I am still a little upset.'

'And no wonder, after having repelled invaders so splendidly. Why don't you sit here, beside the fire, with me as your watch–dog to fend off any hostile forces?' Thankfully Mercy sank down beside him.

'I should not have come,' she said. 'Charlotte was certain that my background would make no difference, but it does. And I am so afraid my being here will cause trouble. Mrs Pritchard, for one, is not at all pleased to have a laundress as a fellow guest.'

'Although it may be discourteous of me to say so, Mrs Pritchard's opinions are not quite as important as she imagines. Charlotte is a sound judge of character, and she is pleased to call you a friend. I hope, upon further acquaintance, you might look upon me in the same light. You will have no more trouble.' He spoke with the absolute self-confidence of the privileged, and Mercy believed him. 'So, no more talk of wishing you had not come. Promise?' He looked at her quizzically.

'I promise.'

Later, it was Lord Alston who took her in to dinner, and who remained by her side during the rest of the evening. Mercy wondered if such single-minded attention was quite proper. Despite her problems with Peter, she was a married woman and Lord Alston, she understood, had a wife. Only as the evening drew on, and she regarded her fellow guests more closely did she realize that, though most of the others admitted to being married, none had come with their partners. The discovery brought back a hint of uneasiness, which she tried to shrug off. If Peter considered himself freed from marital ties why shouldn't she?

However, she did not find it so easy. She discovered that she could not throw off the responsibilities of marriage. The ties binding her to Peter were too strong.

Breakfast next morning was a very casual meal, with everyone helping themselves from the selection of chafing-dishes on the sideboard. Lord Alston was spooning a generous helping of kedgeree on to his plate as she entered.

'Ah, Mrs Lisburne. You slept well, I hope?' he greeted her.

'Extremely well, my lord, thank you. There's no sign of Charlotte yet?' she observed, looking round.

'No, nor likely to be for some time. My cousin is not renowned for being an early riser.'

'Oh.' Mercy was at something of a loss, uncertain of the form on such occasions.

'We are free to enjoy ourselves this morning. Do you ride, Mrs Lisburne?'

'Not with any decorum,' she replied.

He laughed. 'Then, when you have finished your breakfast, will you permit me to be your escort for a country walk?'

'But you are dressed for riding, my lord.'

'I can go riding any time I like. I have never before had the honour of escorting you and believe me I find that prospect infinitely more preferable. Or perhaps you would prefer to go for a drive?'

'A walk, I think. It's such a beautiful morning.'

'A walk it will be.'

The air was heavy with the scents of autumn, of mouldering leaves, of wood-smoke, and of the ripe verdant smell which marked the end of the year. Mercy drank it in and felt an unexpected pang of nostalgia. Since her marriage her life had been bound by town and sea, she had gone into the countryside only rarely. She took in a deep breath and let it out again with a sigh.

Lord Alston laughed. 'I have seldom heard such a contented sound,' he said.

'It's this air, the smell of it. It brings back such memories of my childhood.'

'Yet surely you were poor? Those memories should be unhappy ones.'

'Oh no, not all of them. There were happy times too, especially at this time of year. Gathering nuts from the hedgerow, for example, and blackberries!'

'I can see you are still very much a country-lover at heart, Mrs Lisburne. I am too; I am delighted you chose to walk this morning. How enjoyable it is to find someone who shares one's own interests! To walk by one's self is no pleasure.'

'I am sure you would have no difficulty in finding a companion to keep you company, my lord.'

'Maybe not, but I know I wouldn't have found any other companion to be so charming.'

'Oh dear! That sounds terribly as though I were fishing for compliments.'

'I hope you were. I'd be delighted to discover that fishing was one of your accomplishments; it is another favourite pastime of mine.'

'Then I am afraid I must disappoint you, my lord,' laughed Mercy. 'Fishing for compliments is, I regret, my only acquaintance with the sport.'

'Oh good! In that case I'll teach you the other variety. There is some excellent coarse fishing to be had on this estate. We'll have our first lesson tomorrow.'

He seemed so pleased at the prospect that Mercy could not help smiling. She was finding being in his company extremely easy. For all his aristocratic ancestry he clearly did not care a fig that she had once been a laundress. With his easy manners and his total disregard for the difference in their origins he reminded her of Peter in the early days of their courtship. The thought was not a happy one and she hastened her step to escape from her painful memories.

The remainder of the day passed surprisingly easily. Charlotte had arranged an excursion to Glastonbury for her guests, and Mercy knew she could rely on her friend's formidable presence to keep the likes of Zena Pritchard at bay. Most of all, though, it was Lord Alston's attentiveness that silenced the malicious tongues and allowed Mercy to enjoy herself. He was her constant companion during the outing, then again at dinner she found him by her side.

Only after dinner did the atmosphere seem to go flat. The inevitable bridge game broke up early, the gentlemen went half-heartedly to play billiards, and an effort to organize dancing came to nothing. Mercy was quite glad to retire to bed with a book. Her rest did not last long, however. She was awakened from her sleep by running feet and shrieking from the corridor outside. Alarmed, she leaped out of bed and, pulling on her dressing-gown, she opened her bedroom door. At first the corridor was empty, then Archie Nicholson and Charles Wentworth rounded the corner. Minus their jackets, they were racing each other, carrying Lilian Manning and Zena Pritchard pick-a-back respectively. At Mercy's door Archie Nicholson tripped, bringing down the others in a heap on the carpet.

'This is our version of steeplechasing, and much more enjoyable,' explained Charles Wentworth as, laughing and shrieking, they disentangled themselves. 'Won't you join us, Mrs Lisburne?'

The bedroom door opposite opened, and Lord Alston, clad in a maroon silk dressing-gown, looked out. 'If you wish to take part in the fun I'm sure you will have no difficulty in finding a cavalier for yourself,' he said.

Mercy was aware of the hopeful note in his voice. At the same time she caught the strong smell of alcohol coming from the struggling group on the carpet. There had evidently been some hard drinking going on after she had left the party, and she had no wish to get involved. Apart from that, she felt it was an absurdly childish pastime for adults to indulge in.

'Thank you, no,' she said. 'I am rather tired. I'll leave you to your games.'

Not bothering to hide his regret Lord Alston bade her good night. As she closed her door she heard Zena Pritchard's voice exclaim waspishly, 'Why on earth did you ask the Lisburne woman to join us, Charlie? We're being jockeys, not bags of laundry.'

There came a bleat of inane laughter, followed by more shrieks as their silly race continued. The noise of the quartet's activities kept Mercy awake until the early hours, then she heard Lilian Manning and Captain Nicholson whispering and giggling together until the sound was cut off by the closing of a single door. Zena Pritchard's bedroom door, closed too. Mrs Pritchard was not alone. The low murmur of voices, male and female, laughing and giggling, and the clink of glasses, continued for some time. Mercy thought she recognized the man's voice as Charles Wentworth's. Longing for some quiet, so that she could go back to sleep, she waited for the sound of his departure. It never came. Eventually the voices ceased, and Mercy was able to settle down again.

She was beginning to understand now why no one at the country house-party was with their spouse, and she began to feel uneasy once more. Was infidelity an accepted part of these occasions? Angry as she was with Peter, she had never really considered being unfaithful to him. She wished, yet again, that she had never come to Upper Lee.

—

If anyone had any regrets about the excesses of the night before it was not evident at the breakfast table.

'We thought we'd make up a riding-party to go as far as the gorge today,' announced Zena Pritchard, ignoring Mercy completely. 'We can count you in, can't we, Lord Alston? You're a great rider.'

'I am afraid I must decline your kind invitation. I'm otherwise engaged. Mrs Lisburne and I are going fishing.'

'Are we?' said Mercy, surprised. 'I know you said something about it, but I didn't think you were serious, my lord.'

'Of course I was serious. I do hope you aren't going to disappoint me.'

'No, of course not. It sounds very enjoyable.'

'Fishing?' Mrs Pritchard's voice was suddenly full of enthusiasm. 'What a splendid idea! That sounds much better than riding. We'll join you and make up a fishing-party instead.'

'I had no idea you were so keen on coarse fishing, Mrs Pritchard.'

'Of course I am, my lord. I love it!' Mrs Pritchard shot a jubilant look at Mercy.

'Then you must have Charlotte's water bailiff. I had spoken for the fellow's services this morning, but I'm sure you'll make better use of him than we will. Mrs Lisburne and I are only going still-water fishing in the Home Pool – far too tame for an experienced angler like you.'

'Oh but…' Zena began to protest.

Lord Alston held up his hand.

'I insist,' he said. 'Now, if you are ready, Mrs Lisburne, shall we go?'

Mercy left the room with Lord Alston conscious of Mrs Pritchard's indignant gaze boring into her back. She would have been less than human if she had not revelled a little in her triumph.

As Mercy crossed the hall her glance fell on the table where the morning's delivery of post was neatly laid out. There was nothing for her, she had already looked. It was foolish of her to look a second time, but she could not help hoping. She had left her address at the Villa Dorata, so that Peter could write to her if he wished. Only, he had clearly not wished. Swallowing, her disappointment she went to fetch her coat.

The fishing proved to be a soothing diversion, with Lord Alston a very patient tutor.

'I am afraid our catch is rather meagre,' she said, observing the two small tench and the undersized rudd in the keep-net.

'Did you enjoy yourself? That is the main thing,' said Lord Alston.

'Yes,' she said, without hesitation. 'What about you?'

'How could I help myself, in such company?' he replied.

At once she regretted having asked the question. There was an admiration in his eyes she did not want to recognize. She was honest enough to admit that she found Lord Alston's attentions flattering and a boost to her battered pride. What she sheered away from was the painful question of where such admiration was going to lead. She had no wish to be party to the adulterous games that occupied the other guests.

'Hadn't we better be getting back to the house?' she said. 'We'll be late for lunch.'

'Does it matter…?' began Lord Alston, then he paused. 'You are quite right, Mrs Lisburne. It is high time we went back,' he said.

Gradually, during the next few days, it was assumed that Lord Alston was Mercy's permanent escort. They were partnered at dinner and at the bridge table; when dancing provided the entertainment in the evening no other man presumed to ask Mercy for a waltz or a veleta.

At first Mercy accepted the situation, but uncomfortably, not knowing how to avoid it. It had not escaped her notice that the other guests had paired up too. Oh, very discreetly, but there was no ignoring the muffled whispers at night and the furtive thud of bedroom doors closing. Mercy's new-found freedom clearly had its dangers, and it bothered her in case Lord Alston expected similar favours. To her relief he made no such demands.

The last evening was spent playing a particularly rowdy game of hide-and-seek. It surprised Mercy that adults – and seemingly sophisticated adults, at that – could take part in such rough-and-tumble infantile games. She recognized them for what they were, an excuse for a sort of mildly lecherous behaviour. She wondered if the participants were naive enough to see them as no more than horseplay. She doubted it. For that reason she was reluctant to join in, but by the final evening her resolution was worn down.

'Oh, do come along, Mercy!' Charlotte urged her. 'You can't really want to sit in the library with a dull old book while the rest of us are having such fun.'

'I'm quite content, really I am,' Mercy replied.

'Guests in my house are ecstatically happy, or having a wonderful time, or enjoying themselves no end. They are never just content! I regard the word as an insult! Put that book down and join the fun.'

Charlotte in this mood was hard to deny, so Mercy did as she was told with a resigned smile.

'Charles Wentworth is "he", and it is permissible to hide anywhere in the house except the servants' quarters. Right, Charlie! I've managed to drag Mercy out of the library so we are ready. How long are you giving us?'

'Up to a count of thirty, then I come. Off you go!' answered Charles.

Feeling more than a little foolish Mercy hurried out with the rest, and found herself a hiding-place behind one of the long dining-room curtains.

'You'll be discovered immediately,' said a voice behind her.

She turned and saw Lord Alston. He put his finger to his lips and taking her hand led her out of the room and along a small corridor she had not noticed.

'This leads to the garden-room. No one uses it at this time of year,' he whispered. 'Quick, in here.'

He hustled her into a long cupboard in which hung mackintoshes. Squeezing in beside her he closed the door. It was cramped in there, among the waterproofs, making it necessary to stand very close together. Lord Alston's arms began to creep about her waist and he pulled her closer. She felt his hold tighten as his body pressed against hers, and his mouth began to explore the softness of her neck. Mercy stood very still, not certain what to do. She wanted to pay Peter back for hurting her, yet she had serious misgivings about what was happening.

'I— I think I hear someone coming,' she whispered in desperation.

'No one will find us here,' murmured Lord Alston, his hands beginning to stray upwards to her breasts. Distressed, Mercy tried to move away. She wanted none of it.

Voices in the corridor outside made him halt. In a moment the cupboard door was wrenched open and Charles Wentworth, aided by a jubilant Zena Pritchard, declared, 'Found, the pair of you!'

Mercy felt her face go scarlet, but Lord Alston merely laughed and said, 'That was rather caddish of you, Wentworth, to find us so quickly.'

'The night is young,' Wentworth replied, a knowing leer on his face. 'It wouldn't do to leave you too long too soon.'

The game continued, with Lord Alston being Mercy's shadow, to her increasing disquiet. Each time they shared a hiding-place his caresses were becoming more importunate, his ardour more evident. It took all of Mercy's ingenuity to fend off the more excessive of his attentions. When finally it was time to retire she could not fail to see the blatant desire in his eyes. Lord Alston had changed from being a reassuring friend into a would-be seducer, and the transformation horrified her.

As she prepared for bed she listened tensely for the discreet tap at her door. When it came it was an urgent rapping, causing her to freeze. She knew Lord Alston found her attractive, and she had enjoyed his company, but tonight he was demonstrating all too clearly just how badly she had misjudged the situation. It had been stupid and naive of her to think she could restrict their relationship to a mild flirtation. Matters were rapidly slipping beyond her control.

The knocking at her door was becoming insistent, it must be audible to the whole house. She could not stand it any more... She would speak to him, reason with him.

She opened the door.

Mercy had no chance to speak. Lord Alston, clad in his maroon silk dressing-gown, stepped into the room with complete assurance, pushing the door shut with his foot. He swept her into his arms straight away, forcing her backwards until they collapsed on the bed.

'Please – please, no,' she gasped, trying to struggle out from under his weight.

He did not hear her. 'You've no idea how I've waited for this.' His voice was low, his breathing heavy as he pulled her dressing-gown away from her shoulders.

'Please, stop—' began Mercy, then she was silenced by the demands of his mouth.

Desperately she tried to struggle, but she was trapped on the bed by his body, her arms pinioned by her own dressing-gown.

Now his hands were at the neck of her night-gown, pulling and tugging, only to find his efforts defeated by the demure Peter Pan collar, and the rows of insertion lace. At once he turned his attention to pulling it up. Memories of the Orchard Laundry and Albert Hoskins flashed into her head, sweeping away all indecision. She knew without doubt she was not going to let this man, duke's son or not, have the pleasure of her body. With a terrific effort she managed to free one arm.

'No! Stop!' she cried again, hitting out at him.

Lord Alston looked down at her, his face flushed, his eyes bright with excitement.

'So you still mean to tease me, eh? Well tease away, we've got the whole night ahead of us, and I intend to make the most of it.'

He meant it, too! Mercy was desperate now.

'I'm not teasing! Please stop!' she begged again, without response.

Her night-gown was crumpled up round her waist. Lord Alston's excitement was increasing to the point where she knew there would be no hope of restraining him. Shades of Albert Hoskins haunted her. She stretched out her hand and found the water-jug on her bedside table.

The shock of the cold water was enough to make Lord Alston gasp and loose his hold on her. Mercy took her chance to push him off the bed, scrambling off the other side herself, pulling down her clothes as she went.

Lord Alston was sitting on the floor, water dripping off his head.

'What was that for?' he demanded in aggrieved surprise.

'You wouldn't stop!' she cried. 'Time and again I said no, but you wouldn't listen.'

'You didn't want me to listen. You were teasing. You were as desperate for it as I was.'

'No, I wasn't!'

'Oh come, my dear! What do you think we've been doing the whole evening? After all those cosy moments together, the times we squeezed so seductively into cupboards and dark corners. What the devil did you expect to be the outcome?'

'I— I'm not sure.'

'Well I am! You were inviting me to your bed as clearly as if you'd handed me an engraved invitation.'

'No I wasn't… at least, I didn't mean to.'

'Didn't you? Then you must be the most innocent, naïve woman I've encountered. And for goodness sake put that thing down! You're in no danger. I'm no rapist.'

Mercy put down the heavy silver-backed hairbrush she had been wielding like a club. She realized, with some surprise he was more hurt than angry. Honesty got the better of her.

'I'm sorry,' she said. 'I suppose it must have seemed as though I was leading you on. Perhaps I was, only when it came to it… well, I suppose my marriage ties are too strong. It was mainly my fault. I'm sorry.'

Lord Alston rose slowly to his feet, brushing trickles of water from his face.

'You're honest, I'll give you that. I only wish you'd given matters a bit more thought and realized what you were doing. I feel an absolute fool.'

'Oh no!' protested Mercy. 'I'd hate you to feel like that. I like you far too much.'

'That's something, anyway. Though if you douse men you like with freezing water to cool their ardour I can't imagine what you'd do to someone you disliked.'

'That's easy to answer. I hit them with flat-irons.'

'You what?'

'I hit them with flat-irons. Or to be more accurate that was what I did to my former employer when he got too familiar.'

'Then I must consider myself to be fortunate. Did the poor fellow survive?'

'Yes, luckily. He was just a bit singed, the iron was hot, you see.'

Lord Alston gave a bark of laughter. 'Then I was definitely fortunate.' He turned and made for the door. 'All that remains now, I suppose, is for me to offer my abject apologies for having misunderstood your intentions. I feel I have insulted you, which is the last thing I wanted.'

'You haven't insulted me, and anyway, I acknowledge it was partly my fault.'

'That's very handsome of you. Not many women would say such a thing.'

'As well as an apology I owe you my thanks. This is the first time I've been anywhere without my husband. I didn't expect to enjoy myself, but I have, because you've been so kind. I'm very grateful.'

'You're a generous woman, Mercy Lisburne, and a most unusual one. You make me very regretful that we couldn't enjoy a far closer relationship.' He spoke wistfully, almost sadly. Then he gave a sudden smile. 'Don't worry, I'm not going to start making advances again. You've dealt my self-esteem a bit of blow, though. I think you should make amends. Come to the ball I'm giving at my place in Dorset next month.'

Mercy looked at him doubtfully, 'I'm not sure,' she said.

'No strings, no obligations. Just come as a friend. Charlotte will be coming; I know she'd be delighted to have you join her party. There's no need to give me an answer now. Think about it. I'll make sure you receive an invitation.' He paused at the door. 'We're still friends, aren't we?' he asked.

'We're still friends,' she assured him.

It was a long time before Mercy got to sleep that night. Memories of the evening and of the disastrous misunderstanding haunted her, making her go crimson again and again. Lord Alston had taken her rebuff well. She decided she liked him very much. Nevertheless, she had no intention of attending his ball.

The Villa Dorata felt strangely quiet when she returned. It was good to see the children again, she had missed them, but away from the nursery the place felt gloomy. It took her some time to ask Agnes the question that had been bothering her.

'Peter's not at home?' she said.

'No! He's up in London for a few days to visit his tailor and shirtmaker; then he's going shooting in Norfolk.'

'Norfolk? Who does he know there?'

'Some people called Grant.' Agnes paused ominously. 'I understand they are friends of Mr and Mrs Hewson,' she said.

That was enough for Mercy. Next morning, when the elegantly engraved invitation to Lord Alston's ball arrived in the post Mercy did not hesitate. She wrote at once accepting, just as she went on accepting the other invitations to race-parties and shooting-parties and country weekends which suddenly came through the letter-box. Her engagement book filled with extraordinary speed, and she looked at it with satisfaction. The invitations were to her and her alone. She was a person in her own right now, not merely the wife of Peter Lisburne. She no longer needed him. She could manage alone.

Chapter Ten

Joey strode up the gravel drive of the Villa Dorata, his face set with grim determination. He was not going to be fobbed off a second time. The trim parlourmaid who answered his urgent ringing at the front door took him rather by surprise, he had been expecting the sour-faced old buffer who had turned him away the previous day. The expression on the maid's face was no more welcoming.

'Tradesman's entrance is round the back,' she said haughtily.

'I'm not a tradesman. I've come to see Mrs Mercy Lisburne.'

'Mrs Lisburne is not at home,' was the prompt reply. A little too prompt for Joey's liking.

'I know Mrs Lisburne's in. I've just seen her drive up in her car. So I'll see her now, if you please. I've an urgent message for her, and if you don't want to get your marching orders, along with old misery-guts who answered the door to me yesterday, I suggest you go to her at once.'

'She wouldn't dismiss Mr Rogers,' the maid said disparagingly.

'Oh no? Just go and tell her Mr Joseph Seaton wishes to see her urgently.'

The maid looked at him doubtfully, then said, 'Very well, but wait here on the doorstep.'

She was back in a surprisingly short time, her face rather pink.

'The mistress will see you now, sir,' she said. 'Will you be kind enough to come this way.'

It seemed to Joey that she led him across a vast expanse of marble floor, then up a huge winding staircase, but such was his desperation to see his sister the details of his surroundings were a mere blur.

'Mr Seaton, ma'am.' The maid showed him into a pretty sitting-room, then departed.

'Joey! Such a surprise!' Mercy rose to her feet, her arms outstretched towards him. He thought she looked more beautiful than ever in her rust-coloured gown. The fashionable Russian style, with its simple lines and rich embroidery, suited her. Only when she released him from her embrace and held him at arm's length did he notice the faint lines of strain about her eyes. She looked pleased to see him, but she did not look happy.

He took hold of her hands. 'I'm here because I've some bad news.'

Her grip on his fingers tightened.

'Bad news? Is it Blanche? Ma? Lizzie?'

'Blanche. Some sort of a seizure.'

The colour drained from her face.

'Is she seriously ill? Have you called the doctor? I'll come at once. I'll just get my coat.'

Joey restrained her as she made for the door, shaking his head.

'It's too late,' he said quietly. 'Blanche is dead. She died yesterday.'

'Dead? She can't be!' Her eyes widened with shock.

Joey understood her disbelief. Difficult, quarrelsome, cantankerous, there had been a steely quality about Blanche that made her seem indestructible.

'I'm sorry,' he said softly. 'Come on, you'd better sit down.'

He led her to a sofa and sat beside her, his arm comfortingly about her shoulders.

'She died yesterday, you say? Then why did you leave it until now? Why didn't you come and fetch me?'

'I did come. I was told you weren't at home.'

'But I was!'

'I was sure you were, only there was no getting through to that butler fellow. I left a message.'

'I didn't get it,' she cried desperately.

'I thought not. That's why I came back today.'

'I still don't understand. If Rogers had given me your message I'd have come. I might have had time to be with her, to see her again for one last time.'

'Maybe he thought I was some disreputable character, out to threaten you.' Joey attempted to lighten her distress.

'No, Rogers wouldn't fail to deliver a message off his own bat. He was ordered not to give me your message, and I can guess by whom. I'll never forgive her! Never!'

'Her? Your mother-in-law, do you mean? Surely she wouldn't have done such a thing?'

'Agnes Lisburne is quite capable of doing such a thing, and she disliked Blanche. But she shouldn't have got her own back this way. It's too cruel.' Mercy's face suddenly crumpled, and the tears began to stream down her cheeks. The lump in Joey's throat threatened to choke him, as he pulled her close to him in shared grief. How long they clung together like that he did not know. It was Mercy who moved away first, mopping her eyes with a totally inadequate handkerchief.

'Tell me what happened... about Blanche, I mean,' she said. 'Were you there?'

'At the end, yes. Seemingly Blanche collapsed in the street, outside the Oak, appropriately enough. It was Harry Dawe who brought her home.'

'She didn't suffer, did she?'

'No, she was unconscious most of the time, though she rallied a bit soon after I got there. Her mind was quite clear for a spell. She had me dig this out of a hidey-hole she'd got in one of the rafters. Said she'd been keeping it for you because you were the only one in the family who would appreciate it.' Joey rummaged in his pocket and took out a small brown-paper parcel.

He watched his sister open it to reveal a small book of poems by Shelley. Inside, on the flyleaf was written: 'To Blanche Elizabeth, on her sixteenth birthday, from her loving Mama. 12th June, 1863.'

As she turned the pages a card fell out. It was a photograph of a young girl dressed in a plaid dress with the absurdly wide skirts of the previous century. On her head she wore a matching soldier-style hat, while her feet were smartly encased in neat white boots. Written on the back was the name 'Blanche'. There was a surname too, but it had been scored out so heavily it was indecipherable.

Joey drew in his breath sharply, his attention caught not by the evidently fashionable clothes of the girl, nor by the fine house in the background. It was her face that made him gasp.

'It's incredible!' he exclaimed. 'It could be you! But look at the name - Blanche! It's the Old Un, isn't it? It must be. Wasn't she pretty? And do you see that posh house behind her? You don't think those stories of hers were true, do you?'

'I think they might have been.' Mercy smoothed the photograph with gentle fingers. 'She does look pretty there, doesn't she? And happy.'

'And well off. I don't know anything about fashion in those days, but she certainly isn't dressed like a pauper, is she? I don't think she's standing in front of a workhouse, either. When you think of what she became... I mean, it makes you wonder what happened, doesn't it?'

'Whatever it was, it must have been terrible for her. Poor Grandmother.' Carefully Mercy put the photograph back in the poetry book.

'Thank you for bringing them,' she said, her voice still husky with weeping. 'They must have meant something very special for her to have kept them all these years, her last links with her old way of life. I'll treasure them always.'

'I knew you would, and so did Blanche. That's why she wanted you to have them.' Joey rose to his feet.

'You aren't going yet, are you?' asked Mercy in alarm.

'I've got to get back to give Queenie a hand with the suppers. It's too much for her on her own, and her father's so poorly he can't help.'

'Are you liking it in Paignton?' Mercy knew few details about his latest job.

'Yes, fine,' he replied, too heartily to convince his sister.

'You haven't told me when the funeral's to be,' said Mercy.

'Ah yes, the funeral.' Joey paused on his route to the door. 'The thing is, she didn't want any of us to go.'

'Not to go?'

'Yes, quite definite she was. "I am not having folks howling and bawling over me," she said. "You will all be glad to be rid of me, and I shall be glad to go, so there is an end to it!"'

'But we weren't glad to be rid of her,' protested Mercy. 'At least, I'm not, and I know you're not.'

'I told her that, but she wouldn't change her mind. "I will come back and haunt any of you who disobey my wishes," she said, all la-di-da and precise to the end. The doctor was very taken with her. He said it was the most impressive deathbed he'd attended in a long time. Ma and Lizzie were scared out of their wits. You won't get them within a mile of the cemetery on Wednesday.'

'Wednesday... that's when it's to be?'

'That's right.' Joey shuffled awkwardly. 'Look, Sis, just because she doesn't want us there, that's no reason for her to have a pauper's funeral. Could you see your way to chipping in with the cost? I tried getting some out of Pa, but you know what that's like, and Ma and Lizzie never have a brass farthing between them, in spite of the money you send.'

'Of course I will. I should have offered. I'm sorry.' Mercy looked stricken.

'So I can tackle the undertaker, can I?'

'Yes, please. Make sure she has a decent funeral, one fit for the Blanche in the photograph. Don't worry what it costs, send the bill to me, and the doctor's bill, too.'

'No, I'm paying my share.' Joey was adamant. 'I've enough.'

'Very well, we'll split the expenses, if that's what you want.' She smiled at him, still somewhat tearful. 'Thanks for coming. You've no idea how good it is to see you again.'

'And you, Sis. We'll have to get together again soon, eh?' His voice lacked conviction. Somehow he did not think he would be seeing too much of Mercy in the future. Although she had been back to Fernicombe Cottages of late, her visits had been fleeting and unsatisfactory. There was a brittleness about her these days which made her seem more of a stranger than ever. He did not dare ask her how she really was or if she was happy.

'That would be lovely.' She reached up and kissed him. 'Take care,' she whispered. 'Give my love to Ma and Lizzie and everyone. Tell them I'll come to see them soon.'

'I will,' he promised, giving her one last hug.

Only as he walked away from his sister's house did its magnificence register with him. He could only bring her sitting-room into sharp focus, but that was enough. The tasteful furniture, the pictures on the walls, the modern gramophone standing open, its records strewn casually on the table. Above all, it was the sense of space and the clean smell of everything which impressed him. No hint of stale cooking and bad drains, just polish and fresh flowers. He liked that.

The contrast between Mercy's way of life and his existence with the Dixons cast a gloomy shadow over him. As he made for the tram back to Paignton his depression deepened so much he almost forgot to call in at the undertaker's. The result was that he had to retrace his steps. By the time he returned to the lodging-house he was late and in a bad mood.

Queenie was in the kitchen when he arrived. Her plain face was crimson with the heat as she frantically peeled a small mountain of potatoes. Her air of harassment made him feel guilty. Peeling potatoes was one of his jobs.

'There was no need for you to start those. You knew I'd come. I'm only a bit late,' he snapped.

'Just thought I'd make a start to help you out.' She turned and stirred at something on the stove, pushing a strand of hair from her perspiring brow as she did so.

She looked tired, and her gentle uncomplaining response filled him with remorse.

'Thanks,' he said. 'Sorry I bit your head off. I missed my tram and – well, you know how it is.'

'Yes, I know.' She gave him a quick smile of sympathy. 'Things can't be easy for you at the moment. The kettle's nearly boiling, I'll make you a cup of tea.'

'No! Give me a minute to change and I'll make you one. And leave those danged tiddies alone. I'll do them.' He stopped and gave a grin. 'Lor', my sister would give me a thump round the ear if she heard me calling them tiddies. My apologies, Miss Dixon! Leave those potatoes alone, if you will, and I will give them my undivided attention when I return.'

'You gurt fool!' he heard Queenie laugh as he hurried upstairs.

In record time he was back in the kitchen. He made the tea and, placing his hands on Queenie's stout waist, he pushed her gently but firmly away from the potato stack.

'Sit down!' he ordered, 'and drink your tea while it's hot!'

'You tell her, boy. She might take some notice of you.' Stan Dixon shuffled in, one hand clutching at the doorpost for support. He looked more grey and ill than ever. 'How're things going?'

'Everything under control,' replied Joey.

'In that case I think I'll go and have a lie down for a few minutes. If you need me just give a yell.'

'We will!' Joey assured him.

It was a nightly ritual, this offering of assistance. Stan was far too sick to do any work, and they all knew it. Joey's promise to call him if necessary had been a polite fiction. However, it seemed to satisfy Stan's pride for he gave a nod of his head, and turned, painfully slowly, to leave the room.

Queenie watched his progress, her eyes full of concern.

'There's a fresh pot of tea here, Dad,' she said. 'I'll bring you in a cup.'

Stan was having to concentrate too hard on moving to turn his head.

'That would be grand,' he said.

Joey, too, watched Stan's movements anxiously. In the short time he had been with the Dixons the older man's health had deteriorated. It did not seem right for a decent man like Stan to suffer so. Suddenly the whole world seemed tinged with gloom. He picked up the vegetable knife. If it were true that hard work drove away the miseries then he had an assured cure waiting for him in the form of the heap of potatoes.

The remedy was only a partial success. The visit to Mercy's house had unsettled him far more than he had expected. He could not help comparing her existence with the way he lived now. Both he and Queenie worked like slaves, yet somehow the place never seemed clean. Life was one unending battle against dirt, vermin and the grime of poverty. It was a long way from the gracious living at the Villa Dorata, or even the Devonshire Hall. The place was too dingy and squalid to be called a boarding-house. It was a common lodging-house!

At that moment Joey came to a decision. Running a lodging-house was not the sort of future for him. He wanted something more. Mercy had always encouraged him to better himself, and so had old Arthur. They must have thought he had some special quality that would make him get on in the world. Well, he would prove they were right. He would look for a new job!

'Am I getting a cup of tea today or next week? I'll be dead of thirst by the time you get round to pouring it!' demanded an aggrieved voice.

Joey came out of his reverie with a start. One of the lodgers was waving a battered enamel mug under his nose.

'Sorry, Arnold, I was miles away,' he said, filling the mug from the large teapot he still had clutched in his hands.

'Well, before you drift off again remember to have a look round for those of us who want a refill,' replied Arnold, more amenable now he had got his second cup of tea.

'I will,' promised Joey.

'What was all that about you going somewhere?' asked Queenie, as together they collected up the dirty dishes.

'It was only old Arnold having a moan because he wanted more tea and I was daydreaming.'

'Thank goodness! For a minute I thought you were leaving!'

He should have told her then. It was the ideal opportunity to let her know he was planning to leave, but somehow he could not. The anxiety in her voice when she thought he was going had been so unmistakable, and her subsequent relief so obvious that it had brought him up sharply. How were the Dixons going to manage when he had gone? He owed them a lot. There was no way he could leave them in the lurch. He would have to make sure Queenie and Stan were all right before he quit.

When Wednesday came Joey went home for his grandmother's funeral.

'I'll be glad when 'er's gone, honest I will,' said Lizzie, shuddering as she looked at Blanche's coffin, balanced on its trestles, in the parlour. ''Er shouldn't be in 'ere, not in the room where us 'as to eat. 'Tidn't right.'

'You're getting fussy in your old age, aren't you? You always eat in the kitchen anyway,' Joey pointed out brusquely.

'Tis a nice coffin,' remarked Ma conversationally. 'Lovely polish on the wood. Must have cost a pretty penny.'

'Well, us all knows who's footing the bill, don't us?' said Lizzie waspishly. 'Lady Muck! She only comes 'ere to look down on us. Now 'er's flinging 'er money about again.'

'I notice you don't object when she flings it in your direction,' Joey observed. 'And as you seem interested and since you aren't willing to pay your share, Mercy and I are dividing the costs between us.'

'What money've I got to waste on fancy funerals? I've got two childer to keep...' began Lizzie, spoiling for a fight. Fortunately, before she could say any more the clip–clop of horses' hooves in the lane outside announced the arrival of the hearse.

''Tis yer!' cried Ma unnecessarily. 'Where's your pa? Oh where's your pa?'

John Seaton appeared from the garden, silent and taciturn as ever. For once he was absenting himself from the Oak long enough to see his mother's coffin carried from the house. How Blanche had ever

174

managed to produce such an oafish and self-centred son was a mystery to Joey. True, she was not the easiest of women, but having seen her early photograph, he was certain she must have had just cause for being cantankerous. There was no denying that her life – all their lives – would have been much easier if only his father had been a bit more amenable and had utilized some of his undeniable intelligence. He guessed the unknown man who was his paternal grandparent had a lot to answer for!

The whole family stood at the gate to watch the hearse depart on its short journey to the village churchyard, the black horses going at a sober pace, the plumes on their heads dipping and swaying in time with their hooves. No villagers followed the funeral carriage as they usually did. Blanche had not been popular. Instead they stood at the roadside or looked on from their gardens as her coffin passed.

Joey found the sight of the black-draped coffin going on its last solitary journey incredibly moving. It looked so forlorn. He opened the garden gate and stepped out into the lane.

'Don't say you'm going after 'er!' exclaimed Ma in horror.

'Only as far as the churchyard.'

''Er said 'er'd come back if anyone did. Bain't 'ee afraid, boy?'

'Blanche didn't frighten me when she was alive. She certainly doesn't frighten me now she's passed on,' replied Joey.

He spoke with an airy assurance which remained with him until they entered the churchyard gates, then it evaporated. To his shame he found himself observing his grandmother's interment from behind a convenient hedge, hardly close enough to hear the intoning of the vicar's voice. He told himself he was abiding by Blanche's last wishes, he refused to admit he had given way to any stupid superstitious dread. Nevertheless, when the vicar finally closed his prayer-book, and Matt Nethercott, the sexton, began shovelling the earth into the grave, he was glad he had stayed to say goodbye to the old girl.

He was about to leave when a sudden movement caught his eye. A young woman, dressed in black, moved out of the shelter of the opposite wall and began to walk away. He had no difficulty in recognizing Mercy. He ran to catch her up. Too late, only the roar of a motor engine receding along the lane betrayed that she had ever been there. Joey was pleased she had come. He understood why she had not called at the cottage: sorrow and the quarrelsome atmosphere at home went very ill together. He and Mercy genuinely mourned the passing of the old lady. They had both loved her. Somewhat belatedly, he hoped Blanche had realized it.

Thrusting his hands deep into his pockets he turned round and headed home to say goodbye to Ma. Then it was back to the Dixons.

'Glad to have you back, boy.' Stan clapped him on the shoulder as he shuffled past.

'I've only been gone since breakfast,' grinned Joey.

'All the same, we missed you. Don't know how we'd manage without you, and that's the truth.'

Joey's conscience gave a nasty twinge. He was glad Stan did not know that in his coat pocket he had both the *Torbay News* and the *Directory*, bought for their 'situations vacant' columns.

His plans for the future turned out to be purely academic. He could not find another job! The trouble was that he was reluctant to cause the Dixons any distress by admitting he was looking for other employment, which meant he could only follow up likely adverts in his scant free time. By the time he got there, not surprisingly, the jobs had gone. It looked as though he would be working at the lodging-house for the rest of his life.

He was hurrying along Palace Avenue one day when a familiar voice hailed him.

'Joey Seaton! I don't believe it! It can't be!'

'Ted Cox! Of all people!' He stared at the cheery, towheaded fellow with disbelief. Then in a trice they were both laughing, and slapping each other on the back and talking at the same time.

Ted Cox was a couple of years older than Joey, a seniority which had entitled him to be a waiter in the *table d'hôte* room at the Devonshire Hall Hotel, where they had met. That is until Ted's career, like Joey's, had come to an abrupt end thanks to the efforts of Mr Bell, the under-manager.

'What're you doing here in Paignton?' Ted demanded.

'I work here. What's your excuse?'

'I don't need an excuse, I was born here,' Ted grinned. 'So where are you working, then?'

'At a place in Church Street.' Joey was loath to admit he worked in a lodging-house. 'You're looking very spruce and prosperous, you old devil.'

'It's the sea air and good living!' Ted patted his stomach, which was already showing a tendency to bulge beneath his waistcoat. 'I don't know why we're standing here like this when we could be catching up on the news in comfort. How about a quick one in the Globe?'

'A very quick one,' said Joey. He had come out to fetch some medicine for Stan and he did not want to be away too long.

Soon they were sitting in the bar parlour, regarding identical glasses of old and mild.

'So, how've you been getting on since you and old Mabel parted company?' asked Ted, after half of the cool liquid had slid down his throat.

'Not so bad. Could be better, though.'

'You want to try a life on the ocean wave, like me. Transatlantic liners, and all that.' Ted took another swig at his beer.

Joey stared at him. 'Is that what you're doing?' he asked.

'It certainly is. New York to Plymouth, Plymouth to New York, on the White Star Line.'

'What do you do?'

'Same as I did at the Devonshire Hall, only, now I do it with a nautical air,' Ted grinned. 'Why don't you give it a try? I could get you a job.'

'Are you serious?'

'Of course I am.' The cheerful grin faded from Ted's face as he leaned across the table. 'They're always on the look out for properly trained blokes. The living conditions aren't up to the Devonshire Hall, naturally; and the chief steward's a bit of a tartar, but he's fair. I'd sooner have his sort than old Mabel's any day of the week. Into the bargain, you see something of the world. And the people you meet! You would not believe some of the folks I've served. I used to think the Devonshire Hall was classy, but it's nothing compared to on board ship, especially working in the first-class dining room.' Joey was dazzled. He had never thought of going to sea.

'And you think you could get me a job?' he asked.

'Never doubt it! I'm not saying it'd be top-notch to start with, mind. Probably in the crew's mess in the beginning, where the money's not too great. But you wouldn't stay there for long. You're good at your job, and you'd soon learn the ropes. You'd be where the big tips are in no time. Look, I go back to Plymouth tomorrow. Come with me.'

'Oh I couldn't, not so soon.'

'Why not? While you're young and with no ties it's a great life.' Ted looked at him with sympathy. 'And if you don't mind me saying so, it'd probably be an improvement on the job you've got now.'

Joey gave a grin. 'You don't have to tell me!' he said. 'And if you could get me a job I'd jump at it. But the folks I work for have been good to me. I wouldn't want to leave them in the lurch. I'd have to make sure there was someone to take my place before I left.'

'Oh well, if that's all…!' Ted's face cleared. 'There's no problem. I'm coming home again in three weeks. You should have found someone to take over by then. It'll give me time to tackle the chief steward about taking you on.'

'I don't know how to thank you.'

'Don't even try. You'd have done the same for me. Now, how about another pint?'

But Joey shook his head. 'Sorry, Ted,' he said, rising to his feet. 'I've got to go.'

'If you're sure? See you in three weeks, then. Come up to our place, bag and baggage. We live in Winner Street. You can't miss the house. It's got a green front door, and a knocker like a clenched fist. The landlord's hand, my dad calls it. We'll travel to Plymouth together.'

All the way back to the Dixons Joey could not hold in the grin that kept breaking out on his face. He had never expected anything like this to happen. It was like a dream come true. He knew Ted would do his best for him.

Next morning Joey awoke to the thought that sometime during the day he must tell the Dixons he was going. But when? There just did not seem an appropriate time to spring it on them. He decided on the middle of the afternoon, when they usually had a cup of tea together, a pleasant lull in the hectic activity of their day. He hated himself for spoiling the pleasant mood of the, but he knew there was no help for it. 'I've got a bit of news to tell you,' he said.

'Oh yes? Come into a fortune, have you?' wheezed Stan.

'Something apart from that. I met an old pal yesterday, a fellow I used to know at the Devonshire Hall Hotel. He's working on the transatlantic liners now, the ones that go from Plymouth. He reckons he can get me a job.'

A heavy silence fell on the shabby room.

'You mean you're going to leave us?' asked Stan.

'Well, yes.'

'I— I thought you were happy with us.' Shock had drained some of Queenie's normally high colour from her face.

'I am,' lied Joey. 'You've both been grand to me, and treated me well. It's just…I would like to see a bit more of the world while I'm young.'

Another silence settled on the room. At length it was broken by Stan.

'Only natural, I suppose, boy,' he said. 'We're going to miss you, though.'

'Yes,' agreed Queenie, in a strange, choked voice. 'We'll miss you. When— when do you go?'

'In three weeks.'

'So soon?' Queenie shot an alarmed look at her father. Joey interpreted its message clearly enough. It was a look of panic. It said, How on earth are we going to manage?

'You needn't worry. I won't leave you in the lurch,' he said hastily. 'I'll make sure you get someone decent to take my place. We'll find someone easily in the time.'

'That's good of you, boy. We'll be lucky to find someone who works as hard as you, though,' said Stan.

'We won't find anyone like you.' Queenie's voice was a mere whisper, and Joey saw, to his distress, that her eyes were filled with tears. He saw something else too, a hurt and an unhappiness which went far beyond the loss of an employee.

Perhaps it was just as well he was going. For some time he had had the suspicion Queenie was getting too fond of him. He liked her well enough, but that was all. It was not just that she was plain. He had known lots of plain girls who were grand company, but with all her virtues poor Queenie was too much on the dull side to appeal to him. Yes, it was a good thing he was going. His departure was saving her much more unhappiness in the long run.

It was doubtful if Queenie appreciated the situation, however. For the rest of that day she went about with a face that was pinched and drawn. Stan, too, was clearly shaken by the prospect of Joey leaving.

In spite of the gloom about him Joey's spirits took an upward turn. He could not help himself. He began to count off the days before his new life would begin. Only seven more days to go… six… five…

179

Queenie's brisk hammering at his door woke him, as it did every morning.

'Time to get up!' she called.

Even before Joey opened his eyes his first thought was, In four days' time I'll be on my way to Plymouth.

Still barely awake he rolled shivering out of bed. Bleary-eyed, he lit his candle, and groping for the jug, poured some water into the tin bowl. There was no time for much of a wash, that would come later if he got the chance. For now he would make do with an icy splash. At least it woke him up enough for him to concentrate properly on getting dressed. He had one leg in his trousers when he heard Queenie cry out.

'Joey!'

There was such panic in the way she called his name that he hastily thrust in his other leg and ran, buttoning himself up as he went.

Queenie was standing in the doorway to Stan's room, giving little moans of anxiety. Joey moved her to one side and went in. He half guessed what he would find. Stan was lying in his narrow iron bed as if asleep, only no sleep was so still or so permanent. Just to make sure, Joey bent down, his ear close to Stan's mouth, listening intently for the least sound of breathing. There was none. He looked back to where Queenie still stood in the doorway. Sympathetically he shook his head.

'Dad!' said Queenie, then again, as though she hoped to rouse her father she repeated, 'Dad! Dad! Dad!'

Joey steered her out into the corridor and closed the door. By now most of the lodgers were appearing from their sleeping-quarters in various stages of undress.

'Stan?' asked the one called Arnold.

Joey nodded.

'I'll just pull my boots on then I'll go for the doctor, shall I?' Arnold paused only long enough to give Queenie a little pat on the arm, before he hurried away.

In low whispers the news was spread throughout the house.

The subdued voices hushed as Joey guided a stunned Queenie downstairs and into the back parlour. It was bitterly cold in there, so he lit the fire and turned up the gaslight. Queenie was shivering convulsively, in spite of the blanket he put round her shoulders. One of the lodgers produced some brandy, but it would have remained in her hand if Joey had not raised it to her lips. He greeted the arrival of the doctor with great relief, not for Stan's sake – he knew Stan was beyond help – but for Queenie's. He had never seen anyone so numbed by shock.

'Upstairs?' The doctor raised his eyes upwards. In a few minutes he was back again.

'It was expected,' he said, 'Pity! He was a fighter, was Mr Dixon. A sad loss for you, Miss Dixon. You have my deepest sympathy.' There was no response from Queenie, so he turned his attention to Joey. 'Are you some relation, young man?' he asked.

'No, sir. I just work here.'

'Do you know if Miss Dixon has any relatives? Someone who would come and give her a bit of comfort?'

'I've never heard her mention any family, nor Stan – Mr Dixon, either.'

'Hm, in that case the best thing I can do is give her a sedative to make her sleep.' The doctor picked up the cup that had held the brandy and sniffed at it. 'Yes, a good sleep is what I can promise her. In the meantime see if you can discover any relations, particularly female. A young woman should not be on her own at a time like this.'

'I will,' promised Joey. 'And don't worry, I'll look after her.'

'Good.' the doctor regarded him keenly. 'I'll come and see her again tomorrow. I'll bring the death certificate then.'

Joey soon discovered it was one thing promising the doctor that he would look after Queenie and quite another actually doing it. He had never had to deal with a situation like this before. Finally, in desperation, he called in Mrs Morris, who lived next door. She was sympathetic and willing enough, but she was also extremely stout and far from young. By the time she had got Queenie undressed and into bed she was out of breath and puce in the face.

'If you needs me, just call, my 'andsome, and I'll come running,' Mrs Morris assured him.

Looking at her vast girth he doubted it, but she had meant it kindly. Then he went back to administer the sedative to Queenie. Time and again he had questioned her gently, asking did she have any family whom she would like him to contact, all without response.

It was a morning the like of which Joey had never encountered, and heartily hoped he would never encounter again. A death in the household or not, there were still twenty-odd men who had a long hard day's work ahead of them and who needed to be fed before they went. Somehow the kitchen range was lit, the men were fed and went on their way, and he was left to clear up.

First, though, he went to the dresser drawer where Stan Dixon had kept his papers. After a long and careful search among the bills and receipts, however, he unearthed nothing. It seemed that Queenie had no one in the whole world upon whom she could rely. There was only him!

When she awoke next morning she was vague and distant. Joey thought it was merely the after-effects of the sedative, but the day progressed and there was no improvement. Although she resumed her normal duties she was like an automaton. All the formalities of death fell to Joey.

'I'd like to come to the funeral,' said Mrs Morris, when she came to ask after Queenie. 'When did you say it was?'

'Saturday,' replied Joey. 'Saturday at two o'clock—' He broke off abruptly. He had just remembered – on Saturday he should be on his way to Plymouth and a new life. He took one look at Queenie, at her numb face and her lifeless eyes and he knew that Plymouth and his new life would have to wait.

'You're too soft for your own good, you know that, don't you?' said Ted good-naturedly, when Joey told him the news. 'It's not the end of the world, though. We'll just postpone our plans, that's all. It'll be about three months before I'm home again. I'll look you up then and see how you are fixed.'

'Thanks, that would be grand,' said Joey gratefully, then he added, more gloomily. 'Though by then there probably won't be any jobs left.'

'Don't be such a misery!' Ted gave him a friendly thump on the back. 'If you don't get in with White Star there are plenty of others. Lots of liners call at Plymouth to drop off the mail. All you'd have to do is hang about the shipping offices along Millbay Road for a spell, you'd soon get fixed up.'

Joey left Ted feeling more cheerful than he had dared to hope. His plans for a new job and a new life were not cancelled, they were merely postponed. He found the thought a comforting one as the time arrived for Stan's funeral.

At the graveside Joey looked at Queenie with increasing anxiety. There had been no tears, no hysterics, no outburst of emotion. Her unnatural silence worried him. It was as though she had blanked out her mind to the reality of her loss. 'Earth to earth, ashes to ashes, dust to dust.' The familiar words brought Blanche's lonely funeral back to his mind. Two deaths in such a short time were hard to bear, and he felt his throat contract. Queenie's arm was linked inertly through his and he gave it a sympathetic squeeze. There was no response. Even when the moment came to scatter the first earth upon the coffin Queenie made no attempt to take the trowel offered to her by the sexton. It fell to Joey to put it in her hand and guide her movements so that she cast some soil into the grave.

'Poor maid, you wouldn't think it would affect her like this, would you?' said Mrs Morris in a low voice as, back at the lodging-house, Queenie sat bolt upright and oblivious in her chair. 'Let's hope her comes out of it soon.'

'She'll snap out of it now the funeral's over,' he said with a conviction he was a long way from feeling.

It was late that night when he finished his chores and he dragged his weary limbs up the stairs. On the landing he came to an abrupt halt. Through the chinks of the ill-fitting door filtered the glow of candlelight. In his room he found Queenie.

She was sitting on the end of his bed, shivering with the cold in her long calico night-gown. She looked up as he entered, and he saw that the blank dazed expression which had been so familiar of late had disappeared.

'Joey,' she said, her eyes filled with pain. 'Joey, my dad's dead!' Slowly the tears began to trickle down her plain face, gathering strength until they became a flood.

Joey made no attempt to quell them. He was too thankful to see a natural reaction. He knelt by her side, not knowing what to say to give her comfort.

'He was a fine man,' he said at last. 'One of the best.'

'Oh, he was! For all he was so ill not once did he complain. And he was so good to me! He never raised his hand to me...' On and on went the reminiscences in an unending stream, punctuated only by gulping sobs.

Listening to the normality of her grief, Joey felt the load of responsibility slip from his shoulders. In its place came awkwardness. Sorrowing or not, it was not proper for Queenie to be alone with him in his room so late at night, and certainly not when she was clad only in a nightgown. Her heavy breasts were pushed against the white calico in a way which made him feel distinctly uncomfortable.

'You'd best get back to your own room now and try and get some rest,' he said, attempting to drape his jacket over her shoulders.

Queenie pushed it away, ignoring his words.

'What am I going to do, now that Dad's gone?' she wept. 'You won't go and leave me, will you, Joey? Not now! Not when I'm by myself!'

It would have taken a harder heart than Joey's to resist the pleading and misery in her voice.

'I'll stay,' he promised. He tried to add, For a while, at least, but Queenie flung her arms about him.

'I knew you'd stand by me,' she wept.

Even though he was feeling increasingly ill at ease, Joey had no option but to put his arms about her. He could feel the warmth of her through the thin cotton, and the soft flesh of her plump body yielded to his hands.

'You should try and get some sleep.' He tried to dislodge her grip, without success.

'No, don't send me away. Let me stay with you.'

'That wouldn't do at all, and you know it,' he said, with growing desperation.

But Queenie's hold did not slacken. 'Please!' she begged. 'Please let me stay!' In her distress her pleas were getting louder until Joey feared she would wake the whole household.

What could he do? He had to let her stay!

'All right! All right!' he whispered urgently. 'Keep your voice down.'

His bed was a narrow one, no more than an iron cot, with scant room for the two of them. Queenie's close proximity proved to be more arousing than he had ever anticipated, and her gratitude unexpectedly intoxicating. Afterwards he never knew if his actions had been prompted by sympathy, a wish to give comfort, or simply by animal need. Whatever his motives he found himself caressing Queenie's smooth skin, his hands travelling over the pillowy softness of her ample curves. Soon there was no holding back. He rolled on top of her and thrust himself into her, the urgency of her response increasing his excitement.

At last his passion waned, leaving him breathless and with a growing sense of self-reproach, which was not lessened by Queenie's ardent whispering of, 'Joey! Oh Joey, my love!'

He lay awake for a long, long time, appalled by what had happened. In the end he could not bear to lie there any longer in the cramped bed, with Queenie's bulk slumbering beside him. In bare feet, so as not to wake, he crept downstairs and began the day's work a good hour before usual.

He dreaded Queenie's arrival on the scene. What should he do? What could he say to her? Self-reproach racked him. To his surprise there were no recriminations from Queenie. Black did not suit her, it made her seem too pale, otherwise she appeared to be astonishingly normal.

'You've got the stove going nice and early, I see,' she said. 'It'll give us a good start.' She put on her apron and began slicing bread.

Joey watched her with astonishment. Surely she was going to make some mention of what had happened between them? All the day long he waited tensely for her to heap recriminations on him. Finally, when she did not, his own shame forced him to broach the subject.

'Queenie, about last night...' he began. 'I want you to know that I'm sor—'

'You don't want to worry yourself about that,' she broke in swiftly. 'After all, it takes two, don't it?'

'Yes, I suppose so.' He gave a wry grin. 'I've been feeling rotten about it. Thanks for taking it this way.'

'You daft fool, what other way should I take it?'

She smiled at him, and that smile swept away his brief feeling of relief. It was too full of adoration. Then Queenie turned back to her work so calmly he wondered if he had seen things in her smile that were not there.

Day followed day without Queenie ever referring to what had happened between them. Joey began to relax. It had been an isolated incident, it had not meant anything, no harm had been done. He even let himself begin to dream of working on a transatlantic liner once more. As soon as he found someone to replace him at the lodging-house, then he would be off like a shot. First he would have to tell Queenie, though, she had to know that he intended to leave eventually. Not looking forward to what was to come he went in search of Queenie. He found her, as ever, in the kitchen.

'Can you spare a minute—' he began. 'Hey, are you all right? You look really poorly.'

Queenie did not have time to reply. With a little gasp she rushed out into the yard, and he could hear her vomiting in the privy.

'You get yourself up to bed,' he said, when she returned, limp and wan. 'I can manage by myself.'

'No, I'll be all right. It's nothing,' she answered.

'It didn't sound like nothing. You go and rest.'

'I don't need to,' she insisted. 'It's happened before. I'll be fine by the end of the morning.'

'Then you should see the doctor—' he got no further. 'What do you mean, it's happened before?'

'Well, it's— it's happened before.' She would not meet his gaze.

Suddenly he went cold. Recollections of his sister, Lizzie, being ill in the mornings came back to him, and the implications.

'Oh no!' he groaned. 'Oh no! Not that!'

'I'm— I'm— afraid it is,' said Queenie in a small voice. 'Couldn't it be something else? Colic, or a bilious attack or something?' he asked desperately.

She shook her head. 'I'm sorry,' she whispered, a tear slowly coursing down her cheek.

Joey rose, swallowing hard. 'There's no need to apologize,' he said, attempting to sound cheery for her sake, though goodness knows, it was the last thing he was feeling! 'As you said yourself, it takes two. Well… well, here's a turn up for the books.'

'Joey, I expect you're angry, and… and…' Her voice petered out, then rallied again. 'There's no need for you to worry, I can manage.' The words were brave, but there was no mistaking the anxious appeal which shone mutely from her eyes.

'A fine opinion you seem to have of me, I must say!' He pretended to sound indignant. 'No, we'll get married sharpish! It's a good job we're nice and handy for the church.'

'Oh Joey!' Queenie somehow managed to beam with happiness and weep at the same time. For two pins Joey could have wept with her, only, there would have been no joy in his tears.

'You'd best come home with me sometime soon, to meet my family. We'll have to go anyway because I'll have to have their consent, me only being a slip of a lad.' Somehow he had adopted this silly jocular voice and he could not get rid of it. Queenie did not seem to notice anything amiss.

'Will they object?'

'Object? No, they'll be only too glad to get rid of me!'

'Oh Joey!' said Queenie again, smiling at him with love and devotion.

He saw that look and his heart sank. Accusations he could have stood, recriminations he could have borne. What he was going to find the most difficult to tolerate was the adoration. That was going to be almost too difficult to bear.

Chapter Eleven

'The afternoon post, Madam.'

Rogers proffered Mercy her half-dozen letters on a silver salver. He did so with the exaggerated care he always gave to her mail these days. Ever since the day when Joey's note telling her of Blanche's illness had failed to reach her Mercy's correspondence had been delivered with punctilious efficiency. Surprisingly it was Peter who had brought about the change. In a rare anger, he had delivered a biting reprimand which had brooked no misinterpretation. The butler had turned white as he replied, 'Yes, sir.'

Peter's interview with his mother had been more private but no less effective. For days afterwards Agnes had been tight-lipped and silent, visibly shaken by the fact that her son had dared to rebuke her in such a way.

Mercy had been touched by Peter's concern for her, as well as surprised at his unexpected forcefulness in tackling the matter.

When she had thanked him for taking her part so promptly he had replied, 'What else did you expect me to do? You're my wife. It is up to me to look after you.'

She had not known what to say. It had been quite a while since he had shown any marked concern for her. Before she could think of the right words Peter continued, 'And even if the message had not been so important it should still have reached you. To hinder someone else's private correspondence or interfere with it in any way is despicable.'

His last sentence swept away her growing feeling of tenderness towards him. He was reminding her that once she had interfered with his private papers and lived to rue the day. Obviously, he had no intention of forgiving her, even though she was willing to forgive his far greater transgression. The brief moment of affection between them was lost and, as Mercy took her letters from Rogers, she could not help a pang of regret.

A quick glance at the envelopes told her of their contents. Mostly they were invitations to dine, the last, though, bore Joey's scrawl.

She read the letter twice. Once was not enough to take in the enormity of its news. Married? Joey was married? Barely eighteen and he had taken on the responsibility of a wife and, if she were reading between the lines correctly, a child!

'It's not possible! It's just not possible!'

Mercy strode about her sitting-room, too distressed to settle, the sheet of cheap notepaper clutched in her hand. That Joey could have thrown away all his hopes and prospects so completely seemed incredible. The daughter of his late employer, Joey had written. She wondered about this Queenie who had so unexpectedly become her sister-in-law. Already she was seeing her as some forward, voracious creature who had got her claws into Joey.

The one hopeful line in the whole letter had come at the end: 'We are going to keep up the family business and run it together,' he had written.

The family business! At least that sounded as though he might have some prospects. For the first time Mercy realized that she had no idea what trade her brother was following. Not a very prosperous one, judging by the look of him when he had called. On an impulse she rang the bell.

'Tell Jenkins to bring the motor round in quarter of an hour,' she instructed the maid. 'I want to go to Paignton.'

Church Street, when she found it, proved to be a busy, bustling area of mainly older properties, many still thatched. One side was dominated by the rich red sandstone of the church, while at the other, down the slope, a brewery belched out pungent steam. So this was the area where Joey lived and worked.

Her one fear was that she might encounter her brother by chance. She did not want that, it would appear as though she were spying on him. In an effort not to appear conspicuous she strolled along, looking in shop windows, glancing covertly at the numbers to determine where Joey lived. There was a thriving greengrocer's that she hoped might be the right place, or the neat little dairy. It was almost too much to hope that it might be the extremely busy inn... Then she saw the number she was looking for and she almost groaned aloud in her disappointment. The tall house was shabby and dilapidated, with peeling paint and more than one of its windows broken and boarded up. The faded letters on its wall might say 'Beds, Breakfasts, Dinners, Teas' but she recognized it as a common lodging-house, and a none too successful one by the look of it. Mercy's last scrap of optimism faded, as she wondered at the mess into which her young brother had got himself.

Peter was at home when she returned – a rare event. He glanced up as she entered the drawing-room.

'You look tired,' he said. 'Have you been far?'

'Only to Paignton.' She slumped on to a sofa.

'Paignton must have become much more exhausting since I was last there. Here, let me pour you a sherry.' He rose and set the drink on the table beside her. 'You shouldn't do so much, you know. You are wearing yourself out,' he said solicitously.

He sounded so kind, quite like the old Peter, not the distant stranger with whom she had been sharing her life of late. She could not help saying, 'I'm not tired, I'm worried about Joey.'

'Your young brother? Has he got into some sort of a scrape?'

'He's married! Here, read this!' And she handed him the letter.

Peter scanned it carefully.

'He's far too young,' he stated. 'What on earth will they live on? Have you any idea what this family business is?'

'That's why I went to Paignton today, to see what I could find out, and it is worse than I'd anticipated. The business is the most awful run-down old lodging-house. It can't be making any money. It looks almost like a slum.'

'The stupid young fool! The best favour we can do for your brother is to try to get him out of his predicament. I'd have thought there was a good chance of getting the marriage annulled, especially when you take into consideration Joey's age. I'll put the matter before the lawyers tomorrow, shall I? Just to sound them out, of course. No names or anything like that.'

He was really concerned about Joey. But that was typical of Peter. At least, it was typical of the Peter she had married.

'I only wish we could,' she said. 'Unfortunately I think there is a complication.'

'A compli— Oh, you mean a child on the way?'

'Yes. Why else the haste? The sudden change of plans? In the last letter he wrote to me, not many weeks since, he was talking of going to sea.'

'I see what you mean. It's just such a shame. A young fellow throwing everything away like that. Is there anything I can do? Money, perhaps?'

'I— I thought I'd send him some as a wedding-present.'

'Make it a decent sum.'

'A hundred pounds?' she suggested tentatively.

'Will a hundred be enough to make any difference?'

She was forced to smile. 'Unless they go mad it should make a deal of difference,' she said. 'That's more than two years' wages for most working men.'

'I didn't know. You forget, I haven't your wealth of practical experience.' He smiled at her in return, then took her hand in his. 'It seems a long time since we've sat alone together like this.'

'Too long,' Mercy said softly.

'It's very pleasant here, just the two of us.'

'It is indeed.' She relaxed against him. 'It is so peaceful, and we can see the entire bay, with all the ships going back and forth. Doesn't it make you want to be out there, on the *Tango* or putting the *Jasmine* through her paces?' she teased gently.

'Not at the moment. I am extremely content where I am, thank you.'

That was the reply she had wanted him to give. His hand increased its pressure on hers and she gave it an answering squeeze.

'You know, we never did go away on a trip together, did we? I've even forgotten where we decided to go,' he said.

'I don't think we made up our minds. I seem to remember the Mediterranean being mentioned, and possibly Portugal.'

'Let's go to the South of France!'

'Are you serious?'

'Why not? We seem to have drifted apart during these last few months; we see almost nothing of each other. Let's spend some time together, and have fun, the way we used to do. What do you say?'

'Yes, please,' she said. 'Let's go away.'

'That's splendid!' He smiled his old, boyish smile, then he said softly, 'I've missed you, Mercy, do you know that?'

She shook her head.

'I only know that I've missed you,' she whispered, and she raised her face to him, hoping he would kiss her.

He did not. Instead he traced the outline of her face with one finger. 'The mother of two lively boys, and yet still so beautiful. It's incredible,' he sighed.

'Now I have to say something on the same lines to you, do I?' she smiled. 'Something about you being too absurdly youthful and athletic-looking to be the father of a growing family?'

'That will do until you can think of something better,' he replied gravely.

And they both began to laugh.

'Where shall we go, on this trip of ours? Monte Carlo? Nice? Cannes?' Peter asked.

'Oh, I don't know. I'll leave the choice to you.'

'Very well, I'll see to it. Only, I'm not going to tell you where I have chosen. It will be a surprise.'

Peter made love to her that night for the first time in months. Afterwards, lying in his arms, everything in her existence seemed to be perfect. They had hurt each other and now they had forgiven those hurts. Deliberately she closed her mind to recollections of Tilly and of the girl in Brittany. They were the past, and she was looking to the future. A future she wanted to spend with Peter.

In the midst of her present contentment Mercy was still worried by Joey's marriage. She hoped he would invite her over or make some other arrangements for her to meet his new wife, but although a suitably grateful 'thank you' letter came in response to her wedding gift, there was no suggestion that they should meet. Finally, she was driven to make the first move.

'I will be in Paignton next week,' she wrote. 'Can I take the opportunity to call on you?'

The reply, when it arrived, was equally formal.

'We would be delighted to see you. Would three o'clock be a convenient time for you?'

The visit was a disaster from the word go. Joey was visibly uncomfortable at her presence, although he greeted her with words of welcome.

'And this is the missus,' he said with forced joviality. 'This is my Queenie.'

Mercy was stunned at the sight of the plain, stolid young woman. No one could have been further from her vision of a painted trollop. That Queenie was in an agony of embarrassment was all too evident.

'I'm very pleased to meet you,' Mercy said at last. 'I have brought you some flowers. I hope you like chrysanthemums.'

'Oh! Oh yes! Thank you! They're lovely!' Queenie took the hothouse blooms and looked about her in desperation, not knowing what to do with them. She put them on the table, then had to move them to set down the tea-tray, then had to move them again because she had put them on her own chair.

'Here, give them to me. I'll put them in the kitchen, in some water.' Joey snatched them up with more than a hint of impatience.

'Haven't you poured the tea yet?' Joey demanded, when he returned to the cramped back-parlour.

'No… I was waiting for you.' In her eagerness to oblige Queenie's hand shook.

'Watch out! You're spilling it everywhere!' It was there again, that note of irritation in Joey's voice when he spoke to his wife. Then he said in an easier tone, 'Oh, never mind. A drop of tea on the floor won't hurt, will it?' And Queenie had shot him a look of pure adoration.

So Joey did not love his wife, but his wife loved him. Mercy wondered how their matrimonial tangle had ever come about.

'The wedding present you sent us was very generous,' said Joey.

'Yes, very generous.' Queenie's voice echoed her husband's.

'I hope it will come in useful,' replied Mercy.

'Oh it has!'

'You mean you have spent it already?'

'We've bought this place, it was a bargain at the price! A real investment!' Joey sounded cheerily confident, and Queenie beamed at him with proud approval.

'It's always good to own the roof over your own head,' said Mercy weakly. If that roof doesn't leak, she added silently. She thought they were mad. It seemed to her that her brother had merely compounded the mess he was in.

She was relieved when she could decently take her leave. The room, the surroundings, the whole situation depressed her. Most of all, though, it was the smell! It evoked a part of her life she wanted to forget – the smell of poverty.

Joey showed her to the door. There was one more thing she had to know.

'I suppose there is a baby on the way?' she said.

'Yes,' he replied.

All the way home the hopelessness in his reply haunted her.

–

Peter was extremely occupied these days. It was the centenary of the Torbay Royal Regatta and the preparations seemed to need an inordinate number of committee meetings and conferences. Mercy did not mind. If he were happy, so was she. She decided to take the opportunity of a quiet afternoon by herself to catch up on her correspondence. She was just finishing a letter when the sound of voices in the hall reached her. One was unmistakably that of Charlotte.

'The Honourable Miss Dawson-Pring and Captain Nicholson to see you, ma'am,' announced the maid. But Charlotte was already on her way.

'This is a lovely surprise,' said Mercy, rising to greet them.

'It is good of us, isn't it?' concurred Charlotte. 'All the more because we have brought you a gift. It's a gramophone record of that new tango, "Jealousy". You haven't got it, have you?'

'No, I haven't. Thank you.' Mercy took the flat package, somewhat bemused.

'Beware of Greeks bearing gifts; there is an ulterior motive, I'm afraid,' said Archie.

'Oh dear, perhaps I had better not accept this.' Mercy pretended to hand the present back.

'When you hear what the favour is I'm certain you'll push us both through the door and throw the wretched record after us,' said Charlotte. She lowered her voice conspiratorially. 'We want you to save Archie here from total ostracism. To look at this fellow, so handsome and upright in his smart uniform and shiny buttons, you wouldn't think he was a social misfit, would you?'

'No, I wouldn't, and I don't believe it, either,' laughed Mercy.

'I'm afraid it's true, Mrs Lisburne,' confessed Archie, a look of exaggerated shame on his face. 'I can confess it to you, because I know your discretion is absolute, but naturally it's not something I want to get around. My shameful secret is I can't do the tango!'

Mercy collapsed into fits of laughter.

'Oh horror!' she exclaimed dramatically. 'And you an officer of His Majesty! How dreadful!'

'What I need, Mrs Lisburne, is a lady of kindness and patience to take me in hand, one who is a superb dancer, and one whose gentleness of spirit will not prompt her to kick me in the shins every time I tread on her foot. Naturally we thought of you.'

'Oh flattery! Flattery!' exclaimed Mercy.

'Never mind that,' said Charlotte. 'Personally I think you would need your head examined if you agreed to take him on. He has no aptitude at all. Nevertheless, will you try, as a favour to me and to save my toes from further punishment?'

'When you put it like that I can hardly refuse, can I?' replied Mercy.

Already she had put the record on the turntable, and was winding up the gramophone. After a preliminary hiss the music started.

'Dum *dum* dumdum *dum* dumdum *dum*.' She began humming the tune, and after a moment raised her arms to an imaginary partner and began to dance.

'That's it! Archie, look at her feet!' ordered Charlotte. 'Slow, quick, quick, slow. Come on, try it.' She dragged him to his feet, and, in line, the trio began pacing out the dance.

'This is no good, I'm doing the lady's steps,' protested Archie.

'Then turn round and do them backwards, you idiot! Oh, the record's finished! Wind it up again, Mercy, and we'll try once more!' Charlotte was at her most imperious. 'Now, have a go with Mercy as your partner. Ready? Begin! Slow, quick, quick, slow!'

'Mrs Lisburne is much easier to dance with than you,' observed Archie. 'She doesn't turn it into a battle of wills.'

'Not in that direction, you silly man!' Charlotte protested, as the dancing couple somehow finished up wedged in a corner of the room.

'I was concentrating so hard on my feet I forgot I had to steer as well!'

'I think we'd better draw a diagram for this imbecile, don't you, Mercy? Have you got a pen and paper handy?'

'In the bureau,' gasped Mercy, breathless with laughter.

'Physical training, navigation, and now geometry! I'd sooner be on manoeuvres, honestly I would,' grumbled the luckless Archie.

'Stop moaning! You'll manage well enough when you follow my diagr—Oh no!' Charlotte's words ended in a yell of distress as she knocked over the ornamental silver inkstand.

'Your lovely skirt! You've got ink down it!' cried Mercy.

'It would happen to this outfit, my particular favourite! The ink has ruined the velvet! Just look at it!'

Mercy was already ringing the bell.

'I'll send for Stafford,' she said. 'She's a marvel with stains.'

'It had better be dealt with straight away,' said Stafford when she arrived. 'Will you be kind enough to come with me, ma'am, and I'll see what I can do.'

'Archie, you're to keep practising while I'm gone,' ordered Charlotte over her shoulder, as she was shepherded away by the maid.

'She doesn't give up, does she?' said Archie with a wry smile. 'On this occasion I think she's wasting her time, and yours. When it comes to dancing I'm a regular duffer.'

'No, you're not,' Mercy contradicted. 'Try to remember that dancing is supposed to be fun. Let's give it one more try, and this time forget about the steps. We'll just move round the room in time to the music.'

'You're a glutton for punishment, I'll give you that. Right, that's the gramophone rewound. And off we go... I think I'm beginning to get the hang of it... Now for that tricky bit Charlotte was trying to teach me...'

'No, not yet!' cried Mercy, but her protest was in vain. Archie, in attempting the new step, caught his foot in the rug. He lost his balance, and collapsed on to the sofa in a hysterical, undignified heap, with Mercy underneath him.

'Get off, you're squashing the breath out of me,' laughed Mercy.

'I can't move!' Archie, too, was almost helpless with mirth. 'My foot's entangled in the fringe of the rug. Oh, this won't do! What would anyone think if they came in?'

'What should people think?' demanded a male voice. 'The truth seems pretty obvious to me.'

Over Archie's shoulder Mercy saw Peter's tall figure outlined in the doorway.

'Hello, darling,' she said. 'You are home early.'

'Yes, too early. Or maybe I've arrived just in time. Really, Mercy, you disappoint me. I would have thought you had sense enough to be more discreet when you have a rendezvous with your lover.'

'Lover? You are joking!' Her smile faded. There was no humour in Peter's voice, only coldness and anger, and hurt.

'Hey, Lisburne! What do you think of catching me in a compromising situation with your wife?' called Archie cheerily, turning his head. 'Why, the wretched fellow's disappeared. He might have given me a hand to get to my feet.'

'Oh! Get up, please,' begged Mercy.

'I'm trying to. What's the fuss about? Surely your husband knows this is only a lark. Oh lord, he didn't seriously think we were…?' At last Archie realized that the joking was at an end, and stood up.

'He did!' exclaimed Mercy, scrambling to her feet. 'He thought we were making love!'

'In his own house? Surely not! Oh, don't take on so. I'll go after him and explain. He'll be back in a minute laughing like a drain, you'll see!' Archie rushed from the room and down the stairs.

Archie ran out of the door, but as he did so the Daimler shot past, heading towards town.

He came back in, panting at his exertions.

'I'm afraid I missed him,' he puffed. 'I expect he's heading for his club, the bolt-hole of all misunderstood and misunderstanding husbands. I'll go and ferret him out, then I'll drag him back here, eh? And on the way I'll make sure he stops off at the florist's and buys you the biggest bunch of roses in the place!' For a moment the cheery expression left his face as he looked up at her. 'Can I say how sorry I am that this has happened? I feel very much to blame.'

'Please don't,' said Mercy, in a small voice, 'it isn't your fault. It is a stupid misunderstanding, but please… if you could hurry?'

'Of course. I'm on my way now.'

'What on earth is all this rumpus about?' Charlotte appeared at the head of the stairs wearing one of Mercy's dressing gowns. 'Why has Archie deserted me? He can't hate learning the tango that much!'

'It isn't any laughing matter! There has been a terrible misunder-standing.'

'And Archie ran off in a huff?' Charlotte was incredulous.

'No, of course not. We were practising the tango together when we fell over, and Peter came in and— and—'

'Jumped to the wrong conclusion,' finished Charlotte. 'Really, Mercy, there are times when I wonder at the common sense of that husband of yours. As if you would be carrying on a torrid affair here, of all places; and with me only along the corridor. Now stop looking so tragic this instant and send for some tea. On second thoughts…' Charlotte scrutinized her friend's face more closely. 'On second thoughts make that brandy. We may as well make ourselves comfortable while we wait for Archie to bring home your misguided spouse.'

They waited a long time. When Archie finally returned he looked rather hot and bothered.

'A slippery customer, your husband!' he said. 'I chased him all over town without catching up with him. Don't worry, though. I've left letters addressed to him everywhere likely and unlikely, asking him to contact me most urgently.'

'What a storm in a teacup! I had no idea that Peter could be so unreasonable,' remarked Charlotte.

'He's not unreasonable! Not normally!' Mercy leapt to his defence.

'Then how do you explain his behaviour at the moment? If that isn't unreasonable I don't know what is.'

Mercy made no reply. She could not explain to her friend how new and fragile was the reconciliation between her and Peter. Too fragile to withstand the least suspicion of betrayal.

'The minute he gets in touch with me we'll have the whole silly business sorted out in double-quick time, you'll see.' Archie spoke with a conviction and optimism that Mercy wished she could share.

'It makes me thankful I haven't got a husband to bother about,' stated Charlotte. 'They seem to be far more trouble than they're worth, even the nice ones, like Peter. Is that the time? I'm afraid we must be off now that I'm decently clad again. I'm out to dinner tonight. A charity affair, all lukewarm food and clothes smelling of mothballs. Rest assured, my dear, Archie will start his game of "Hunt the Husband" again first thing in the morning, and then I will give the silly man the dressing down of his life.'

'Why?' protested Archie. 'What have I done to deserve that?'

'Not you, you idiot! Peter!' Charlotte gave a groan of exasperation, and propelled the young officer down the stairs.

They had no sooner left the house than the drawing room door opened, and Agnes emerged.

'I had intended to spend a restful afternoon with my embroidery. However, that was not to be,' she said with disapproval. 'All the dashing about and running up and down stairs. The place was like a bear garden.'

It was on the tip of Mercy's tongue to point out that much of the activity had been caused by Peter and his jumping to conclusions. She did not, though. Instead she said, 'I do not see how people going up and down stairs can possibly interfere with embroidery.'

'I only ask for a little consideration!' snapped Agnes. 'Obviously I hope for too much!' And she swept out of the room, a picture of hurt indignation.

Mercy waited until she was well clear before she also left. She had too much on her mind to dwell on Mrs Lisburne's imagined grievances. It was long past midnight when she heard the Daimler return. She lay in bed, hoping in vain for Peter to come to her. When he did not she rose and, putting on a robe, went quietly along the corridor. Peter had taken to sleeping in a room on the far side of the house – more final than his sleeping in the dressing-room. There was a light showing under the door when she reached it. For a moment she listened, making sure that Poole was not about, then she knocked. 'Peter,' she said softly. 'Let me in.'

Immediately the light was switched off.

'Peter!' Her voice was more urgent now. 'I must talk to you. Please open the door.'

Complete silence was the only reply. She turned the handle. The door remained shut. In one final effort she rattled at it, but Peter made no response. All she could do was return to her own room before she woke the rest of the household. Her disappointment was bad enough to bear, she did not want to add humiliation to it. But now her predominant emotion was a growing anger.

She awoke determined not to hang about the house waiting for a chance to explain things to Peter. If he wanted explanations then he would have to seek her out. She opened her diary and checked engagements for the day. Her life was going on undisturbed.

Eventually, she encountered Peter in the hall, as she was going out and he was coming in. She would have let him pass with an impersonal, 'Good afternoon. What a lovely day!' but it was he who stopped.

Dismissing the ever-present Rogers, he said, 'Is that all you have to say to me?'

'What else is there?' she asked sweetly.

'You don't feel you owe me some explanation?'

'Explanation!' cried Mercy. 'Oh, at last we've come to it, have we? For hours I've been waiting, quite prepared to give an explanation, but where were you? Sulking at your club or some similar hide-out. Well, I am afraid I have not the time for such explanations now. I have an appointment. It's your turn to wait, kicking your heels.'

She moved towards the door, but he caught hold of her arm.

'For heaven's sake!' he said, his voice low. 'What did you expect me to think, finding you with Nicholson in that way?'

'I expected – I hoped that you might have trusted me enough at least to hear my version, instead of dashing off in high dudgeon, not caring how much you embarrassed poor Archie or humiliated me.'

'Are you saying that you are not having an affair with Nicholson?'

'Oh for goodness' sake, use your common sense!' she exclaimed, her patience at an end. 'Is it likely that I would have an assignation with my lover here, where anyone might interrupt us at any time?'

'Then what were you doing?'

'Very well, for the sake of peace I will tell you. We had fallen over. Archie and I were dancing and we overbalanced.'

'Dancing? A likely story!'

'Since you clearly do not trust my word then ask Charlotte.'

'Why should I ask Charlotte?'

'Because she was only yards away, in my dressing-room, having a stain removed from her skirt.'

'I know Charlotte. She'll say anything to help a friend.'

'Now you *have* gone too far!' Mercy rounded on him furiously. 'I can't force you to believe me, and frankly I am not particularly interested whether you do or don't. Question Charlotte if you like! Question Stafford! Question your mother!' she added, suddenly noticing the drawing room door move a few inches. 'You may as well come out, Mrs Lisburne. You'll be able to hear much better out here in the hall.'

'There is no need to be impertinent!' Agnes emerged with dignity. If she was feeling embarrassed at being caught listening she did not show it.

'One benefit of your eavesdropping is that we don't need to explain matters,' said Mercy, ignoring her comment. 'You heard what's been going on, now perhaps you will explain to your son that I was not alone with Captain Nicholson yesterday afternoon.'

'I really do not know how I am expected to know any such thing,' said Agnes haughtily.

'By your usual method of leaving the drawing room door open so that you can hear what is going on.'

'I will not be insulted in my own home.' Agnes began to stalk away. 'If your wife and her friends choose to concoct some cock-and-bull story about ink-stains, then it is no concern of mine.'

'Ink-stain? What is this about ink?' asked Peter.

For once Agnes appeared ruffled by her slip of the tongue.

'I have no idea what you are talking about,' she said. And she would have walked away.

'Mother, I would know the truth. Was Charlotte Dawson-Pring here at the same time as Archie Nicholson?' There was a steel in Peter's tone which Mercy had never heard before.

Agnes almost quailed before her son's anger. 'I— I suppose so. Well, yes, she was.' Then she rallied. 'And if you have quite finished this inquisition I would be obliged if you would let me leave,' she said, with more of her usual asperity.

'How can I apologize?' said Peter quietly, after she had gone. 'Just saying I'm sorry is – is woefully inadequate. I've been hasty and unjust, and so many other things. I ask you to forgive me.'

Mercy should have been relieved to hear his words but somehow the right emotions evaded her. The last twenty four hours had left a bitter wound. He had been too quick to condemn, and she had forgiven him too often. She had no more forgiveness left to offer.

'If you had only listened, given me the benefit of the doubt...' Mercy's voice was low and bitter.

'You will forgive me, won't you? Please?' He held his hands out to her.

She backed away. 'I may have done once, when I was young and naive, but not any more. You didn't believe me, and you didn't trust me. How can I forgive that?'

Keeping her head high she left the house. She did not look back.

A burning resentment made Mercy go ahead with her afternoon's plans. She would carry on as usual, just to show Peter that she did not care. In this determined mood she left to join Charlotte at the Devonshire Hall Hotel. She was late, and the fashion show, for which she had a ticket, had already begun.

'You haven't missed much,' Charlotte hissed in her ear. 'Some tolerable skirts and blouses, and a walking costume in which I would not be seen dead. The best is still to come.'

Mercy settled in her seat and made herself concentrate on the elegant well-corseted figures that swept past in an increasing variety of clothes. If her friend thought her chatter a little forced or her face rather strained, she made no comment.

'I am going to be extravagant,' Mercy announced, when the show came to an end.

'I am delighted to hear it. What do you propose to do?'

'Buy something new. I like the look of that peacock-blue silk.'

'An excellent choice. You should look absolutely superb in it.'

'I thought I could wear it at the Melba concert next week. What do you think? Would it be suitable for an afternoon performance?'

'I think that there will be more eyes on you than on the celebrated Madame Melba. You have got your ticket, I hope? I understand they are as rare as hen's teeth. I only got mine through sheer belligerence.'

'There is no need to worry on that score. Lord Alston has invited me to join his party.'

'Ah!' said Charlotte knowingly. 'So he's back from Switzerland, is he?'

'I presume so. I received a letter from him the other day.' Mercy deliberately kept her voice nonchalant. In fact, until this afternoon, she had been going to decline his invitation. Now she was determined to accept.

'Bully for you!' said Charlotte softly. 'From that I presume you have finally caught up with that husband of yours.'

'Yes!' said Mercy, in such a forbidding tone that even Charlotte did not feel inclined to question her further.

There was little sign of Peter during the next few days. It was as though the brief idyllic reconciliation had never happened, and Mercy struggled hard to put it from her mind. The easiest way was to throw herself wholeheartedly into the social whirl once more, and so she found herself accepting practically every invitation that came her way.

Apart from the thin veneer of 'keeping up appearances' her marriage was over. So what was left to her? She had nothing else, she would be a social butterfly.

Chapter Twelve

'I am going as Boadicea,' announced Charlotte. 'You could show more interest.'

'More interest in what?'

Charlotte groaned dramatically. 'I knew you weren't paying attention. I want to discuss something of importance. Your costume for the fancy-dress ball is becoming a matter of great urgency.'

'Oh, the ball,' said Mercy.

'There's no need to say it in that bored way. It is for charity. The Ivywood Clinic is a very good cause, and it promises to be quite a social occasion, so kindly make your mind up what you intend to wear.'

'How about a laundry-maid's costume?'

'Don't be flippant. It is a matter which requires serious thought.'

'Oh, I don't know! You think of something for me!'

'You sound as though you aren't interested.'

Mercy nearly retorted that she was not. But at least the ball would fill in an evening. That was all she required of anything these days.

'I know, I'll go as a butterfly,' she said. It seemed a particularly appropriate costume.

Charlotte, however, saw no underlying significance in her choice.

'A splendid idea! We had better get you to Madame Cecile immediately. If she is to concoct a ravishing creation for you the least we can do is give her enough time to do the job properly.'

'My dear, you look marvellous!' said Charlotte approvingly, when she saw the completed result. 'I meant to be impressive and magnificent as the Warrior Queen, now that I'm beside you I simply feel dowdy and insignificant.'

'Never that!' laughed Mercy. 'I am sure the real Boadicea was never so imposing.'

'Flattery is all very well, but it is you who turns the heads.'

It was true, no matter how Mercy tried to deny it. Beneath the lights of the ballroom she shimmered like an iridescent jewel. All eyes were upon her.

'I suppose there's no hope that you would let me sign my name against every dance, is there?' asked Lord Alston, taking her dance programme from her.

'And be accused by every female in the room of monopolizing you? No, thank you,' smiled Mercy.

'I suppose I'll have to reach a diplomatic compromise.' He scribbled his name beside three, then, as he handed back the card with its tiny tasselled pencil, he gave an elaborate bow, in keeping with his Elizabethan costume. The colourful doublet and breeches suited him, making him an unexpectedly dashing Sir Francis Drake.

'And now, if you will permit me...' Archie held out his hand for her dance programme. 'There!' he said, scribbling away. 'I'm far more greedy than Alston, here, though I see he's got in before me for the Lancers, the lucky devil!'

'Rank, dear boy! That's all it takes,' said Lord Alston calmly, as the orchestra struck up the opening bars of the first waltz. 'Now, this is my dance, I think, so would you do me the honour, Mercy, my dear?' He held out his arm to her, and together they went on to the ballroom floor.

Theirs was a small party to start with, then gradually, as the evening continued, Lord Alston or Charlotte would invite some other friend or acquaintance to come and join their circle. The noise and the laughter coming from their corner of the room grew in direct proportion to the number of people who congregated there.

Mercy was in demand for every dance, until her feet ached and her head throbbed. She would gladly have sat out, if importunate hands had not drawn her back on to the floor again and again. As the tide of noise rose steadily it became increasingly difficult to hear what anyone said, and she found herself laughing at inaudible jokes simply because others were laughing too. There was something horribly empty about it all.

But one man stood apart from the hilarity. He was an acquaintance of Charlotte's, and no doubt she had introduced him to the others but Mercy had not caught his name. Now he was standing next to her, very tall and upright, not taking part in any of the conversation. There was a slightly disdainful air about him, as if he found the proceedings far too frivolous, and was wishing himself elsewhere. She could sympathize with him. At that moment Archie leaned towards her, telling her something evidently meant to be funny, but which she could barely hear. At the end she dutifully laughed loudly, not having understood any of it. At the sound of her laughter the man looked in her direction, and she caught impatience and near contempt in his gaze.

Slightly annoyed, she could not help being intrigued. He seemed so out of place. He had an air about him of having far better things to do with his time, an attitude that was rare in the circles in which Mercy moved. She found her attention going back to him again and again. He was about as tall as Peter, but there all similarity ended, for his hair was dark, and his movements, when he did move, were precise and energetic, quite unlike Peter's. Even his costume, of leather breeches and a short green jacket adorned with stag's horn buttons, set him apart from anyone else by its authenticity. He wore it with ease, as though well accustomed to be dressed in such a way. In all the time he was under Mercy's observation he hardly spoke to anyone, and she wondered if shyness might account for his off-hand manner. There was only one way to find out, so she decided to take the initiative. She leaned towards him.

'Your costume seems very realistic, sir. You look ready to climb the Swiss Alps,' she remarked.

At her words he executed a stiff bow in her direction. He inclined his head towards her. 'Your pardon, there is such a din I did not hear what you said.'

Beginning to regret having made her overture Mercy repeated her words. Although this time he evidently understood them the disdainful expression remained on his face.

'Then I regret I would be most inappropriately dressed, for my costume is German, and it is worn for hunting wild boar,' he replied. His voice implied that it was something any fool should have known.

Mercy refused to be put down by him, even though she felt rather silly.

'My apologies. I have just proved that I've visited neither Switzerland nor Germany. However, I congratulate you on your perseverance. To my ears your German accent is perfect.'

'That is because I am German,' he said, not bothering to conceal the contempt in his tone.

Mercy felt her face go scarlet with anger and humiliation. How dare he make her out to be such an idiot! She searched for some sharp retort. But he had turned away, and was now leaning against a pillar, staring into space.

A snatch of music warned everyone that the Lancers were about to commence, and Lord Alston came to claim Mercy.

'Who is that man in the green jacket?' she asked as they made up their sets.

Alston glanced over his shoulder. 'Oh, the German? He's Gunther von Herwath, one of Charlotte's finds.'

'She need not have bothered finding him. He's very disagreeable!'

Alston chuckled. 'You've crossed swords with him, have you? He can be a bit abrupt when he's a mind.'

'Abrupt? He was downright rude!'

'Rude! Oh I say, that won't do! I'll go and have a stern word with the fellow!'

'Please don't bother.' Mercy put out a restraining hand. 'He's not worth it, and if you go now you'll only spoil the set. I wonder why he bothered to come to the ball, when he makes it abundantly clear he is hating every minute.'

'I suppose he felt he had to. After all, the whole point of this evening is to raise funds for his clinic.'

'*His* clinic?'

'Yes, Ivywood. He runs it. He's a doctor, and a darned good one, I believe. Oh, we're starting! Off we go!'

The intricacies of the dance left no time for Mercy to dwell on the shortcomings of Gunther von Herwath. By the time the final set was done, and they returned breathless and exhausted to their seats, she noted that he had gone. Apart from that she did not spare him another thought.

It was gone midnight when Lord Alston's car drove her up the drive of the Villa Dorata. They reached the front door just as Peter was getting out of the Daimler. He could not fail to recognize the Rolls, and his nod of acknowledgement in its direction was terse.

'You've had an enjoyable time?' he asked, as he and Mercy walked up the steps together.

'Tolerably so, thanks.'

'It was a fancy-dress affair, I believe.'

'Yes, it was. In aid of one of the TB clinics.'

'How very worthy. I'm intrigued by the portion of costume I can see beneath your wrap. What did you go as?'

'A butterfly.'

'How charming.'

The conversation between them was very civilized, very polite – it could have been taking place between strangers.

Peter absently handed his hat and scarf to Rogers. Mercy did not know where he had been. She did not ask.

'Is there anything you would like before you retire? Shall Rogers get you a drink, or something?' he asked.

'No, thank you. I'm very tired. I'll go straight away up to bed.'

'I think I'll do the same.'

Shoulder to shoulder they climbed the stairs. At the top, as if by unspoken agreement, they stopped.

'Good night to you, Mercy.'

'Good night to you, Peter.'

They turned and walked in opposite directions. Only a few yards of floor, corridor and walls separated them. It might as well have been a continent.

Charlotte arrived the next morning, looking incredibly energetic for someone who had not got to bed until the early hours.

'The ball last night was an unqualified success!' she announced heartily.

'Do you mean socially or financially?' asked Mercy, feeling she had not weathered the lack of sleep as well as her friend.

'Both, I hope, though I was speaking financially. The Ivywood Clinic's funds now show a marked improvement.'

'Let's hope the temper and manners of its director follow suit.'

'You mean Doctor von Herwath? Isn't he absolutely charming?' She caught Mercy's eye. 'Well, perhaps not all of the time. He doesn't suffer fools gladly...'

'As he demonstrated very clearly last night.'

'I'll admit he can be impatient; but such an interesting person. These men with a mission so often are. I must confess I'm rather taken with him, and I am determined to help him in every way I can.'

Mercy regarded her curiously.

'Doctor von Herwath doesn't sound like the usual candidate for your aid,' she said.

Charlotte came as close as she was able to looking coy. 'You've got to admit he is exceedingly attractive.'

'No, I've not got to admit any such thing. You be as smitten as you like, I shall go on thinking he is most unpleasant.'

'Oh really! I despair of you!' Charlotte returned to her normal brisk self. 'Even if you don't agree with me about the man you have got to admit that his clinic is an extremely worthy cause. Ivywood is run by a charitable trust, you know. The patients don't pay a penny piece. No one is ever turned away because they are too poor to pay for treatment.'

'Charlotte, I know you of old. You are leading up to something.'

'Not for myself. For those poor suffering souls—'

'Charlotte!'

'Very well! I have decided to have a charity tea at my house in aid of Ivywood. It will be in two weeks' time, and I am relying upon you to help me.'

'You want me to carry the trays of tea?'

'Don't be silly, dear. I have plenty of staff who can cope with that. No, I intend to have a few tastefully laid out stalls and that sort of thing. I thought you could be a gypsy fortune teller.'

Mercy burst out laughing. 'I know nothing about fortune telling, and I doubt if I could learn in two weeks. If you'll forgive me, I'll give your charity tea, worthy though it is, a miss.'

'You're letting your dislike of Doctor von Herwath put you off. He's a first-rate doctor. And he works at the clinic for a pittance, even though he could command top fees if he chose to set up in private practice. He has helped so many people.'

'Don't tell me this miracle-worker has discovered a cure for TB!' exclaimed Mercy. Then she regretted her facetious outburst. 'Of course, he can't have done!' she said quietly. 'I'm ashamed I said that. TB is not a subject for sarcasm. I'm sorry, I'll do what I can to help. But no fortune telling!'

'Then how about selling lucky white heather – in gypsy costume, of course?' asked Charlotte, brightening visibly.

'All right, I'll be a gypsy hawker, since you're so set on it,' laughed Mercy. 'Are you sure you don't want me to boil the water for the tea in a black pot over a fire of sticks in the middle of your lawn?'

Charlotte's elegant house in the Warberries was filled with the hum of voices and the clatter of teacups. Mercy circulated among the visitors, very conscious of her vivid red and yellow gypsy skirt, and of the heavy rings of gold in her ears.

'Would you care to buy a bunch of white heather?' she asked tentatively. 'Only threepence a bunch.'

It was remarkable how many people did not hear her, or ignored her if they did.

'You have to be more forceful, my dear,' said Lord Alston, putting a sprig of heather in his buttonhole and dropping a sovereign into her purse. 'Use all your gypsy wiles. Oh, and put the price up. This lot can afford a shilling for a good cause!'

He was right, of course. She set out to be more persuasive. Her new tactics proved to be most successful, so that twice she had to replenish her basket. She was beginning to enjoy playing her role. Eventually she was left with only one last bunch of heather. Although the afternoon was drawing to a close, she noted the arrival of a latecomer.

Determined to sell the last of her wares, she hurried over.

'Buy some white heather, sir,' she pleaded. 'Only a shilling to you, sir.'

'And how much would it be to anyone else?' the man asked. His accent was clipped and uncomfortably familiar.

She looked up and saw his eyes were very clear and hazel, and they held recognition and slight scorn.

'A shilling,' she replied frankly, in her normal voice.

'I thought so. Well, I suppose I must buy it, though I do not usually encourage such superstitious nonsense.'

He paid for his heather then walked away. Mercy watched as he crumpled the sprig in his hand and then threw it contemptuously into the fire. He proceeded to stand with his back to the fireplace, his hands behind him, looking exceedingly bored. Then he stalked out.

'Isn't it marvellous that Doctor von Herwath could come?' enthused Charlotte, when they met later in the garden room.

'I wonder that he bothered. He made it all too obvious that he was utterly bored.'

'I expect he is tired, caring for those patients every day.'

'Charlotte, it's not like you to make excuses for someone. Nevertheless, in spite of what you say I think he is a most disagreeable man, and please don't involve me in anything connected with Ivywood ever again!'

The last place Mercy expected to encounter Doctor von Herwath was at the skating rink. She had some qualms about going roller skating in the first place. For all it was the latest craze, it did not seem to be a proper sort of activity for a mature married woman. Her acceptance of Charlotte's invitation had something to do with the knowledge that Peter would not have approved.

The rink was on the pier, a flat expanse that doubled as a venue for roller skating in winter and as the foundation of a tented concert hall during the summer. Mercy was not the only married woman in the party, Lilian Manning was there, and Zena Pritchard, neither of them accompanied by husbands. Instead, Charles Wentworth lent his languid presence to the group, and proved to be an unexpectedly able skater.

Upon greater acquaintance Lilian could be an amiable companion, she was so cheerful and good-natured. The same could not be said of Zena, although she treated Mercy with more civility than she had done at their first encounter at Upper Lee. Mercy had declined Charles's offers of assistance. She preferred to make her own way round the rink slowly and steadily, keeping a wary eye on her fellow skaters. It was as well she did, for Lilian dashed about the place in a madcap fashion, not caring if she fell over or cannoned into someone. Zena proceeded more carefully. Mercy suspected that her caution was more to give her an excuse to hold on to Charles than lack of ability. As for Charlotte, she skated as she did everything else, competently and efficiently.

There was no denying that their group dominated the rink. At times Mercy felt embarrassed at the lack of consideration her companions showed towards the other skaters, charging about as if they were the only people there. And they were far and away the noisiest. She felt sorry for the other citizens of Torquay who had paid their few pence to enjoy the speed and challenge of being on roller skates only to find themselves gradually ousted from the rink. Most gave up and went home; a few bystanders lingered at the edge to watch. Unfortunately one of these onlookers proved to be Gunther von Herwath.

Mercy was concentrating on her skating when the accident occurred. It was Lilian's scream which caught her attention. Lilian had been screaming all afternoon, but this was different. This time there was pain and terror in her voice. Mercy turned to see her crumpled on the ground, a white-faced Charles Wentworth trying to support her. Even at a distance Mercy could see the red blood beginning to stain Lilian's skirt, as well as the ground, at an alarming rate.

'Do something, Charlotte,' Charles was pleading. 'For heaven's sake do something!'

Charlotte remained immobile, her face ashen. As for Zena, she was clutching at the surrounding fence, in a half faint.

Hampered a little by her unaccustomed skates, Mercy sped over as fast as she was able.

'Oh help her, someone! She's bleeding to death!' In his panic Charles was giving Lilian ineffectual pats on the arm.

'No, she is not bleeding to death!' Mercy said emphatically, dropping to her knees beside the whimpering Lilian. She hoped she was right. The gash on Lilian's hand was deep, right down to the bone, and the wound was bleeding in great spurts. 'Have you got a large handkerchief, Charles? Here, hold her hand up, while I try to stop the bleeding... Charlotte, your scarf, if you please... and fetch Doctor von Herwath, he's just gone along the pier.'

Still Charlotte did not move. She seemed mesmerized by the growing pool of blood. In the end Mercy had to send a small boy after the doctor. All the time she had been pressing hard below the cut with her thumbs, and talking encouragingly to the semi-conscious Lilian. Slowly the terrible gushing began to ease, as with great relief Mercy saw Doctor von Herwath come striding towards them.

'What has happened?' he asked, then continued without waiting for a reply, 'Ah, a cut, and a very nasty one.'

Mercy half expected him to make some remark about this being the inevitable result of fooling about on skates, but he did not.

'There, let me see...' he said. He regarded Mercy's makeshift bandage. 'Ah yes, this is good. I will simply bind this a little tighter for you now, then I think we had best take you to the hospital to have it seen to properly. You, sir! I presume you were driven here? Go and fetch your car! Quickly, someone! Give me a scarf or something absorbent to use as a bandage...'

He did not need to ask. While Charles dashed off, eager to help, Mercy had already been tearing strips from her cambric petticoat.

Doctor von Herwath took them without comment, just as he accepted her help unquestioningly. While he worked he talked calmly to Lilian.

'You have been very brave. It must have been an alarming experience for you. Happily it looks far worse than it really is. I must say, you chose to have your accident at exactly the right moment, when there was someone nearby who knew what to do.'

Mercy thought he was referring to himself. She was surprised to find him looking in her direction.

Charles came hurrying towards them, the chauffeur, his arms full of rugs, following behind.

'The car's here,' he puffed. 'We've got it as close to the end of the pier as possible.'

His arrival seemed to galvanize Charlotte into action.

'Then let's get this poor girl to hospital at once,' she declared, taking over as though she had been in charge from the start. 'Wrap those rugs about her. Charles, you and Adams shall carry her to the car. The doctor and I will follow on behind. Don't worry, Lilian, my dear, I'm coming to the hospital with you.'

Lilian, however, seemed distressed by this arrangement. Doctor von Herwath noticed her reaction.

'Miss Dawson-Pring,' he said. 'Is that lady over there not one of your party?' Everyone looked towards the edge of the rink, where Zena sat, pale, trembling and forgotten.

'She looks very shaken,' the doctor continued. 'It is my advice that you get her home quickly. This lady here can come to the hospital in your stead.'

'Nonsense—' began Charlotte.

Doctor von Herwath did not let her finish. 'There is no time to argue,' he said. Turning briefly to Mercy he said, 'Come!' and set off after the injured Lilian at a great pace.

In spite of the seriousness of the situation Mercy had to bite back a smile as she trotted behind him. She had never seen Charlotte so nonplussed before. The doctor's manner certainly brooked no contradiction.

When they reached the hospital the sister on duty would have shepherded Mercy into a waiting-room, if the unfamiliar surroundings on top of the shock she had already suffered had not unnerved Lilian.

'Don't leave me!' she begged weakly, clutching at Mercy.

'Let the lady stay!' said Doctor von Herwath.

212

The sister obviously objected to such unorthodox procedure, but because she dared not say anything she expressed her indignation by bustling about in a flurry of carbolic and starched cotton.

'I can't go on calling you "this lady". What is your name?' demanded the doctor. It was the first remark he had made directly to Mercy since they had left the pier.

'It is Mercy Lisburne. *Mrs* Lisburne,' she stated.

'Mercy. How appropriate,' he said, ignoring her careful emphasis; and he almost smiled.

Before she could reply the duty doctor arrived. That both men knew each other well was immediately apparent.

'A very neat piece of work,' remarked the duty doctor, as Lilian's emergency bandage was removed. 'You are a very fortunate young lady, having such a first-rate fellow on hand at your accident.'

'Little of the credit is mine,' said Doctor von Herwath. 'Mrs Lisburne had the matter well under control by the time I got there.'

'You did?' The duty doctor glanced up briefly at Mercy and smiled. 'In that case, should you ever need to go out to work, we'd be glad to have you.' He was only half joking.

Mercy thought how ironic it was that now she had no need of employment she was being offered a job. She could remember very clearly a time when she was desperate enough to have considered anything. Nursing would have seemed a marvellous opportunity.

Lilian's wound had scarcely been dressed when a nurse announced, 'Mr Manning is here, sir.'

This was the first time Mercy had ever seen Lilian's husband, and she found it hard to imagine the pale studious-looking man who entered married to the effervescent Lilian. Yet clearly he was fond of her, the look of anxiety on his face as he saw his wife lying there was proof enough. More surprisingly, Lilian evidently had far more regard for him than she ever betrayed when she was in the company of Charlotte's set. At the sight of him she exclaimed, 'Henry, oh Henry, I needed you so!' then promptly flung her good arm round his neck and burst into tears.

Mercy watched the scene with an unexpected throb of pain. Once she and Peter had been as loving, a very long time ago.

'I think we can safely leave Mr Manning to look after Mrs Manning for a few minutes while she recuperates,' said the duty doctor, tactfully ushering everyone else out of the room. 'Have you a car waiting, Mrs Lisburne? Or would you like me to call a taxi for you?'

'We sent the car away,' said Mercy, 'and to be honest I think I would like to walk for a while.'

Now that the excitement and drama was over she was beginning to feel rather shaky. What she needed was some fresh air.

'A good idea. I will join you,' said Gunther von Herwath. 'Where did you learn to cope so well in an emergency?' he demanded suddenly, 'it is not something you learned in the company of Miss Dawson-Pring and her friends.' His command of English was almost faultless. Only his clipped accent betrayed the fact that it was not his first language.

'It was simply common sense. As for coping – I was extremely thankful to see you come hurrying up. I doubt if I could have bandaged Lilian's hand firmly enough to have stopped the bleeding properly.'

'You would have managed.' Doctor von Herwath spoke with complete assurance. 'You say you used only your common sense, yet you did exactly the right things. Most importantly, you did not panic at the sight of blood.'

'I have three brothers and a sister, all of whom had their fair share of accidents and disasters when they were small. I suppose I've grown used to binding up cuts and gashes.'

'Your nurse must have been a woman of sense and enlightenment to have left you to deal with the injuries of your brothers and sisters. Though I suppose she might equally have been lazy, and not shown much concern for her charges.'

'I'm afraid you are wrong on both counts,' laughed Mercy. 'We didn't have a nurse. We were far too poor.'

'You do surprise me. I took you for a lady of wealth. You dress so elegantly and you seem much at home in the company of people like Miss Dawson-Pring.'

'I am fortunate in having a very generous husband.' Mercy paused for a brief moment, conscious that she did not often think of Peter in such a complimentary way these days. 'When he married me I was working in a laundry,' she continued.

'I think you are not being serious with me.'

'I promise you, I am speaking the truth,' smiled Mercy.

'How remarkable!' He paused, as though considering what she had said. When he spoke it was explosively. 'Then why do you waste your time so?' he demanded.

'I beg your pardon?' Mercy was quite startled by the violence of his expression.

'Why do you waste your time with frivolous people like Miss Dawson-Pring and Mrs Manning? It can have been no easy matter, rising from your humble background. It must have taken determination and intelligence – yes, and courage too. I have seen how calm you can remain in a crisis. Yet, with these excellent qualities you insist upon behaving in a silly, frivolous manner.'

'I object to being called silly or frivolous, sir!' Mercy retorted indignantly.

'I expect you do,' he said. 'You can't deny it, can you? The playing at being a butterfly or a gypsy beggar, and all the other mindless amusements of the well-to-do lady! Those are no occupations for a woman like you! You are wasting your abilities, and that is wrong!'

'Really, sir, I've never heard such impertinence!' Mercy's anger was all the sharper because, in her heart, she agreed with him.

'I speak the truth!' He uttered the words in such a matter-of-fact manner that she found herself unable to argue.

Instead she said coldly, 'There is a taxi over there. Would you be kind enough to hail it for me? I have walked far enough.'

He did as he was requested without comment. Silently she got into the car, and reached out to close the door, only to find him holding it firmly.

'It is time you stopped frittering away your life,' he said. 'I shall expect you at Ivy wood tomorrow to see the work we do. Two-thirty would be convenient.'

Mercy opened her mouth to protest, but she was too late. He had slammed the door shut and ordered the driver to move off. She sat bolt upright in her seat, too tense to relax against the cushions. Her encounter with Gunther von Herwath had left her feeling as if she had been grappling with a whirlwind. Part of her was furious at his dictatorial manner, while the rest of her agreed with everything he had said. He had put her dissatisfaction clearly and succinctly into words. Her life was empty and useless. And she knew it. Her early years had been spent struggling to survive. She was used to fighting. Now, there was no fight, no struggle, no purpose. Doctor von Herwath had offered her a solution, though offered was something of a misnomer. It had been more of a command.

She told herself that she would certainly not go to Ivywood the next day, that wild horses could not drag her anywhere near that awful man.

What else will you do, if you don't go? asked a persistent inner voice. Visit your hairdresser? Spend an hour or two playing bridge? Would that really be more interesting than going to Ivywood?

She postponed her hairdressing appointment, cancelled her bridge afternoon, and ordered the car for two-thirty the next day. Being late would be her gesture of independence. She had no intention of letting this German doctor think she automatically danced to his tune.

Chapter Thirteen

The entrance to the Ivywood Clinic was immediately off the road. It had once been a private residence and like so many houses in Torquay it was built on the side of a steep hill. From the outside it seemed a modest enough place, well maintained but very plain. The solid oak door bore a shining brass plate engraved with the words THE IVYWOOD CHEST CLINIC, ADMINISTERED BY THE IVYWOOD TRUST, REG. CHARITY. Underneath it said MEDICAL DIRECTOR – DR GUNTHER von HERWATH. His name was followed by a bewildering array of letters. The qualifications of Doctor von Herwath were certainly impressive. Mercy pushed open the door and entered.

The interior of Ivywood was suitably hushed, and a faint odour of carbolic hung on the air. Nevertheless, it was bright and cheerful. The cream walls looked freshly painted, and there was a well cared for air about the place. A middle-aged woman in a spotless white overall was watering a flourishing selection of pot plants. As Mercy entered she turned and put down her watering jug.

'Can I help you?' she asked with a pleasant smile.

'My name is Mrs Lisburne. I think Doctor von Herwath is expecting me.'

'Ah, yes, Mrs Lisburne. The doctor said you'd be coming. He is with a patient at the moment, so he asked me if I would show you into the sitting room. I am Miss Beech, the receptionist, secretary, clerk, oh, and gardener too, when the need arises.' She laughed, indicating the row of flowerpots. 'Doctor von Herwath is a great believer in having plants in the clinic. His theory is that we must pay attention to the needs of our patients' spirits as well as their bodies, otherwise they have no chance. He has some very interesting ideas, does the doctor. We are so lucky to have him, really we are.'

All the time she had been talking Miss Beech had been guiding Mercy across the entrance hall and down a short flight of stairs. Now she opened a door and ushered her into a large room, bright with spring sunshine. From the huge window it was possible to see the whole of Torbay.

'Will you sit down?' Miss Beech indicated one of the numerous comfortable armchairs in the room. 'As you see, no one is in here now. The patients are resting. Fresh air, nourishing food, and lots of rest! That's what Doctor von Herwath always insists upon. He's quite a martinet about it.'

'I'm sure he is,' said Mercy.

Miss Beech smiled at her tone.

'He does have his funny ways, doesn't he? You'll get used to them when you've been here a little while.'

'I'm only here on a visit,' protested Mercy.

Miss Beech smiled again. She seemed to smile rather a lot.

'I said exactly the same thing myself,' she said. 'Yet here I am, working at Ivywood for a fourth year. Once Doctor von Herwath meets someone whom he thinks will fit into our little team he can be most persuasive. I had better warn you, he has decided you would be good for Ivywood and Ivywood would be good for you.'

'Doctor von Herwath seems to be taking a lot on himself!'

'Oh, he said it in the nicest way. He chooses his helpers with such care. It's an honour to be asked, truly it is.'

Mercy could not agree, but she felt that any objection would be a waste of breath – Miss Beech had about her the beaming certainty of a dedicated disciple.

Gunther von Herwath entered the room at that moment. He moved briskly, his white coat flapping, the papers in his hands fluttering with the draught he created.

'It is quarter to three,' he observed. 'I said to come at half past two. Of course, I knew you would be late.'

'I nearly didn't come at all,' retorted Mercy.

'Nonsense, you always intended to come!'

'I certainly did not!'

Instead of replying the doctor turned to Miss Beech.

'The post has just arrived,' he stated. 'I am expecting the medical notes for Mr Blake.'

'Of course, Doctor von Herwath! I'll go immediately and look!' Miss Beech hurried away.

'Does everyone leap to your orders?' asked Mercy in exasperation.

He regarded her steadily, the intense gaze of his hazel eyes making her uncomfortable.

'We have twenty patients here,' he said. 'Most with families who depend upon them. Goodness knows, we cannot promise to cure them! But at least we can help them, ease their suffering; and sometimes, if we are lucky, we can extend their lives. With so much depending on them the staff at Ivywood have far too much sense of responsibility to waste valuable time in arguing. You have seen our sitting room where our patients congregate. Now I will take you to the dispensary.' He set off at a great rate.

'Aren't you wasting valuable time showing me round?' asked Mercy, trotting to keep up with him.

'If you are to help here you must know where everything is and how it is used. Have you noticed the covered terrace?' he continued, ignoring her protests. 'It runs the whole length of the front of the house. The patients spend much time there, filling their lungs with good fresh air. And here is the dispensary. We pride ourselves that no other clinic in the town has one so adequately stocked or up to date. Now we will go to the kitchens and see the domestic arrangements.'

He took Mercy through the house at a terrific rate, yet somehow managing to explain the various functions and services so well that by the time they had finished and returned to the sitting room she could not help being impressed. By now there was a dozen or so people in the room. One occupant proved to be a small, spare man, whose face bore the hectic flush of his complaint. He looked up and grinned as they entered.

'What've you been roped in for, missus?' he asked breathlessly. 'You'll 'ave to watch yourself with the doctor, you know. Before you know it you'll be working 'ere, 'e'll be treating you like a dog, and you'll get no thanks for it. No, nor any wages, either.'

'You don't want to take any notice of this fellow,' said Doctor von Herwath without rancour. 'He thinks because he is our oldest inhabitant he can say what he likes.'

''Course I do! 'E's been trying to polish me off for four years and not succeeded yet! That entitles me to speak my mind.' The small man grinned and held out his hand. 'Matt Thoms is the name, and pleased to meet any friend of the doctor's. You mind my warnings now.'

Mercy took his hand in hers. It was hot and light, and so frail she might have been clasping dry twigs.

'Thank you for putting me on my guard, Mr Thoms,' she smiled.

'I reckon you've got his measure. But if you 'ave any trouble, you just tell me. I'll soon sort 'im out. I ain't afraid of 'im just because 'e wears a white coat.' The words were belligerent, but said with a wide smile.

'If you keep on like this, Matt, we will have no one working for us,' the doctor pointed out calmly. 'You should be encouraging Mrs Lisburne, not trying to frighten her away.'

'You've got a point there. Goodness knows it's a treat just to look at 'er! I only want 'er to know what she's letting 'erself in for.' Matt Thoms winked up at Mercy and said in a stage whisper, ''E's all right really, is the old doc, but someone's got to keep 'im in 'is place, else 'e'll start thinking 'e runs the show.'

'Whereas everyone knows that Ivywood is really run by you, Matt.' Doctor von Herwath smiled down at the little man. It was the first time Mercy had ever seen him smile.

'You've got it in one, me old mate.' Matt winked again.

'Well, Mrs Lisburne, will you join forces with me, and help me cope with the likes of Matt.'

'So you are asking me at last, Doctor,' she retorted. 'Up till now you've been ordering me to help you.'

'That's telling 'im, missus!' chuckled Matt.

'You will come?' persisted the doctor.

Mercy relented. She knew she wanted to come to Ivywood. These people needed help. They were all so desperately sick, she could see that. But she did not know what she could do.

'I've no nursing qualifications,' she said.

'You do not need them. We have enough nurses. I have another job for you. We will go to my office and discuss it.'

Mercy sighed. 'You've gone back to ordering me about again,' she said.

Doctor von Herwath gave a very Germanic bow.

'Mrs Lisburne, would you do me the pleasure of accompanying me to my office?' he said.

'There, what did I say? You've 'ad a good influence on him already,' chortled Matt Thoms.

'Sadly it didn't last long,' admitted Mercy ruefully, regarding the back of Gunther von Herwath as he strode from the room. 'I suppose I must be grateful that he actually asked me. It would be wanting too much to expect him to wait for my reply. Goodbye for now, Mr Thoms.'

'Cheerio, ducks. 'Is office is at the top of the stairs, if you don't catch up with 'im.'

It was as well the cheery little man had given her directions, for by the time Mercy reached the door there was no sign of the doctor. Mounting the stairs she found him in a small, cluttered office, already reading some notes. The door was open so she entered. He had not noticed that she had been left behind.

'This is what I want you to deal with,' he said, putting a sheaf of papers into her hand.

She looked at the papers. The first was from the wife of a patient. She was in danger of being evicted because she was behind with her rent. She wanted to know how soon her husband could be released and get back to work. Another was from a man, desperate for advice because, while his wife was in Ivywood, he was finding it impossible to cope with going out to work and at the same time care for their five small children. The others were in a similar vein, people with problems because their loved ones had fallen sick and had to be admitted to Ivywood. It was all too painfully familiar. Memories of Fernicombe and the struggle to survive came flooding back.

'It is a heart-rending collection,' said Mercy quietly.

'Yes, it is,' agreed the doctor. 'Such burdens would weigh down a fit person; you can imagine what they do to the gravely ill. You must deal with them!'

'I beg your pardon?'

'Deal with them! That is to be your function here.'

'How—' Mercy began to protest in vain.

'You are ideally suited for the job. We cannot pay you, of course, though a small part of our funds will be made available to help you in your work. You must see Miss Beech about that side of things.' He opened a folder and began reading the contents, seeming to forget she was there.

'Am I to presume that I am dismissed?' demanded Mercy.

'There is something else you wish to say?' He appeared to be bewildered by her attitude.

'Yes there is something I wish to say,' she retorted. 'I will work here. I will do the job you want, to the best of my ability. All I ask in return is a little more civility from you. Nothing much. Simply more requests and fewer commands.'

'How will things ever get done?'

'They'll get done all right. You try it and see!'

'Very well, I will try. You will begin on Monday...' He almost smiled. 'That was not a very good try, was it? Would you be kind enough to begin on Monday?'

'No, I will not!' said Mercy, her brisk tone matching his. 'I will come every morning and I intend to begin tomorrow. Good day, Doctor von Herwath!'

She left half expecting him to call after her with some further instructions. When he did not she permitted herself a satisfied smile – she had got the measure of Doctor Gunther von Herwath.

For the entire journey home she wondered if she had been mad to accept. She had not the least notion of how to set about her new job. At the same time she was aware of excitement pulsing through her veins at the challenge which lay ahead. At last there was some purpose to her life! She wondered whether or not to tell Peter of her new occupation. Upon consideration she decided against it. He showed no interest in her activities these days, and besides, it was no concern of his.

When she returned to the Villa Dorata Peter was not at home, anyway. The first to greet her was Rogers, with a letter. Recognizing Joey's writing she ripped it open. It was brief and the very first words drove away the brightness of her day.

'Dear Sis,' Joey had written. 'I thought you would want to know that Queenie lost the baby two days ago. She is well enough in herself, but down in the dumps, as might be expected. Your ever-loving brother, Joey.'

So it had all been for nothing! Mercy knew that her first thoughts should have been for her sister-in-law, yet she could not help herself. All she could think of was that her brother had thrown away his future needlessly. She noted that he made no mention of his own reaction. The few terse lines betrayed nothing. Then she thought of Queenie – belatedly, to her shame. Poor devoted, adoring Queenie. The blow must have been devastating. From upstairs in the nursery came happy yells as John and William romped noisily. How would she have felt to have lost either of them?

I'll go to see Queenie tomorrow morning, she decided. I'll take her something pretty, to cheer her up.

Then she remembered that her morning was already occupied. Any visit to her sister-in-law would have to be in the afternoon. Upstairs John and William were still creating a racket. Mercy hurried to the nursery, consumed by an urgent need to see them and hold them – to reassure herself of their existence.

Her first morning working at Ivywood was less hectic than she had feared. Miss Beech turned out to be invaluable, a mine of useful information.

'I don't know why I'm here! You could do this so much better yourself!' Mercy exclaimed at last, fearing that she might have ousted the other woman from the job.

'My dear, I have been attempting to do your job as well as my own for months now.' Miss Beech's eyes twinkled. 'I found it quite impossible to do things thoroughly. Believe me, I am so relieved to have you with us.'

'Good, I'd hate to be treading on anyone's toes... Goodness, is that the time?' Mercy stared at the clock in disbelief. At the Villa Dorata so often the hours went by painfully slowly, yet the entire morning at Ivywood had gone by in a flash.

'So you have not been bored?' Gunther von Herwath was standing in the doorway.

'I've not had a chance. We've not stopped for a minute, have we, Miss Beech?'

'We have not. You've found us a good worker, Doctor,' replied Miss Beech, smiling.

'Of course. You are not staying to have lunch with us, Mrs Lisburne?'

'Regretfully, no.' replied Mercy, securing her hat with a long pin. Doctor von Herwath regarded the frothy concoction of veiling and feathers.

'A pity,' he said. 'That delightful creation you are wearing on your head would have cheered us all up.' Then he walked away without another word.

'Well I never!' Miss Beech was quite astounded. 'A compliment from the doctor. You are honoured, my dear.'

'Are you sure?' Mercy regarded her reflection critically. 'I've a strong suspicion he meant that this hat would give everyone a good laugh.'

223

Miss Beech refused to be convinced.

Mercy decided she did not have time to go home to eat. Instead she lunched modestly at a small cafe, then went into Williams and Cox's to buy a gift for Queenie. She chose a pink Shetland bedjacket as fine as a cobweb and bound with satin ribbon. It was by far the prettiest in the shop, though she honestly could not imagine Queenie wearing it. Remembering the awkwardness that her last floral offering had provoked she bought a basket of fruit instead.

To her eyes the house in Church Street appeared even more dilapidated than before. Joey opened the door to her, and she thought he looked worn out.

'Sis!' His tired face lit up. 'I didn't expect you to call.'

'I thought I'd just drop in and see how Queenie is getting on,' she replied.

'She's taken it badly, poor soul.' Joey dropped his voice to a conspiratorial whisper. 'I'm having the devil's own job keeping her in bed. The doctor says she's to stay there for another week at least, but she's all for getting back to work. She's worried that I won't be able to cope on my own – she's darned near right, too, only, I'll not admit it to her. She's not well enough to get up yet, she really isn't.'

'Couldn't you get someone in to help for two or three weeks?' asked Mercy, then immediately regretted her words.

'I can get them right enough, it's paying them that would prove troublesome,' said Joey wryly. 'Still, that's enough of our problems. Come up and see Queenie.'

He led the way up the uncarpeted stairs into an equally bare bedroom. Queenie was in the large double bed, propped up with pillows. She still looked ashen.

'You've got a visitor,' Joey announced. 'Mercy's come to see you, isn't that nice?'

'Oh yes, lovely!' Queenie tried to echo her husband's enthusiasm, but only succeeded in looking flustered. At the sight of Mercy, so expensively dressed and immaculate, her hand went at once to her hair which hung limply about her shoulders.

'I've brought you some fruit.'

Mercy balanced the basket on the bedside table. It looked exotic and out of place in these shabby surroundings. The bed jacket was no more successful. Queenie enthused about it, fingering the gossamer-fine wool with genuine pleasure, then after she had thanked Mercy she wrapped it up in its tissue paper again, and said that she would 'keep it for best'.

Mercy wondered what constituted 'for best'. She feared the jacket would be consigned to a drawer and never see the light of day again.

'Joey says you've to stay in bed for another week,' she said.

'Oh, that's just him fussing.' Queenie gazed at her husband, her eyes holding all their old mute adoration.

'It isn't only me who's fussing, it's the doctor too,' said Joey firmly. 'So you're staying there until he says you can move!'

'But you've far too much to do, you're looking worn out. He is, isn't he?' Queenie appealed to Mercy.

'He'll manage!' Mercy assured her.

Queenie shook her head. 'It's not right, you having to do so much just because I let you down...' The tears welled up and began to trickle from her eyes.

'You haven't let me down, you silly girl,' Joey patted her shoulder gently. 'We've had a bit of bad luck, that's all. But you're not to make things worse by getting up too soon. You could ruin your health that way, and then where would we be, eh?'

Queenie wiped her face with the back of her hand and nodded. Mercy could not help noticing that though Joey was gentle and kind his behaviour towards his wife held no sign of love. Nor did he mention the hope of other children in the future. It was such a glaring omission she wondered if Queenie had noticed it too. Then she looked at her sister-in-law, and saw the sad despair in her face.

Mercy felt desperately sorry for the unhappy young woman lying there in the bed. She wished she could help, but she could only offer practical assistance. There was no question of her giving them money, she knew better than that. Then she remembered one of the letters she had read that morning at Ivywood, an appeal for help that had clearly been penned with great effort, on cheap paper.

'Once Queenie is on her feet it's going to be a while before she gets her strength back,' she pointed out. 'Ideally, what you need is someone reliable to come and live in for a month, or six weeks, or even longer.'

'Oh yes! Ideally! It would solve all our problems,' Joey agreed ruefully.

'Don't be so sarcastic!' She gave her brother a playful prod. 'It just so happens I think I can be of help. I've just started assisting at one of the chest clinics. We had a letter from the mother of one of the patients, a Mrs Baxter. Her only son is in the clinic, and likely to be so for a long time. She's up in London and can't afford to come and see him, so she wrote pleading with us to find her some work in this area.'

'I don't see how that would help us,' said Joey. 'Well, if she came here it would be ideal. She'd have work, she could live in, and, with her son just a few miles down the road she could see him regularly. It's perfect.'

'And what about the little matter of wages?'

'They'd be taken care of, from a fund at the clinic.' She was not being absolutely truthful, for her plan was to pay the woman's wages herself. To her relief Joey failed to notice anything amiss.

'There's got to be a snag,' he insisted.

'Only that she might refuse to come, though I think it's unlikely.' The letter had been so desperate, the young man was so ill! 'I will write tonight. Can I promise her that she'll have ample time off to visit her son?'

'That you can! It still seems too good to be true.'

As Joey showed her out he looked more cheerful, and Mercy felt a sense of achievement. If everything went well she would have helped her brother and made a start in her new job, all in one fell swoop. She was not sure which pleased her the most.

On this occasion she was lucky. Mrs Baxter accepted both the post and the rail fare with gratitude, and was settled in at Church Street in an incredibly short time.

'Miss Beech informs me you have had a success already,' said Doctor von Herwath. 'You have found a place for Mrs Baxter. That is very commendable. How did you achieve such a miracle?'

'Sheer luck. I happened to know someone who needed some live-in help.' It was no more than the truth, but Mercy felt uncomfortable beneath the German's unwavering gaze.

'It is good that Mrs Baxter will be with her son. I am afraid they have very little time left together.'

'I had no idea!'

'Sadly it is a situation one must become accustomed to here,' said the doctor. 'We can only bring as much comfort as possible, and this you have achieved. You have done well.'

Mercy began to feel quite gratified at this praise, until he added, 'But, Mrs Lisburne, I hope you do not propose to finance all your successes personally. Splendid as it would be, I think Mr Lisburne might protest and take you away from us.'

Mercy was dismayed. 'I didn't... I only... How did you find out?'

'Simply by looking in the account book. If I may make a suggestion, when you write up your report for our trustees I think that against "Finances" you should simply put "Made private arrangements". It will save complications when the auditors come.'

Mercy laughed, relieved that he wasn't angry. 'That's a good idea,' she said. 'I shall certainly do that.'

'Good. You don't have to prove your worth to me, you know. I am convinced that you are capable of carrying out the tasks allotted to you.'

It took a moment for the meaning of his words to penetrate. 'You think I have deliberately organized things, so that I appear successful?' she demanded.

'It would be understandable.'

'I don't care whether it's understandable or not. That's not how it was! And if you have such a low opinion of me then there's no point in us trying to work together.'

She would have stalked out, but he caught her arm.

'I am sorry,' he said.

She stopped in sheer surprise. It was the first time she had heard him apologize for anything.

'I am sorry,' he repeated. 'To have thought such a thing was unworthy.'

She paused. 'Perhaps I was a little hasty. To be honest, in finding a place for Mrs Baxter, I did have an ulterior motive. I wanted to help someone close— Oh, if you must know, my young brother is in difficulties. He has no money and now his wife is ill. I know he would never have accepted any financial help from me, but I wanted to do something for him. Mrs Baxter gave me the ideal opportunity.'

She was not quite sure why she had confided the facts to him. With trepidation she waited for him to give some sharp response. But all he said was, 'Jimmy Baxter will have his mother near him now. That is my only concern. I feel I must warn you, though, that you may not find the other cases of hardship among the patients' families quite so easy to solve.'

'I've already discovered that,' she admitted with a rueful grin. 'Nevertheless, I'll keep trying.'

'Good,' he said. 'I expected nothing less.'

Mercy soon found that her new job took up far more time than the few hours she had originally allowed for it. It became a challenge for her to find a solution to each problem presented to her, to give some help to each patient in trouble. In a few short weeks her life changed completely. Instead of having long empty hours to fill she had not a spare minute. Working with Doctor von Herwath was a constant battle. He was difficult and impatient, wanting things done at impossibly short notice, getting angry when they were not, yet she could not help admiring him. The harder he worked, the harder he expected those under him to work. It was difficult keeping up with his boundless energy and his standards of perfection in everything. But Mercy, swept along by his energy, found herself striving all the harder because of his influence. His tall, lean figure, always active, always restless, became the focus of her day.

At first Peter did not seem to notice any difference in Mercy's daily routine. They scarcely saw each other, anyway. However, one day, when they chanced to lunch together he remarked, 'Have you quarrelled with Charlotte?'

'No, why?'

'I saw her the other day, and when I happened to mention you she was most off-hand.'

'May I know how I happened to enter the conversation?'

'I simply made some joke about the number of times you two play bridge together, and she replied, "Oh, Mercy has far more important games to play these days" in a decidedly sour way.'

'And what explanation did Charlotte give for her comment?' she asked.

'Naturally I didn't question her any further!' Peter seemed irritated at the idea. 'The fact that I don't know where my wife is for most of the time, nor what she is doing, is something I prefer to keep private!'

'I didn't think you were interested.' Mercy helped herself to vegetables.

'Of course I'm interested! You're my wife!'

'A small matter you tend to forget when it suits you.'

Peter dropped his knife and fork on to his plate with clatter.

'I've no wish to quarrel,' he said angrily. 'But when my mother tells me you are never at home, and when your friends complain they never see you, then I begin to wonder how you are spending your days. I have a right to know.'

'And do I have an equal right to know your movements?' asked Mercy sharply. Then she relented. 'Oh, finish your lunch! There's nothing worth quarrelling about, it's very simply explained. I'm doing some charity work. Charlotte's nose is out of joint because I was asked to help and she wasn't.'

'It must be very absorbing work, to take up so much of your time.' Slowly Peter resumed eating.

'It is, though it's exhausting at times.'

'And what do you do?'

'I help the patients at one of the clinics with their family problems – housing difficulties, jobs, children who are left with no one to care for them – all sorts of things.'

'And that is what you've been doing these few weeks?' Peter sounded relieved. 'Why did you never tell me?'

'It didn't seem important.'

'It seems very important to me, and very worthwhile.' He sounded quite pleased, almost proud.

'Oh, it is worthwhile. We could do with more money, of course, though Ivywood has a small fund to aid families. As Doctor von Herwath says, "How can people be expected to recover if they are worried about what is happening at home?"'

'Ivywood? In Warren Road? That's a TB clinic, isn't it?' Peter had stopped eating.

'Yes. It's extremely well run. You'd be most impressed—'

'You don't mean that you go there and actually mix with the patients?'

'Of course I do. Why, what's the matter?' For Peter was staring at her in appalled disbelief.

'The matter? You need to ask? For goodness' sake! Mercy, did it never occur to you that you could catch the disease?'

'You know I never catch anything—'

'And what about the boys? Have you given them a single thought? If you won't consider yourself, you should have at least considered them. You could bring it home to them!'

'I don't think that's very likely.'

'I am afraid I disagree. Goodness knows, there's enough controversy about the number of TB clinics in Torquay! There are always letters in the papers about the patients spitting in the streets and spreading the infection. For you to work among those people, then come home and go straight up to the nursery.' He paused. 'It won't do!'

'I am sure you're being too cautious.'

'And I'm sure I am not! The risk is too great!'

'I'll ask Doctor von Herwath's advice about it, and see what he recommends.'

'There is no need to bother him. I have a better solution.'

'Oh, and what is that?'

'You won't go near Ivywood again. You will write to this Doctor Whatever-his-name-is, and tell him you can no longer assist him.'

'You can't mean it?' She was horrified.

'I assure you that I do!'

'But the work means so much to me.'

'More than your children?'

'No, of course not!'

'Then you have no choice.' Suddenly his voice became more gentle. 'I'm sorry to have to ask you to give this up. I'm sure you were doing a lot of good work. But couldn't you do something similar for one of the other charities? Ivywood must find someone else. I'll tell you what, I'll send a hefty donation to the clinic. How would that be?'

'No!' Mercy protested, close to tears. 'I won't give it up.'

'Why are you being so unreasonable?' Peter cried. 'You are risking the health of our boys, and you know it!'

In her heart Mercy acknowledged that what he said made sense; she was smitten with guilt that she had not given full consideration to John and William; yet some stubborn core within her made her continue to protest.

'I intend to continue working at Ivywood,' she said with determination.

Peter faced her across the table, equally determined.

'Then you give me no option,' he said harshly. 'If you go back to that place I will have no alternative but to forbid you access to the boys.'

Mercy gasped.

'You couldn't! You wouldn't!'

'It would be with the greatest regret.' His voice was low, but his face remained grim. She knew she was defeated.

Later, alone in her room, Mercy wrote her letter of resignation to Doctor von Herwath. It was a difficult task. She was uncertain why she had resisted Peter's request so vehemently. It went deeper than no longer having a sense of purpose. At least, though, she would not have to cope with the dictatorial moods of Gunther von Herwath, of dealing with his impatience, of trying to keep up with his boundless energy. She thought of the days ahead when she would no longer see him – and knew at last why she felt so bereft.

Chapter Fourteen

'You say you can't come to Ivy wood any more? I don't understand. What has happened?' Gunther's voice sounded strange and distant over the phone.

Mercy's fingers tightened their grasp on the receiver.

'Nothing has happened. It's no longer convenient for me to work at your clinic, that's all,' she said.

For a moment only the crackling on the line broke the silence.

'Your husband has made some objection.' It was a statement, not a question.

Flustered by his directness she said in a high, artificial voice, 'Good gracious, why should he do that?'

'I can think of many reasons. I will come and talk to him.'

'No! You mustn't do that!' The idea alarmed Mercy.

'Then we must meet, you and I, and discuss this.'

'No!' she repeated. 'There is nothing to discuss. I cannot work at Ivywood, and that's all there is to it.'

'So, you would leave just when you are beginning to progress with your work?' There was another silence, then he said, 'I will be in the Princess Gardens in one hour.'

'No!' Mercy cried again. 'I can't… It's impossible…' But she was talking to the empty air. He had rung off.

Her resolve held for fifteen minutes… thirty… forty-five… then she could hold out no longer. She rang for Rogers to order the car, only to be told that Peter had it.

'Then get me a taxi! At once!' she cried, already running up the stairs to get her coat.

She was ready long before the taxi was announced, and she prowled about her sitting room restlessly. Suddenly the hands of the clock seemed to be moving at a prodigious rate. Gunther would be punctual, she knew he would, and she was going to be late! If she missed him now she would never see him again, for she knew she would not have the courage – or the foolishness – to contact him once more.

The taxi finally deposited her at the entrance to the Gardens, and she forced herself to stroll casually along between the lawns and flower-beds. As she walked, the folly of what she was doing struck her, but it was too late to go back. Perhaps she would not see him after all? Maybe she was too late, and had missed him? The brisk purposeful stride behind her was unmistakable. She did not turn round. He drew level with her without saying a word, and for a while they continued in silence.

'Why must you leave us?' Gunther demanded abruptly.

'Because of the risk to my children's health. I hadn't considered it fully.'

'Not until your husband pointed it out!' Again it was a statement, not a question. There was another silence. 'Perhaps he is right,' Gunther said at last. 'If you were my wife I would use any excuse to keep you away from other men.'

'Peter didn't mean…' she began, turning to look at him for the first time. Then she faltered, thrown by the sentiment of his words and the bleak expression in his eyes. Hurriedly she turned away again, her pace quickening unconsciously.

'You won't get away from me so easily,' he said, lengthening his stride to keep up with her.

'I don't want to get away from you,' Mercy replied.

Too late, she realized what she had said, but she knew she did not wish to retract one word.

'Good,' said Gunther.

They walked along, not looking at each other, not touching. Their brief exchange had somehow been a declaration of love, and they both knew it. One meeting, a few commonplace words, and their lives had changed.

Along the pier seemed the natural route to take, away from other people. Finally they reached the end, and together they leaned over the railings. Alone, except for a single angler, they gazed down to watch the surge of the clear green water.

'You could defy your husband and continue to come to Ivywood,' said Gunther.

'Oh no!' Mercy's reply was swift and definite.

'You are afraid of him?'

'Of course not!'

'Yet he is forcing you to stay away. Don't deny it, I know it is so. What weapon is he using? It must be something very important to you. Your children? Your husband has threatened to part you from your sons! He is inhuman!' His accent was more pronounced than usual, his consonants more clipped, by the force of his emotion.

'No, he's not,' protested Mercy. 'Normally he's a very gentle, kindly man, but he does love the boys dearly, and his fears for their health are genuine. He isn't using them as an excuse to torment me, I am sure of that.'

'You spring very quickly to his defence.'

'I feel I have to be fair. Please, I would sooner we did not discuss my husband.'

'Very well. I am only too happy to oblige. I must mention him one more time. Does he forbid you working for Ivywood or is it simply your presence in the clinic to which he objects?'

Mercy considered carefully. 'I think it is just my presence in the clinic, and my contact with the patients,' she said.

'Good, then that is one point settled. Miss Beech can send you the case histories by post, and you can work at home. If you have any problems then you can telephone.'

'You make it sound so easy.'

'It is. Compared to our other difficulty it is simplicity itself.'

'What other difficulty?'

'You know perfectly well. How are we to go on seeing each other?'

'We mustn't— We can't!' she began to protest, but her words faded.

'You say "mustn't" and "can't", yet you know the words are nonsense. How can we exist and not see each other any more?'

'I don't know. I only know that we must never meet like this again.'

'You are suggesting that we must part for ever? Such a thing is impossible.'

'Please,' she begged. 'Gunther, please don't make things even more difficult. Let us say our goodbyes and have done.'

'You admit that things are difficult, you call me by my Christian name for the first time, yet you insist that we say goodbye? What sort of a being are you? No, don't answer. I know what sort you are – you are the most beautiful woman I have ever known, the most gentle, the most caring—'

'No! Please stop,' she begged, turning to him and placing a gloved finger gently against his lips.

'I will stop,' he said, taking her hand and holding it in his. 'I will stop, so that you must be the one to say goodbye, and you must be the one to leave, never once looking back at me. You must be the one, because I know that I can't.'

She wanted to go. It was the prudent thing to do, she knew. Yet somehow she could not persuade her lips to shape the words, nor command her feet to take the first steps away from him.

'You cannot do it either, because it is not possible,' he said, quietly releasing his hold. 'So we will leave this place together, and we will meet again tomorrow.'

She did not object. Side by side they walked back along the pier, their feet echoing in unison on the weather-worn planking. They did not touch. There was no need. The unspoken force between them said it all.

'I must get back to the clinic now,' said Gunther, when they reached the road. 'Shall I get you a taxi?'

'No, thank you. I think I would like to walk.' She needed time to sort out her emotions before she went back to the Villa Dorata.

'As you wish. And we will meet here tomorrow at the same time.'

He took her hand, and bowing over it, he kissed it. They turned away from each other, beginning to walk in opposite directions.

'Mrs Lisburne!' Gunther's voice calling after her made her spin round. 'Don't forget about the case histories. Miss Beech will put them in the post this afternoon for you. You can begin work on them tomorrow.'

He was so much the brisk domineering Doctor von Herwath again that Mercy laughed out loud.

'I won't forget,' she said.

For the rest of the day she could not settle to anything, nor could she sleep that night. She knew she was on the brink of something momentous, and the future had become suddenly hazy, uncertain and – yes, she had to admit it – exciting.

Next morning, the fat Manila envelope looked incongruous among the invitations and trivial letters that lay in her place at breakfast.

'A package that size has got to be important,' Peter commented. 'Not going into business, are you?'

Mercy drew in her breath carefully.

'They are case histories from Ivywood,' she said.

Peter's head shot up, and he glared accusingly at her over the top of his newspaper.

'Don't worry, I haven't been near the clinic,' she assured him. 'Doctor von Herwath is going to let me work from home. Miss Beech, the clinic secretary, will send me the details by post.'

'Oh!' Peter sounded somewhat mollified. 'Surely you'll need to speak to the patients at some time or another, won't you?'

'If I do then I will use the telephone.'

'That's all right, then, just so long as you keep away from the clinic and its inhabitants.' Peter disappeared once more behind his newspaper.

'You have no objection, then?' she asked.

'To what? To you doing a bit of charity work from home? No, certainly not, if it keeps you amused. Good lord, is that the time? I've a Regatta committee meeting at the Yacht Club in half an hour. If you will excuse me?'

He rose and, dropping the newspaper on to the table, left the room, calling for Rogers as he went.

Mercy hoped her face did not betray how much she was relieved. If Peter had objected to her continuing to work for Ivywood she did not know what she would have done, but asking him was a risk she had had to take. He would have been far more likely to be difficult if he had found out about it by accident.

Collecting her post, she went upstairs to her sitting room. She meant to deal with her correspondence at once, as she usually did, but somehow the pen refused to behave itself, and the letters became a blur on the page. The image of Gunther's face kept on getting between her and what she wanted to write. She knew so few details about him, other than that she loved him. She loved the abrupt, formal way he spoke. She loved his tall figure, so charged with energy. She loved his humanity, his sense of purpose. She loved Gunther!

Next day he was waiting for her in the Princess Gardens. He was sitting on a seat, his long legs stretched out before him. The sight of him made her want to run to him, yet at the same time she felt consumed with an unexpected embarrassment.

'Your cheeks are pink,' he said, rising to greet her. 'You are blushing.'

'No...' she protested. 'It's just that I have never done anything like this before.'

'You met me yesterday.'

'Yesterday was different.'

'Yes, it was.' He gazed into her eyes, making her long to know his thoughts. 'Yesterday we had a rendezvous, today we have an assignation. That is it, is it not?'

She nodded.

'And you are not comfortable about it?'

'I don't think I am.'

'I am glad!' he declared forcefully.

'You are? Why?' she asked in surprise.

'Because it proves you are not accustomed to having affairs.'

She was shocked into silence. It sounded so blunt and harsh when put in such a way.

'Is that what I am doing?' she asked quietly.

'It is what you are on the brink of doing. Only you know if you intend to continue.'

The responsibility he had just thrust at her was suddenly so over-whelming she did not know how to reply.

'You are involved too,' she said at last. 'The decision is not mine alone.'

'I reached my decision when I saw you for the first time, dressed in that ridiculous butterfly costume and looking so enchanting. I fell in love with you immediately.'

'You did no such thing!' she protested, half laughing, half pleased. 'You thought I was incredibly stupid. And you were abominably rude.'

'Of course I was. I do not usually fall in love so suddenly. I had to conceal my emotions the best way I could, so I was discourteous to you. I am very good at that.'

'Yes, you are,' she agreed, still laughing.

'And you are beautiful.'

'Oh!' She drew in her breath sharply. Colour rose to her cheeks again, and she was aware of her heart pounding.

'You are annoyed that I admit to loving you? If so you must tell me now, and I will walk away for ever.' He spoke hesitantly. She had never expected to hear such hope or uncertainty in his self-assured voice.

'No,' she said. Then more forcibly, 'No, I am not annoyed. I am glad!'

'Good!' He smiled at her. 'If only you knew how much I want to kiss you. But not here, in this public place.'

While they had been talking they had been walking, not heeding where their feet led them. Mercy was a little surprised to find that they were strolling along the beach. How or when they had left the gardens she did not know. It was idyllic, with the sea rushing up the rose-pink sand in little waves. Idyllic, but very public. She wanted to feel his arms about her and to have his lips on hers with an urgency that made her blush; yet, at the same time something held her back.

Gunther observed her carefully.

'I think that perhaps you are relieved we are not completely alone,' he said. 'And I cannot make love to you.'

'I'm not!' she protested in confusion. 'Well, perhaps a little… Oh, I don't know!'

'It is good that you are reluctant. I have noticed so many society ladies who throw themselves into love affairs for no better reason than it is fashionable or that they are bored. I am glad you are not like them.'

'No, I am not,' she said, suddenly really sure of her motives for the first time. 'I am not a society lady, though I admit that I was bored. Falling in love was the last thing I intended. I didn't mean to do it, it just happened, and I am still bewildered. You must forgive me if at times I don't make sense.'

'I would forgive you anything,' he said softly, 'if only you agree to see me as often as possible. It will not be easy. You know how little free time I get, and you, too, have your family obligations, but we will take what few moments we can and spend them together. Do you promise?'

Mercy nodded. 'I promise,' she said.

It was only when she returned to the Villa Dorata that she was tormented by guilt. She was still married to Peter, what business had she loving another man? But, troubled as she was, she knew she could not keep away from Gunther.

As she expected their meetings were erratic. A brief phone call or an enigmatic scribbled message among the day's case notes were usually the only warning she had. When they were together they talked and laughed and argued. His vigour and zeal fascinated her. When she was with him she felt alive, her mind buzzing with ideas.

It was unrealistic to expect a man as vibrant with energy as Gunther to be content with chaste walks on the pier or along Abbey Sands.

Now, whenever possible, their stolen meetings involved driving into the country, far away from Torquay, where they could be alone. Mercy was well aware of the mounting passion in their relationship. She was aware of it in Gunther, and she felt it herself, a growing urge to make love to him fully that was becoming increasingly difficult to resist. Yet resist it she did, to his bewilderment.

'You say you love me. That is so, is it not?' he demanded.

'Yes, you know it is.'

'Then why will you not let me love you properly? You must know how desperate I am for you. Is it that you find that side of loving distasteful?'

'No,' she said softly. 'Far from it.'

'Just what I suspected. I could not imagine you being frigid. You were made for love, my darling, I have known it from the beginning.'

They had driven to one of their favourite spots, the thick trees of the Exeter Forest surrounding them, while below, in the distance there was the blue of Lyme Bay. Alone and secluded, it would have been all too easy to be overwhelmed by emotion, especially when Gunther was kissing her with such fervour. She felt her body begin to melt towards his, her own longing begin to take control. Then she forced herself to move away slightly. Gunther sighed and sat up.

'What is it?' he asked. 'What are you afraid of?'

'I don't know, and that's the truth,' she answered, close to tears. 'I want you, you know that… but somehow I can't…'

Suddenly he smiled down at her, stroking her cheek with one finger. 'I think I know the problem. I have fallen in love with a very moral lady. The world is full of wives who think nothing of being unfaithful to their husbands, yet I have to love one who has a conscience.'

'It's totally illogical, I know,' she admitted, 'when I have already confessed to loving you. But I don't know what to do about it, do you?'

Unexpectedly he began to laugh.

'What can I do except curb my passion and wait?' he grinned. He planted a hearty kiss on her brow. 'There! Does that not show commendable restraint?'

They rose and began packing the picnic things into the car.

'Gunther,' said Mercy contritely, as he held open the door for her. 'I am sorry.'

He gave a wry smile and, taking her hand in his, held it for a moment against his cheek.

'So am I,' he said. 'But I realize that it is easy for me; I am free, while you have so many difficulties to overcome. Don't worry, I will wait for you, no matter how long it takes. I would sooner that than have you come to me with doubts and misgivings in your heart. When we make love it must be because it is what both of us want more than anything else in the world.'

Mercy was touched and a little surprised. Knowing his directness and his impatience she had not expected him to be so understanding. For a fleeting moment she allowed herself to imagine what it would be like to be with Gunther always, free from all other restraints and responsibilities. It was a heady vision, but completely impossible.

'My misgivings have nothing to do with you – they are all to do with my marriage. You must believe that!' she declared in an urgent need to reassure him.

'I do,' he replied. 'Otherwise how could I go on being so incredibly patient?' He took his watch from his waistcoat pocket. 'And now I must get you back home before your husband starts complaining.'

'It doesn't matter if I'm late, Peter is away on a sailing trip. Even if he had been home I don't suppose he would have noticed whether I was late or not. He's too involved with yachting and the Regatta and… and things of that sort,' she amended. She had been going to say 'other women' but latent pride and loyalty to Peter prevented her. He had resumed his association with Tilly Hewson, and in spite of all else the knowledge still stung her.

Gunther concentrated upon negotiating the narrow forest track for a while.

'So your lives are quite separate, yours and your husband's?' he said eventually.

'Yes.'

'Do you think he would mind? I mean, would he be difficult about us?'

Mercy thought carefully. Peter should not mind. He had no right to be difficult, not after his behaviour, yet she was uncertain. Being in this situation was new to her, she was not sure of the rules. Once she would have confidently predicted Peter's reaction to anything, but not now. The severity of his retaliation when he learned that she was working at Ivywood had shaken her. It was possible that he could be equally severe again.

'I don't know,' she admitted. 'I think he might.'

Gunther stretched out and covered her hand with his.

'Now it is my turn to be sorry,' he said.

'What for?'

'For bringing you so many problems. Consider how simple and uncomplicated your life would have been if you had never met me.'

'Don't say such a thing!' she cried. 'Don't even think it! Without you my life would be empty and meaningless and— What's so funny?' she demanded, for he was chuckling openly.

'Because you are saying exactly what I hoped you would say. I should not have spoiled it by laughing, I should have let you go on and on and... Oh, you look so delightful I shall have to kiss you. I can't help myself.'

Eagerly she held up her face in an automatic response, wanting to feel his mouth on hers once again. His lips were warm and sweet, and gave promise of so much that could be hers if only...

A sudden lurch of the car brought them both back to reality, as, still laughing, Gunther struggled to bring the car back under control.

'Now I must concentrate upon my driving,' he declared primly, 'otherwise I will not return you home in one piece, never mind on time, and that would not be a good thing at all.'

—

The problem of how she could reconcile loving Gunther whilst still being married to Peter caused Mercy much anguish. Her marriage was over. She could not help feeling sad that something which had begun with such happiness and optimism should end so abysmally. She feared she had contributed to its failure. She should never have married Peter, but it was too late now. There seemed no solution – separation or divorce were too horrendous to contemplate. She could think of no way out. All she could do was to carry on as normally as possible.

Mercy had not seen Charlotte for some weeks. It was at a bazaar that she encountered her again. As soon as she entered the crypt of Torre Abbey, where the bazaar was to be held, she saw a tall, unmistakably elegant figure moving among the stalls organizing everything with an unhesitating authority.

'Hello, Charlotte,' she said. 'I've come to be of assistance, if I may.'

Charlotte turned, and raised an aristocratic eyebrow.

'Why, it's Mercy Lisburne isn't it?' she said.

'Don't play games! You recognized me immediately,' Mercy replied, suppressing a sudden urge to grin. Charlotte at her most haughty could be faintly ridiculous.

'I wonder you managed to find time to come,' said Charlotte, clearly put off her stroke by Mercy's refusal to be quashed. 'I thought you were constantly busy at Ivywood these days.'

'Then it is high time you renewed your sources of information. I no longer work at the clinic. In fact, I haven't been there in weeks,' said Mercy.

'Oh, is that so?' Charlotte's frosty manner thawed a fraction. She was not prepared to forgive Mercy for ousting her, though. 'I don't think there is anything for you to do, unless you want to be in charge of the ladies' cloakroom,' she said.

'No thank you,' said Mercy politely but firmly.

Charlotte glared at her irritably, but for once a shortage of helpers was jeopardizing her formidable reputation for organizing events. She decided she could cut Mercy down to size on some other occasion. 'You can do the white elephant stall,' she said grudgingly.

With a barely concealed smile Mercy went to her post.

Lilian Manning came hurrying by, carrying a tray of cakes. 'Mercy!' she exclaimed with genuine pleasure. 'How lovely to see you again. Look! I've hardly got a scar!' She extended her hand, flexing her fingers for Mercy to examine.

'Watch out,' warned Mercy. 'Charlotte will never forgive you if you drop those cakes.'

'Whoops! You're right,' giggled Lilian, adjusting the tray, which had slipped to a precarious angle. 'We'll meet and have a nice gossip later.'

She hurried off across the room, and as Mercy's eyes followed her she saw Zena Pritchard busily setting out crocheted mats and embroidered table-runners on the handiwork stall. Charles Wentworth was helping her, as elegant and attentive as ever.

How do they manage it? Mercy wondered. She's married, and they've been having an affair for years, yet no one seems to object, least of all Zena's husband! What were the rules they played by? On the surface did everything have to seem normal and respectable? It did not matter what one did so long as one was discreet. But, after all, discretion was the watchword. She and Gunther had only to be discreet, then her husband could have no objection to their liaison. Why should he? It was not as though he had any feeling left for her. She greeted the incoming surge of customers with considerable optimism. At last she could see some shape to the future.

Mercy happened to be on her way out next day when Peter arrived home. He leapt from the taxi and bounded up the steps.

'I've just heard the most marvellous piece of news,' he said, after he had greeted her.

'You have?'

'Yes. I stopped off at the Yacht Club on my way home to see if there were any messages left for me. You'll never guess what! The *Shamrock III* is coming here for her sea trials in preparation for her America's Cup challenge! Oh, we're going to see some magnificent yachting this summer! Good old Tommy Lipton, he's going to give us all a treat!'

Mercy had a sudden wistful memory of a Regatta when the best and most beautiful yachts in the country had lain at anchor off Torquay, and of a youthful Joey being mad with excitement to see them. It seemed a long time ago. Sir Thomas Lipton had been in town then, along with one of his other splendid yachts. Had that been *Shamrock I* or *Shamrock* II? She could not remember. All she could recall was how magical and unreal the beings had seemed, who lived their lives aboard those sleek glittering craft. How disillusioned she was now. It made her feel sad. 'Sir Thomas is coming too?' she asked.

'Indeed he is, which is why I'm in a bit of a hurry. There's been an extraordinary committee meeting called at the club for this afternoon to organize a proper welcome for him. I'll have to be quick if I'm to make it.'

Her brief mood of nostalgia evaporated abruptly, along with her vague feeling of guilt at leaving the house the moment her husband was coming home. Clearly he could not get away fast enough to attend his wretched meeting!

'If you will excuse me, I must go now,' she said.

'Go? You are on your way out, aren't you? Yes, go by all means!'

She stepped into the waiting car without a backward glance.

Her rendezvous with Gunther was brief and unexpected. Ten minutes earlier a hasty telephone call had summoned her.

'Only for a few minutes,' he had pleaded. 'There's something I must discuss with you. Say you'll meet me at the Rock Walk!'

Her curiosity had been roused, along with her need to see him and be near him again. Now she had Jenkins drop her by the Pavilion, and she walked the rest. As she slowly climbed the steeply sloping terraces of the Walk she was glad of that blazing sunshine, though it made her climb somewhat uncomfortable. At least the sunlight and the heat drove away any ghosts of that long-ago Regatta that might still lurk among the palms and the ilex bushes.

When she was halfway up she encountered Gunther coming down, from the direction of Ivywood.

'Why, Mrs Lisburne, what an unexpected pleasure,' he said, in tones of well-modulated surprise.

'Doctor von Herwath, how nice to see you,' she replied.

There was no one close enough to overhear their little, for which she was grateful. Would anyone have been taken in by their exchange of pleasantries? She doubted it.

'What do you wish to discuss with me so urgently?' she asked, in a quieter, more intimate voice.

'The fact that you look adorable and I love you.'

She laughed.

'Was that so urgent?' she asked softly.

'Yes, to me.' He smiled at her. 'Though I confess I do have something else I want to say. I have to go to a medical conference in Edinburgh at the end of June. Come with me!'

The suddenness of his suggestion took her breath away.

'I couldn't possibly...'

'Why not? It will only be for a few days. Don't you want to be with me?'

'How can you ask that? You know I do! But you know the difficulties!'

'Difficulties are there to be overcome, and I am sure we could manage. We would be discreet, naturally. We would not even travel together. I could go up on the Saturday and you could follow the day after. I won't be totally occupied with lectures, and I am sure you could find something to keep yourself entertained for a few hours. I hear the shops in Edinburgh are excellent.'

'I dare say they are. It's still impossible.'

'Come!' he insisted. 'I've been patient for so long, and now we have our chance. You must come! You must!'

A pulse of excitement was beginning to throb inside her, growing to a tide of recklessness. Why shouldn't she snatch a little happiness? And anyway, they would be extremely discreet.

'If you put it like that I can hardly refuse, can I?' she said breathlessly.

He gave a great sigh of relief.

'Now I am happy,' he said, his voice not quite steady. 'We will be together. It is hard to believe.'

'Yes, it is, isn't it?' She was finding it difficult to credit what she had done.

'You won't change your mind?' Gunther spoke with anxiety.

'No, I won't,' she assured him. 'I can't imagine anything more wonderful than spending those days alone with you.'

He gave another sigh, this time of regret.

'What's the matter?' she asked.

'Time is the matter,' he replied. 'I must return to the clinic. I've got to leave you, and I cannot even kiss you goodbye.'

'Save it,' Mercy said. 'Save all your kisses and all your soft words and all your love, so that I can enjoy them properly when I'm with you in Edinburgh.'

'Edinburgh is beginning to sound remarkably like heaven,' Gunther said smiling.

They stood facing one another, knowing they had to part, but each reluctant to make the first move. Then from the path below came the sound of voices and the crunch of feet on gravel. People were coming, shattering their brief idyll. Coolly, and formally they took their leave of one another and set off in opposite directions.

Mercy's emotions were in a ferment as she considered what she had promised, but she did not regret her decision. The more she thought about it the more she was glad she had agreed to go to Edinburgh with Gunther. Glad, and incredibly happy! As she grew closer to the Villa Dorata she feared her happiness must show on her face. But although Peter was at home when she returned he did not seem to notice anything amiss.

'Did your meeting go well?' she asked politely.

'Splendidly, thank you. We've decided to give a grand dinner for Sir Thomas. He's putting the town in an absolute forefront of international yachting by bringing the *Shamrock* here, it's only right that we should honour him. A dinner seems the most appropriate gesture. Where, though? That is the problem!' Peter went on talking about the plans for the dinner, about which yachts were to be invited to match their speed against the *Shamrock*, about how the harbour berths would need to be reorganized, but Mercy scarcely heard a word. She was far too absorbed by her own plans.

Time passed slowly. Her trip to Edinburgh glowed on the horizon like a golden sun, beautiful, desirable, and seemingly just as inaccessible. June crept by at such a snail's pace that she began to fear the magic date when she was to travel to Scotland, the twenty-ninth, would never arrive.

She told Peter she would be going away for a few days, and he made no objection, though he was so involved with plans to welcome the *Shamrock* she wondered if he had heard her. It came as a bolt from the blue, therefore, when, the day before she was due to depart he remarked to her, 'I hope you've bought a new dress for the occasion.'

For a second she was alarmed, thinking he had discovered about her trip to Edinburgh.

'What occasion?' she asked, hoping her voice sounded calm.

'The dinner, of course.'

'I'm sorry. What dinner?'

Peter looked at her askance.

'Honestly, I've been convinced recently that you've not been listening to anything I said, and now you've proved it,' he complained. 'I'm referring to *the* dinner, the one we're giving to honour Sir Thomas Lipton.'

'Oh, is it soon?'

'Really, this is too much!' he protested. 'It's the day tomorrow, so I certainly hope you have got something suitable to wear. We will be sitting at the top table.'

Now it was Mercy's turn to look bemused.

'You're talking as though I'm going,' she said.

'Of course you're going. For heaven's sake, I've talked of little else for three weeks, so don't pretend to be surprised!'

'But I can't come. I'm going away.'

'Then you must cancel your trip.'

'That's not possible.'

'Why not? What is it? Visiting friends, or something to do with this charity work of yours? If it's so important you can leave on Tuesday, but on Monday you will attend the dinner with me.'

'I can't! I'm going away tomorrow, I tell you!' How could she say that Tuesday was too late? That Tuesday would give her no time with Gunther?

'And I tell you you're not! I refuse to go on my own. Think how it would look!'

'I can't!' Mercy could hear her voice rising.

'Can't or won't? Which is it?' His voice was suddenly very low and furious. 'Goodness knows, things between us are pretty grim, and I'm aware I must take my share of the blame! But you must admit I ask very little of you. I make no attempt to curb your allowance. I make no objections to your friends. I don't even inquire how you spend your time when you are not with me. However, on this occasion I must insist. I will not be shamed in front of all of Torquay by having to attend an important dinner by myself, while my wife goes gallivanting about to goodness knows where! Whatever you think of me in the privacy of our home, I would be grateful if on this occasion you would play the devoted wife in public.'

'And what will you do if I refuse?' she demanded.

He looked at her, a strange expression she could not fathom in his eyes.

'I have no intention of threatening you,' he said. 'It is my express wish that you attend the dinner with me on Monday. That should be sufficient.'

If Peter had put pressure on her or attempted to bully her she would have defied him, but he had not. Instead he had made a reasonable request. She knew he had a point, it would cause comment if he attended the dinner without her. If she let him down now she would be flouting all the rules by which his society existed, the very rules she was relying on to permit her to love Gunther and yet remain the respectable Mrs Lisburne. It was a double standard, there was no denying it, but a double standard she knew she had to maintain.

'I have something suitable to wear,' she said in a dull voice. 'Coral-coloured lace. It's new. I've not worn it yet.'

She had been intending to wear it in Edinburgh, for Gunther.

'That sounds very pretty. I am sure you will look delightful,' said Peter courteously.

She was glad when Peter went out without making any further comment. She did not want him to see her weeping.

She would have to send a telegram because Gunther had already left for Scotland. It was difficult to arrange the meagre words in a way which would hurt him as little as possible. Even so, the scant message seemed terribly spare and inadequate.

When the day of the dinner party dawned, it brought with it an oppressive feeling of foreboding. Mercy thought this was due entirely to her own misery, but the dark mood seemed to have affected Peter too. He, was still reading the newspaper as Mercy came downstairs, and she heard him remark, 'Things seem to have taken a very nasty turn, Rogers. Very nasty indeed.'

'Indeed they have, sir,' replied the butler.

'What's wrong?' asked Mercy.

'A spot of bother on the Continent,' answered Peter. 'It's far enough away at present. Let's hope it doesn't come any closer!' He rose from the table. 'If you'll excuse me deserting you the moment you arrive. I have to get down to the Yacht Club as soon as possible.'

'Yes, of course.' She helped herself to kidneys and bacon, before picking up his discarded paper.

'Archduke Ferdinand of Austria assassinated in Sarajevo', read the headlines.

She had only a vague notion who Archduke Ferdinand was, other than that he was related to the Austrian Emperor. Too concerned with her own unhappiness to bother about happenings in a place she could not even pronounce, let alone guess where it was, she threw the newspaper on one side. Her breakfast suddenly looked less than interesting. She pushed it away and signalled Rogers to bring the coffee-pot instead.

In a town as devoted to yachting as Torquay a dinner to welcome the owner of the famous *Shamrock* dynasty was bound to be the social event of the year. Yet even the benign and genial presence of the guest of honour, Sir Thomas Lipton – friend of kings, grocer extraordinary, and one of the premier yachtsmen in the land – failed to dispel the general mood of apprehension. Phrases such as 'Europe's a powder keg' and 'What's the Hun up to now, do you imagine?' kept drifting across the dinner table.

Mercy's already low spirits were not helped by the atmosphere of unease.

However, she chatted amiably, smiled until her face felt it must crack with the effort, and laughed at the appropriate moments, determined Peter should not find anything to criticize in her conduct. By the time the dinner party finally came to an end and they returned home she was exhausted.

'A successful evening, didn't you think?' remarked Peter, as they climbed the stairs together.

'Very!' she agreed, 'How do you rate Sir Thomas's chances of winning the America's Cup this time?'

'Excellent I would say, if the international situation doesn't spoil things.'

'You think there is going to be real trouble? Just because the Austrian archduke was assassinated in some outlandish place? Everyone says it was the work of a fanatic.'

'So it was, and all this fuss will soon die down again, you'll see. Sir Tommy'll get his crack at the America's Cup.' He sounded very hearty, as if to compensate for his burst of pessimism.

'That's all right then. I'll say good night now.' She began to move towards her bedroom.

'Mercy!' The sudden urgency in Peter's voice made her swing round.

'What is it?' she asked, wearily stifling a yawn.

'Oh nothing. Just "Good night".' He hurried off towards his own room, leaving Mercy wondering what he had really been going to say.

She was dreading the return of Gunther, yet looking forward to it at the same time. It felt like years since she had last been with him and felt his arms about her, she could not wait to be with him once more. All the same, she knew he would be hurt and angry because she had not gone to Edinburgh. She was right. When they met again, out in the country beyond the town, his face was white with suppressed pain and fury.

'Why?' he demanded. 'Why did you not come? Was one of your children ill? Was it a matter of life and death?'

'No,' she admitted. 'I had to attend a dinner with Peter.'

'A dinner! You disappoint me! You break my heart, and all for a dinner?' He could scarcely believe it. 'I thought you cared for me. How wrong I was!'

'No you weren't!' she cried. 'Of course I love you! You must never doubt that!'

Gunther was insistent. 'You gave in to him, with no thought of me!'

'It wasn't like that!'

'How? Did your husband threaten you?'

'Certainly not. It's not in his nature to be brutal.'

'He threatened you once before, to make you leave Ivywood.'

'That was only because he was afraid for the boys. He would never have been so severe on his own account.'

'How quickly you leap to his defence! If he is so reasonable then why did you give in? Why did you not come to me? I would not have let anything or anyone come between us in the same circumstances.'

'It's easy for you to say. You're free! Please try to understand. This dinner was so important to him, and he could not have attended it alone. He asks very little of me, as long as we maintain the illusion that ours is a united family. Though there must be many marriages like ours, I doubt if many husbands are as truly tolerant as Peter. He could make things very much more difficult for us. Have you ever considered that? He never inquires where I've been or who with. He didn't even insist I attend the dinner with him – he asked. That was why I agreed in the end, although I was desperately disappointed.' She was surprised by her heated defence of Peter. Was it her troubled conscience asserting itself or old loyalties dying hard? She said quietly, 'We've missed being in Edinburgh, but there will be other opportunities in other places.'

'Will there? I doubt it.' Gunther sounded very pessimistic. 'Though I suppose you are right. It wouldn't do for you to provoke your husband into being more dictatorial.'

He had not understood her motives, but Mercy did not correct him. She was more concerned by an underlying note of anxiety in his voice, one she had never noticed before.

'Is something else wrong?' she asked gently.

'You can ask that? Have you not read the newspapers?' He leaned disconsolately against a farm gate and gazed at the rolling green hills beyond. 'You must realize that there is likely to be a war in Europe.'

'So people say. It won't concern us, will it?'

'I am afraid that Germany is heavily involved, which does concern me. And though Britain is an island, she too has allies on the Continent. If they get embroiled so will she.'

'Are you saying that our countries could be at war?'

'Yes.'

She stared at him, shocked by his blunt answer. For the first time she was beginning to appreciate the dark clouds that had been gathering.

'You – you needn't be involved, not you personally. You are a doctor, not a soldier,' she said hurriedly. 'You could stay here. You would be safe!'

The twin prospects of war and losing Gunther were almost too much for her.

'There are so many complications.' Suddenly he reached out and grasped her in his arms. He said in a low emotional voice, 'I can't bear the thought of losing you. I love you, and I want you with me always. Leave Peter. You don't love him, you love me. He has no feelings for you. How can you bear to be locked in a marriage that is all sham and deceit? Have the courage to be honest. Come away with me!'

'Where could we go?' she gasped.

'I have been offered a position in America, in Baltimore – someone I met in Edinburgh. We could start new lives there, lives where we could be together.' Mercy was shaken by the enormity of the suggestion, even though, secretly, it was something she had dreamed about. 'Peter would never agree to a divorce!' she exclaimed.

'Then we will simply live together.'

'And the children! What would happen about my children?'

'Perhaps your husband would let them come with us. You are always saying what a reasonable fellow he is.'

'No!' cried Mercy. 'He would never allow it.'

'Perhaps not at first, but in time… I know it is a hard decision, but you do want to be with me, don't you?'

'Oh yes!'

'Then promise me you will think about it. I ask nothing more at this moment. Only that you will consider coming to America with me. I would prefer it to be as my wife, but if not, then as my love and my life.'

'I'll think about it.' She found she was shaking, and he pulled her closer so that she rested her head against his chest. 'It sounds so wonderful. If only there weren't such difficulties… I'll think about it, I promise!'

In the following days she thought of little else. The decision tormented her night and day. But for John and William it would have been easy, she would have gone with Gunther at once… Or would she? Her marriage vows still tied her to Peter, the ghosts of what had once existed between them. The knots were tied far tighter than she had realized. Yet she loved Gunther!

The tumult in Mercy's head was not helped by the news in the papers. Each day it grew increasingly grim. Mercy read about it avidly now, trying to grasp what was happening, but all she could really understand was that the chaos that now reigned in Europe was increasing her dilemma.

'Can you not give me a decision yet?' Gunther asked. 'I have been patient. If we are going I feel we should leave soon, swiftly and with no regrets.'

How could she have no regrets? Mercy felt as though she were being torn into little pieces. That night, she tossed and turned in her bed, too tormented to sleep. Finally she rose and went into the night nursery. In the glow of the night-light she looked down on John, slumbering so peacefully in his small bed, a tattered woolly rabbit clutched in his hand. Then she turned to William in his cot. Restless as ever, he had kicked off his covers, and gently she replaced them. Then she knew there had never been any dilemma, she had only thought there was. She could never leave her children, not even for Gunther.

A movement behind her made her start, until she realized it was Peter standing there beside her.

'Two minds with but a single thought,' he whispered.

'I just came to see if they were all right,' she whispered back.

Peter seemed to think this perfectly reasonable, even though the boys' nanny was only in the next room.

'Grand little chaps, aren't they?' he said. Mercy nodded, unable to speak. Together they left the nursery, closing the door quietly behind them.

'Grand little chaps,' repeated Peter, 'I hope all this war nonsense comes to nothing, for their sakes.'

Again she could only nod.

'I'm afraid it will come, though. The war, I mean,' he went on. 'Mercy, I must tell you… I've been trying to tell you all day… If war comes – or maybe that should be when war comes – I've decided to join the Army. In fact, I've as good as signed up already.'

'Peter!' She stared at him aghast.

'I felt I had to.' He gave an apologetic grin. 'Just thought I'd let you know. It needn't affect you. Mother can cope with the boys, she's not nearly as frail as she pretends. You go ahead with your own plans.'

Mercy felt the colour drain from her face. He knew! He knew about her and Gunther, and about the terrible decision that had been tearing her apart. She looked into his eyes, expecting to see accusation. There was none. Instead he looked sad. She drew in her breath sharply.

'There's no need to trouble your mother,' she said, keeping her voice carefully under control. 'I'll be here to look after the boys. Yes, and her too, if need be.'

'Good,' said Peter. 'I wasn't sure.'

He leaned forward and kissed her on the cheek, the first intimate gesture he had offered her in months.

'Good,' he said again.

They stood staring at one another, not certain what to do or what to say. Then finally they went their separate ways to their own rooms.

Mercy telephoned Gunther next morning to give her decision; she did not feel strong enough to tell him face to face.

'It is as I expected,' he said, and he sounded unhappy.

'I'm sorry.'

'Yes, so am I.'

'What— what will you do now? Go to America?'

'No, I will go back to Germany. There is a special train on Saturday for the German hotel workers in the area. I will be on that.'

'Do— do you want me to come and see you off?' The tears were running down her face.

'No, I think not. I am not sure I could bear it. We will say our goodbyes now, like this. You know I will always remember you… Goodbye, my love…'

Mercy tried to reply, but her sobs choked out the words. At last she heard a click as he hung up. Gunther had gone!

Chapter Fifteen

War was declared on the fourth of August. On a day in high summer Britain and Germany became deadly enemies.

For Mercy it had the unreal horror of a nightmare. Appalled, she listened to people referring to 'dirty Huns', and the threats, half jocular, half serious, of what our troops were going to do to them once they met up. Gunther was a Hun! A short time ago he had been respected and admired. Now, because of some incomprehensible international tangle he was the object of hatred and scorn. To Mercy the pain of her divided loyalties was almost unbearable, the more so because she had to keep it to herself.

Peter did not wait. He joined the Army immediately.

'You don't have to go!' she protested.

'My son knows where his duty lies!' Agnes snorted. 'He's not going to be backward when his country needs him.'

'His country doesn't need him,' cried Mercy. 'The recruiting offices are full.'

'I feel I should go,' said Peter quietly. 'It's hard to explain… I can't expect some other fellow to do a job I should be doing myself. Besides, it will be over by Christmas, everyone says so.'

Mercy wanted to argue with him, to persuade him to stay, then she saw the determination in his face and knew it was no use.

'Of course it will!' declared Agnes vehemently. 'Our boys will be more than a match for a lot of silly foreigners. I shall, of course, come to see you off tomorrow, Peter. You and all our other young men.'

'And what of you? Are you coming to see me off, too?' Peter said, after his mother had left the room.

'Do you want me to?' Mercy asked uncertainly.

'Yes, I do.' Then more vigorously. 'I would like it very much.'

'In that case I will certainly come.'

The scene at the railway station was a noisy one, with a brass band and cheering crowds accompanying the hundreds of young men who were heading towards Devonport to begin their service life. Agnes took one look at the throng, and withdrew to a more sedate and elegant distance. Mercy, however, stood her ground.

'Did you see the boys?' She had to shout to be heard above the din. 'They did so want you to see them waving their flags. They're with your mother. Somehow she managed to find a vantage point in the Grand Hotel, I don't know how.'

'Yes, I saw John and William, waving away like fury.' Peter's face grew serious. 'I hate leaving them. I'm going to miss them very much, you know. Take care of them for me, and Mother, too. Oh, and Mercy...'

'Yes?'

A whistle blew, and the guard waved his green flag.

'Yes?' she repeated.

'Take good care of yourself as well, my dear.'

On an impulse Mercy raised her face to kiss him, but already the train was pulling away, and all she could manage was the briefest touch of her lips on his cheek. She had never imagined that Peter's departure would be such a wrench. Inside her she felt the aching void increase, something she had not imagined possible, and she was aware of a terrible sense of foreboding.

Gunther and Peter, both gone to war! What if fate threw them together? What if one killed the other?

Nonsense, she told herself sternly. Gunther's a doctor, he won't be anywhere near the fighting. And besides, it'll be all over by Christmas.

'I beg your pardon?' asked the woman next to her, whose plump body was pressed against hers in the crush.

'I said it'll be all over by Christmas,' said Mercy, embarrassed to realize she must have been talking aloud. 'That's what everyone's— My goodness! Queenie! What are you doing here?'

The plump woman turned towards her, her face streaked with tears.

'Why, Mrs Lisburne... Mercy... I didn't know it was you standing there beside me,' she said.

'What are you doing here?' asked Mercy again.

'Why, seeing Joey off. Didn't you know he'd joined up?' Her words were almost drowned in a welter of sobs.

'Joey?' Mercy was aghast. 'He hasn't gone as well?'

Queenie nodded, rummaging in her pocket for a crumpled handkerchief.

'I didn't know— I didn't even get the chance to say goodbye to him!' cried Mercy, hurt that he had not told her.

'He made his mind up sudden, like. We— we went up to Fernicombe this morning. He wanted to say goodbye to his family, meaning to come to you after, but his Ma was in such a state... Poor Joey, he couldn't take any more goodbyes... Oh, there's not going to be any shooting, is there? He won't be in any danger, will he?'

'I don't suppose he'll hear a gun fired in anger,' said Mercy, wishing she believed her own words. 'But what about you? How will you cope while he's away?'

'I'll manage all right, thanks. Mrs Baxter's still with us. After her boy died she didn't have the heart to go back to London, so she stayed on. Besides, trade's falling off, what with the building business being slow, and lots of the men joining up. All the same, I'd better be getting back.' Queenie scrubbed at her eyes, making them even redder.

'Remember, if you need anything just let me know,' said Mercy.

'Thank you, but we'll manage,' said Queenie shyly. 'Goodbye.' And she was swallowed up by the crowd.

Gunther, Peter, and now Joey! It seemed to Mercy that the wretched war had already stolen so much from her, and it had scarcely begun. She was thankful she still had her work for Ivywood to keep her occupied. Then one morning a letter arrived from the new medical director, thanking her for her valuable interest in Ivywood, but stating that her services were no longer necessary. The only reason given was that present policy at the clinic was considered to be 'too Germanic' and was therefore to be revised.

The injustice and the narrow-mindedness of this statement made Mercy speechless with fury. It was some time before its effect on her own life became apparent. What would she do with herself now, without Ivywood?

Agnes Lisburne had no such problem. The outbreak of war seemed to affect her like the sniff of gunpowder to an old warhorse. She was suddenly consumed with such energy it was as if she had decided that her war efforts alone were going to bring about victory. She began by drawing up a regime for the household of such austerity it provoked revolution in the kitchen before the first week was up.

'Mrs Lisburne is very eager for us all do to our best in these difficult times, Mrs Clark,' said Mercy soothingly to the cook. 'I can understand your problems, and I'll have a word with her. In the meantime, perhaps there are a few more ways you can think of to cut down. We could have more fish instead of meat perhaps, and maybe margarine as an alternative to butter on certain days?'

'Margarine instead of butter? In my kitchen?' The cook was horrified.

'It would be for the upstairs table as well as the servants' hall,' prompted Mercy.

'Well, if you and Mrs Lisburne are willing to make the sacrifice too, that's different,' said Mrs Clark, slightly mollified. 'As for the rest, I'll see what I can manage.'

'I'm sure you'll cope splendidly,' said Mercy. She anticipated her mother-in-law's reaction to finding margarine on her tea table with relish.

As she expected, Agnes was outraged. The idea that she would have to make sacrifices, as well as other people, had not been obvious to her.

'Don't you think we should show a good example?' asked Mercy.

'One can take things too far!' stated Agnes, her voice full of disapproval. 'It is all right for the servants, they are used to doing without.'

The incident marked an end to Agnes's attempts to reorganize the domestic arrangements, instead she took up committee work. There was soon scarcely a Force's Comfort Fund or a War Savings League that was not blessed with her presence. In this work she was encouraged by Charlotte. Mercy watched them, but could not find it in her heart to equal their energetic enthusiasm.

'You should make more effort, you really should!' Charlotte admonished her. 'Anyone would think you didn't want us to win this war.'

Conscious that, for her, there would never be any victory, no matter which side won, Mercy smiled politely and said, 'I've been doing my bit, seeing to the house and the children. That's quite enough for me.'

'No, it's not,' said Charlotte flatly. 'You are capable of much, much more. Do something worthwhile.'

Mercy felt a stab of pain. Charlotte's words were uncomfortably reminiscent of Gunther's.

'Feeding my family is worthwhile,' was all she would reply, leaving Charlotte to stamp away in disgust.

Peter came home for a few days' leave after his initial training period. Mercy was pleased to see him, yet at the same time there was an awkwardness between them that was hard to dispel. She was quite glad when Agnes chose to monopolize him, revelling in the glory of having a soldier son to show off to her less fortunate acquaintances.

'It's a wonder Mother doesn't fit me with a halter and parade me up and down Fleet Street like a prize horse,' he grumbled amiably, collapsing into an armchair after a particularly exhausting outing with Agnes.

'She's very proud of you, and no wonder,' said Mercy. 'You look extremely distinguished in your uniform.'

'I'm glad I look the part at least. Mother seems to think this is all some gigantic pageant. Well, let her enjoy herself while she can, I suppose.'

'What do you mean by that?'

'Only that this war can't go on being an interesting pageant for much longer. The real soldiering will begin when I get back to camp tomorrow.'

'You are being posted overseas?'

'Yes.'

'Do you know where?'

'Not yet. All troop destinations are secret.'

'But it's too soon!' she protested.

'What is too soon?' asked Agnes, coming into the room.

'My trip abroad,' said Peter.

'You are going abroad? How very nice for you.' Mercy had to bite back a cry of protest. How could Agnes be so stupid? Could she not imagine the consequences?

There was no more personal talk for Mercy and Peter that evening, thanks to Agnes's continual presence. When Peter departed on the train next morning there was a lot left between them that was unsaid. Mercy watched him go with distress, thinking of all her lost opportunities during the recent few days. She should have reached out to him more, attempted to bridge the gulf between them. She knew she would never regret loving Gunther, nor would she ever apologize for having done so, but Peter was going into such danger. Surely there were words of understanding that could have been exchanged between her and Peter that would have gone some way to heal the rift? It was too late for spoken words now, she would have to write them.

Reading the newspaper each day became a kind of penance for Mercy. She would avidly scan the columns, knowing that for her the only good news would be the end of the war. At first the articles, particularly in the local papers, were light enough, almost trivial. The war seemed a distant inconvenience. Then, from a place in Belgium called Mons, came the first reports of casualties from the Front. By the autumn wounded soldiers were arriving in town, and more than one local family received the dreaded message informing them of the death of a loved one. The war had suddenly reached Torquay.

'You must do something towards the war effort,' Charlotte insisted yet again.

'I've plenty to occupy me,' Mercy replied.

'I dare say you have. That's not the point. Keeping house and playing with your children won't help to win the war.'

'I'll do my bit, never fear.'

'See you do!' Charlotte sounded quite fierce. 'Now I must dash. There's a party of Belgian refugees to be met at the station, and taken to their lodgings.'

Mercy felt unsettled after her friend had departed, she knew Charlotte was right. It was no use trying to retreat into her own little world, pretending the terrible events outside were not happening. She would have to act. Next morning she called at the Recruiting Office.

'I am afraid you have left it a bit too late to join the Voluntary Aid Detachment, Mrs Lisburne. The local requirement has already been most adequately met. If you had only come sooner.' The woman regarding her across the desk sounded vaguely reproving.

'Surely, with the wounded coming in, isn't there something?'

The woman ruffled the papers in front of her officiously. 'There are shortages in some parts of the country, of course, if you would be prepared to move.'

'I'm afraid I can't. I have two children.'

'Well that's an end to the matter!' The woman snapped shut the file.

'But I must do something,' cried Mercy, unconsciously echoing Charlotte's words, 'is there nothing else? Couldn't I be a ward maid?'

'Ward maids are usually inexperienced young girls, not mature married ladies. You would find such a post quite unsuitable.'

'Nevertheless, I am prepared to serve in such a situation.'

'My dear Mrs Lisburne,' the woman replied, in the manner of one addressing a willing but none too bright child, 'it does you great credit that you wish to do your bit, but I assure you, you would find the position of ward maid not at all to your liking.'

'How can you be so sure?' snapped Mercy, her patience at an end. 'I am no stranger to scrubbing floors and similar tasks. If ward maids are also in such an overabundance I am quite prepared to tackle laundry.'

The woman regarded Mercy's well-cut coat and her elegantly gloved hands.

'Very well, Mrs Lisburne,' she said, in some bewilderment. 'Report to the Town Hall as a ward maid tomorrow.'

Torquay's fine new Town Hall had been converted into an emergency hospital and Mercy entered nervously.

'Are you sure you know what you're letting yourself in for?' asked the nurse who took charge of her.

'No,' said Mercy. 'But I'm not afraid of hard work and I'll not faint at the first bit of mess.'

'Thank goodness for that! At least, you're being realistic!' The nurse gave a grin. 'Most of the ladies who volunteer to work here expect their duties to consist of doling out arrowroot gruel and laying cool hands on fevered brows. Come on, I'll put you with Grant. She's a sensible soul and will show you what to do.'

Grant proved to be a quiet capable girl of about nineteen, and at first she seemed in awe of her new charge, until Mercy's ability at cleaning earned her respect.

'You're awfully good, Lisburne,' she commented shyly.

'It's not the first time I've done messy jobs,' admitted Mercy, then she eased her aching back and admitted ruefully. 'Though not for a long time, I'm sadly out of practice.'

'I wonder you didn't train straight away to be a VAD. You'd be absolutely splendid.'

'I did try. I left my application too late.'

'So did I, but we'll get our chance soon enough. Half of the VADs here won't last the course.'

Mercy soon discovered that she knew a good few of the VADs. Dignified ladies who had graced many of Charlotte's charity functions, they had volunteered their services in the first flush of patriotic fervour.

It was as well she did not expect Agnes to approve of her new occupation, for she would have been disappointed.

'A ward maid!' Her mother-in-law gave a shudder of horror. 'Have you no regard for your standing in society?'

'Some of the other ward maids are from very good families,' said Mercy. 'Like me, they're waiting their turn to train as VADs.'

'And do you think it will come?' asked Agnes. 'There seems to be more than enough volunteer nurses about, as far as I can see.'

'Oh yes, it will come.' Mercy spoke quietly. 'We've a long way to go in this war yet.'

This defeatist comment earned her a reproving look from Agnes.

At first Mercy found her new duties exhausting, she was surprised and ashamed at the way her recent years of easy living had softened her. Gradually, though, her protesting muscles and aching feet grew accustomed to the rigours of being a ward maid and she found herself enjoying her work. Not all of the newly trained volunteers were so fortunate. Some of the VADs, who had signed up in a cloud of rosy idealism found the reality far too distasteful and began to drop out.

A new batch of casualties had arrived at the Town Hall straight from field hospitals at the Front. As they were being brought into the ward Mercy was busy refilling one of the great urns that had to be kept boiling day and night to supply essential hot water. She paused in her work, thinking how pathetic the poor men looked, so dirty and dishevelled, many with the Flanders mud still on them.

'This lot would arrive today of all days!' declared Nurse Chapman, who was in charge. 'When we're short-handed! The doctor'll be on his rounds in a minute, so get these lads cleaned up and comfortable as soon as possible,' she ordered a group of VADs. 'It's going to be a bit of a scramble. Do your best.'

Working in pairs, they began attending to the wounded. Mercy was just resuming her own work when she heard a disturbance behind her. Turning round she saw two VADs standing beside one of the beds.

'Oh come on, Simpson,' one was saying to the other. 'Hasn't this poor soul suffered enough without you taking your time over him?'

'Surely you can see? He's crawling with lice!' The other woman spoke in terms of horrified disgust. 'I can't take any more of this awful dirt. They shouldn't be sent to us in this state, really they shouldn't!'

'Stop being so stupid, Simpson!' the other VAD sounded stern. 'You know I can't manage on my own.' But she was talking to thin air, Simpson had fled.

Mercy did not think twice. She stepped forward.

'Tell me what to do,' she said.

The VAD, who was a small middle-aged woman, looked at her in surprise for a brief second, then smiled.

'Who says the age of miracles is past?' she said. 'Let's begin by cutting away his uniform.'

'Sorry… I'm a bit… mucky.' The soldier was too weak to open his eyes as he spoke, and his voice was barely more than a whisper. 'Forgot… to take… my loofah!'

The VAD and Mercy exchanged glances over the man's bed. They had not realized he was conscious, let alone capable of speech, not with the massive wound in his thigh that was seeping blood through the field-dressing.

'Never mind,' said Mercy. 'Matron'll be along in a minute to see whether you prefer Pear's toilet soap or Castile.'

A faint smile twitched at the man's lips. 'You can… scrub my… back…' he whispered.

'We're going to have to watch out for you,' the VAD addressed the soldier cheerily. But for the second time within minutes she was talking to herself. The man had slipped into unconsciousness.

Mercy and the VAD worked together for the rest of the afternoon, making their way down the twin line of beds, removing the filth and vermin of war as they went. The doctor had already begun his preliminary examination of the new patients. As he approached, his retinue following respectfully in the rear, Nurse Chapman came hurrying ahead into the ward to check on progress. At the sight of Mercy working with the VAD her brows knitted.

'What are you doing?' she demanded.

'Helping me, thank goodness!' said the VAD. 'Simpson ran off, she's had all she could take. We're managing fine, honestly we are.'

Nurse Chapman looked doubtful for a moment, then said, 'Oh all right, carry on. Only, for goodness' sake don't let Matron catch you! When the doctor comes round hide in a cupboard or something.'

Mercy did not get the chance to hide. They happened to be attending to a patient near to the door when in walked the doctor, matron and all.

'Why is a ward maid doing the duties of a VAD?' demanded Matron in a voice of doom.

'It was an emergency, Matron,' Nurse Chapman explained hurriedly. 'Allenby's partner was suddenly taken ill, so… er…'

'Lisburne' supplied Mercy in a hurried whisper.

'So Lisburne stood in. She seems competent, and Allenby is experienced—'

'Lisburne? I know you, don't I?'interrupted the doctor. 'Didn't you bring someone to Casualty once? A skating accident or something.'

'You've got a good memory. That was some time ago,' admitted Mercy.

'Yes, it was. Von Herwath was with you, as I recall. I seem to remember you did some pretty good first aid work then. What the devil are you doing messing about as a ward maid? You should be nursing!'

Not waiting for her reply he swept on to his next patient. Matron followed him, a look of pained affront on her face. It was bad enough for a doctor to forget protocol and directly address a lowly ward maid, but for a ward maid to have the temerity to reply was an affront to the structure of hospital discipline.

Mercy could sense Allenby and Nurse Chapman shaking with silent laughter beside her, and she chewed fiercely at her lip to stop herself having a fit of the giggles. When Doctor, Matron, and their acolytes had departed the three of them collapsed into an hysterical heap.

'Enough hilarity, ladies,' gasped Nurse Chapman, remembering her dignity. 'Back to work. And Lisburne, I think we can expect to see you among the VADs soon.'

'I hope so,' said Mercy fervently. 'I do hope so.'

The very next morning she was summoned before Matron. She was to begin her VAD training immediately!

-

It was a long, cold winter. The lighting restrictions which darkened the streets made it seem even more dreary and dismal than normal. In addition to everything else Mercy suffered agonies from chilblains. Despite the discomfort she was determined not to give up her nursing. At last she felt as though she was doing something worthwhile.

Accounts of the war in the newspapers were cheerful enough, but their optimism made Mercy feel uneasy. The reports of easy victories and excellent conditions did not seem to tally with the comments of the men she was nursing.

By the time spring came it seemed as if they had been at war for ever. Even the dignified atmosphere of the Villa Dorata was disrupted by Agnes filling the place with parcels being made up for the troops, or groups of women dutifully folding bandages.

It was midsummer when Peter came home for a brief leave. Mercy looked forward to seeing him again with an eager excitement which surprised her, yet somehow the happily anticipated days did not fulfil their promise. To begin with Peter was different. She had expected that, of course. She was not surprised that he seemed older, more serious, and that much of his old boyishness had gone. What she found less easy to understand was a certain withdrawal in his manner. She sensed it had nothing to do with the past difficulties of their marriage. It was the war. He never spoke of his experiences at the Front. It was a part of him that was completely divorced from life at home.

For the first time in an age he made love to her, if such hectic thrusting urgency could be called love. Mercy found his lack of consideration, so completely out of character for Peter, the most upsetting thing of all. She wished they could talk more, but somehow there was too little time and he was too distant.

On the day before his leave ended Mercy chanced to encounter Rogers coming out of Peter's dressing room. Poole had long since joined up, so the elderly butler had assumed the duties of valet while Peter was home, and now he stood outside the door, an expression of acute distress on his face.

'Is anything wrong?' she asked.

Rogers swallowed hard, clearly grappling with extreme emotion.

'I was about to commence packing for Mr Peter, Madam, and I asked him if there was anything special he needed, and he said— he said, "I'd be grateful if you could get me a large tin of Keatings".'

It was a measure of the butler's distress that he referred to Peter in the old familiar way, instead of the proud 'Captain Lisburne' of recent months. Mercy could understand why he was so upset. The idea of the ever fastidious Peter needing anything as distasteful as flea powder clearly upset him greatly. But Mercy had tended enough men straight from the Front not to be shocked.

'I'll buy some on my way to the hospital,' she said.

'Oh thank you, Madam!' Rogers's relief was evident. 'I shall endeavour to pack it carefully so that Mrs Lisburne does not see it.'

'Good.'

Mercy smiled at him, and Rogers gave a brief grin in return. One unexpected benefit from the war was the greater understanding between her and the butler.

Peter departed on a cold, rainy day more appropriate for October than August. Mercy sensed he was almost glad to be going, as though he was relieved he would no longer have to keep up any pretence.

Another year came and went. Casualty lists mounted, the names of places like Ypres, Marne and the Somme were on everyone's lips, and there was still no hope of peace. Mercy was astonished at how cheerful the wounded soldiers remained, even though most of them were destined to return to the trenches again as soon as they were fit. Boredom was a great problem once they had begun to recuperate, and so Mercy sacrificed her beloved gramophone and took it into the ward, along with as varied a selection of records as she could find. The brief musical interludes were tremendously popular, and were soon nicknamed 'Mrs Lisburne's Half Hour'. Only once did these impromptu concerts cause any dissension.

The gramophone was in the charge of a corporal from Plymouth, who proudly operated it from his wheelchair.

'Danged if I can read what this label says,' he declared. 'Darned thing's in a foreign language. Hang on, I can make out the name— Franz Lehar. Oh, that'll do.'

'No it won't!' exclaimed one soldier. 'He's a bloody Hun, isn't he? Us don't want none of their rubbish in here!'

'He'm Austrian, not German, you gurt fool. He wrote *The Merry Widow*.'

'I don't care what he wrote. He's still a Hun!'

'Got some good tunes in it, has *The Merry Widow*.'

'What's wrong with a British tune?'

'Austrian, German! Don't make no difference. They'm all vermin!'

'No, you can't say that! There's good and bad among them, same as there is with us,' stated the corporal reasonably. 'My brother's a prisoner in Germany. He's in a prison hospital and he wrote to say he's being really well looked after. He says if the same doctor had treated him in civvy street it'd have cost him a fortune. Funny thing, this German doctor knew Plymouth well, he was joking with our Stan asking him if he fancied a night out in Union Street. Knew Torquay, too. Used to work at one of the TB clinics or sommat.'

Mercy had been passing through the ward during this exchange, but she stopped stock still at the corporal's words.

'Funny old world, isn't it?' commented someone.

'It is that!' agreed the corporal with a sigh. 'A decent bloke like that doctor, and what has to happen to him? He gets run over by a car and killed! Our Stan says everyone, prisoners and Germans, was in a terrible way about it. What a waste, eh?'

Mercy was the only one who found the lively rhythm of the waltz out of place and shocking. It could not have been Gunther! No doubt there had been lots of German doctors working in Torquay before the war. It did not have to be Gunther!

She forced herself to voice the question.

'The doctor who was killed, you don't happen to know his name?'

The corporal stopped beating time to the music. 'Sorry, Nurse, our Stan didn't stay. I could write and ask him, though there's no knowing how long it would take.'

'Thank you – there's no need.'

'Might he have been a friend of yours?' The corporal looked at her with sympathy. 'Perhaps it's better for you not to know for certain – it's not as if you could do anything. Shame, though. He saved our Stan's life.'

'Yes, you're right.' Mercy managed a brief smile, and left the men to the music.

It did not have to be Gunther who had been killed, but it was. Instinct told her so, and a stunning pain overwhelmed her. She had no recollection of leaving the ward. When her senses came back to her she was in the sluice room, among the bedpans and the steam, and she was crying.

Eyes red with weeping were no novelty during those dark days. Nurse Chapman noticed Mercy's and merely asked kindly, 'You all right, Lisburne? You can take a break and brew up some tea, if you like.'

'No thanks, I'm fine,' Mercy lied, and went back to her work.

She was not fine, of course. Her thoughts kept returning to Gunther, to his long muscular body broken and bleeding, to his boundless energy stilled for ever by a stupid accident. That night and for many nights to come she wept herself to sleep. Her grief she had to keep to herself, but for the first time in that long and terrible war her loyalties were no longer divided.

1917 brought with it tighter and tighter food restrictions, and though the news that America had entered the war was cheering, people were too exhausted to be overjubilant. It was also the year in which Peter celebrated his thirtieth birthday. He was master of his own affairs at last, but too involved with fighting in 'The War to end all Wars' to pay much attention.

It was Mercy who had to cope with this new responsibility. Agnes kept a tight control on the finances until the last possible minute before reluctantly handing over the reins. The advent of war might have lessened hostilities in the household, but Agnes Lisburne was determined to demonstrate her continuing disapproval of her son's marriage to the bitter end.

To her annoyance Mercy proved to be an able manager where money was concerned, so robbing her of any chance to gloat over her daughter-in-law's incompetence.

A persistent tapping on her bedroom door woke Mercy one afternoon.

'I am sorry, Mrs Peter,' apologized the ever-faithful Stafford. 'There's a telephone call for you. I said you that you'd been on duty all night, and that you were asleep and couldn't be disturbed, but the person at the other end said it was most urgent, and she sounded so upset.'

'She?' Mercy emerged from her cocoon of bedclothes and blinked in the afternoon light. 'Oh, very well. Put it through to my sitting-room, please. I'll take it in there.'

Pulling on a robe she shuffled drowsily into the other room. Sleeping at odd times of the day was one part of nursing to which she could never become accustomed.

'Hello,' she said.

'Mercy? Oh Mercy!'

Mercy's weariness dropped from her immediately.

'Queenie?' she said sharply. 'What's happened?'

'It's Joey... A letter came...' Over the line all Mercy could hear was a series of incoherent gasps as Queenie struggled to share her news. She made out only the words 'official' and 'posted missing'. They were enough.

'I'm on my way,' she said, ringing off. She hurried back into her bedroom.

Stafford was there.

'Oh dear, I was afraid it was bad news, Mrs Peter,' she said with concern.

'Yes, my brother. I must go to Paignton at once.'

'Very well, Mrs Peter. I'll get out your grey linen dress, shall I?'

Mercy found it slightly incongruous, having a lady's maid when she considered some of the tasks she performed in the course of her nursing duties. There was no help for it, though, because Stafford had nowhere else to go and would never get another situation at her age and in wartime. On this occasion Mercy was grateful for the maid's help. Her mind was so consumed with anxiety she could not concentrate. Eventually, she found herself knocking on the peeling door of the lodging-house in Church Street. It was opened by the dour Mrs Baxter, who stood by without a word, and let her in.

Queenie was sitting in an armchair in the back room when Mercy entered. At the sight of her visitor she rose to her feet, tried to speak, and collapsed in tears. It was Mrs Baxter who, still without speaking, took a letter from the mantelpiece and handed it to Mercy. The words stood out black against the paper, harsh and dreadfully official.

'I regret to inform you that your husband, Private Joseph Seaton, is missing, presumed killed in action.'

It was the 'presumed killed' that caused Mercy to catch her breath. He could not be dead, not Joey. He was too young, he had seen nothing of life. She wanted to say words of comfort to the heartbroken Queenie, instead she found herself clutching at her sister-in-law and sobbing too. Mrs Baxter brought them some tea so laced with brandy that at the first mouthful they both coughed and spluttered. By the time she had finished her cup Mercy, for one, felt calmer and able to think more clearly.

'It's not definite, you know,' she said encouragingly. 'It only says "presumed". There must be a lot of confusion over there, so how can they possibly know where everyone has got to? How can anyone say who is alive and who isn't.'

'What can we do...?'

Mercy had been pondering on these questions. She did not think she could bear simply to sit still and wait.

'I'll write a few letters,' she said. 'My husband, for one, might be able to discover something. I refuse to give up hope, and you must do the same!'

Queenie gave a watery promise, struggling to hold back a fresh flood of tears.

It was easy, writing the letters, seeking the best sources of information. While she was doing those things Mercy felt active and hopeful. It was afterwards, when she could only wait, that despair took hold. Week slipped into week until nearly a month went by. Just when she felt that she could stand the uncertainty no longer the telephone rang and this time it was an ecstatic Queenie who spoke.

'I've had a letter from Joey! He wrote it himself! He's alive!' she cried.

For Mercy the room swayed about her precariously, so that she was forced to grasp the table to steady herself.

'Thank God!' she said fervently. 'Is he all right?'

'He was wounded and taken off to a hospital behind the lines. That was why no one knew where he was for a while.'

'And is his wound serious?'

'He's lost his right foot!'

The blunt way Queenie said the words made Mercy gasp with horror. She sat down suddenly, the phone still clutched in her hand.

'Oh no!' she exclaimed. 'Poor, poor Joey! That's terrible!'

'No it's not!' declared Queenie, unexpectedly jubilant. 'He's coming home, and they won't be able to send him off to fight again, will they?'

'I— I suppose not.' Mercy was shaken by her reasoning. 'How is he?'

'On the mend, he says. And once he gets home we'll really get him better. Oh, isn't it grand news?'

'Yes, wonderful news,' Mercy agreed. She thought of her lively young brother hobbling about on crutches. How would he cope? she wondered. But that was a problem for the future. The main thing for now was that he was alive and coming home!

The letter that came from Peter later that week made no reference to Joey – Mercy's note must not have reached him. She did not notice the omission, however. She was too startled by his news.

'I've had a slight collision with a German shell, which did not do my arm any good,' he wrote. 'It's nothing too desperate, it's what is enviously referred to here as a "cushy Blighty", because it means I will get some home leave.'

He was coming home! Mercy felt intense relief. Her next reaction was to wonder how she could arrange time off so that she could be with him.

How much older he looks! These were Mercy's first thoughts when she saw Peter waiting at the station forecourt.

He saw her coming and smiled, holding out his right arm to embrace her. Only then did she notice that his other arm was in a sling. He held her tightly, his lips tasting cold on hers. He took a deep breath. 'Just smell that air! The sun, the salt and the sea! Who couldn't recuperate under these conditions! It's probably even better the further away from the trains you get!'

'It certainly is. I don't know why we're standing here, among the smoke and smuts from the railway engine. Let's go home!'

'Home! How wonderful that sounds!' His words were almost whispered and his face grew serious, his hold on Mercy's hand tightening. Then almost as swiftly he was smiling again. 'Come on, my friend!' he urged the taxi driver. 'Let's get going! I don't want to spend any more of my leave at the station!'

It was a very light-hearted evening. John and William could not get enough of their father's company, and followed him like two small shadows. Over-excited, they protested loudly when the time came for them to go to bed.

'What's this? Mutiny in the ranks?' demanded Peter, in mock fury. 'To bed this minute! And I'll follow behind to make sure you obey orders! Forward march! Left, right, left, right...' The three of them headed for the stairs, followed by Nanny who was laughing and shaking her head.

'Peter is in splendidly high spirits!' exclaimed Agnes, for once approving. 'And after all he has gone through, too!'

Privately Mercy thought that there was a forced note to Peter's joviality. As the evening wore on she was more and more convinced that she was right. For all he continued to joke and be amusing she sensed he was having to work hard at his light-hearted mood, and that it was a strain.

Then she realized how foolish she was being. Peter had been wounded and had doubtless had a rough time, no matter how little he tried to make of the affair. Now he was home it was only natural that he should need to adjust.

That night, after Agnes had gone to bed, they went up the stairs together. At the top Peter made as if to sleep in his old room again.

'There's no need,' said Mercy in surprise. 'You didn't use that room on your last leave.'

'Perhaps it would be better, all the same. I'm such a restless sleeper these days I'd only disturb you. Good night, my dear.' He bent and kissed her on the cheek then walked off along the corridor.

Hurt, disappointed and humiliated, she made her way to her own room and to the huge empty bed. Things had not been perfect during his last leave, but she had felt that they had made a big step forward towards being reconciled. And she did want to be reconciled; she was surprised how deeply she felt about it. It was as if the dangers and difficulties of the war years had reawakened her earlier feelings for him and caused the old rift between them to fade.

Mercy knew he was not sleeping well at night. When he came down to breakfast at nine or ten o'clock his face was pale and his eyes were heavy with weariness. He was restless when he was awake, too, seeming unable to settle, setting out on walks or picnics and excursions, only to be overcome by exhaustion.

'You are doing too much,' protested Mercy one day, when he slumped into an armchair, white with fatigue after having walked miles along the cliff top.

'For heaven's sake, I've only got a wounded arm!'

'Which is still a part of the rest of you, thank goodness! The whole of your body had to stand the shock when you were wounded, you know, not just that one limb. Give yourself a chance.'

'It is a simple enough injury, I ought to be able to cope with it.'

'I wouldn't call that a simple injury.'

'It is compared to what a lot of other fellows suffered!' He gave a sudden grin. 'All the same, perhaps you're right. Maybe I'm expecting too much of myself. My arm's given me a good bit of pain, naturally, though not nearly as much as the time I dislocated my elbow playing tennis. That's probably why I'm not taking it too seriously.'

'I'm not suggesting that you make a career of being an invalid, just that you relax more, and don't push yourself so hard.'

'Very well, I'll do as you say, Nurse. I'll be ever so good.'

'See that you do!' she said, pretending to be stern.

She was pleased to see that for a day or two he did make an attempt to follow her advice and he seemed more calm. Then gradually his restlessness returned. She felt her own anxiety creep back, a certainty that something was wrong. Never once did he suggest returning to her bed, and she was disappointed. It was strange, because during the day he was polite and cheery and considerate, even affectionate. Only at night did a barrier seem to come between them. It had been her great hope that on this furlough the final divisions keeping them apart would be broken down. She wanted to be his wife properly, and her great fear was that Peter would go back to Flanders without knowing how much she wanted his love again.

She lay, tense and miserable, in the vast expanse of bed for what seemed an age; then she could stand it no longer. Getting up, she put on her robe and went to Peter's room. He was sitting up in bed reading when she entered.

'We must talk,' she said.

'What about?' he asked.

'Us. Things are wrong between us, and I want to put them right before it's too late.'

He did not reply, but simply put down his book and looked up at her. Feeling absurdly nervous she sank on to the edge of the bed. There was one shadow she had to dispel.

'I had news of Gunther von Herwath a while back,' she said tentatively. 'At least I think I did.'

'Aren't you sure?'

'I think it must have been him, everything fitted. One of the patients at the Town Hall heard from his brother who is in a prison hospital in Germany. The German doctor who treated him said he had once worked in Torquay in a chest clinic.'

'I suppose it could be von Herwath.' Peter sounded guarded. 'I dare say the Red Cross could make inquiries for you.'

'It would do no good. He was killed in a car accident.' There was a brief silence.

'I'm sorry,' said Peter quietly. 'You… you cared for him very much, didn't you?'

'Yes,' said Mercy, her voice little more than a whisper. 'It was over some time ago, though.'

'Was it? I was never sure.'

'We had no future together, even if the war had not come along. I think I realized that from the beginning.'

'Thank you for telling me.'

272

'I told you for a purpose.'

'You did?'

'Of course I did. I wanted you to know that Gunther wasn't between us any longer. He is what's keeping us apart, isn't he?'

'Yes... No... Partly...'

'Then what else is it? For heaven's sake tell me so that I can do something to put it right! I want us to be together again. I hate this coldness between us. I know I'm to blame as much as you for the start of it, but when you were home last time I thought you wanted me again and that everything was going to be all right. But it isn't is it? And I want to know why? What can I do?' Emotion surged up in Mercy, spilling over as tears cascaded down her cheeks. 'What can I do to put things right?' she repeated.

'Nothing!' Peter pushed back the bedclothes and stood up. He strode to the window, his back to her.

'Don't do that,' she pleaded. 'Don't turn your back on me. There must be something I can do so that we're happy again.'

'It's nothing to do with you,' he protested. 'Now, for pity's sake go away!'

'No!' She was adamant. 'Not until I find out what's wrong. Don't you want to make love to me any more?'

'Of course I do.'

'Then why do you keep away from me?'

'You wouldn't understand!'

'I could try!' she cried desperately. 'Can't we sleep together again? That doesn't seem much to ask.'

'No!' exclaimed Peter. 'No! No! I've told you, I'm far too restless, I'd keep you awake. Now go away, please!' There was a desperate pleading in his voice, and she noticed he was clutching the curtain with his good hand so tightly the knuckles had gone white.

A hint of understanding swept through Mercy.

'Is it memories of when you were shot keeping you awake?' she asked gently. 'You mustn't be ashamed of that. It's only natural for it to stay with you for a long time. It does with most men. I've seen it in the hospital. It will go in time. Until it does please let me be with you. Don't be alone.'

Still he did not turn towards her so she slid her arms about him, resting her head against his back.

'Don't be alone,' she repeated. 'I'm here.'

Peter turned to face her with an abruptness that almost overbalanced her. Only his good arm, about her so suddenly, prevented her from falling. For a long, long time they stayed in each other's embrace, neither moving nor speaking. When at last Peter spoke his voice was tight with emotion.

'I'm sorry,' he said with an effort. 'I didn't want to hurt you. It's just impossible to forget. I try to shut it out, but it's always with me. There's no escaping it, even over here. The bombardment goes on and on, you see. Ceaseless noise which seems to get right inside your head. There was so much destruction, Mercy! So many good men mown down like so much corn at harvest time. And for what? Can you explain it to me? Fifty men I lost in one day. Fifty decent fellows with families and loved ones at home! How can their deaths have made the world a better place? What is it all about? What is it all for? I wish I could understand... Dear God, how I wish I could understand...!' Now that the barrier was down the words came out of him in a stream – the horror, the suffering, the squalor, the all-pervading mud.

Mercy listened appalled. She had heard the patients at the hospital talking about their experiences often enough, and so she had a better idea than most of the conditions at the Front. Even so she was shocked by what she heard, shocked at what Peter and others like him were being forced to endure. She continued to listen without interruption. She held him more tightly, offering him the silent comfort of the warmth of her body.

Somehow, she was not aware when or how, they had slipped on to the bed. With one arm still about Peter, she pulled the covers up over them both, cocooning them in comfort and security. Slowly, painfully, the nightmarish litany came to an end as exhaustion overcame him. The tight grip of his hand on hers was painful. Her arm, trapped now by the weight of his body, was agonizingly cramped. She would not move, though, for fear of disturbing him. Not until his anguished shuddering breaths had grown deep and regular, and she knew for certain he was asleep, did she stealthily ease her aching limbs. Then, curling her form close to his, she too fell asleep.

It was dawn when she awoke. In the half-light she turned her head, to find him looking at her.

'You're still here,' he said softly.

'Of course. I said I would be.'

'I'm glad. I'm sorry you had to listen to such rubbish. It wasn't fit for your ears. I should never have burdened you with it. I'm thoroughly ashamed of myself.'

Mercy propped herself up on one elbow and gazed down at him.

'Did it help, talking about it?' she demanded. 'Do you feel better for having got it out of your system?'

'Certainly I do, but—'

'Then there is no but about it. You bottled up too much horror! You must never do it again. There's little enough I can do for you, goodness knows! At least share your troubles with me. It's not much to ask.'

'Yes it is. It's asking a great deal to burden you with all that. Nevertheless, you are right. It's too much to hold in at times.' Gently he pulled her back on to the pillow. 'It's gone now, though. The nightmare's gone for the present. Let's think of more pleasant things.'

'Such as?' she asked, her finger tracing the outline of his cheekbone.

'Pleasant things that should have been occupying us throughout this leave. We've wasted so many opportunities!' With his good hand he was trying unsuccessfully to undo the tiny pearl buttons on her nightgown.

'Drat these things,' he said softly. 'I had to tackle fiddly little buttons like this on our wedding night, I recall. You should have learned better by now.'

Smiling, Mercy came to his assistance, not only unfastening the buttons but pulling off the garment completely.

'Then maybe we should make up for lost time,' she said.

The last part of Peter's leave was a golden time. Their days were long and sun-soaked, their nights were filled with love-making. It could not last, of course. Wonderful as it was it had to end.

There were many families saying farewell on Torquay Station. Separate little groups clustered round kit-bags and suitcases, isolated from each other yet sharing their fears, their hopes, their dreads.

The clatter of the railway signal made Mercy's heart grow cold. The London train was coming. Peter was leaving. The puffing arrival of the engine prompted a surge of activity on the platform, farewell kisses, last desperate embraces.

'I'll be back,' repeated Peter. They exchanged one long lingering kiss through the train window, then slowly and relentlessly the train pulled away.

'Hello, stranger!' Nurse Chapman greeted Mercy when she returned to work. 'It must be nice to be some people, taking long holidays.'

'It'll be the last I get for an age. I've mortgaged my days off for the next hundred years, I think.'

'But was it worth it?'

'Yes, oh yes!'

'In which case I won't inquire any further, me being a pure and innocent spinster. It's back to work for you, my girl. Just you wait until you see how many bedpans and bottles are waiting for your attention.'

At first it seemed strange being back in the hospital again. Mercy felt disorientated and disorganized. The routine soon came back to her, however, and before the month was out Peter's leave had assumed a hazy glow of unreality.

Newspaper reports of the war continued to be optimistic. There was talk of 'the end being in sight'. This cheery attitude made no difference to the numbers of casualties. They continued to stream in at a distressing rate. The food shortages were becoming severe, and to make matters worse flu epidemics were sweeping in waves across the country.

'I was just boasting that I'd escaped this latest bout,' gasped Mercy, emerging from the lavatory where she had just been sick. 'Talk about pride coming before a fall.'

'You might still come out of this with your pride intact,' said Nurse Chapman. 'It's the third time you've lost your breakfast recently. How long is it since your husband went back? Have you considered that you might have nine-month flu?'

'Don't be silly,' protested Mercy. 'That's not possible.'

'Come on, when did you last have the curse?' demanded Nurse Chapman cheerfully.

'I can't remember… A while ago… Ages ago! Oh my goodness, you could be right!'

'I'm always right!' said Nurse Chapman with a self-satisfied grin. 'Oh drat! That means we're going to lose another good nurse!'

Mercy scarcely heard her. She was too busy grappling with this latest revelation. She was pregnant again!

Chapter Sixteen

His foot hurt! It caused the bile to rise in Joey. His foot had gone, blown to smithereens by a shell at Ypres, and yet it still caused him agony. Even when it was not paining him he could often feel it. Then he would look down and see his shin ending in nothing, only the surplus inches of his trouser leg turned up and secured by a safety-pin to keep them out of the way. He lay back in his chair and closed his eyes. Think of something else! Not the pain! Anything but the pain! Think of the future! Make plans!

In those dark early days, when his life had been an alternate blur of agony and morphine-induced torpor, he was convinced he had no future. He had seen himself begging for pennies at the roadside, the words 'Crippled ex-soldier' scrawled on a card round his neck. But that had been in the early days. With recovery had come a smouldering anger, and with it a grim determination to shape his own destiny.

At every step of his life so far fate seemed to have dealt him a loser's hand. Surely he was worthy of more? Well, he was not going to let circumstances trample him in the dirt, he was going to fight back! He was intelligent enough. And now he had the determination, thanks to the bitter fury which gnawed away inside him.

But how? It was one thing having the desire, achieving it was very different. There was one advantage of his present condition, it gave him plenty of time to think. He had long ago discovered thinking and planning were by far the best opiates for the anguish he was suffering, in his leg and in his heart.

Slowly and deliberately he turned the various options over in his mind, searching for something to give him a start. Eventually, exhausted by pain and his mental efforts, he fell asleep.

Queenie was in the room when he awoke.

'There, you've had a lovely sleep,' she said, smiling fondly at him.

Her smile irritated him. She was enjoying fussing over him and pampering him. Sometimes he thought she was glad he had been disabled, because he needed her, it made her feel indispensable.

'I wasn't asleep!' he snapped. 'Can't I close my eyes without you thinking I'm asleep?'

She flinched at his tone, and at once he felt ashamed. She meant well, did old Queenie. She could not help it if she got on his nerves. He would have managed very badly without her. She attended to his every need, nursed him, cared for him. 'You're right, I was having forty winks,' he admitted more gently, 'I just didn't want you to catch me at it.'

The smile came back to Queenie's face.

'I don't know why you feel that way. Sleep's the best thing you can do.'

'Sleep seems to be the *only* thing I do these days.'

'That's not true. You're always reading or busy with something. If you're rested now, how about a little airing? Just as far as the beach and back. It's a lovely afternoon.'

He gritted his teeth at her choice of words. A little airing! It made him feel like a babe in arms, or else some senile old duffer in a bath chair. With great self-control he contained his irritation.

'That's a good idea, if you're sure you can spare the time,' he said.

'Of course I can spare the time, if it's for you,' replied Queenie.

They made their way at a steady pace, Queenie pushing the wheel-chair. Joey hated this mode of transport, but it was either that or stay indoors all the time. He was working hard at getting about on crutches, often pushing himself beyond the bounds of his still fragile endurance. In spite of his efforts his mobility was limited, and he knew it would be a time yet before he was able to go any distance.

The way to the beach was fortunately level, through Victoria Park, then down Torbay Road with its modern houses and shops.

Halfway along the Esplanade Joey said, 'This seat will do fine. Have a rest.'

Somewhat thankfully, for she was rather out of breath, Queenie put the brake on the wheelchair and settled herself on the seat. To Joey's relief she did not begin talking, for the moment he was quite content looking at the view. The warm russet-pink of the sand seemed to glow against the clear translucent green of the sea and the pale blue of the sky.

'Would you object if I sat beside you?' asked a female voice.

Looking up he saw a neatly dressed middle-aged woman.

'No, not at all! Please do!' Queenie moved up with her usual awkward flutterings.

'Oh, how nice to rest!' The woman spoke with evident relief. 'It's been such a lovely day I was tempted to take a walk, and I'm afraid I've rather overdone it.'

'A little sit in the sun is what you need,' said Queenie shyly.

'It is indeed, and I've been so lucky. I'd not expected such lovely weather so early in the year.'

'You're just visiting Paignton, then?' asked Joey.

'Yes, I'm here for a few days to see my son. He's at the hospital at Oldway. He was so badly gassed, poor boy.' The woman's voice faltered slightly. 'He was at Passchendaele… And you?' she inquired.

'Ypres,' said Joey shortly.

The woman shook her head sadly, then she turned her face up towards the sun. 'This is such a lovely part of the country.'

'You've never been here before?' asked Joey.

'No. Well I've never gone in for holidays much. If this war has had any benefit it's at least made us travel more. If poor George hadn't been in hospital I'd never have come here. I'll come again, though. I'm quite determined about it, once the war is over and George is fit again. We're going to come back and really enjoy this lovely beach, and the pretty countryside.' The woman gave a little laugh. 'I don't suppose we'll be the only ones, either, what with all the hospitals and nursing homes in this area. You'll see, after the war there'll be a great rush of folks coming here for their holidays because of it.'

'I'm glad we'll be able to thank Kaiser Bill for something,' said Joey. 'A bit of extra trade's always a good thing.'

'Well, now that my feet are rested I think I'll give a bit of extra trade to a tea-shop. I've found ever such a nice one. Lovely cakes. How they manage it with all this rationing I don't know! The only trouble is it's right at the other end of town. I wish there was one a bit closer to the beach. But we can't have everything, can we?' The woman rose and gazed out across the sea. 'Oh, how I envy anyone lucky enough to live here! Still, I'll have to do the next best thing and come for regular holidays. I'd best be off. Goodbye, I'll leave you in peace now.'

'She seemed a nice person,' said Queenie, after the woman had gone.

Joey did not reply. He scarcely heard her. The chance conversation with a complete stranger had achieved what all his puzzling and pondering had failed to do – given him an idea for his future. It was so obvious he was a fool not to have seen it before. So many people were getting to know the area, and finding out what it had to offer, there was bound to be a boom in the holiday trade after the war. This was what he should be working towards – getting a foothold in the tourist business. His choice of phrase brought a smile to his face, but for once it held no trace of bitterness. He had too much to think about! Why should he wait until after the war? The demand was there now! All those families who were coming down to see fathers or brothers. What did they need? Somewhere clean, cheap and comfortable to stay! Somewhere pleasant where they could get a decent, inexpensive meal! There were places like that in Paignton, but not enough! There was plenty of room for more, even now in wartime.

'You're very quiet!' Queenie's voice broke into his thoughts. 'You're feeling all right, are you? You've not got overtired.'

'I'm fine,' he replied, more cheerful than he had been in a long time. 'I'm just thinking something out, that's all.'

'You and your thinking and your reading!' said Queenie fondly. 'It's a wonder your poor brain doesn't ache. Let's go home now, shall we? I've got a nice piece of ray for your tea. If you fancy it?'

'That sounds a bit of all right,' replied Joey. 'Could you manage a few chips as well?'

He was rewarded with a beaming smile.

'Of course I can! Oh, it's good to see you getting your appetite back again!'

Now that he had a germ of an idea to work on Joey could not let it go. Every day it gnawed at him. Two things were immediately clear to him - he had to act quickly, or he would lose his best chance of succeeding, and he would have to move from the lodging-house. Church Street was fine and convenient for many things, but most visitors would head towards the sea and the beach; that was where the money would be made.

It did not take him long to decide what he wanted – a small cafe with a few rooms to let for bed and breakfast. That was only to start with, of course. Once he had got it established he would expand the business, more tables, a decent restaurant, maybe even building up into a proper hotel… A top rate hotel like the Devonshire Hall! Now that would be something!

One invaluable asset he did have was Queenie! She was a good cook, and she worked harder than anyone else he knew. There was Mrs Baxter, too. She would probably stay with them, so there would be no staff problems in the beginning. With the three of them working together he did not doubt that they would succeed.

To provide the capital he would have to sell the property in Church Street and… Here his dreams invariably crumbled. Property was not selling well, not while the war continued. His scrutiny of the papers had told him that much. And even if he found someone eager to take on the lodging house he would get next to nothing for it, it was in too bad a state of repair. One thing he was determined not to do was to go to Mercy for help – not until he had some capital to put into the venture. Black despair overwhelmed him. What was the point of dreaming and making plans? He had no money! He could not even get about on his own!

The problem of his immobility caused Joey more anguish than anything else. He was making progress, but too slowly to satisfy him, so he worked out a regime of his own, far more severe than anything the hospital advised, to get himself walking again. To this end he did exercises, forcing into action muscles that had been inactive for so long. Arms, back, stomach, his one good leg – daily he forced them to work again. He would go out alone, too, setting himself daily targets to reach on his crutches.

One of his greatest challenges was closest to home. The steep lane running alongside the house was rough and rutted, here and there the red bedrock showed through precariously.

On this particular day it had been raining, and the lane's uneven surface was slimy with mud, causing his crutches to slip. More than once he had to put out a hasty arm against the rough-hewn wall to stop himself from falling. At last he stopped, tired and sweating. The muscles in his arms and shoulders were already like red-hot wires, his back was one massive ache. Before he made the return journey he would have to rest. Thankfully he leaned back against the wall and closed his eyes.

'Are you all right, mate? Do you need a hand, or anything?'

He opened his eyes to find a stranger regarding him with some concern. The man was a little older than himself, not so tall, and decidedly more prosperous-looking. His navy-blue pinstripe suit was a little flashy, but not cheap, anyone could see that.

'I'm fine, thanks,' lied Joey. 'Just having a bit of a breather.'

'You're not going to try to get up there, are you?' The stranger nodded towards the slope.

The incredulity in his voice acted as a spur to Joey. 'Yes, why not? I'll manage fine once I've had a bit of a rest,' he said with assurance.

'Well, I know I'd not tackle it in your place. Where did it happen?'

'Ypres.'

'Ah, that sounded to be a very nasty do. Me, I missed it all. A dodgy heart!' The stranger patted his well-tailored chest. 'I'm not sure whether I'm glad or sorry. I don't fancy what I've heard about the war; but then I feel a bit out of it, if you know what I mean.'

'Yes, well, I'm out of it too, now.'

'Very true, and with good reason. Can't they do something better for you than those two bits of wood?' The man glanced down at Joey's crutches.

'I'm in line for an artificial foot. They say they're so good you even get corns, but that's still a bit in the future. There's a good many ahead of me in the queue. Until then I have to go on my peg-leg. All I need is a bloomin' eye-patch and a parrot.'

Joey refused to accept the stranger's pity and the man gazed at him with renewed respect. 'You're cheerful enough about it, I must say.'

'Not much choice, really. I've got to look to the future.'

'I agree with you! Take your chances and look to the future! Think ahead! Now, cars – they're *my* business – they're the future! Horses are a thing of the past! Only fit for chasing foxes and improving rhubarb! When this war's over the roads are going to be swarming with cars. They'll be big business, and I intend to have my share. I've already got one garage and I'm on the look out for another.'

'To buy when the war's over?'

'To buy now! There's no point in waiting until peace breaks out. All those poor sods who've survived the war'll be coming home wanting jobs or to run businesses, and there won't be enough to go round, you mark my words. So I'm acting now. If I wait I'll lose my chance.'

Joey's tiredness slipped away from him.

'Do you know, that's exactly how I feel,' he said. 'My problem is a lack of cash.' He glanced down. 'And the lack of a good leg.'

'From what I've seen you're managing on one pin pretty well. If you can do that, you can do anything. OK, so you've only got one foot. Well, my advice is don't let the grass grow under it! I don't intend to be caught napping. That's what I'm doing here – looking at a possible site.'

'I didn't know there was a garage down here.'

'There isn't. I was thinking of building one. It's not on, though, not here.' He indicated the small builder's yard behind them. 'Not enough space for what I intend to do, and the access is bad. I need to be on the top of the hill, on the road up there.'

'I'll sell you the house on the corner,' said Joey jokingly.

'Is it yours to sell?'

'It's mine right enough. I wish it wasn't. It's falling down and I can't afford to repair it.'

'As a salesman you've a lot to learn, my lad,' the man smiled. Then his face grew serious. 'Look here, I know you were only kidding, but maybe it's not such a daft idea, if you really mean you want to sell.'

'I mean it, all right.'

'In that case let's have a closer look. Have you had a long enough rest?'

'I'm fine now. Let's go,' said Joey, feeling slightly bewildered by the unexpected turn of events.

Declining his companion's offer of a hand up the hill he doggedly stumped his way, step after painful step.

At the top the man regarded the house with interest.

'This looks promising,' he said. 'The position's fine. Just what I'm looking for. Freehold or leasehold?'

'Freehold.'

'Good. Could still do with a bit more space, though. What's at the back?'

'It's a fowlyard. The old fellow in the house across the road owns it.'

'Even more promising. Do you think he'd sell?'

'He might, if the price was right.'

The stranger nodded thoughtfully.

'Hm, this needs a bit of careful consideration. Look, this is my card. Raymond Hodges is the name. If you give me your name and address I'll be in touch. I might make an offer for your place, I might not, it depends. You do understand it would just be the site value, don't you? The house is no use to me. It would have to come down.'

'I understand,' said Joey.

'And a lot hinges on whether the old fellow's willing to part with his hens. As I say, I'll be in touch, if that's all right with you?'

'It's all right,' said Joey faintly, still bemused. Then more definitely he said, 'In fact it's fine, and I look forward to hearing from you, Mr Hodges.'

Raymond Hodges shook hands with Joey. 'Good luck to you,' he said. 'I hope we can do business. I like a man who knows his own mind.'

Joey watched him walk away. By the time the nattily suited figure had turned out of sight towards Winner Street he was already wondering if he had dreamed the whole encounter. But no! In his hand he held a piece of pasteboard upon which was printed: 'Raymond Hodges – Finest quality new and second-hand cars. Speedy motor repairs. Agent for Dunlop tyres.' And underneath was an address in Torquay. Raymond Hodges was real enough, but had he meant what he had said? Would he really get in touch?

A week later the letter came. On the type-written page set out clearly in black and white was an offer. A good offer. Better than Joey had dared to hope. His first action was to hobble to the local post office and phone Mercy.

'What's the matter? Is something wrong? Is Queenie ill?' she asked anxiously, when she heard his voice.

'No, of course not,' he reassured her. 'Just because I've phoned you doesn't automatically mean bad news. To tell the truth, Mercy, I'd like to have a talk with you about a little matter of business. Is there any chance you can come over?'

Mercy caught the eagerness in his voice. He had not sounded so bright and enthusiastic for a long time. 'I'll come this afternoon,' she said. 'I'll get a taxi just this once. A woman in my condition shouldn't be expected to struggle on the bus in order to visit her wounded brother.'

'Your condition?' In his excitement Joey had forgotten his sister was expecting again. 'Oh yes! How're you keeping?'

'I thought you'd never ask,' chuckled Mercy, noticing the omission. 'I'm fine, thanks. I'll see you later.'

When she arrived Queenie showed her into the back parlour, where Joey was sitting, then hurriedly left them alone.

'She's still a bit scared of you. Daft, isn't it?' he said.

'She's just naturally bashful,' replied Mercy, though she doubted if shyness was the true reason for her sister-in-law's hasty withdrawal. She had noted Queenie regarding her already prominent bulge, and seen the look of wistfulness that had crossed the other woman's face.

'You're looking well,' observed Joey. 'Being in the family way certainly suits you.'

'I know it does. I feel absolutely marvellous. There's nothing like the prospect of a baby to brighten life up.' She paused. 'I don't suppose you and Queenie have news on that front, have you?'

'Certainly not!' Joey said shortly. 'Queenie's got enough to do pushing me about. She couldn't manage with a baby as well. How's Peter?'

The determined way he was changing the subject was not lost on his sister.

'Peter's fine, thanks. At least, he was according to his last letter.' She gazed at him steadily. 'Now we've got all the polite formalities over and done with, let's get down to really important matters. What do you want to talk to me about?'

'How do you fancy being my business partner?'

'I'll tell you better when I know what the business is.'

'A cafe and little guest-house combined. There's a property going on Torbay Road that would be ideal. It's been on the market for a while, so I've a good chance of getting them to drop their price a bit.'

'A cafe and guest-house? This is a bit sudden, isn't it?'

'Not really. I've been thinking it over for ages. Look, I've even done the costing for the furnishings and equipment we'll need.' He laid a list of figures in front of her.

'Goodness, you *are* serious! You've certainly gone into the matter thoroughly!' She was impressed.

'Of course I have! I've got to get out of the lodging house business, Sis! I'm never going to amount to anything here. And now's the time to make my move. A cafe and guest-house are exactly what I want. We'll build the trade up gradually, then when we're on a sound footing – and not until – we'll expand. I want it to be like some of the continental hotels I saw when I was on stand-by behind the Lines. Family-run they were, with good cooking and a bit of class. They'd started from

285

small beginnings, I reckon, and so can I. A bit of hard work to begin with… But it would be great!'

Mercy looked at his face, so alight with zeal. 'What about this place in Torbay Road?'

'The position is ideal. Between the beach and the station. Couldn't be better. It's got a good frontage on the road, too, so folks wouldn't be able to miss us. It used to be a shop, and according to the advert it's got a fair bit of living-space with it, four bedrooms and good attics. Of course I haven't had a chance to look it over properly, not being too mobile; from what I've seen in passing it looks in pretty good order.'

'It certainly sounds good,' she said. 'It would need a lot of hard work to get going, though. How do you think you'd manage? You admit yourself you aren't particularly mobile these days.'

'I'm not. But don't think I intend to stay like this. I'll be fitted for my artificial foot soon, then I'll be standing on two legs just like anyone else. Until then, if I can't work standing on my own I'll lean against something. If I can't lean I'll sit. If I can't sit I'll jolly well lie on the floor – but I'm going to succeed!'

The intense emotion in his voice shook Mercy. She had never heard her brother so determined about anything.

'There is the question of the money,' she reminded him.

'I'm going to sell the house. I've had a good offer. Then there's my pension for this!' He patted his wounded leg. 'It should be enough to keep a smallish wolf from the door, and for the rest…' He paused.

'Is this where I come in?' asked Mercy.

'Yes. If you could see your way to coughing up the rest! You could either have it as an ordinary loan, and I'll repay you regularly at a recognized rate of interest, or else you could have a proper share of the business. The decision is yours.'

'How very kind of you!' Mercy smiled at his businesslike manner. 'I notice that you say "I" all the time and never "we". What does Queenie think of all this?'

There was the merest hesitation. 'I haven't told her.'

'Not told her?' Mercy was appalled. 'Joey, you've got this far with your plans and you've never once consulted her? That is awful. This place is her home, even if you don't think much of it. She lived here long before you came on the scene, don't forget!'

'All right, there's no need to jump on me,' snapped Joey.

'Yes, there is, because it seems I'm the only one who ever calls you to order. Queenie never would! She's a nice woman, and she deserves some consideration. Far more than you give her!'

'All right! All right! I'll tell her about my plans.'

'No you won't, Joey! You'll discuss your plans with her! There's a difference!'

'And what do I tell her about your part in this?'

'Nothing, because it's nothing to do with me.'

'You mean you won't help me?' Joey was dismayed.

'I don't know yet. I'll give you my answer after you've consulted Queenie.'

'Queenie always falls in with my plans,' said Joey, impatient again. 'Why won't you give your decision now, or at least say you'll think about it?'

'Queenie might disagree this time. It's a pretty momentous step. And I refuse to consider the matter until she has agreed to it fully, without you bullying her into it.'

'I don't bully her!' protested Joey indignantly.

'You do a passable imitation at times.'

Joey glared at his sister for a moment, then he grew shamefaced.

'I don't mean to,' he said. 'I suppose I've got a bit short in the temper lately.'

'You've had your reasons,' Mercy said more gently. 'Talk things over with her; but calmly, mind! I'll come back in a couple of days. If she is in agreement, then we'll discuss the matter further.'

'If that's the way you want it, Mercy.' He paused and looked at her sheepishly. 'And thanks!'

'You haven't anything to thank me for yet,' smiled Mercy, rising to go. 'Oh, and one more thing. Don't let Queenie know you've talked to me about this before you mentioned it to her. She'd be terribly hurt! As far as she's concerned this is just an ordinary family visit!'

'All right! You're the boss, Sis! You always were!'

Mercy gave a derisory snort. 'Liar!' she said cheerfully, and kissed him on the cheek. 'See you in two days.'

Queenie did not ask the purpose of Mercy's visit. It would never have occurred to her to do such a thing. All the same, Joey felt obliged to offer some explanation.

'She came over to ask after Ma and Lizzie. She hasn't heard from them in some time,' he improvised.

'Oh…' Queenie accepted his account totally.

'Are you busy? Too busy to give me a push as far as Torbay Road?' Joey asked suddenly. He had to broach the subject sometime. Now was as good as ever.

'Of course I'm not too busy,' Queenie beamed.

'Right, then let's go. There's something I want to show you.'

The For Sale board was still on the property when they got there.

'Nice looking place,' remarked Joey.

'Yes, it is.'

'Someone with a bit of go could really make something of it, couldn't they? It's an ideal spot for a cafe or something like that.'

'Yes, it is.' Queenie sounded a little bewildered. She could sense there was a hidden significance in Joey's, and she was at a loss to know what it was.

'Wouldn't it be grand if we had somewhere like this?'

'But this is far beyond us!' she said hastily, suddenly nervous.

'Is it? Don't you think the three of us – you, me, and Millie Baxter – could run a place like this? I think we could turn it into a smashing cafe. A really smart one, with tablecloths and matching cups and saucers. Maybe even flowers on the table. What do you think of that?'

'It sounds lovely.' For a moment she was carried away by the picture he painted. Then she added. 'It sounds ever so grand, though. Far too grand for us.'

'If I'm grand enough to get my foot shot off for my country then surely I'm grand enough to run a flaming cafe!' retorted Joey angrily.

'Of course you are. I only meant… I meant that it would cost a lot… More than we've got…'

He had upset her, which was the last thing he wanted. 'Maybe not. Not if we sold the place in Church Street,' he said more quietly.

'Sell the house? We couldn't!'

'Why not? It's ours to sell.' Seeing the stunned expression in her eyes he tried another tack. 'You know, a good cook like you is wasted running a lodging-house. Just think of all the lovely things you could make if we had a cafe – the scones and the pies and the fruit cakes – the stuff you love doing but don't get time for.'

'I'm not good enough… not for a cafe.'

'You are! You're a first-rate cook, and I'll have something to say to anyone who argues! I defy anyone to better your gingerbread!'

'Oh!' gasped Queenie, torn between pleasure as his praise and terror at the enormity of his ideas. 'We haven't enough money...'

'Not right at this moment, we haven't. Funnily enough there was a fellow came round the other day. He was looking for a property like ours to turn into a garage. He was offering a pretty good sum – one I don't see us bettering.'

'Did you accept?'

'Without consulting you?' Joey looked aghast at the idea. 'Tell you what! Just for the fun of it let's look round the back.'

'We shouldn't... It's not right... Let's not...'

In spite of her protests Queenie allowed herself to be persuaded into pushing Joey to the lane at the back. She protested more when he reached up and opened the gate.

It swung open to reveal a modest garden leading up to the rear of the building. Queenie hung back fearfully, so Joey was obliged to propel himself by pushing his hands along the wall. He reached the back area and peered in through the window.

'Queenie, come and see this!' he urged.

Reluctantly she joined him, pressing her face against the glass.

'Oh!' she gave a sigh of awe. 'The whole kitchen's lovely, it would be ever so easy to keep clean. It hasn't got a sink, though! How funny! There isn't anywhere to wash up.'

'There is!' said Joey! 'Here in the scullery. Have a look!'

Queenie looked. She regarded the large shining stoneware sink, the gleaming taps, the ample draining boards, the draining rack for the crockery, and compared them to the cracked, dilapidated equipment she was forced to use.

Joey watched her face.

'The stove looks efficient,' he remarked. 'I bet it would give you all the hot water you want.'

Her face brightened at the prospect of constant hot. But it dropped again. 'We still couldn't manage it,' she said sadly. 'Whatever we got for our place, it would never be enough to buy this.'

Joey allowed a moment to elapse before he answered.

'I wonder if Mercy might lend us some?' he said, as though he had just thought of the idea. 'Or maybe she would care to be a partner in the business. What do you think?'

Queenie did not reply. She had gone back to have another look at the kitchen.

Even if Mercy had not already made up her mind to help financially she doubted if she could have withstood the eager pleading in her brother's eyes. The moment she was shown into the back parlour, two days later, his desperation seemed to reach out to her.

'All right,' she said laughing, before he could say a word. 'How much do you need?'

They spent the whole afternoon talking finance. Queenie blenched at the sum Mercy offered to lend them.

'That's an awful lot? Can you spare it? I'm sure we could manage with less.'

'I dare say you could,' said Mercy. 'But it will give you a bit in hand to tide you over any difficult patches. And it's to be a straight loan, without interest. You'll be doing all the work and so you deserve the profits. Besides...' She eased her back, which was beginning to ache. 'I've enough to bother about at the moment without getting involved in business affairs.'

She regretted her casual remark immediately, for a shadow crossed Queenie's face. Joey, however, was too overwhelmed by his sister's generosity to notice his wife's sadness.

'Are you sure? I mean, it is a lot of money,' he gasped.

'Don't worry, I'm not going to lose it, am I? And I can spare it at the moment. Peter gives me a very generous, and I'm spending very little on myself these days. Before you get carried away, though, hadn't you two better have a proper look at the place?'

'I'll go and see the estate agent now!' Joey was already reaching for his crutches.

–

'I believe you are looking at the property with the idea of running it as a business as well as a home, Mr Seaton?' remarked the agent, opening the front door for Joey and Queenie.

'Yes. A cafe.'

'Oh, ideal! You couldn't have a better spot. Let me show you the kitchen and service area.'

For over an hour Joey hauled himself from room to room, up and downstairs, opening doors and windows, peering into cupboards. It did not matter that he was covered in perspiration or that his body was one great ache with fatigue. He drove himself on to the point of exhaustion.

'Does this property seem to meet with your requirements?' asked the agent tentatively, when at last there was nothing more to examine.

Joey pulled a doubtful face.

'I must warn you, this type of building is very much sought after,' the agent said hurriedly. 'I'll do my best to hold it for you while you consider it, but if someone else makes a definite offer...'

'What do you think, Queenie?' Joey turned to his wife.

Poor Queenie was too alarmed to make such a momentous decision.

'It's up to you, dear,' she said.

'The place seems satisfactory enough.' Joey chose his words carefully and with deliberation. 'We could make something of it, given a chance. Sadly, I think we're going to have to say no. Very reluctantly, mind. It's the price, you see. It's a bit above our touch, I'm afraid.'

'The price? And... and is that your only objection?' Emotions between hope and desperation flickered over the face of the young agent. Joey guessed it had been quite a time since he had made a sale. 'Well, I suppose I could approach the seller, with a view to a reduction. He is a very reasonable gentleman, and when I explain the sacrifices you've made for your country... Yes, I think I can assure you he'll reduce the price.'

'By how much?' asked Joey.

'Fifty pounds,' was the prompt reply.

'We'll have it,' said Joey.

It took him a full week to realize the enormity of the step he had taken; a full week of bemused disbelief. When he finally came out of his dazed state it was to realize how much there was to be done. In the same week that the contracts were exchanged his discharge from the Army came through.

The day when they moved into the house in Torbay Road was the most thrilling of Joey's whole life. He felt that finally he had put a foot – his only foot, as he wryly observed to himself – on the ladder of success. After the excitement came the hectic activity and the problems. A major difficulty was having to master the bureaucratic web that would ensure they would have food to offer their customers. There were moments when even he wondered if he had taken on too much.

One thing was certain, he would never have managed without Mercy. Quite apart from her financial help she was a constant source of encouragement and advice. At first she always deferred to Queenie, until she finally realized that her sister-in-law was quite out of her depth in matters of decor and furnishing, and happy to leave the choice to others.

Decor! That was Mercy's fancy word for the paint on the walls, and the lino on the floor. Fancy or not, she certainly had a flair for making the ordinary look special. Mercy had suggested covering the plain deal tables they bought with red checked cloths to give a continental air to the place. It was Mercy who had ordinary butter muslin made into curtains, draping them until they looked like something out of a smart magazine. The pictures brightening the plain walls, the pot plants bringing a refreshing touch of greenery to the darker corners, they were all found by Mercy.

Buying crockery proved the greatest setback. Thanks to the general shortages it seemed impossible to purchase any sort of china in quantity, never mind something attractive. It threatened to delay their opening.

'I'll have to have a word with Mercy. Perhaps she'll have a few ideas,' he said, when yet another potential supplier was unable to help.

'I don't think we should trouble your sister!' said Queenie. 'She's doing too much. Have you forgotten she's having a baby?'

'It's not an easy thing to forget, with her being as big as a house end,' he blustered. In truth, he had come close to overlooking his sister's pregnancy. 'As for being unwell, she's as strong as an ox, is our Mercy.'

'She's been looking very peaky lately,' Queenie insisted, so firmly that Joey began to feel uneasy.

When next he saw his sister he felt decidedly ashamed. She did look pale, and there were dark shadows under her eyes. He should have noticed sooner, only, he had been too involved with his own affairs.

'You're going to have to start taking it easy,' he said. 'You're looking washed out.'

'Thanks! That's really boosted my morale.' Mercy managed a smile.

'I mean it. You haven't long to go now, have you?'

'Only four weeks, hopefully.'

'Right, from now on we're going to manage by ourselves.'

'Does that mean you've managed to find your cups and saucers? Oh good! I needn't make any more inquiries. And just when I thought I was on to some for you, too.'

'You were?' exclaimed Joey. 'Where?'

'But you don't need my help, you've just told me so.'

'Don't be daft. I was thinking about you. Tell me about this crockery.'

'Someone told me about a guest-house in Teignmouth. The owners are selling up and retiring and they've probably still got their crockery. Do you want me to make inquiries?'

'Certainly I do!' stated Joey, forgetting his concern for his sister's health in his excitement. 'Find out what else they're selling, while you're about it. Don't forget we've got four guest bedrooms to furnish.'

'Are you sure about all four?' Now it was Mercy's turn to look concerned. 'Do you and Queenie have to sleep in the attic? Think of all those stairs.'

'If I get stuck Millie Baxter'll help Queenie give me a push. She's sleeping up there too, in the next room. Besides, soon I'm getting a nice tin foot. I go to get fitted next week.'

'Oh well, I suppose you know best. I'll see what I can find in Teignmouth.'

'Take a taxi, Mercy!' Joey urged.

'Don't you know there's a war on? I'll go by bus.' Two days later Queenie paused in her task of cleaning the windows and exclaimed, 'Fancy! There's a furniture van pulling up outside. Oh, and Mercy's getting out!' Joey looked out of the window. And there, sure enough, was Mercy coming towards the front door. Behind her two removal men were already lowering the tailgate of the van. Queenie hurried to open the front door.

'Stand by to receive furniture!' Mercy announced, as she entered. 'I went to the house in Teignmouth, and I managed to get a couple of bedroom suites. That's all they had that were suitable, and even they are a bit old-fashioned. But they are in good condition, and lovely wood, so I hope they'll do to get you started.'

'Of course they'll do!' cried Joey enthusiastically. 'Did you just get bedroom furniture?'

'I got a whole load of china, too. Some nice stuff, although it is quite plain – white, with a blue and gold rim. And I got some kitchen equipment…'

Her voice tailed off oddly, causing Joey to look at her sharply.

'Are you all right?' he asked. 'You look washed-out.'

'Just a bit tired. It was rather a rush.' Mercy put a hand against the wall to steady herself.

'Here, sit down before you fall down.'

Joey's warning came none too soon, for Mercy crumpled into a nearby armchair, and lay back, her face ashen, her eyes closed.

'Queenie!' yelled Joey in a panic. 'Queenie! Millie! For heaven's sake come!'

Both women came running. Millie Baxter took one look at Mercy and went for the smelling salts and the brandy, while Queenie lifted her sister-in-law's feet on to a stool and began fanning her with a newspaper. The smelling salts did the trick. Mercy gasped and spluttered, then her eyes opened.

'Sorry to be such a fool,' she said limply, waving away the brandy. 'I just came over faint for a minute.'

'You haven't any pain, have you?' asked Queenie anxiously.

'Don't worry, the baby's not trying to make an early appearance.' Mercy summoned a smile. 'It was just a fainting spell, that's all!'

'Brought on by doing too much!' said Queenie. 'You've got to stop, really you have.'

'Yes, you must!' Joey insisted. 'We're very grateful for all your help. I can't even begin to say thanks – but you're not to do anything more for us, do you hear?'

'I enjoy it, though!' said Mercy. 'It's been fun and—'

'I'm glad to hear it. All this dashing about on buses! It's got to stop. We don't want to see hide nor hair of you until after the baby's born, and that's final!'

When Mercy had fully recovered, Joey made sure she went home by taxi. Perhaps it was as well he did. At the end of the week a telegram arrived from Torquay. It said: 'Jennifer Blanche born twenty-eighth May stop Both well stop Love Mercy.'

Jennifer Blanche! Mercy had called her daughter after their grandmother. How the Old Un would have liked that. Not that she would have shown it. She would have responded with some pithy comment. The thought made Joey smile.

–

For a while things went so smoothly Joey feared it could not last. He was right. The long-awaited arrival of his artificial foot did not turn out to be the blessing he had expected. He had been so looking forward to getting it; a bit of time to get a comfy fit, a bit of effort until he got the hang of it, and at last he would be standing on his own two feet again. Reality was very different. He had not expected to experience so much difficulty learning to move his leg so that his foot touched the ground effectively. He would fail to manoeuvre properly and trip or overbalance, or else he found himself becoming exhausted because he was raising his knee to exaggerated heights at every step. He was also not prepared for the discomfort as the foot, padded as it was, chafed against the tender flesh of his stump until it was raw. His determination to walk forced him on past the limits of his endurance, until he could have wept with the pain.

Finally the doctor ordered him to take things more easily.

'The way you're going, my lad, you'll raise an abscess on the stump, and that will be the least of your troubles!' he had said sternly. 'It's not something you can do overnight. You've got the rest of your life to get the hang of walking with a new foot, so what's the rush?'

The rush was the urgent need to get the business started, and have some money coming in as soon as possible. His immobility was a terrible setback, for now who would wait on the tables? He had pictured himself doing it – a more mature version of the dashing figure he had been at the Devonshire Hall. He had allowed himself the added appeal of a limp, his proof of his service record, but that was all. It had been a pointless dream. He could not manage it, and now he would have to bring someone else in. The extra expense would be little short of disastrous.

As he sat, racking his brains despairingly, his gloomy thoughts were broken by the entrance of Millie Baxter.

'What about my aprons?' she said.

'Aprons?' He stared up at her in bewilderment.

'Yes. I want decent ones. Nice white ones with a frill.'

'What aprons? What the heck are you talking about?'

'My aprons!' She spoke loudly, as though addressing an imbecile. 'For when I wait on the tables. I've got a tidy black dress.'

'Wait on the tables? You?'

'Yes, of course. You can't and she won't, so there's no one else, is there?'

For a moment Joey was speechless. The thought of Millie, with her taciturn manner, serving the public was so ludicrous that he nearly laughed out loud. Then he thought again. What choice did he have? Millie it would have to be!

'You can have what aprons you like,' he said. 'You'd better go and choose them yourself.'

'And caps? Fancy ones?'

'Yes, get some caps as well.'

To his amazement Millie came as close to smiling as he had ever seen her. She actually *wanted* to be a waitress! Whether she would be any good remained to be seen. Joey could not imagine her waiting at tables, but then there were times when he could not imagine the business opening. It seemed like an impossible dream. Eventually, with excitement and trepidation, he hung up the 'Open' sign, wondering when and if the customers would come. He had barely time to hobble back indoors before an elderly couple arrived.

'It says bed and breakfast outside,' said the man. 'Would you have a double room for a couple of nights? And we'd like a meal, too.'

Seaton's Cafe and Guest House was in business!

Chapter Seventeen

Mercy cradled the baby in her arms, rejoicing in the soft warmth of the small body against her, relishing the slight pressure of the tiny head under her chin. To think she now had a daughter! Jennifer Blanche! Would old Blanche have been pleased, she wondered? She was not sure. There was never any certainty about the way her grandmother would react. There had been no other name for the child, though. She was old Blanche to a T and had been since the very first day.

She hoped Peter knew. She had sent a message as soon as she could, but there was no knowing when or if it had reached him. She wondered how long it would be before Peter saw his daughter. The cold thought that he might never do so she pushed to the back of her mind. The war was nearly over! Fate could not be so cruel, could it? Oh, how she wished the fighting would end, and he could come home.

A few more months, and then, on a chill November day, the whole country erupted in one great outburst of joy. The Armistice had been signed! There was peace at last!

'I suppose you're hoping your husband'll be home for Christmas,' said Queenie.

'There's not much chance of that, I'm afraid.' Mercy pulled a face.

'What a shame! I can't think what they still want soldiers for, now that it's all over.'

'I suppose it's going to take a time, getting everyone back.'

'Maybe you're right. It does seem a shame, though, your little boys not having their daddy home for Christmas. Poor man, he hasn't seen the baby yet, has he? Where is she? Haven't you brought her to see us?'

'Not today, I'm afraid. The weather's too cold.' Mercy was only partly telling the truth. She did not like bringing the baby when she came to her brother's house. The bleak look in her sister-in-law's eyes whenever Queenie held Jennifer made her uncomfortable. In that childless household she felt quite guilty. Changing the subject quickly she said, 'How's business?'

'Mustn't grumble,' replied Joey, stumping in. 'We're doing all right.'

Mercy had her doubts. Although the cafe was heated the rest of the house was freezing. There could only be one reason for such meagre fires in this weather – economy.

'Yes, we're doing all right,' Joey repeated. 'Of course it takes time to build up a reputation for good food, but I reckon we're well on the way.'

'I'm glad to hear it.' Mercy rose to leave.

'Thanks for coming.' Joey walked with her to the door. He was moving more easily these days, and she commented upon it.

'Yes, thank goodness,' he grinned in reply. 'I don't trip over nearly as often. I still need my crutch, just to steady myself. I intend to do without it by the summer. You can't have a crutch in a busy cafe, it'd just get in the way.'

It was impossible not to admire his optimism, even though Mercy feared the business was not doing well. Surviving this first year would be the great test for her brother. What he needed was something to tide him over the lean period while the cafe was getting established.

She stopped suddenly on the door step.

'Catering for parties!' she exclaimed.

'Who is?' demanded Joey, nearly colliding with her and regaining his balance with difficulty.

'You could! You could do outside catering! Providing sandwiches, cakes and so on for people's parties and celebrations. Those little savoury pies that Queenie makes are delicious, they'd be ideal!'

'It's certainly an idea.' Joey looked hopeful. 'How would we deliver the food, though?'

'I could come and drive for you.'

'You would, too!' Joey laughed. 'No, you've given me the idea, that's enough. The rest's up to me.'

'Well, if you decide to try it get your advertisements out now. It's the right time, with Christmas coming on.'

'I will, don't worry! Thanks a lot, Mercy. For everything, not just for this. For everything going right back to when you used to keep me at my books and made sure my neck was clean. But for you I'd still be working in Sam Prout's tiddy field—'

'Potato field,' she corrected, touched by his words.

And they both laughed.

–

For Mercy the Christmas celebrations that year had an odd, unreal feeling to them. The festivities were the most joyous for years because the war was over, although there were still severe shortages and restraints. But Peter was still away in the Army. With three children in the household the festive season at the Villa Dorata was lively enough, but she missed him. It was peacetime, and Mercy felt that he *ought* to have been with them.

Early in the New Year the telephone rang. It was a highly delighted Joey.

'Just thought I'd let you know that your idea for doing outside catering is proving a life-saver,' he said. 'We were having a bit of a lean time, though I didn't like to admit it, then along you came with your brainwave. We've been doing a nice steady trade over Christmas, and it looks like continuing – coming-home parties for fellows leaving the services mainly. What's even better is that we're getting more and more business through personal recommendation. Beats an advert in the *Paignton Observer* every time.'

'Oh, I'm so glad!' Mercy felt a great sense of relief.

'Yes, I think it's going to prove a good back-up to the rest of the business. And it's all thanks to you!'

'Not to mention Queenie's cooking!'

'And my organizing ability! Don't forget that!' Joey said so emphatically that she laughed. 'Now, how are things with you? When is that husband of yours coming home?'

'At the end of March, isn't that wonderful? I only heard this morning.'

'I'm glad to hear it. You'll be glad to have him back, I know. I bet the boys are thrilled to bits.'

'Indeed they are. John's already started to cross the days off on the calendar.'

'He can't have got far if you only heard this morning. Now don't forget, if you're planning a big party to welcome your Peter home I know just the firm to do the catering!'

'You must give me their address sometime,' Mercy answered wryly, leaving Joey still chuckling when she put down the phone.

It seemed that March would never come, then, at last Mercy found herself waiting yet again on Torquay Station. The boys, smart in their sailor suits, fidgeted with impatience, while Mercy walked up and down, rocking Jennifer in her arms. Eventually the train puffed in, cutting off the warm spring sunshine, casting the platform into shadow.

Peter had lost weight! That was all she had time to observe before he clasped her in an embrace so tight that Jennifer set up a wail of protest.

'Poor little mite! Did you get squashed?' Keeping one arm still round Mercy he addressed his new daughter, gently caressing the baby's plump little cheek with a tentative finger. 'Oh, you're beautiful! Beautiful like your mama! No man ever had a better welcome home present!' Then he turned his attention to John, who had been jumping up and down and tugging at his father's sleeve in an attempt to gain his attention. 'Now who is this huge young man who seems so eager to speak to me?'

'It's me, Papa! It's John!' cried the boy.

'John? It can't be! John was only little, and you're a big fellow. So big I don't think I can throw you up in the air any longer. Let me try!' To John's noisy delight he picked up the child and swung him skywards. 'Goodness, what a weight! I'll have to put you down. Now, William here will be much easier!' He reached for his other son, but the younger boy backed away. 'Let's see if I can throw you in the air too,' he persisted. William's response to being picked up was to scream, 'No! Don't want to!' so vehemently that Peter quickly released him. 'What's the matter? Did I hurt him?' he asked Mercy anxiously.

'No, I'm sure you didn't. It's – it's just that he hasn't seen you for a while. He's a bit shy.'

'Shy? Of me?' Peter was astounded at the idea. He crouched down to the level of his younger son, who was trying to hide behind Mercy. 'Don't you remember me?' he said persuasively. 'Don't you remember your Papa?'

William merely turned his back on his father and buried his face in Mercy's skirt. Peter rose, distress on his face.

'Well I'm blessed!' he said quietly. 'I didn't expect that.'

'Don't forget, he's only five,' Mercy explained gently. 'And he hasn't seen you for over eighteen months. That's a long time in his little life. You can't blame him for not remembering you.'

'I suppose not.'

'I remembered you, Papa!' put in John, quick to seize the advantage. 'I remembered you very clearly.'

'Yes, you did, and I'm grateful.' Peter took him by the hand. 'Let's go home now and see if Grandmama's forgotten me.'

John thought this was a great joke, and giggled all the way to the car. Mercy was not so amused. She had seen the hurt look on her husband's face, and she felt the incident had marred the pleasure of his homecoming. Not for long, though. The welcome awaiting him at the Villa Dorata dispelled all shadows. Rogers even managed to produce some champagne. It seemed strange, having Peter home and knowing that he would never be going away again – not to war, at least – just as it was strange seeing him in civvies. How quickly she had come to associate him with Army uniform.

Their love-making that night was at first filled with urgency, as if they were unaccustomed to having time to satisfy their loving. Only gradually, as the night wore on, did their passion become more leisurely, interspersed with contented slumber, letting them take pleasure in each other again in a way they had not done since the early days of their marriage. Briefly, only briefly, did Mercy allow herself to think of the period when she and Peter had seemed to be drifting irrevocably apart. It had taken a terrible war to heal that rift. The shadow of it was with them still, in spite of the way the anxious war years had served to close old wounds and soothe old hurts.

William continued to be a problem. Always more introvert and temperamental than his elder brother, he steadfastly rejected Peter's friendly overtures with all the self-willed obstinacy his five years could muster.

'Why does he do it? That's what I can't understand. There's John who's only delighted to have a game of ball in the garden with me, or come to see how the *Tango* is getting on, yet William avoids me as though I were a monster. People will think I ill-treat him, or something.'

'John is older, and he's easy-going, like you. He can cope with change much better than poor William. Try to see it from his point of view. He's had a lot of upheaval in his little life recently. Firstly Jennifer arrives, and he is ousted from being the baby of the family. Then a large stranger comes to live in the house with him.'

'I'm not a stranger, for pity's sake! I'm his father!'

'To him you must seem a stranger. Just let him come to you in his own good time, then everything will be all right!'

'It's about time he went to school,' Peter said, anger tingeing his hurt.

'Please let's get over one hurdle before we tackle the next,' she begged.

'Is that what I am – a hurdle to be got over?'

She grinned suddenly. 'I'm not sure who deserves the title most, you or William. After due consideration I think it's a draw.'

Slowly Peter began to smile.

'Maybe you're right,' he said. 'And I'll take your advice and let things take their course, for all it's such a blow to my pride. I've spent the entire war dealing with grown men, and handling them very well, if I may say so, yet now I find myself unable to cope with my five-year-old son.'

'I think an entirely different approach is needed. Imagine how different your Army career would have been if your battalion had consisted of five-year-olds instead of adults.'

'Perish the thought! I would have surrendered to the enemy long since!' Peter laughed. He flung his arms about her and swung her off her feet. 'How lucky I am to have you! For all you've given me a difficult son.'

'I don't find him difficult,' replied Mercy, putting her arms about his neck. 'And the giving was not entirely mine. If I recall you had something to do with the production of William.'

'Did I?' He pretended to consider. 'So I did! Perhaps I can't put all the blame for any little difficulties on to you.'

'No, you can't.' She began to plant a succession of light kisses along the line of his jaw. 'Besides, there soon won't be any little difficulties, you'll see.'

'At this moment I can't see anything or anyone but you,' he said, the pressure of his arms tightening about her.

Mercy melted against him contentedly. Things would soon sort themselves out, and once they did the future would be so rosy! The years ahead appeared to her as an idyllic glow.

–

The rosy future had to be postponed. Just as everyone was getting used to having Peter home and being a complete family once more,

Agnes became ill. She had fallen victim to the fresh outbreak of flu that was sweeping the country. Mercy felt guilty. At the beginning of the epidemic she had been so concerned with protecting the children from it that she was scarcely aware of the threat to the older woman. For Agnes was old! Mercy realized it with a shock as she gazed down at her mother-in-law lying in bed. She seemed to have shrunk in size, almost as though she were diminishing before their eyes.

Outside the bedroom the doctor's expression grew grave.

'You were a VAD, I believe, Mrs Lisburne,' he said to Mercy. 'I am sure you're perfectly well aware of how little we can do at this stage. Her lungs are my chief concern. Already she is experiencing difficulty in breathing. In any other household I would recommend hiring a trained nurse, but under the circumstances...'

'I will look after Mrs Lisburne myself,' Mercy said.

'She could not be in better hands, I'm sure.' The doctor gave a brief smile. 'My only warning is don't wear yourself out! You don't want to get ill yourself.'

'I'll be sensible,' promised Mercy.

For nearly a week Agnes grew steadily worse. For as long as she could Mercy tended her, listening to the rasping breath hour after hour, watching the woman in the bed tossing and turning feverishly.

'You can't keep this up!' said Peter firmly. 'It's foolish to try.'

'I can manage. Stafford is helping me,' Mercy insisted.

'There's no need for you to manage! We are perfectly able to employ professional help.'

'It doesn't seem right, having your mother attended by strangers while I'm here.'

'And it doesn't seem right you wearing yourself out if it isn't necessary. Doctor Evans agrees with me. He has given me the names of two nurses he can thoroughly recommend, one for day duty, one for night. It's all arranged, there's no more to be said!'

Mercy was a little hurt and annoyed at his high-handed attitude, then she realized she was being unreasonable. She was tired, she had to admit. Wryly she noted to herself that she had to get used to a husband who tended to issue commands. The old easy-going Peter had been left behind somewhere in Flanders, it was a much more decisive Peter who had come back.

Against all the odds Agnes recovered, but she never regained her former robust health. Her heart had suffered, and she tired easily.

Her days now were spent sitting in her chair or sleeping. Agnes had become a semi-invalid, reduced to bouts of self-pity in which she would announce she was moving to her house in Chelston because she was no longer wanted at the Villa Dorata.

Mercy felt sorry for her, an emotion she had never expected to feel for her mother-in-law. There was something pathetic about this once domineering woman now reduced to a husk of her former self.

There was no question of Agnes living alone, of course; she was not well enough, but Mercy did not have the heart to say so. Instead, she pointed out that the house at Chelston was already let. Agnes would have to wait until the lease expired before she could move in. That day never came.

–

Gradually, the scars of the war years healed and life began to return to normal. It was not the normal of before the war, however. Somehow the tranquillity and even tenor of life in those pre-1914 days never returned. Things seemed to move more swiftly, and there was more dissatisfaction and agitation, probably because there was so much unemployment. Even the nurses employed to look after Agnes had been embarrassingly grateful to get a permanent job. Now that the VAD hospitals and wartime nursing homes were closing there was no need for so many fully trained medical staff.

Peter was conscious of the problems too. It was not unusual for strangers to come knocking at the door, men who had been under his command, and who were now in difficulties. There were letters, too, asking for help, which he never denied. In fact, Mercy suspected that he was spending a fair bit of money assisting his old soldiers.

Sailing continued to be Peter's overriding passion, and he spent a good deal of his time at the Yacht Club.

'I'm beginning to think you live there,' teased Mercy one day.

'Well, we've got to get the old club back on an even keel again. The place has got a bit run-down during these last few years.'

'It's not alone!' retorted Mercy, pointedly running her hand along a peeling windowsill.

'Yes, I agree. The house needs redecorating, inside and out.'

'All of it?' gasped Mercy.

'Certainly. The place hasn't seen a lick of paint since – since 1913 at least! I thought we'd have the outside done golden-yellow, as it used to be years ago. What do you think?'

'It sounds delightful. How nice it will be to see the old place spruced up once more.'

'Good! Then I'll get on to the decorators at once. Do you really object to me spending so much time at the Yacht Club?' he asked suddenly.

She had to smile. 'Of course not. You enjoy it so much.'

'There's a chance you'll be able to enjoy it with me, and not just as a guest. It's been proposed that ladies be allowed to become associate members! What do you think of that?' He sounded so thrilled with the idea that Mercy was forced to quell the laughter which rose in her.

'That's tremendous news,' she said gravely.

'Yes it is! It's high time, too! It hasn't been put before the committee yet, and of course there are bound to be a few who'll oppose it. I shall fight for it, though, don't worry. As soon as the motion is carried and on the books naturally I shall put you forward for membership!'

'Thank you, darling.' Mercy kissed him on the cheek.

'Talking of sailing and all that, have you had a look at old *Tango* recently?'

'Not for a while, no.'

'I went over to see her last week. Being laid up has done her no good at all, so I thought I'd put her in for a complete refit.'

'A refit?' The laughter died from Mercy's face.

'Yes, I did consider just having her overhauled, but she's in too bad a state. Besides, her engines need bringing up to date. There's been a lot of progress since she last put to sea, poor old girl.'

'That will cost a lot, surely?'

'It won't get any cheaper for waiting. There's a berth free down at Noss, and men available. To be honest I think they could do with the work now the war's finished.'

'It's admirable of you to give employment to those men,' Mercy said, keeping her voice calm. 'But wouldn't it be better to wait until we've had the house done, and spread the bills a little?'

'No, I do not! I doubt if the *Tango* is seaworthy now, so that would mean her being laid up for another twelve months, deteriorating all the time. Not to mention the fact that we could not use her. I can't understand you. I thought you would be pleased.'

Mercy found it hard to explain her objections. While Peter was in the Army she had managed to run the household pretty economically. Now he was home he had taken complete charge of their finances and she was growing alarmed at the rate they were spending money. Not all of it was Peter's fault, of course. They had more wages to pay as servants returned from the services, and they lived better now that thriftiness was not required as part of the war effort. Nevertheless, their expenses had increased out of all proportion.

'I am pleased. You know how I'd love to see *Tango* back in the water, only I think it would be wiser to wait a while.'

'Ever the prudent housekeeper!' he said, kissing her cheek, 'I'll admit you've done a marvellous job, keeping the household going and solvent while I've been away. However, that time is over. There's no need for you to worry your head over bills and expenditure and similar boring things. I'm here to take charge. You've enough to do looking after the children and Mother.'

Silently Mercy fumed at his condescension. But to speak out would only provoke a quarrel, which was the last thing she wanted.

'Very well,' she said. 'Have *Tango* rejuvenated, if it makes you happy.'

'Good!' Peter's face beamed. 'Of course it makes me happy. Why shouldn't I have fun modernizing *Tango*? You are having fun modernizing the house!'

Mercy agreed he had a point. She was thoroughly enjoying refurbishing the Villa Dorata. Peter fully approved of her ideas.

'You've done marvels!' he exclaimed a week later, regarding the newly finished dining-room. 'It's as if you'd let the sunlight in! I'd never realized how cheerful the place could look.'

'Yes, very cheerful, if you like ladders and dust-sheets and chaos.' Much as she was pleased with his approval the amount they were spending still bothered her. 'Peter, we've already done so much. Let's leave the upper floors for now.'

'And spoil the ship for a ha'p'orth of tar?'

Unfortunately there was more than a ha'p'orth of anything involved. They had other expenses, too, the boys' school fees, for instance. These were not exorbitant while they attended the local prep school, but it would not be long before John went off to school to Blundells in Tiverton, then the costs would increase. Mercy felt uneasy. It was all too much like the early days of their marriage. She hoped history was not going to repeat itself. Time and again she tried to get a fuller view of their finances, but Peter always fobbed her off.

Despite her other activities she made a point of visiting Joey regularly. He was doing so well now it was a pleasure to see him so happy. And she had to admit that she found his new business interesting.

'Flourishing, that's what we are!' Joey informed her contentedly. 'At last the cafe's got going. We're getting a good bit of trade in morning coffee, teas and light lunches, even out of season, and that's what I've been working for.'

'Well, you seem to have got it,' said Mercy. 'There wasn't an empty table as I passed, which is good, on such a rainy day.'

'Yes, Paignton finally knows we're here!' Joey gave a chuckle. 'I reckon it's all thanks to the pier burning down, you know.'

'How can you say that?' asked Mercy, in astonishment.

'It was the crowds who came to see the fun. If you'd seen the people packed along the Esplanade watching the flames, you'd know what I mean. The best free entertainment the town's had in years. Afterwards, when it was over, everyone was gasping for a cup of tea, and that was when Seaton's was discovered!'

'You idiot!' Mercy laughed.

'You think I'm joking, don't you? Well, maybe I am, but only a bit. There's no denying that in the couple of years since then our business has gone on improving. The outside catering's flourishing, too. We've got a few good regular orders – masonics, friendly society suppers and that sort of thing – and they help no end. We've taken on a woman to help Queenie in the kitchen. I've even had to get a girl in to help me serve at these outside do's.'

'Yes, I've seen her.' Mercy was not sure she liked her brother's new employee, Angie Bolton, for all she was bright and hard-working. The girl was too conscious of her own attractions, and the look in her eyes when she had gazed at Joey had been rather too bold and enticing. 'Wouldn't Millie help?'

'She can't be in two places at once, and, anyway, you just try ousting her from the cafe and see where it gets you. That's her territory, that is, and woe betide anyone who interferes. While we're on the subject of Millie,' he said, 'don't you think it's time I took over paying her wages?'

Mercy looked at him in horror. 'How did you know about that?'

'By doing a bit of ferreting! It's puzzled me for a long time, how her wages have been paid so regularly, especially when I knew that Ivywood place closed ages ago. I tried my darndest to find out who was responsible, but no one seemed to know. Then I met a lady who used to work at the clinic, Miss Beech, and she said a Mrs Mercy Lisburne had been in charge of that department, and suggested I should contact her. The silly thing was, it never occurred to me to ask you in the first place. I thought you'd only worked for Ivywood for a couple of weeks. But no, says Miss Beech, you were in charge of the clinic's welfare work for quite a while. I put two and two together. Why on earth did you never say something?'

'I'd almost forgotten I was paying Millie,' admitted Mercy. 'Besides, you worked so hard to pay back the money you borrowed, I thought it was a good way to help a little more.'

Joey shook his head in disbelief.

'What can I say?' he demanded, and for a moment Mercy wondered if he was going to be angry. 'At every turn you've helped me out. Those days are over now, though. I'm standing squarely on my own two feet, even if one of them is tin. I owe you for Millie's wages, at least going back to the start of Seaton's. Hang on a minute while I get my cheque-book—'

'No, there's no need. I don't want it, honestly!' Relieved as Mercy was that at least she had not offended her brother, it took all of her powers of persuasion to get Joey to keep the money.

'All right, it'll be your share in the business,' stated Joey. 'On one condition! If ever you need help – it sounds daft, I know, but it could happen – then you're to come to me first. Do you promise?'

'I promise,' agreed Mercy, though in truth she thought the day would never come.

–

Time drifted by and Mercy's life assumed a comfortable pattern, with nothing to mar her contentment. Even the wrench of John going away to school had its unexpected benefits for, once parted from his more ebullient brother, William became more outgoing. The wary relationship between him and Peter mellowed, and to Mercy's great relief, eventually warmed into real affection. Jennifer was a joy to them all. She had developed into a placid little girl, with such a sunny disposition that Peter jokingly wondered if they had been right to call her after her great-grandmother.

The *Tango* became a focus for the whole family, with long leisurely trips during the school holidays which somehow never seemed to be marred by foul weather or fog, or even much rain. It was a wonderful time. Mercy hoped it would never end.

But at 3 a.m, one morning, harsh reality entered their world with a noisy hammering at their bedroom door. Bleary-eyed, Mercy tried to focus on the clock. The urgent knocking continued, and an anxious voice called, 'Captain Lisburne! Mrs Peter! Oh please wake up!' Peter was out of bed in a trice, pulling on his dressing gown as he went. Mercy was hard on his heels. Agnes's nurse would not have awoken them without good reason.

'I am very concerned about Mrs Lisburne,' said Nurse Mellor urgently. 'I've already telephoned for Doctor Evans. I hoped I acted correctly?'

Peter was already dashing along the corridor ahead of them, so Mercy replied, 'Of course. You think it is that serious?'

'I'm afraid so, Mrs Peter.'

Even before Mercy entered the bedroom she could hear the harsh rasp of Agnes's breathing. Alarmed, she glanced questioningly at the nurse, who simply shook her head sadly.

'Is there nothing you can do for her?' demanded Peter of the doctor, when he came. 'Shouldn't she be in hospital?'

'It would be disturbing her for no purpose. Far better to keep her here, in familiar surroundings, with her loved ones near.' Doctor Evans spoke kindly, but the snap as he closed his leather bag seemed to have a terrible finality about it.

It was a long, dreadful night. No one woke the servants, they appeared of their own accord.

Blessedly, the children slept on. Everyone else was wide awake and tense, waiting for the inevitable moment. It came soon after dawn. A pale light was illuminating the sky, and the birds were starting to sing. It was then that Agnes stopped breathing.

Mercy mourned the loss of her mother-in-law far more than she had anticipated. They had never got on well, she would have been a hypocrite if she had said otherwise. Yet she missed her. Agnes had been an integral part of her life for a dozen years or so. It was hard to imagine the Villa Dorata without her.

Peter's grief surprised her too. Agnes's death had not been entirely unexpected, she was elderly and had been in ill health for some time. Nor had his relationship with his mother ever been a loving one. Nevertheless, he appeared numbed by his loss. All during the funeral ceremony his face was bleak and grim, a natural enough expression under the circumstances, as was his silence all the way back from the cemetery. What Mercy was not prepared for was the way his numb withdrawal continued for days afterwards.

The funeral was over, replies had been written to the messages of condolence, John had been driven back to school, and Mercy settled down to the quiet existence required by being in mourning. She, was writing letters in the drawing room one morning when a visitor was announced. It was Arthur Conway, the family solicitor.

'Mr Conway, this is an unexpected surprise,' she greeted him.

'Good morning, Mrs Lisburne.' He shook her hand. 'I'm sorry to disturb you. It was Captain Lisburne I wanted to see.'

'No doubt Rogers has gone in search of him. In the meantime, please sit down. Can I offer you a drink? Or some coffee?'

'That's very kind of you, but no thank you.' Arthur Conway sat down in a chair opposite her.

He was a lean, upright man, very correct in his manner, very self-assured. Today, however, Mercy felt that he was ill at ease. When Peter entered the room he rose with evident relief and said, 'Ah, Captain Lisburne! You are an elusive gentleman. I have been trying to contact you for some time!' The slight reproof in his voice was alien to his normally formal demeanour.

'I suppose you have.' Peter spoke abruptly. 'Very well, come along. Let's get it over with.'

They went from the room, leaving a puzzled Mercy sitting there. It was not her intention to eavesdrop. At first she found the rumble of male voices coming from the next room intrusive, so she rose to close the window. Once she heard the conversation more clearly, though, she froze, her hand on the latch.

'It can't be postponed any longer, Captain Lisburne!' Mr Conway was speaking quite sternly. 'You are only compounding the complications. Probate should have been applied for days ago. We must go ahead.'

'Why?' demanded Peter. 'I know what the outcome will be! And precious little comfort there is for any of us!'

'That may be so, sir. I appreciate your reluctance, things will not improve by trying to ignore them. The formalities must be observed.'

'Oh, do what the devil you like!' Peter sounded as if he were at the end of his tether. Then more calmly he added, 'My apologies, Conway. None of this is your fault, so I've no cause to snap at you. We'd better get on with it then. Where? Here in the dining-room?'

'If it would be convenient. There are no outside beneficiaries so perhaps the household could be summoned? With the exception of the children, of course.'

Mercy could not think what it all meant, only the mention of beneficiaries suggested something to do with Agnes's will. Now she considered it, she supposed there had been rather a delay in reading the will. She had barely stepped back from the window before Rogers entered.

'Your pardon, Madam. Captain Lisburne sends his compliments, and asks if you would be kind enough to join him in the dining room.'

Mercy went into the next room to find Mr Conway seated at the head of the table, an array of papers in front of him. Peter was gazing out of the window, his back to her, as if trying to disassociate himself with what was going on. A certain amount of whispering and shuffling outside announced the arrival of the servants. When Peter finally sat down opposite her his eyes steadfastly refused to meet hers.

'We are here to read the last will and testament of Mrs Agnes Gertrude Lisburne, who died on the 3rd day of October, in the year of our Lord, 1923,' began Mr Conway, adjusting the pince-nez on his nose. 'I suggest we continue without further delay.' He smoothed out the folded document before him and began to read. 'I, Agnes Gertrude Lisburne, née Penthorp, being of sound mind…'

His voice droned on, announcing the bequest of minor sums of money and personal mementoes to each of the servants, larger amounts to Rogers and the senior staff. Then came the division of her jewellery and more personal effects among the children, the bequest of her diamond brooch and the string of pearls that had once caused Peter such embarrassment to Mercy. To Peter was left the contents of the house, some mementoes of his late father and…

Mercy sat expectantly, waiting for these relatively minor items to be dealt with first. Not that she had any expectations for herself. She had been surprised that Agnes had left her anything at all. No, her hopes were for Peter and the children.

'…And finally the set of pearl and gold shirt-studs formerly the property of the late Mr Harold Lisburne. This being duly signed by me, Agnes Gertrude Lisburne, on this twelfth day of July.''

Mercy was astounded. That was the end of the will! Already the servants were leaving the dining-room. They were leaving silently because they were under the iron control of Rogers, but she could sense what a buzz of excitement they were holding back.

'Is that all?' she asked, astounded, when the three of them were alone.

'I am afraid so,' replied Mr Conway.

'But what of her stocks and shares? Her house at Chelston? Her capital?'

The solicitor looked anxiously at Peter, who simply waved a hand at him to continue.

'I regret to say they are all gone, Mrs Lisburne.'

'Gone? How? Why? They can't be!'

'I am afraid they are.'

'Why was I never told?' she demanded. 'Why?'

Peter looked uncomfortable. 'I wanted to spare you,' he said. 'I hoped things would improve.'

'But they haven't, have they?' she cried, incensed at being kept in ignorance of the state of their finances yet again. 'How much longer did you intend to keep quiet about it?'

Arthur Conway interrupted with a discreet cough. 'Unfortunately the late Mrs Lisburne's finances were the victims of the troubled times in which we live. The root of the trouble was that her husband, the late Mr Lisburne, invested most of his money in railways, mainly abroad. At the time these were splendid investments, of course. There was no way he could have envisaged the terrible events ahead.'

'You mean the war has caused the trouble?'

'Not really the war. You see, most of Mr Lisburne's investments were in the Imperial Russian railway system.'

'Russian? Surely—'

'Yes!' broke in Peter angrily. 'There is no Imperial Russian Railway, not now the Bolsheviks have taken over and claimed everything.'

'Then those stocks are worthless now?'

'They're waste paper.'

Mercy considered for a moment. The Bolshevik Revolution happened in 1917, the year in which Peter had his thirtieth birthday.

How ironic that he should gain his inheritance and then unknowingly lose it within months.

'What has Agnes been living on since then?' she asked.

'Her capital,' said Mr Conway. 'That was why the Chelston house had to be sold. Also, she did have an annuity, so during her lifetime she had few worries.'

'Thank goodness for that! At least we won't be paupers.'

Still angry, she rose to go. 'Please sit down again, Mercy.'

She took one look at Peter's white face and sank back into her chair.

Unnoticed, Mr Conway gathered up his things and crept away.

'You haven't told me the worst yet, have you?' she said. Her eyes fixed on him with mounting concern. 'Let me guess. It wasn't just your mother's money that was invested in Russian railways, was it? It was our money, too!'

'Yes.'

'So what have we been living on for the last five years?'

'Our capital… and Mother's annuity helped with the household expenses.'

Mercy tried to speak, but distress and anger blocked her words.

All she could do was to demand again, 'Why on earth didn't you tell me?'

'And have you worried about something that was not your concern? Certainly not!'

'Not my concern? How can you say that?'

'It was up to me to handle our finances. The responsibility, and the blame lie with me.'

'For heaven's sake, we're man and wife! We should share such problems!' In spite of her words she felt resentful. 'Oh Peter! The refurbishing of the house and the refit for the boat. Why did you go ahead with them when you knew this had happened?'

'I didn't think the revolution would last! I was sure the Bolsheviks would be overthrown and things in Russia would return to normality eventually.'

'Oh Peter, Peter, Peter!' Mercy could only shake her head in disbelief at such misplaced optimism. 'Well, *Tango* will have to go, and *Jasmine*, too. We can't afford to keep them now.'

'They've already been sold.'

'And still you said nothing to me?' Mercy exploded into anger. 'What else is there? There's bound to be other things you're keeping to yourself. We're no doubt up to the eyes in debt, are we?'

'No, we're not!' Peter snapped. 'That's one thing I've struggled against. I remembered how distressed you were about it last time.'

'I suppose I must be grateful for that. Have you told me all the bad news, or do you plan to surprise me with something else?'

'There is one more thing.'

'I guessed there would be!'

Peter took a deep breath.

'I had hoped... in fact, I was relying on Mother's annuity to help us out... I didn't realize... I've only just discovered it was for her lifetime only. It ceased on her death.'

Mercy's anger faded as swiftly as it had arisen, driven away by mounting fear.

'Then what income have we?'

'None.'

'And capital? Or assets?'

'None. Only the house.'

'Then what are we going to do?'

'I don't know.' The words were spoken in utter despair. 'Oh God! We're in such a mess, and it's all my fault! I was a fool, putting such trust in things going back to how they were. I should have known the world would change. But I wanted everything to be beautiful and perfect for us. The war years were so hard, with me away and you struggling here alone. I couldn't bear to see you living in a shabby house, or deprived of the lovely things I know you enjoy. When we were first married, one of my greatest pleasures was to give you the beautiful things you'd never had. I wanted to go on giving, making sure you never had to do without again. And now it's all gone wrong. We're ruined, and I am to blame!'

The desolation in his voice wrenched at her heart, making her regret her harsh words and angry tone. Again he had kept things from her, but he had done it to protect her. Amidst her anger, distress and shock she had to remember that, no matter how misguidedly, he had borne all this trouble alone for her sake. She held out her arms to him, holding him close, her head pressed tightly against his chest.

'The only thing I blame you for is remaining silent for so long. You should have shared these problems with me, not kept them to yourself.

Never once did I have the slightest inkling you had so much worry on your mind. It was wrong of you, my darling, but I know you were only trying to protect me, and I love you all the more for it.'

'Do you?' He sounded so surprised and relieved. 'I was convinced that you'd despise me for making such a mess of it.'

'No, never that!' she whispered, her arms encircling him even more tightly.

They clung together, speechless in their anxiety. It was Mercy who spoke first.

'We'd better start working out our future, don't you think? We do own the house, don't we? It hasn't been mortgaged?'

'Not yet, thank heaven! It's still ours.'

'Then why are we worrying? At least we've got something left.'

'I'd like to hold on to the house, if we can. Maybe we could rent it out, and go to live abroad for a while. They say Kenya's a marvellous place, lots of opportunities, wonderful climate.'

'Kenya!' Mercy was taken aback at the enormity of the idea. 'It's such a long way, and what would we do?'

'Farming out there seems pretty popular.'

'We'd need money to start us off!' Even to her own ears her words sounded defeatist and she knew despondency would get them nowhere. 'Well, if we're setting out to have a new life in a new country we'll have to get ourselves organized,' she said more heartily. 'We'd better start by reading every book about Kenya we can lay our hands on, to see what we're letting ourselves in for. And adventures don't come cheap. We must see how much money we can raise. The staff will have to go; that will be the hard part. We won't need all this furniture in Kenya, though. We'll pick out what we want to keep and sell the rest.'

'You mean, you'll come?'

'Try and stop me!'

She held out her hands to him, and he grasped them, too full of emotion to speak.

–

It was a bad time for selling. Mercy's jewellery fetched very little and paintings and furniture went for a fraction of their value. 'Trade is slack,' was the usual cry, alternated with, 'There's no demand for such old-fashioned pieces these days.' Even the car did not reach the price they had hoped. Worse still, no suitable tenant came forward to rent the Villa Dorata.

'It's no use, we're going to have to sell the house,' said Peter reluctantly. 'There's no other way. I only hope finding a buyer is easier than finding a tenant. I'll tell the estate agent to put it on the market immediately.'

Their meagre finances were dwindling alarmingly so Peter tried hard to find a job, but there were too many men in the same situation. Time and again he was turned down.

'We'll just have to make our start in Kenya a bit less ambitious,' said Mercy, when he returned home after yet another fruitless interview.

'Less ambitious? If we cut back our plans much more I can see us reduced to living in a mud hut with a strip of beans to cultivate,' he replied bitterly.

'Many successful people have started with less.' Mercy was determined to be optimistic, though it took a great deal of effort. If she were honest the thought of going to Africa made her heart sink. She knew enough about farming in England to realize how difficult it could be to wrest a living from the soil. She doubted if it would be much easier in Africa, especially with insufficient capital and no experience. The trouble was she could think of no alternative.

'I nearly forgot, here's a nice fat envelope for you from the Colonial Office.' Somehow she kept her voice cheerful. 'It will be the information you asked for about growing sisal and coffee in Kenya.'

'I'll read it after dinner.'

Peter took the package and threw it disconsolately on to the table that held their growing collection of books, maps and pamphlets about Kenya.

Mercy was making the dinner when an urgent ringing at the front doorbell pierced the stillness of the kitchen. It had been years since she had done any cooking, and she was enjoying herself. The long trek to the front door was less enjoyable. She had never before appreciated how far it was from the servants' quarters. The last person she expected to find on the doorstep was Joey — an undeniably angry Joey.

'Right, I want to know what all this is about!' he declared, waving a newspaper under her nose.

She was as taken aback by his arrival as his forceful greeting.

'This is what I mean!' Joey stabbed his forefinger at a page of the newspaper. 'Is this your house, in the "For Sale" column, or is it not?'

'Yes, certainly it is… Why, what's the matter? Oh, do come in, we can't talk on the doorstep!' She stood back, and Joey limped into the hall.

'You ask what's the matter! You! I like that!' Joey flourished the paper angrily once more. 'Come on now, Sis. What's happened? Why are you selling?'

'Is something wrong?' Peter came hurrying downstairs. 'Who's this?'

'It's my brother, Joey. Don't you recognize him?'

'Ah yes! Well brother or no brother, I won't have you shouting at my wife!' Peter snapped. 'So you can mend your manners now or get out!'

'I'll get out when I've had a few answers, and not before. I want to know what's happened to make you need to sell this place,' retorted Joey.

'Do you indeed? Then let me point out to you it's none of your business. Now get out!' Peter's face was white with anger.

'It is my business! Mercy's my sister, and if she's in some sort of trouble I want to know about it!'

'Do you indeed!' The two men were facing up to one another so belligerently Mercy was afraid they would come to blows.

'Oh, do calm down, the pair of you, and stop being silly,' she said, unconsciously adopting the same tone of voice she used on the boys when they were squabbling.

For a moment longer her husband and her brother continued to glare at one another, then Joey suddenly grinned.

'We'd better do as she says, otherwise she's quite capable of giving us both a clip across the ear,' he said.

'I'm sorry. I shouldn't have rushed in here like a bull in a china shop, it was just seeing the advert so unexpectedly.' He turned to Mercy. 'You promised, Mercy! You promised you'd come to me if you needed help. And you didn't!'

'I know. I'm sorry… Look, our dinner's nearly ready. Come and have something to eat with us, and we'll talk.'

'I'd like to…' Joey looked questioningly towards Peter, who gave a stiff nod of agreement.

'That's settled then! Come on!' said Mercy.

Joey followed her, with Peter bringing up the rear. They ate in the small room which had once been Rogers's domain. Joey's eyebrows rose when he saw the modest surroundings. They rose even further when Mercy served up the meal, but he said nothing, not until they had begun eating.

'Right!' he said. 'No servants, and selling the family home! That's got to mean money trouble! So what happened? I'm not being nosey or interfering,' he said to Peter. 'I want to help.'

'It's kind of you,' Peter answered quietly, clearly reluctant to discuss their affairs with anyone, even Mercy's brother. 'All the same, there's nothing you can do.' He did not add that Joey was hardly qualified to advise him on financial matters, but the thought hung unspoken on the air.

'How do you know until you tell me the problem?' Joey insisted.

'Peter's right.' Mercy laid down her knife and fork with a gesture of despair. 'You wouldn't be able to help. We've had a bit of bad luck, and to cut a long story short, all our capital has gone.'

'In that case what you need is something to tide you over, until you get on your feet again.' Joey leaned forward eagerly. 'I've got a bit tucked away. I was planning to buy the house next door and expand Seaton's, but you're welcome to it. It's not a fortune, only a few hundred. Still, it should help.'

'Oh Joey, we couldn't take your money,' Mercy said, deeply touched.

'Why not? I took yours!' Joey said cheerily. 'And very useful it was. You've a share in the business, don't forget. Without you two I would never have got started. So why shouldn't I come to your rescue, for a change?'

'We appreciate the gesture,' broke in Peter. 'Nevertheless, we must say no. We've made up our minds to sell the house and go out to Kenya, to try our hand at farming.'

'Kenya? Farming?' Joey stared at him incredulously. 'Do you know anything about farming? Or Kenya, for that matter?'

'Not much. No doubt we'll soon learn,' Peter replied. Joey's sharp gaze went from his sister's face to that of her husband, and he said, 'If you'll forgive me for saying so, neither of you looks overjoyed at the prospect. It's a big step to take and a long way to go for something you're not keen about. Isn't there something else you could do? Something less drastic?'

'Such as?' demanded Mercy gloomily.

'You've thought of letting the place?'

'Yes, and got no response. To be honest we'll be lucky to get a buyer, and I don't see us getting anywhere near the asking price,' she said, her gloom increasing.

'And what will you do if the house doesn't sell?'

'I don't know, honestly I don't! I suppose we can always take in lodgers.' Mercy said with bitter humour. After a moment she looked up. 'That's not a bad idea, you know,' she said. 'We've enough bedrooms and plenty of space. A family guest-house! Something modest!'

'That's an idea!' Joey regarded her eagerly. 'But a family guest-house? It can be a lot of hard work for a very poor return. No one knows that better than me!' 'Then we'd better make it an hotel,' said Mercy.

As soon as the words were out of her mouth there was a dramatic silence.

'Now that *is* a good idea!' Joey was staring at her, his face suddenly tense.

'A top-class hotel, with the best of everything, catering for the cream of society!' Mercy's imagination was catching fire.

'Right,' agreed Joey. 'Make it really smart! Have the latest in everything!'

'And superb food, and comfortable bedrooms...'

'With washbasins...'

'Maybe even a cocktail lounge!'

'What, in each bedroom?'

'No, you fool! You know what I mean!'

'If you have a cocktail lounge you'll have to have a barman who really knows how to make white ladies and corpse revivers, and who shakes them with style...'

'Just like they do in the films...'

'This all sounds very well, but it's of no help to us!' Peter's voice brought Mercy and Joey up with a jolt. They had been so caught up in their excitement that they had not noticed his apathy.

'It could be!' said Mercy. 'Don't you see? Turning the Villa Dorata into an hotel could be just what we need.'

'What do we know about the hotel business, for a start?' asked Peter.

'You and I know nothing!' Mercy admitted. 'Joey does, though. Maybe he could advise us… or better still, come in with us. Would you, Joey?'

She hardly needed to ask. Although he was struggling to keep his face impassive Joey's eyes burned with enthusiasm.

'Like a shot! You know I've always wanted to run a decent hotel,' he replied.

'And what about you, Mercy? Do you think you would really like the hotel business?' Peter asked.

She gave the matter careful consideration.

'Yes, I think I would,' she said. 'Certainly more than farming in Africa. And I've found it interesting, being at Joey's… That's a point! What would you do about Seaton's?'

'I could get someone in to run it,' her brother replied. 'Or else I could sell the whole lot and put the money into this place.'

'Which brings us to the knotty problem of finance! Where's the money going to come from for these grand plans of yours?' demanded Peter.

'From the bank,' said Joey cheerily.

'And you think they'll give it to us, just for the asking?' Peter's tone was sarcastic.

'I can't see them turning us down. You've got the house to offer as security, and I can throw in Seaton's – that's if I don't sell it, of course. It doesn't match up to the Villa Dorata, but it's doing very nicely.'

'I don't see why we're having this discussion!' Peter sat back abruptly in his chair. 'It's not as though this hotel idea is anything more than hot air.'

'I don't agree!' Mercy exclaimed. 'The more I think about it the more I like it! It's a definite possibility…' She paused, for the first time noticing his grim expression. 'Doesn't the thought of running an hotel appeal to you?'

'No, it does not! I loathe the idea of complete strangers wandering about my home!' He was so emphatic that she was startled.

'But, darling, there'll be strangers here if we sell!'

'True, but I won't be forced to watch! I'll be in Kenya!'

'Then there's no more to be said!' Mercy struggled to hide her disappointment. She looked down at the food congealing on her plate. 'Goodness! The dinner's cold! It's inedible! I'll clear away and do us some bacon and eggs instead.'

'Don't bother for me, thanks. I'm not hungry.' Peter rose to his feet. With a brief 'Good night' to Joey, he left the room.

'Don't cook specially for me.' Joey rose too. 'Queenie'll have supper waiting, and if I don't eat it she'll get in a tizzy, thinking I'm sickening for something.' He managed a smile, although his disappointment too was very visible. Mercy knew how he felt. For a brief moment they had had a wonderful vision, but their hopes and dreams had been swept away.

'You'll get your first-class hotel one day, don't worry,' she said, as she kissed him goodbye.

'If you say so!' He gave a faint grin, 'it was a nice idea while it lasted, though, wasn't it?'

'It was,' she agreed. 'Very nice!'

Between her and Peter the subject of hotels was not mentioned again. However, Mercy found she could not put the thought from her mind. When Peter was not home she wandered through the house, looking at the rooms – so many of them now unused, planning which could be used as guests' rooms, staff quarters, public rooms. Part of what was now the servants' accommodation could be made into a lovely flat for their own use… The more she considered the facilities, the more the villa seemed suitable for conversion. It was not over-large, of course. Still, in time they could extend. She grinned to herself, she was beginning to think like Joey. Then she sighed. Such a pity! It was a lovely idea! And one she couldn't forget.

–

The people who came to view the house were few, and for the most part they exclaimed at its size and the difficulty of running it with the present servant problem. The only man who showed any real interest was a bombastic fellow in a loud suit, who, ironically, wanted it for an hotel. Peter winced openly as the man condemned the place as old-fashioned, criticized the decor, and sniffed contemptuously at the grounds.

'The man's a philistine!' he declared to Mercy as they went to bed that night. 'Did you hear him? Knock down the walls to make most of the ground floor into one enormous dance hall indeed! "Bringing the place up to date" he called it! I've got a different name for it!'

'I think he may have been trying to get us to drop the price,' said Mercy. 'He's certainly the most hopeful prospective buyer we've had so far.'

'More's the pity!' Peter thumped his pillow with unnecessary violence before he settled down. He did not sleep, though. For a long time after they had switched out the light Mercy sensed he was still awake. Eventually he said, 'I've been thinking about this idea of going to Kenya.'

'Oh yes...?'

'We shall miss this place when we go, won't we? And our friends...? I'm not desperately keen on going, are you?'

'Not really, no!'

There was a long pause, then he spoke again.

'That fellow this afternoon was the absolute end, wasn't he? The thought of having to sell the Villa Dorata to him makes my flesh creep... In fact, I hate the idea of selling it at all. At least if we ran it as an hotel ourselves it would still be ours... and we wouldn't be knocking the drawing room about to make a dance floor for flappers to cavort about on, would we?'

Mercy was suddenly wide awake.

'Certainly not,' she replied. 'Peter, darling, does this mean you want to turn the house into an hotel?'

'No,' he said flatly. 'But I've thought about it and it seems to be the lesser of an awful lot of evils. That is, if you and your brother haven't gone off the idea.'

'I certainly haven't, and I'm pretty sure Joey's still enthusiastic.'

'Right, then the three of us had better get together as soon as possible, to see what can be done.' He gave his pillow another thump and settled down, putting an end to all discussion about their future for the moment.

For a long time after Peter had gone to sleep Mercy lay wide awake. Sleeplessness was something she had grown accustomed to of late, as her worries and anxieties thrashed about in her mind. This time it was different. This time she felt as if a great load had been lifted off her shoulders; for a long time she spent the night hours thinking and planning, until she finally drifted off into a deep and relieved sleep.

Chapter Eighteen

'This seems rather a lot. Are you sure this expenditure is necessary?' Peter regarded the pages in front of him, his brow furrowed.

'What are you referring to in particular?' There was a hint of impatience in Joey's tone.

'Most of it, if you want the truth. Take heating the bedrooms, for example. Surely it isn't necessary, not for every one? You say yourself the summer is getting nearly as busy as the winter. Couldn't we manage with less?'

'No,' Joey said firmly. 'We want guests all year round, don't we? Winter and summer? Cold weather and hot? Therefore we need to heat the bedrooms.'

'Every one?' insisted Peter.

'It's easier in the long run. We'll get the mess finished in one go, and overall it will be cheaper. I've looked at the steam heating systems which are on the market and this is the best!' Joey pushed a catalogue across the table. 'I've put a mark against the radiators we're having, and according to the plumber they'll be here—'

'You've actually ordered them?' Peter cut in.

'Yes, I have.'

'It never occurred to you to consult us?' Peter's voice was icy. 'I understood ours was a three-way partnership!'

'For heaven's sake! We needed heating pipes so I ordered some! I don't know what the fuss is about!' Joey slumped back in his chair.

He did know! Mercy could tell from his air of sulky defiance. It was exactly the same expression he used to adopt as a small boy, when he was in the wrong but refused to admit it. Only, he was not a small boy any longer, he was a grown man. This was not the first time in their new partnership he had overstepped the mark. She understood his officiousness stemmed from his enthusiasm and determination to make the hotel a success. And there was no denying that when it came to the hotel business he was the one with the experience. Nevertheless, his somewhat domineering attitude did tend to rub Peter up the wrong way. The early planning, the organizing of the bank loan, and the drawing up of the partnership had gone smoothly; it was only when the Villa Dorata began being converted into the Villa Dorata Hotel that the friction began. Poor Peter, she feared the alterations to his beloved home were proving far more than he had expected. He was still deeply attached to the house, while Joey saw it only as a place ripe for conversion, and so they disagreed.

'It is a very good system,' she said. 'And I agree with you about the style of radiator, it's the best possible choice. In future, however, I think we must confer over everything except the most minor things. Imagine what would have happened if all three of us had ordered heating systems.'

'We'd have had the cosiest guests in the country,' said Joey.

'And the biggest coal bills,' added Peter. Then suddenly they all grinned, and the tension was broken.

Mercy was relieved. The clash of wills between her husband and her brother was something she had not anticipated. She hoped it would only be temporary. She had to admit that she was finding the activity exciting. She was enjoying the planning and the organization, and, in addition, she was looking forward to actually running the hotel. It was all so new and stimulating. Even more, it was a definite way out of their financial difficulties. She had no doubt about it! She was just as determined as Joey that their hotel was going to succeed. Sometimes, though, she thought Peter still had doubts.

'We're going to have to charge an awful lot to cover the cost of this work,' he remarked, when they were alone. 'Do you think we'll get enough people willing to pay so much?'

'Of course we will! Just look at the list of distinguished visitors in the *Torquay Directory* every week. We live in a very popular spot.'

'Won't the really wealthy take themselves and their money to the South of France, or somewhere like that?'

'Some will, I dare say, until they hear about the Villa Dorata Hotel. The luxuries and amenities of Nice or Cannes, with all the comforts of home. They'll come flocking, you'll see!'

'When you put it like that I don't see how they can resist,' Peter smiled. 'Now, what's this you're working on?'

Mercy put down her watercolour brush, and held up the painting for him to see.

'It's a design for the new cocktail lounge. What do you think of it?'

'Very nice indeed. Very Japanesey. Rogers's old pantry will be quite transformed. I never realized I had such a talented wife.'

Mercy looked up at him. 'You don't mind, do you?' she asked. 'About having a cocktail lounge? It's not… too slick, in your opinion?'

'No, of course not,' he smiled. 'Especially when it will be so tastefully decorated. We must be up to date. Never let it be said the Villa Dorata Hotel was old-fashioned.'

'And what about the hotel? No regrets?'

'Certainly not. Looking at it dispassionately it was the only choice we had! That idea about going to Kenya was so much moonshine now I think of it. What do either of us know about farming in Africa? It would have been a disaster. Here, at least, we've got Joey to guide our faltering footsteps towards success.' He reached out and brushed a stray strand of hair from her forehead. 'You mustn't worry about me. I'll soon get the hang of things.'

She smiled back at him, reassured.

In the weeks which followed there was no time for doubts. They seemed to start work at seven in the morning, and didn't finish until ten at night, or later. Joey saw so little of his own home Mercy wondered that Queenie did not complain. But then, when had Queenie ever complained about anything Joey did?

Gradually the Villa Dorata was transformed, until it was almost ready for its new role.

Mercy regarded the entrance hall critically, then felt a sense of satisfaction. She was glad that while they had been forced to sell much of the furniture they had managed to hold on to the Waterford crystal chandelier and the set of pretty brocade chairs. Along with the pleasing sweep of the staircase they ensured that the guests' first impressions of the Villa Dorata Hotel would be of timeless elegance.

'What do you think?' she asked Joey. 'There'll be a flower arrangement on the side-table, of course. Tasteful yet welcoming, that's the effect I've been working for.'

'Very swanky,' said her brother, with the minimum of enthusiasm. He had petitioned for up-to-the-minute upholstery in tan leather, and coloured parchment lampshades.

Mercy chuckled. 'All right, you don't have to tell me your true opinion,' she said. 'What have you got there?'

'It's the advertisement to go in the *Directory* and the *Express*, applying for staff. Do you approve? Peter says it's fine.'

Mercy read what he had written. 'That looks splendid! Just imagine! We're looking for staff already! We'll be opening before we know it.'

'Excited?'

'Yes, and a little scared!'

'You've no need. You'll take to it like a duck to water, you'll see.'

'I'll have to! The alternative is to sink!'

A small crowd of girls and women was waiting outside the tiny room, once a cloakroom, which had been designated as an office. From her position at the desk Mercy could hear their voices, some nervous, some excited, some frankly curious about their surroundings. Whatever their attitudes they wanted the same thing – work! Feeling quite nervous herself she called in the first applicant.

It was a long morning, interviewing one person after another. Anxious not to make any mistakes, she scrutinized references, looked each would-be employee steadfastly in the eye to detect any signs of shiftiness – and was careful not to make any acceptances until she had seen everyone! It was an exhausting process, but she felt she must be getting near to the last candidate.

'And what is your name?' she said, turning to a fresh sheet in her notebook as the door opened once again.

'Dolly Tucker. Mrs Dolly Tucker.'

The voice was bright and ebullient and it struck a familiar chord in Mercy's memory. She looked up and found herself facing a stout woman of her own age. For all there was uncertainty on the plump face, even a hint of awkwardness, the round blue eyes twinkled boldly.

'Dolly!' Mercy exclaimed, leaping to her feet so suddenly she sent a sheaf of papers drifting to the floor. 'Dolly Dyer, of all people!'

'I didn't think you'd recognize me, ma'am.'

'Recognize you? How could I help it? You haven't changed! Oh, yes you have! There's rather more of you than there used to be!'

'That's true! There's always been plenty of me. More than enough to go round, my Tom says,' chuckled Dolly. Then added belatedly, 'ma'am!'

'For goodness' sake, stop all this ma'am business! It's me! Mercy! Have you forgotten?'

A resounding sigh escaped from Dolly's stiffly corseted frame.

''Course I aven't forgotten,' she said. 'I just wasn't sure 'ee'd want to remember, you being so grand and everything.'

'Oh, never too grand to remember you!'

Mercy had a sudden impulse to hug the portly woman in front of her, an impulse she subdued, feeling unaccountably shy. She was overwhelmed by delighted emotion at meeting her childhood friend again. It occurred to her that in the intervening years no other female had shown her the same companionship and affection as the cheerfully vulgar Dolly. Until this moment she had not realized how much she had missed her comradeship. Dolly's face smiled until her cheeks positively glowed. 'There, I know'd I was right. My Tom said I shouldn't come, that I'd just get upset because 'ee wouldn't want to know me no more. I know'd better, though! I know'd 'ee wouldn't 'ave changed, not that much!'

'And how is Tom? He is an electrician, isn't he? If he's kept to his trade he must be doing very well these days. Almost everything has become electrical.'

The cheery smile flickered and almost faded.

'Yes, 'e's still a 'lectrician,' Dolly said. 'And real good at it. If only 'is 'ealth would let 'im we'd be real prosperous.'

'I am sorry. What was it? The war?'

Dolly nodded. 'Gassed 'e were. Oh, not real bad, like some of they poor souls. Not even bad enough for a disability pension 'ccording to the War Office, but then the War Office don't have to listen to the poor man wheezing and gasping to get a breath of air down 'is lungs, do they? Sometimes 'e's fine, able to work like the best, then it turns windy or the sea mist comes in and 'e can't 'ardly breathe.'

'So you need a job! Right, you've got one!'

'Just like that?' Dolly was delighted. 'Oh thanks! I don't care what 'tis!'

'Which job can I give you? I know! How would you like to look after the linen? You'd be in charge of everything, from issuing clean sheets and towels, to checking the laundry, to seeing to repairs. Would you like that?'

'Would I?' The glow was back on Dolly's face. 'Yer, if old Ma 'Oskins loses a pillowcase or summat, can I ring 'er up and be all snotty-nosed to 'er over the phone?'

327

'Ma Hoskins? Surely she's not still about?'

'Yes 'er is! Nagging the girls worse than ever. I nearly went for a job back there again, but my Tom says, "You'm not going back to any bleedin' female slave-driver. Us'll starve first!".'

'And the awful Albert?'

'Oh 'e died a few years back. Of something nasty! They should have pinned a medal on who ever gave it to 'im, I reckon!'

'You really haven't changed, have you?' Mercy laughed. 'And yes, you have my express permission to be as snotty-nosed as you like to old Ma Hoskins!'

'I'd really enjoy that, I would! If I could afford to I'd work for 'ee for nothing, just to be allowed to do it!' Dolly put on an affected voice. '"Missus 'Oskins? This is the Villa Dorata 'Otel 'ere, and h'I wants to know what the bleedin' 'ell you've done with h'our pillowcases!"'

'There'll be no need to work for nothing, I assure you. I still haven't worked out your hours yet; you'll be paid a deal more than you'd get from Ma Hoskins!'

'That's grand! That's real grand!' Dolly seemed quite overcome. 'Oh, and there's one thing I've got to say! There won't be no familiarity from me, nor no gossip neither. You'm Mrs Lisburne to me now, and that's what I'll call 'ee. They days when you was Mercy Seaton are forgot! At least, I idn't going to mention 'em ever!'

'That's very good of you, Dolly.' Mercy was touched at such thoughtfulness. 'Thinking it over, though, I'm not sure I want those days forgotten entirely. I'd like a good gossip about them sometime when we're on our own and have got a minute to spare. And for goodness' sake call me Mercy! At least, when we're on our own. I suppose it would be better if you addressed me as Mrs Lisburne in public, though, for the sake of staff discipline, if you wouldn't mind.'

'Staff discipline! Oo, 'ark at 'er!' grinned Dolly delightedly. 'I'm that pleased to see 'ee again I'd call 'ee anything 'ee like! Now I'd better go. You'm still got 'alf a dozen chewing their finger-ends off out there.'

It had been a jolt seeing Dolly again. A pleasant one, but a jolt nevertheless. It brought back Mercy's early days at the Fernicombe Cottages, and at the Orchard Laundry. They had been hard times, yet looking back they were not all gloom. There had been a comradeship among the girls that she had never seen among her wealthier companions. Maybe having to struggle against poverty brought people together. Certainly her bond with Dolly seemed to have endured and she found she was looking forward to working with her old schoolfriend.

The hotel was nearing completion. Much to Mercy's relief the building alterations were finished, even the installing of the heating system. She was heartily glad to see an end to the noise and the dust and the chaos. In place of the builder's lorries there were now delivery vans jamming the drive. Furniture, carpets, glassware, crockery, linen... the list seemed endless. By some miracle a place was found for everything and the Villa Dorata began to look less like the scene of a minor earthquake and more like an hotel.

Now that the hotel was almost complete they had to organize how they would run it. The threat of clashes between Joey and Peter had long since prompted them to portion out the responsibilities equally. Basically Mercy had charge of the housekeeping side of things, Joey controlled the dining room and kitchens, while everything outdoors, such as maintenance of house and grounds, the tennis-courts, and garaging for cars, fell to Peter. The management and administration they proposed to share, and already they found it necessary to hold regular meetings to thrash out hotel policy.

'Having dealt with the printing for the hotel,' said Peter at one of these meetings, 'I suggest we go on to something really important – it's high time we thought about our wine cellar.'

Joey was scribbling down notes. 'I'll see to it, don't worry,' he said.

His words were greeted with such a profound silence he looked up. 'Well, what's wrong with that?' he demanded.

'Nothing,' replied Peter. 'Only, haven't you more than enough to do?'

'Whereas you haven't! I suppose you feel better qualified to decide on wines and spirits than me?'

There was an angry edge to his voice, and Mercy felt bound to intervene. 'You must admit it would make sense to have Peter in charge,' she said. 'I know you used to serve wines and spirits at the Devonshire Hall, but you were only there for a short time, although you learned a lot. Peter, on the other hand, has been drinking wine and learning to appreciate it since he was a boy.'

'There's no need to make me sound such an old soak,' Peter remarked.

For a moment it looked as though Joey was going to disagree. Then he changed his mind. 'Very well, if you really want the job,' he said.

Mercy was relieved. Joey's taste in wine was awful, and she had dreaded telling him so. She was happy for Peter's sake, too. It was a job after his own heart.

'Where will you begin?' she asked.

'I'd like to get a really good house wine to start with,' Peter said. 'I doubt if any of the local wine merchants have sufficient choice. I'll probably approach some of the shippers direct. Of course, the ideal thing would be to go over to France and buy straight from the producer, that way we'd know exactly what we're getting.'

'Why don't you do that? It would certainly make our wine list something special,' Mercy said.

'What, when we're so busy? It's impossible!'

'Why don't the pair of you go?'

They looked at Joey in astonishment.

'And leave you to cope alone?' exclaimed Mercy.

'I can manage for a few days. Come to think of it, a break for all of us wouldn't be a bad thing. Once we open we're going to be run off our feet. It's now or never if we want a short holiday. I could go when you come back.'

'It sounds a marvellous idea.' Mercy looked at Peter. 'It would be a bit of a busman's holiday for you, darling, going round vineyards all the time. Would you mind?'

'I think I could put up with it,' he said gravely.

'What about you and Queenie?' Mercy asked Joey. 'Where will you go?'

'Oh, Queenie's not much of a one for going away. She's happier staying in Paignton. I'll probably go off somewhere on my own.' Something in his voice made Mercy look at Joey sharply, but he turned his gaze away. Puzzled, she wondered what plans he had in mind that prevented him from meeting her eyes.

–

Not until they were actually motoring through the softly rolling countryside of the Loire district did Mercy really believe they were in France. They went at a leisurely pace, combining their search for good wines with exploring the area. The days had an unreal, magical quality about them.

'It's because we're entirely on our own,' said Peter. 'How many times have we promised ourselves a trip like this, with just the two of us? Well, at last it's happening! No children, no friends, just us!'

'A second honeymoon?' suggested Mercy. 'Perhaps in a way it is. Honeymoons are times of transition, aren't they? And when we get home our lives are certainly going to be very different.'

'I confess my definition of a honeymoon is not quite yours. I think mine has something to do with the moon glinting on the Loire, the château on the hill silhouetted against the night sky, and you and I sharing a superb supper for two.'

'What moon? What chateau?' demanded Mercy laughing. 'It's still broad daylight.'

'Have patience. Daylight doesn't last for ever.' He smiled down at her with so much love in his expression that she had no alternative but to kiss him. She could not help herself.

Their return home was the signal for Joey to take his brief holiday. He had still not confided his plans. He murmured vaguely about touring and 'seeing a bit of the country'. It was unlike Joey to be evasive. One thing was certain, he was not taking his wife with him. On the phone Queenie confessed, uncharacteristically, to being understaffed and overworked.

'It's not poor Angie's fault, she couldn't help being taken ill so suddenly,' she said.

So it was Angie Bolton who happened to have been struck by a mysterious illness and on the very day of Joey's departure, too. Mercy felt troubled. Angie was bright, pretty, and definitely had her eye on Joey. When he returned, though, Mercy said nothing. She hoped her fears were groundless.

–

The opening of the Villa Dorata Hotel was scheduled for the beginning of June. There were several people booked in for that first day. The entire staff, from Mercy, Peter and Joey, to the bootboy, were on tenterhooks, waiting to see who would be the first guest to cross the doorstep. A dozen times Mercy checked personally to make sure the rooms were in order, the curtains draped correctly, and the towels immaculate. Every approaching car engine was interpreted as an approaching taxi, every phone call feared as a cancellation.

As it turned out, their very first guest did not have a booking at all. A taxi drew up at the front door, and one man emerged, bearing a much-travelled suitcase. Approaching Joey, who was on duty at the reception desk, he asked, 'Would you have a single room free for about a week? I'm afraid it's short notice. I only made my mind up to come at the last minute.'

'We have indeed, sir. Here is our tariff.' Joey handed him a card bearing the list of charges. 'I hope it is satisfactory?'

'Yes, perfectly all right, thank you.' The man barely bothered to look at the prices. 'I suppose you'll want me to sign the register? My name is Dobson.' He was middle-aged and nondescript in appearance. The only thing of note about him was the faded bronze of his skin, a sign that he had spent some considerable time in the tropics. To Mercy, Peter and Joey, however, he was a very special. He was their first guest!

'Before you are shown your room, Mr Dobson,' said Peter, stepping forward, 'we would like to make a small presentation. This is our very first day as an hotel, and you are our first guest, we would like to mark the occasion.'

It fell to Mercy to hand over the inscribed crystal goblet and wish him an enjoyable stay.

'I say!' said Mr Dobson. 'Oh I say!' He looked completely over-whelmed. 'Oh I say!' he repeated yet again. 'I didn't expect anything like this.' Then he gave a beaming smile. Seeing his evident pleasure Mercy, for one, found herself relaxing. Their first guest was so delighted it had to be a good omen.

In one respect their first day was inauspicious – the weather let them down. They had planned a special reception for their grand opening, and being June, it was hoped the specially invited guests would be able to stroll on the rose-entwined terrace and sip their cocktails. Being a typical English summer, the day proved to be rain-lashed and bitterly cold.

'Never mind, once they've got a couple of Harry's sidecars inside them they won't notice if it snows,' said Joey confidently.

'I hope you're right and that Harry's going to earn his keep!' replied Mercy. She had serious misgivings about paying a barman an exorbitant wage simply because he could mix decent cocktails.

'You're getting to be a proper penny-pincher,' Joey chuckled. 'Don't worry, Harry'll be worth his fee. We were darned lucky to get him. He'll be a real asset, you'll see—Oh lord! Will you look at that fool!' Joey's attention swung to a waiter who, resplendent in black bow-tie, was passing with a tray of canapes. 'Don't you know better than to wear a white hankie in your top pocket? What're you trying to do? Be mistaken for a guest?'

Crimson-faced, the young man removed the offending item, and stuffed it in his trouser pocket.

'Everything looks absolutely splendid,' said Peter, coming up and surveying the scene. 'I hope people turn up. It's a foul night.'

'Well, to start with we've got the resident guests, including Mr Dobson, and they're certain to come.'

'That's not very many.'

'For our first week we're doing very well! Don't be such a pessimist!' Mercy tucked a white carnation into the lapel of his dinner-jacket. 'Our reputation will soon spread. That's why we've invited so many people to our "grand opening"!'

'Yes, of course. I must confess I'll be heartily glad when tonight's over, and this venture is under way.'

'Please don't dread it. There's nothing to worry about.' She squeezed his hand reassuringly. 'Just talk to people as you normally do and everything will be fine.'

'I hope you are right.'

Mercy was certainly right about the success of their cocktail party. Despite the unseasonal weather, just about everyone who had received an invitation had come. The first to arrive, Billie and Cynthia Shaw, yachting acquaintances of Peter's, made straight for the cocktail bar. Noticing their destination Joey winked triumphantly at Mercy. Soon the *chic* new cocktail glasses were being refilled all round and the canape trays replenished.

Lord Alston was one of the first to arrive. He wandered about the place with undisguised curiosity and admiration.

'Well I'm blessed!' he said eventually. 'What a remarkably good job you've made of it! Took a bit of courage, I dare say, having the old homestead knocked about. It'll be worth it, though. And you're not too big. I can't stand big hotels, the sort where you need a map and compass to get from the bar to the billiard-room. I must get a copy of your tariff before I go. I've got a little dinner party planned, just a few old friends, they'd love to eat here.'

Mercy knew Lord Alston had a superb dining-room of his own which was perfectly adequate for entertaining. He also had an excellent cook who was more than capable of producing superb dinners.

'What a good friend you are,' she said, smiling. 'We'll make sure your evening here will be a memorable one.'

'I'm sure you will, my dear. But I mustn't monopolize you, much as I would like to. You go off and mingle with your other guests, while I see what else your barman chappie – what's his name? Harry? – has in his repertoire.' As Lord Alston moved towards the bar Lilian Manning and her husband came hurrying over.

'We've been exploring your hotel, isn't it disgraceful of us!' Lilian announced cheerfully. 'Everywhere looks so nice! You must tell me who made your curtains, the way they hang is an absolute dream!'

'Our curiosity was not an idle one, Mrs Lisburne.' Unlike his wife, Henry Manning looked awkward. 'Dash it all, I'm not sure what the form is on an occasion like this. Would it be all right to discuss business?'

'You see, we've never known anyone who owned an hotel before!' Lilian slid her arm through her husband's and snuggled closer. 'We think it's absolutely thrilling!'

'I'm not sure of the form either,' admitted Mercy, smiling. 'So if there is something you want to discuss just go ahead.'

'We wondered if you are proposing to take permanent guests. You see, I have an elderly aunt—'

'She's an absolute dear!' Lilian broke in. 'But getting on a bit, poor love. It's crazy, her living alone in her great big house, so she's been looking for somewhere where she would be comfortable and well looked after. She won't come to us, although we've begged her. I suppose she doesn't want to impose. Now, if she were here, with you, it would be perfect.'

'We wouldn't want you to feel obliged to take her, simply because we're friends,' added Henry Manning hurriedly.

'I think it's nice of you to consider us,' Mercy said. 'Why don't I give you our list of terms? Then you can consult your aunt, and bring her to have a good look round. Come whenever it suits you, and there will be no obligation on either side.'

'That sounds marvellous!' The slightly embarrassed look left Henry Manning's face, to be replaced by a shy smile.

'She'll adore it here, I know she will!' declared Lilian. 'Oh, isn't this fun?'

Mercy was inclined to agree with her, though she suspected Lilian had little idea of the hard work involved. She had not appreciated how exhausting it could be being pleasant all the time.

'You'll get used to it,' Joey assured her. 'It becomes second nature after a while.'

'Well, in my inexpert opinion the whole evening is going remarkably well,' said Peter. 'Far better than I'd dared to hope. I had a most interesting chat with Mr Dobson. Do you know, he lived in Hong Kong for years? He did a lot of sailing out there. Fascinating!'

'Right, then let's go and see how many other fascinating people we can talk to, and how much business we can drum up,' stated Joey drily.

'Is that what we're supposed to be doing?' Peter looked dismayed. 'I'm afraid I've just been chatting.'

'Don't take any notice of him,' said Mercy. 'We'll just continue to chat. If Joey wants to bring in sordid matters of business, then let him!'

She was certain he would let no chance slip by. Joey was definitely not overawed by the smart people at the reception. He regarded them as potential customers, and treated them with brisk friendliness, betraying no sign of the young boy who had once picked stones for a living. What he thought of the guests privately she was not sure, though from time to time she suspected that she could detect a derisive gleam in his eyes at a particularly inane laugh or silly giggle. He drew plenty of admiring female glances himself, she noticed, and no wonder. He looked very handsome in his dinner jacket. She felt proud of him.

'We're never going to be millionaires with that attitude!' Joey groaned in mock despair. 'Ah well, back to our posts!'

It was characteristic of Charlotte to arrive late. She entered, and paused in the doorway, a dramatic figure in black and silver. When Mercy went to greet her she flung her arms about her.

'My dear!' she murmured brokenly. 'My dear, you're bearing up so well! So brave! So very brave!'

'And what have I to be brave about?' Mercy asked.

'Why, my dear! All this!' Charlotte waved a hand, encompassing the entire company.

'I'll admit I was nervous at first. I thought no one would come on such a beastly night,' said Mercy, deliberately misunderstanding her. 'As you see, my fears were completely groundless.'

'That was not what I meant, as well you know. You may put on a smiling face, but you don't fool me! I know you too well! I know that inside you are all anguish! Suffering for the rape of your beautiful home!'

335

This was too much for Mercy, and she hooted with laughter.

'Oh Charlotte, you are funny!' she giggled.

'Well you are! You must be!'

'I'm not, I assure you. I think that running an hotel is going to be fun! Extremely hard work, but fun! I confess, the more I think of it the more I like the prospect of the years ahead. Apart from anything else, it will be a challenge. Surely you, of all people, can appreciate the enjoyment in that?'

'No, I can't,' said Charlotte flatly. 'Having to alter one's whole way of living! Being nice to perfect strangers every day. I think it sounds awful. Peter will hate it even if you don't!'

There Charlotte might have a point, conceded Mercy privately, and she glanced over towards her husband. He was animatedly chatting with a couple of friends and some of the hotel guests. She recognized the stocky figure of Mr Dobson from Hong Kong, so she guessed they were talking yachting. Certainly, they were all absorbed in the conversation.

'Peter certainly doesn't look like a man having a miserable time,' she said.

'He's not one to betray his true feelings to the whole world.' Charlotte was not going to give up her point of view. 'And nor are you, though I can see you are determined to pretend otherwise. And I shall do my utmost to help you, no matter what you say. I will get all my friends to come and stay here. They'll rally round—'

'It's very kind of you,' Mercy broke in. 'But I must make one thing clear. Much as we want to encourage people to come, we've no wish to have you regard us as one of your good causes. We would welcome any friend of yours here, you know we would, but only if they really want to come. Please don't go round dragooning people into spending their holidays at the Villa Dorata.'

'Would I do such a thing?'

'Yes!'

Charlotte gave an indignant sniff. 'There isn't only you and Peter to consider, you know. There's that poor brother of yours. That limp of his tears my heart. After all he's done for our country...

'And Joey has no wish to be regarded as a good cause either!' Mercy warned firmly. 'If there's one thing he hates it's being thought of as an object for charity – because he's not! He's perfectly capable of working for his living, and so are we! We're planning to do an honest job honestly, and I see no reason why we should feel any shame or distress about it.'

'If you feel so strongly about it…!' Charlotte was clearly taken aback by the force of Mercy's comments.

Mercy was somewhat surprised at herself. Not so long ago she, too, would have seen their present situation as a disaster. Having striven so hard to belong in the privileged, leisurely world inhabited by Charlotte and her ilk it was quite astonishing to find she did not at all mind leaving it.

'There! Now I've got that off my chest, won't you have something to drink? You could try one of Harry's cocktails, or whatever else you prefer.'

'The cocktails look intriguing.' Charlotte removed one from a passing tray, all the while her eyes firmly fixed on Joey. 'I'd no idea you had such a handsome brother, you know.'

'Oh yes, a handsome *younger* brother,' Mercy stressed with a grin.

'All right, there's no need to be so emphatic. I don't go in for cradle-snatching. Besides, he's married, I believe. I must say his little wife is very smart.'

Mercy was puzzled. She had never considered her sister-in-law to be either little or smart. Certainly not in the new dress she had bought for the occasion. The style was fashionable enough, but the fabric, a maroon sateen, had not been a happy choice for Queenie's plump figure. Then she saw the direction of Charlotte's gaze. Joey was talking to Lord Alston, and by his side was Angie Bolton. A very trim Angie Bolton, in an elegant black lace dress which suited her slim figure to perfection.

'That's not Joey's wife, it's Miss Bolton,' she said, in a casual voice.

She was annoyed at Joey for inviting the girl and for making such a fuss of her in public. It had been a hard enough job getting Queenie to come to the reception in the first place, without him humiliating her. Mercy made up her mind to have a sharp word with her young brother – then she had second thoughts. It was Joey's business, after all, and what right had she to interfere? The memory of Gunther was suddenly very vivid. She did not think of him often now, but she knew that, for her, some small part of him would always live on. No, she was the last person to advise someone else on how to conduct their marriage. Instead she went in search of Queenie, to give comfort and reassurance, and to persuade her to come out of her hiding-place.

She was not successful. Queenie had taken refuge in the wireless lounge, and insisted she was quite happy listening to Henry Hall and his orchestra. When Mercy returned to the party she was struck by the noise, the persistent hum of people having fun. Outside, the summer rain lashed against the windows. Inside everyone was enjoying themselves, she could see it in their faces, she could hear it in the timbre of their voices.

Across the room she caught Peter's eye. He raised his glass to her, and silently mouthed the words, 'To success!' Smiling, she raised her own glass and replied, 'Success assured!'

Chapter Nineteen

Dulcie Manning gazed about the lounge, her pale blue eyes taking in the comfortable chairs upholstered in pretty chintz, and the numerous bowls of fresh flowers.

'Who lives here, did you say?' she asked.

'Our friends, Captain and Mrs Lisburne,' her nephew, Henry, explained patiently for the third time. 'It's an hotel, a very nice one, and we wondered if you would like to stay here.'

'Won't your friends mind me coming to live with them?'

'No, they would be very pleased,' said Henry.

'How extraordinary! I wouldn't like it if a perfect stranger come to live with me.'

'That's because you don't own an hotel, and Captain and Mrs Lisburne do,' Henry answered.

'I don't think I would like to own an hotel!'

Henry Manning shot Mercy an apologetic look. Admirable though his patience was he did not seem to be getting through to his aunt. Then suddenly Miss Manning said briskly, 'Very well, I'll come and live here – but only if I can have the room with the nice fluffy pink rug!'

'Certainly you can have that room,' said Mercy, much relieved they were making progress at last.

'Good, then we'd better go home to get my things! Come along, Henry! Come along, Lilian! Don't dawdle!' Miss Manning set off for the front door at a great rate.

'Thank goodness that's settled!' exclaimed Lilian, as she and Henry hurried after the old lady. 'This is one of her bad days, she isn't always like this. You'll find she's a dear really.'

'I'm sure you're right,' replied Mercy. She wondered if they were going to regret having Miss Manning as a permanent guest. It was too late to do anything about it now, though.

'So the Mannings' aunt is definitely staying?' queried Peter, as Mercy entered the office. 'Good, I'll make a note of it. A few more like her would be good for business.'

'I'm not so sure—' began Mercy. Before she could express her doubts she was interrupted by Joey's voice raised in anger.

'From the left, you fool!' he was yelling. 'How many times do I have to tell you to serve from the left?'

Mercy raised an inquiring eyebrow.

'Your brother is holding a training session for some of the waiters in the dining room,' Peter explained. There followed a metallic crash, as though from a dropped tray, and the unmistakable sound of falling cutlery. 'Seemingly he's having problems.'

'He's really hard on those poor souls. I'm surprised, I never thought he had it in him to be such a perfectionist.'

'If he's not careful he's going to achieve the exact opposite of what he intends. One thing we don't want is nervous waiters. Trembling hands and serving food do not go together.'

'Gawd, 'ark at your Joey — I mean Mr Seaton,' remarked Dolly, appearing round the corner. ''E'm really going for some poor soul! And to think of the times I've clipped 'e over the ear'ole!'

'I wouldn't recommend you trying it now,' advised Mercy.

'I won't,' grinned Dolly. 'Though I reckons someone should go to the rescue of the poor lad as is getting the sharp end of 'is tongue! But that's not what I come for. I come to let you know the missing laundry's turned up. Got sent over to the Marine Spa by mistake, would you believe! Does that mean I can phone Ma 'Oskins and complain?'

'Complain away,' smiled Mercy. 'Only, please use the phone in the porter's room, well away from innocent ears.'

'She's right, you know,' said Peter, as Dolly hurried away.

'What, to complain about the missing laundry?'

'No. Someone should have a word with Joey about his attitude. He's far too hard on the staff.'

'Yes, you're right. And I suppose the someone had better be me.' Mercy gave a sigh. 'He's sure to accuse me of interfering. We did agree that staff training was to be his province.'

'That doesn't mean we have to remain totally silent. I've an awful suspicion we may have already done that once too often over the appointment of the chef.'

'Over Lucien?' She looked at him in astonishment. 'What objections can you possibly have to him? He cooks superbly, and he has impeccable references.'

'Yes, his cooking and his references are fine. I wish I could say the same about the man himself. There's something about him which makes me feel uneasy. I can't explain it – he hasn't done anything or said a word out of turn – I only know that if he had been under my command in the Army I'd have had a quiet word with the sergeant major to keep a watchful eye on him. And speaking of sergeant majors, things have gone very quiet in the dining room. He must have finished the training session. Would you prefer it if I had a word with Joey?'

'No, I'll tackle him.'

'Brave girl. If you need any help just yell.'

'Help? I don't need any help with my own brother. Dolly isn't the only one who's clipped him over the ear, you know.' Mercy chuckled. The smile soon left her face as she entered the dining room to find her brother looking like thunder.

'Idiots! That's what we've taken on!' he complained. 'You'd think some of them had never seen a knife and fork before, never mind tried to lay them on a table.'

'You are a bit impatient with them, you know.'

'Impatient? How can you say such a thing? I repeat myself time after time, and still it doesn't go in! I shudder to think how they'd have fared at the Devonshire Hall under old Mabel. Once was the only telling you got there.'

'And once is all you'd need. You're quick to pick things up, haven't I always said so? You must remember that not everyone is as bright as you.'

Joey's angry look slowly melted into a grin.

'Don't stop,' he said. 'I can take all the flattery you care to dish out.'

'It's not flattery, it's the truth. The trouble is that being quick-witted yourself sometimes makes you intolerant of anyone slower. A bit of encouragement works wonders. Haven't you found it so at Seaton's?'

'No, can't say I have. No encouragement of mine would make a jot of difference to Queenie or Millie. And as for Angie, she's so bright she…' his voice tailed away. 'All right, Sis, point taken. I'll talk to them all like a Dutch uncle, and see if that works.'

'It will depend on how many of them understand Dutch,' replied Mercy, making a quick retreat as her brother suddenly advanced on her, a wet mopping-up cloth in his hand.

341

'Tut-tut, such hilarity won't do!' said Peter with mock severity as she sought refuge in the office. 'What will people think?'

'Does it matter what people think?' she asked.

'Does it matter? Just listen to the woman!' He pretended to be shocked. 'The whole of civilization as we know it is founded upon what people think!'

'Nonsense!' said Mercy, then she kissed him lightly on the top of the head, and hurried back to her own duties.

As she ran upstairs Peter's jocular words rang in her head, making her think seriously about them. Now the hotel was under way it was interesting to note other people's reactions to their altered circumstances.

Their real friends, such as Charlotte, Lord Alston and the Mannings had proved they did not care at all. Some acquaintances, however, had been less generous. Recently Mercy had found herself cut dead or treated to the frostiest of greetings, by people who, less than a year before, had been only too delighted to welcome her into their homes. Strangely enough, in the very worrying months when the finances at the Villa Dorata had been at their most critical, these same people had been mostly sympathetic, even kind. Only the news that the Lisburnes were going into the hotel business had brought about the chilly transformation.

Mercy found it odd that genteel poverty should be regarded as socially quite acceptable, but actively doing something to avoid that poverty was not.

Uppity rubbish! One of Blanche's favourite phrases rang in her head so clearly it was as if her grandmother had actually spoken to her. Yes, Blanche would have made short shrift of those with such disparaging airs and graces. She would have been right, too, Mercy decided. Opening an hotel had not lost her the friendship of a single person she cared about. The standoffish attitude of a few snobs was not worth the loss of any sleep.

The reaction of her children to their new way of life was a different matter. It had been varied. Jennifer was young enough to find the novelty of the situation exciting. William, too, had taken it remarkably well. Ever a boy who liked order and familiarity his first question had, 'Does this mean I'll have to go to a different school?'

'No, you won't need to change,' Mercy had assured him.

'That's all right then.' His relief had been evident. 'I wouldn't have wanted to leave my friends. And we'll still be living here, won't we?'

'Yes, but things will be rather different, I'm afraid.'

He considered for a moment. 'Not as different as going to live in Africa, though. I'm not sure I would have liked that. As for this hotel thing, well I suppose it can't be helped. When Jenson minor's people lost their money he had to leave school and start work as an office boy. It must have been awful!'

Mercy did not know Jenson minor, but she felt grateful to him. His plight had clearly left a marked impression on William, making her boy feel quite fortunate by comparison.

Oddly enough it was John, normally so easy-going, who found the situation the hardest to bear. At first he did not say much, but it became marked that he now spent as little time at home as possible, preferring to holiday with friends or go on camping trips organized by the school – anything sooner than spend time at the Villa Dorata. When he was home he became quite surly and difficult.

'Why should I have to do anything simply because some beastly strangers have taken over our house?' he protested one day when Mercy asked him to move his bicycle from the the terrace.

'They aren't beastly. Most of them are jolly nice,' his mother replied. 'Far too nice to fall over your bicycle and hurt themselves.'

'Oh, I hate being poor!' John strode angrily about the room. 'Why did Father have to lose all our money!'

'Your father did no such thing!' retorted Mercy. 'It was the combined effect of the war and the Russian Revolution, as well you know. Lots of other people were affected too and are in a far worse state than us. We're the lucky ones!'

'I don't think we're lucky! And I loathe living in abject poverty!'

Mercy tried not to laugh.

'I realize this flat is somewhat smaller than we're accustomed to, yet I wouldn't call it abject poverty,' she said. 'I consider it to be very pleasant and comfortable.' Then seeing that her words had no effect on her son she continued, 'Shall I tell you what abject poverty is? It's being packed in an overcrowded cottage that's damp and insanitary, with a smelly earth privy in the garden and a pump by the back door. It's breaking your back working for ten hours a day, then walking three miles home because you haven't the few coppers for the bus fare. At your age your Uncle Joey was out in all weathers, clearing stones from the fields. Many a time I've seen him crying because his hands hurt him so much, but it didn't stop him being out again at first light. We depended on the few pence he brought home, and he knew it. No matter what state his hands were in, he had to go! Squalor, hunger and ugliness, they are part of abject poverty! But worst of all there's having no hope! Knowing you're trapped by circumstances and there's no way of escape, no matter how hard you try!'

John stared at her, his eyes wide. It was not often she spoke to the children of her early days. In truth, Mercy was startled herself. She had not intended to speak with such intensity.

'I didn't know... I hadn't realized...' John said.

'You still don't, not really,' Mercy answered softly. 'And that's the way it should be. You and William and Jennifer, you'll never live the sort of life I did when I was young. Believe me, having to run an hotel is a very small price to pay for escaping conditions like that!'

John said nothing, he merely look uncomfortably red in the face. Then he said very quietly, 'I'll go and move my bike,' and left the room.

Mercy continued to gaze out of the window, too wrapped up in her thoughts to notice the white-capped waves in the bay, or passing gulls which swooped and skimmed over the water. How strong was her fear of poverty! She had never recognized it before, not until she had spoken to John, but it had always been there, she saw that now. Reaching out she picked up the tablecloth she had been taking to the linen-room before John's bicycle had diverted her attention. With her fingers she traced the embroidered monogram in the corner. 'Villa Dorata Hotel' it read in stitched letters. Three words that suddenly meant security. She was being given a second chance to escape poverty. It was a chance she had no intention of letting slip by!

The problem of being dropped by certain quarters of society no longer bothered her. In its place came the far more delicate problem of those acquaintances whose enthusiasm for the Villa Dorata Hotel had increased.

'It's getting beyond a joke. I thought I'd better show it to you, Mrs Lisburne,' said Harry, 'it being the end of the month. He handed her a bar bill.'

'Are you saying Mr and Mrs Shaw haven't paid anything since we opened?' she asked incredulously, scanning the sheet of paper in her hand.

'Not one penny. Normally I wouldn't have let it go on so long without mentioning it, but seeing as they're such particular friends of yours...'

That was the point. As far as Mercy could remember the Shaws had not been particular friends of theirs, not until the opening of the hotel. She and Peter had known the Shaws, certainly, and she could recall being at the same dinner parties and other functions from time to time. But particular friends? No! Yet since the Villa Dorata Hotel had opened its doors for business Billie and Cynthia Shaw had been in most nights, full of compliments for the decor, the atmosphere and the cocktails – especially the cocktails, as the bill now in Mercy's hand bore witness. It was astronomical.

'I wasn't sure whether to give it to you or Captain Lisburne, it being Mr Seaton's night off,' said Harry.

'You did right, bringing it to me. I'll see to it. Let me know as soon as they come in, please.'

'Right oh!' Cheerily Harry returned to his bar to prepare for the evening.

Mercy looked at the bill again and felt decidedly uncomfortable. So far, she had never had to deal with anything like this. Difficulties with customers had tended to be very minor up till now. What made this situation more embarrassing was knowing the Shaws socially; but it could not be allowed to continue, the bill was too excessive. She could have handed the matter over to Peter, of course, only she knew how much he would have hated dealing with it.

What would Blanche have said to them? she wondered. Probably something like, 'It is a pity you do not pay as speedily as you drink!' she decided, and chuckled. It was remarkable how often she found comfort in thinking about her grandmother these days, though goodness knows, the old lady had been far from comforting in her lifetime. Mercy decided that on this occasion emulating Blanche might prove a bit abrasive. She would choose a more diplomatic approach instead.

As soon as Harry sent word of the arrival of the Shaws Mercy headed for the cocktail bar.

'Good evening,' she said.

'Mercy darling!' Cynthia Shaw greeted her with a flurry of exaggerated gestures. 'You look absolutely stunning, doesn't she, Billie?'

'Absolutely!' agreed her husband.

'How kind of you to say so,' said Mercy, feeling decidedly embarrassed. 'Especially since I have to broach a somewhat awkward subject. You see, I am afraid you've forgotten to pay your bar account.'

She put the bill on the table in front of them.

'Pay?' Billie Shaw repeated the word as though it were something from a foreign language. 'But Mercy, dear, I didn't think you expected us actually to pay.'

'Didn't you? I can't imagine what gave you that impression.'

'Because we're friends, of course. You really can't charge your friends, my pet,' Cynthia drawled. 'It just isn't done.'

Mercy's embarrassment evaporated rapidly. She could recognize when she was being swindled readily enough.

'Is that so?' she replied sweetly. 'You could be correct. However, you aren't friends of my brother, and since he is a partner in this business, on his behalf I really must ask you to pay. Otherwise it wouldn't be fair to him, would it?'

'I don't think I've enough money on me,' blustered Billie, clearly disconcerted. He had evidently expected Mercy to slink away shamefaced.

'Why don't you look and see?' she suggested, standing her ground.

Muttering under his breath Billie took out his wallet. Mercy was furious to see it was crammed with five-pound notes.

'Why, there's more than enough there to cover your bill,' she cried gaily, leaning forward and deftly extracting the required number. 'Is something the matter?' she asked, as Billie made a cry of protest. 'Oh, of course. You'll want to give Harry a little something for the way he's looked after you all these weeks. Don't worry, I'll deduct it from your change!'

Fury was etched on the couple's faces but the cocktail lounge was filling up, and they were reluctant to make a scene. When Mercy returned with their change they had gone.

'So you actually got some money out of them, Mrs L,' grinned Harry, pocketing his pound note. 'Well done!'

'I could have understood them not paying if they were hard up!' exclaimed Mercy. 'But that wallet was crammed with banknotes.'

'And that was how he intended it to stay. I'll say this, any more of their sort are in for a sad shock if they come here! You're more than a match for any of them, Mrs L.'

'Why, thank you! I shall take that as a compliment, Harry,' replied Mercy. Now the incident was over she felt quite elated, as if she had endured some ordeal and survived.

The confrontation with the Shaws was quite a landmark in Mercy's career: never again was she reluctant to tackle anyone who tried to cheat them.

'You should leave such people to me,' protested Peter, after she had successfully routed one man who had complained about the service only after he had eaten the full five-course dinner without comment.

'No I shouldn't! You are far too nice. You'd be kind and apologetic, and these wretched people would fleece us right, left and centre. They're in a minority, thank goodness, but they shouldn't be allowed to get away with it!'

'What did you say to this one?'

'I told him that the service was free and we only charge for the food, so since he'd eaten every scrap of the dinner he would have to pay for it. He was deliberately trying to get a reduction on his bill, there was nothing wrong with the service. I was watching all the time!'

'You're developing into quite a tigress, do you know that?' Peter chuckled.

'It must be the Blanche in me coming out.' Mercy gave a smile as she remembered a conversation she had overheard between two guests, a pair of 'bright young things'. One had remarked, 'The Lisburnes seem an awfully nice couple, don't they?' To which the other replied, 'He's an absolute sweetie, certainly, but she can be a bit of a tartar!'

If being 'a bit of a tartar' was what it took to make the hotel a success then she was quite happy to continue. Certainly she had seen off the Shaws: they never returned to the Villa Dorata.

Not all their guests provoked conflict, fortunately. Mostly the people who stayed at the Villa Dorata were perfectly charming. One of the nicest proved to be 'Dobbie' Dobson, the ex-colonial officer who had been their very first guest. He had returned again after the briefest of intervals; then, as he had been paying his bill for the second time he had asked if he could stay permanently.

'I don't seem able to settle, now I've retired,' he said. 'I've done the rounds of relations, but never fancied putting down roots anywhere

347

near them. This is the only place that's suited me. Nice country, nice people, good food. I could have my own boat again and go sailing as much as I want. If you've room for me I'd like to make your hotel my permanent billet.'

'We'd be delighted to have you,' Mercy said. 'But perhaps I ought to make it a condition of your stay that you and Peter don't talk yachts and yachting for more than twenty hours out of any twenty-four.'

Mr Dobson grinned. 'I'll do my best, but I can't make any promises,' he said. 'I'll be back in a fortnight then, bag and baggage.'

Mercy was glad for Peter's sake that Mr Dobson was going to be a permanent guest, he so enjoyed having someone with whom to talk boats and sailing. Poor Peter, he sorely missed the *Tango*, although he never complained. He did not even frequent the Yacht Club as often as he used to – he did not have the time. Having 'Dobbie' Dobson in residence was going to be a great consolation.

She had to admit they were lucky in their permanent guests. Among the handful who had made the Villa Dorata their home only Miss Manning ever caused any consternation. Whether Dulcie Manning was mentally vague or merely had a bad sense of direction Mercy was never sure. The old lady had a tendency to turn up in the most unlikely places on the pretext that she was looking for the wireless lounge, or the bathroom, or even her own room. More than once Mercy had found her ensconced in the linen-room with Dolly.

'Let 'er bide! 'Er idn't bothering me none,' said Dolly cheerfully, 'I gives 'er a cup of tea, and 'er sits there for ages, watching me sort the towels, as 'appy as a sandboy.'

'If you're sure?' Mercy was not convinced. 'It worries me in case she wanders away from the hotel and gets lost.'

''Er'll be all right,' Dolly said confidently. 'I don't reckon 'er's as muddle-'eaded as 'er makes out. 'Er just seeks a bit of company when 'er gets lonely.'

'Perhaps you're right. At least when she's with you I know she's all right. We really can't have her wandering into the gentlemen's lavatory again, as she did last week.'

'There, what did I tell 'ee?' Dolly was triumphant. ''Er idn't nearly as muddle-'eaded as 'er pretends!'

Mercy was still laughing as she left the linen-room. The summer season progressed, with the hotel getting busier and busier. The number of bookings for resident guests was very satisfactory, but it was the growing volume of non-resident trade which was most gratifying. Some were summer visitors, of course, birds of passage who came in for an occasional meal or a drink, or to attend one of the regular tea dances, but a goodly number were locals. Many came out of curiosity, interested to see what Torquay's newest hotel had to offer, and the number who began coming again and again was very satisfactory. There was no denying that the cuisine at the Villa Dorata was a definite attraction. Remembering Peter's reservations about Lucien, the head chef, Mercy was convinced he was mistaken. So far the stocky Swiss had not put a foot wrong. He cooked like an angel, and the worst that could be said about his behaviour was that he could be rather morose at times.

It was while Peter and Mercy were having tea in their flat that the internal telephone rang. The day was hot, sultry, and tiring, and they had both crept away for a brief rest before the rigours of the evening, so neither of them was pleased at the interruption.

'I'll answer it, while you pour the tea,' said Peter, reaching out for the receiver.

From where she sat Mercy could hear that the caller was agitated. As he listened Peter's face became more and more grave.

'Clear everyone away from the area,' he said. 'Above all, don't let anyone try to enter the kitchen. I'm on my way!' He leapt to his feet before he had replaced the receiver.

'What's the matter?' asked Mercy.

'The chef's gone berserk!' Peter's reply was given over his shoulder, he was already heading for the door.

Without another thought Mercy followed him. At the bottom of the main stairs they found a knot of people anxiously staring through the dining room door towards the kitchen. Fortunately it was a fine day, so few of them were guests. The head porter was holding the crowd back. By his side, looking decidedly pale, stood Charlie, one of the young under-chefs.

'What's going on?' Peter demanded.

'It's Monsieur Lucien, Captain, he's gone off his head,' replied Charlie, shakily, 'He's got half the kitchen staff trapped in there and he's threatening them with a knife!'

'Is anyone hurt?' asked Mercy, horrified.

'Mickey, the other under-chef, he's got a bad gash on the arm.'

'And he's still in there? Quickly, tell me what happened,' commanded Peter.

'We'd all just come on duty for the evening, and Monsieur Lucien seemed all right at first. A bit quiet and moody maybe, but that's nothing unusual for him. Then, right out of the blue he starts yelling we're all his enemies and plotting against him, and how he's more than a match for the lot of us. That was when he picked up the knife. He lashed out, and Mickey got cut. I took my chance and made a dash for it. He nearly got me, too. Look!' Charlie pulled at the sleeve of his white overall. The stout material had been slashed cleanly and his arm beneath it bore a livid scratch.

Peter whistled under his breath.

'That was a close shave,' he said. 'Now, these unfortunate people in the kitchen, perhaps we can get them out by going through the back entrance?'

'That's no good, Captain. Monsieur Lucien locked the door. The only way's through the dining room,' said Charlie.

'Come and show me! Mercy, you phone the police!'

'No, I'm coming with you. You go and phone!' She gave the nearest waiter a slight push towards the office.

'I don't have to go in there again, do I, Captain?' asked Charlie nervously.

'No, I may want you to explain the way things are in there, that's all. Come on! Make sure you aren't seen!'

The three of them stealthily skirted the dining room. There were two doors to the kitchen, one in and one out, and each had a small glass panel in the top. The sight through these panels was an alarming one. Half a dozen people were huddled in a corner, held at bay by the head chef, who was tensely prowling back and forth in front of them, swinging an enormous carving knife in one hand.

'I'll have to go in, and quickly!' whispered Peter.

Mercy gave a gasp of protest. 'It's far too dangerous!' she exclaimed.

He silenced her with a finger to his lips. 'We daren't wait for the police. That carving knife's getting closer to those poor souls all the time. You two must create a diversion. Stand in the "in" door, and make as much noise as possible. I'll tell you when.'

'No!' Mercy repeated her protest, but again it was in vain. Peter had picked up a marble figurine and was weighing it in his hand as a potential weapon. Then he crept over to the other door.

She had no option but to do as he asked. She exchanged an anxious glance with young Charlie as they armed themselves with metal trays. Then they waited!

The moment Peter gave the signal the pair of them clashed their improvised instruments together hard, yelling and screaming as they did so. Through the glass panel she had a clear view of Lucien swinging round, his glaring eyes blazing in their direction. He never saw Peter come up behind him, nor did he know anything of the marble figurine until it crashed down on the back of his head. Peter had disarmed the chef even as he hit the floor.

A mutual sigh of relief seemed to sweep right through the hotel, and in its wake came an upsurge of noise as people laughed and cried and cheered.

'We'd better restrain the poor man in some way, in case he comes round suddenly,' said Peter, looking anxiously at his handiwork.

Charlie was already on his knees beside the fallen chef. 'It'll be a fair time before he comes round, Captain,' he said, tearing a linen tea towel in strips to bind Lucien's wrists. 'That was a good crack on the head you gave him.'

'I hope I didn't hit him too hard.' Peter sounded worried.

The hall porter had given up trying to restrain the crowd round the dining room door. They rushed forward, engulfing the shaken occupants of the kitchen, and almost smothering them with mingled consolations for their ordeal and congratulations for their deliverance. Everyone was loud in their praise for Peter's bravery. What with tending to the under-chef who had been injured and dispensing tea and brandy to his shocked companions Mercy scarcely noticed the arrival of the police. The first she knew of their presence was when two hefty constables began carrying out the semi-conscious form of Lucien.

'I reckon he's the hospital's business rather than ours, in more ways than one,' remarked the sergeant in charge. 'Don't you worry, we'll take care of him. You did a fine piece of work there, Captain Lisburne, if I may say so. Without your intervention we might have had a very nasty incident indeed.'

There were statements to be made to the police, the injured Mickey to be transported to the doctor, shaken and distressed employees to be ferried home. Then suddenly the hotel was quiet, and Mercy and Peter were alone in the office.

'The police sergeant was right, you prevented a terrible tragedy,' Mercy said. 'You were so brave! You might have been killed, or badly hurt, or...' The sobs that choked her took her completely unawares. She found herself clinging to Peter, tears streaming unchecked down her cheeks, her body trembling violently, as delayed shock beset her.

'It's over! I'm all right! I was in no real danger!' Peter folded her in his arms, and, rocking gently back and forth, soothed her.

'You were in danger...' wept Mercy. 'Terrible danger... and I... I should be comforting you...'

He laughed. 'I like things as they are,' he said, 'in fact, I'd be quite content to stay like this all night.'

'There's no reason why we can't...' Mercy began, then abruptly she pushed away from him with an exclamation. 'My goodness, the dinner! Who's going to cook the dinner?'

Peter released her, a look of almost comic dismay on his face.

'I'd forgotten about that,' he said. 'We'll just have to close the dining room for once.'

'We can't do that! We're fully booked! I'll go and check what's happening in the kitchen.' Mercy rubbed a hand over her tear-stained face, shock forgotten. 'I must look a mess! I'd better tidy up first.'

Not surprisingly the kitchen was not a hive of industry when she entered. Three or four staff were in there, looking bewildered. One was Charlie, who was proudly showing off the cut in his overall.

'Are you sure you feel fit to go on duty?' she asked.

'Yes thanks, Mrs Lisburne, I'm fine,' he beamed. Evidently his active part in releasing his colleagues had done much to restore his shaken nerves.

'I'm glad to hear it,' Mercy said, gazing round. 'We're going to be seriously short of staff tonight.'

She felt this was an understatement. The only workers she had were the pastry chef, a couple of apprentices, and Charlie.

'Begging your pardon, Mrs Lisburne. Who's going to be in charge of the dinner?' Charlie asked.

'Me!' she said, breathing a grateful prayer for Madame Le Clos's patient instruction in Brittany. When she had taken the cookery course she had never dreamed of the uses to which it would be put. How Agnes would have disapproved!

'We had better begin by simplifying the menu,' she continued, pulling open the drawer where she knew the standard recipe file was kept. 'There's nothing written here!' she cried. 'Every sheet is blank!'

'That was Lucien!' explained Charlie. 'He said he wasn't writing down his recipes for us to steal.'

'Ah well, the Villa Dorata dishes may not taste the same as usual, but at least I intend our customers to be fed. We'll do chicken chasseur, that's not too complicated, and as an alternative I see we have pork cutlets. Now for first course there's melon...'

If there had been chaos in the dining room after the siege it was as nothing compared to the frantic activity in the kitchen that evening. Rigid divisions of labour were forgotten as the pastry cook helped with the sauces, the apprentices prepared full dishes, and Charlie seemed to be everywhere at once. As for Mercy, she concentrated on the meat courses, her face growing crimson with the heat, the perspiration trickling down her back in rivulets.

When at last the dinner was over and the kitchen cleaned down to a pristine splendour again, Mercy limped up to the flat. With a groan she collapsed on to the bed.

'Give everyone in the kitchen a five-pound rise! They've earned it!' she moaned.

'Starting with you?' smiled Peter, gently removing her shoes, and massaging her aching feet.

'Especially me! What was the reaction in the dining room? Did anyone comment that the choice wasn't as good as usual?'

'No, not a soul. There were a few compliments about the chicken chasseur, though.'

'There were? Fancy that!' She was genuinely pleased.

'Of course some of the locals knew we'd had a spot of bother. You know how news spreads.'

'Oh dear, that's not so good. It can't have done much for our reputation.'

'I don't know. Those who knew seemed very interested, and wanted all the gory details. Perhaps we should do this on a regular basis – a nice siege, an employee going berserk, a spot of blood about the place – it would do wonders for our publicity.'

'Don't you dare!' Mercy hauled herself to her feet. 'It's going to take all my willpower as it is to get me to the bathroom and into a bath. One such incident and I can cope, make it a regular thing and you'll have to find another substitute chef!'

'Perhaps you're right, we could have too much of a good thing.'

'I'm sure we can! I'm wondering what Joey's going to say about all this in the morning. He'll probably be furious because he's missed the action.' She paused, her hand on the door knob. 'Imagine! This has been our first major crisis! I think we've come through with flying colours, don't you?'

'I do indeed.' He crossed the room to kiss her full on the mouth. 'Don't forget, those colours have still to be flying in the morning. Off you go and get some rest!' And he sent her on her way with a gentle pat on the bottom.

The fracas in the kitchen caused a minor sensation, reaching the columns of both the *Chronicle* and the *Directory*. Fortunately it only provoked a mild curiosity among the local clientele, and soon it was forgotten. With most of the staff fully recovered and a temporary head chef installed, life began to go back to normal. There was no question of Lucien returning, of course, and in time he was replaced by Alphonse, a voluble Frenchman whose only fault was a tendency to swear loudly and at great length in his own language when provoked.

One agreeable after-effect of the siege was the way Joey began to have a greater regard for Peter. Until then Mercy had not realized how ineffectual he had considered her husband to be. Now those days were over, and Joey treated Peter with a new respect, at times even going so far as to ask for his advice.

–

The summer season drew to a close, there was a brief autumnal lull, and then the winter season began.

'I know the summer is increasing in popularity as a time for holidays,' Mercy remarked, 'but winter is certainly going to be more favourable for us, judging by these bookings.'

'So many people want to stay for the whole winter! We're really going to be busy,' said Peter, gazing over her shoulder at the reservations.

He was right. The hotel was pretty full for most of the winter months, and all of those guests expected not only to be fed, looked after and pampered, but entertained as well. At the Villa Dorata they took care to observe every festival with some sort of celebration, from Hallowe'en and Bonfire Night to Pancake Tuesday. Most elaborate of all, naturally, were the Christmas festivities. From Christmas Eve to Twelfth Night there were dinners and dances, parties and cabarets, with entertainers brought down specially from London.

'It's definitely been worthwhile,' said Joey, as, at the end of their first winter, the three of them sat down to take stock. 'The money we've laid out, particularly on entertainments, has been a good investment.'

'So I should hope,' replied Mercy. 'The singer who came for the New Year's dinner-dance alone cost us a fortune. We could have got Beniamino Gigli for less.'

'And I'm still not sure the jazz band was a good idea. Some of our older residents complained about the noise,' said Peter.

'You can't please everyone, and we have had some quieter events, the Strauss evening, for example,' Joey pointed out. 'Though I agree about the noise, we'll have to see what we can do to cut it down, or at least stop it reaching the upper floors. Some sort of a stage with a canopy might be an idea.'

'A very big idea!' protested Peter. 'We're an hotel, not a nightclub.'

'I've been thinking about that.' Joey said. 'Why not have a nightclub as a part of the hotel eventually? When we expand—'

'Expand? Who said anything about expanding?' Peter demanded.

'I'm only planning ahead. It's something for the future. We'll have to get bigger, and my idea is to raise the roof, quite literally. We could make the Villa Dorata higher by one storey, or even two if the foundations would stand it...'

'That would ruin the place!' Peter was aghast. 'And it would never work. Think of the time it would take? How could we run an hotel with all that building and mess about the place! No one would stand for it! We'd lose custom!'

'Then we'd have to close until we were finished. That's what they did over at the Grand Hotel, though it took them nearly a year.' Joey's face was alight with enthusiasm.

'But they didn't do it when the Grand had been open for less then twelve months,' said Mercy, attempting to restore calm. 'I suggest we forget about such ambitious schemes for the moment, certainly until we've paid back a bit more of our bank loan. Let's consider the coming summer instead. What about our publicity?'

'Here's our entry for the *Torquay Guide*; we've already agreed on its wording,' Joey put the paper on the table.

'We really ought to advertise elsewhere, more nationally. I suggest a piece in *The Lady*,' said Mercy.

'If we want to go national the thing is to get recommended by the motoring associations, the AA and the RAC,' declared Joey. 'The motorists! That's where we should be looking for our guests. They're increasing every year – you've only to see the cars jam-packed round the harbour to realize that. We need to be in the AA Handbook.'

'Let's apply at once then,' said Mercy eagerly.

'Don't you think we should go more cautiously?' asked Peter. 'Oh, I agree with everything Joey said. We should certainly apply, but I think it would be better if we gave ourselves more time to get the hotel really established. My view is that we should not aim simply for an 'AA Approved' label, we should go for at least three stars, if not four, from the beginning, and not settle for anything less.'

Mercy was both surprised and pleased at his words. She had never heard him be so ambitious for the hotel before.

'You've a good point there,' said Joey. 'Enter at the top, is that the idea? It makes sense.'

Mercy was doubly pleased. A few months ago her brother would never have approved of any of Peter's suggestions so readily.

'Yes, it does,' she agreed. 'There's nothing stopping us making preliminary inquiries, though, is there? After all, we can't work towards their requirements until we know what they are looking for.'

'We're all agreed we should make inquiries?' Joey looked from one to the other. 'Right, then let's get on. You think an advert in *The Lady* might be a good idea, Mercy…?'

Their meeting was a long one, but fruitful. By the time they had finished they had made their plans for the following months, rectified a few matters that needed attention, and generally sorted out their business affairs.

'I thought Joey looked rather tired tonight,' commented Peter later. 'And no wonder! I can't think why he doesn't get a proper manager for Seaton's. It's not as though his wife is keen on running the business. As far as I can gather that young woman, Angie, sees to most things.'

'She seems very reliable,' said Mercy briefly. She did not really want to discuss Angie Bolton, not even with Peter. It had been her hope that Joey's entanglement with Angie was over, but only the day before she had been proven wrong. The weather had been spring-like, so she had taken advantage of a couple of free hours to enjoy the fresh air. As she had walked along one of the cliff paths, at Petitor, she had noticed two people lower down the slope. Immediately she had recognized them as Joey and Angie. Their arms were about each other, so she had crept off in another direction. They never noticed her.

'Reliable or not, poor Joey has an awful lot of responsibility,' said Peter. 'Mind you, he certainly loves running the Villa Dorata, that much is evident.'

'And what about you?' Mercy asked. 'Do you enjoy running the Villa Dorata too?'

Peter considered for a moment.

'Do you know, I do!' he said.

'There's no need to sound so surprised,' she laughed.

'Yes there is! I was convinced I would never like the life, or get used to it, yet it has turned out quite differently from what I expected. I never realized I'd meet so many interesting people, for a start, or make a good friend like Dobbie. I may be exhausted at times, but I'm never bored. In fact, I feel very lucky. I've managed to hang on to the Villa Dorata, and at the same time a whole new world has opened up for me. I think that's pretty good for a middle-aged father of three, especially when I see the miserable lives some other poor souls have.'

'So you are really happy?'

'Indeed l am!'

The gleam in his eyes convinced her he meant it! Mercy felt relief flow through her. For so long she had been afraid that he was miserable with their new way of life and was keeping his unhappiness to himself. Now, at last, she was reassured. Peter was happy, the children were flourishing, the hotel was prospering. What more could she want?

'Why are you smiling?' Peter asked.

She could not find the words to tell him, so she kissed him instead.

Chapter Twenty

The Villa Dorata's first year as an hotel had ended so triumphantly that for a while no one would admit the second year was disappointing. The summer had been poor, but the winter, the major season, threatened to be even worse. Unsettled weather, jitters on the Stock Market, a generally poor response all round – these were the comments Mercy, Peter, and Joey bandied about at their regular management meetings. They all knew the truth, though; bookings were not as good as they had expected, either for residents or in the dining room.

It was Joey who finally took the bull by the horns. 'We've got to face the facts,' he stated. 'Last year we were the fashionable place, this year we've got more competition. New hotels are opening, and new restaurants. We're no longer a novelty.'

'Do we have to be a permanent novelty?' asked Mercy. 'How do hotels like the Imperial and the Grand manage? They've both been going for donkey's years. I don't see them breaking their necks to join in each latest craze.'

'That's because they don't have to,' said Joey. 'They've both established their reputations, and got their regular clientele. We're still making our way. We've got to let the world know we're here and advertise more. I suggest that we put in our application with the AA now. We'd easily get two stars, probably three, and that would certainly attract a lot of extra custom.'

A thoughtful silence settled on the room, to be broken, at length, by Mercy.

'There's a lot of sense in what you say,' she said. 'But is it what we really want? Our initial intention was to run a really first-class hotel, wasn't it? By accepting two-star classification wouldn't we be lowering our sights simply because business is down a bit this year?'

'We could always start as a two-star and build our way up,' said Joey.

'We should go in at the top! You said so yourself,' pointed out Peter. 'Clawing our way up the grades would not have the impact of having four nice neat stars beside the Villa Dorata's first entry. I think we should give it one more year, a year in which we consolidate the lessons we've learned so far. If, after that, we've made no further progress then we can opt for those two stars. But let's give it a decent try first!'

Mercy was sure there would be an argument from her brother, but to her surprise Joey nodded.

'Right, we'll give it a try,' he said.

'Is that all you've got to say?' she asked, puzzled.

Joey grinned briefly. 'Surprised, are you? Did you expect me to put up a fight? No, I'm with you both all the way on this top-class hotel idea, that's always been my dream. Only, I know from bitter experience real life's not so rosy, and we've got to be prepared to settle for less.'

'Not if we work hard enough,' replied Mercy.

'That's right, not if we work hard enough,' Peter said. 'And in the meantime we'll have to see if we can think up a few novelties, as Joey says, to help us along.'

'How about holding the Devon yo-yo championships here?' suggested Joey, suddenly cheery again. Then he made a rapid escape as the others jeered at him in derision.

-

Dobbie Dobson proved to be a great asset when it came to boosting bookings. He had a large number of friends, a steady stream of whom came to stay with him at the Villa Dorata. Most of them were sailing enthusiasts, even in winter, so Peter was in his element. The only trouble with sea-loving guests was that they were inclined to be unpunctual. Shifts in the wind and missed tides accounted for quite a few absent diners.

'I don't know anywhere else where we'd get this sort of treatment, especially arriving back hours after dinner has finished!' declared Dobbie, regarding the laden trolley as it was trundled into the wireless lounge. 'You are an angel, Mrs Lisburne, you really are.'

'Let's just say that I'm an experienced yachting widow,' Mercy smiled. 'It's not the first time I've been on hand after midnight with hot soup at the ready. Are you sure you don't mind eating in here? I thought you'd prefer it because of the fire.'

'This is grand, thanks,' replied one of Dobbie's friends, an old colleague from his days in the Colonial Service. His teeth were chattering and his hands curled appreciatively about his bowl of hot soup.

Dobbie gave a contented sigh. 'Hot drinks, a welcoming fire, a room to dry our gear! This place is becoming a branch of the Yacht Club.'

'It's something I've long suspected, but you didn't have to confirm it!' laughed Mercy. 'Now, is there anything else you gentlemen need?'

Before they could answer a voice piped up, 'A midnight feast! How jolly! May I join in?'

Mercy swung round to find Miss Manning, clad in a woollen dressing-gown and curlers, standing in the doorway.

'Miss Manning, it's awfully late,' she said gently. 'You should be in bed.'

'Yes, I should, but it's more fun here!' Dulcie Manning regarded the food with round hopeful eyes.

'You are absolutely right, Miss Manning,' said Dobbie. 'Come along and sit here by me, near the fire. What would you like? I can certainly recommend the soup.'

As Miss Manning settled excitedly into her armchair Mercy raised a questioning eyebrow.

'Don't worry,' Dobbie mouthed silently, and winked.

Mercy had to smile in return. Dobbie was such a nice man! She was becoming quite concerned about Miss Manning, though. The old lady was growing increasingly vague; Mercy feared the time was drawing near when Lilian and Henry would have to think of making other arrangements for their aunt. She would be sorry. Dulcie Manning was sweet and gentle, and she was fond of her, for all she was a growing liability.

There was one person at the hotel who was more disruptive than either Dulcie Manning or Dobbie and his numerous friends. It was rare for Mercy to dislike any of the guests, but the moment she had set eyes on Mrs Hetherington she had taken an instant aversion to her. Margo Hetherington was well known as a wealthy socialite. Everything she wore shrieked Paris. Everything she wore also showed a considerable amount of Margo Hetherington, particularly her *chic* but clinging evening gowns.

She had arrived accompanied by one of the most handsome young men Mercy had ever seen, whose sole purpose, in public at any rate, seemed to be to trail behind his companion, a sulky expression on his sun-tanned face. Mercy did not blame the young man for looking petulant. Mrs Hetherington treated him alternately as a servant, to fetch and carry for her, and as a substitute poodle, to be petted and pampered and spoiled. Whether it was the servitude which proved too much, or the pampering, no one ever knew. The young man was seen leaving the hotel one morning and he never returned. In departing he had also taken with him several towels, two new tennis racquets, and a very nice Meissen bowl, all the property of the hotel, as well as a quantity of money, the property of Mrs Hetherington.

Mrs Hetherington was clearly far more annoyed by the lack of a permanent male companion than the financial loss. With eyes that were blatantly predatory, she searched among her fellow guests for a replacement. She eventually set her sights on poor Dobbie, her pursuit of him being so relentless he was at times forced to take refuge down at the Yacht Club.

The cry 'Man-eating shark on the port bow' soon became a code throughout the hotel, a warning to the male guests to take cover. It was all rather amusing and even Dobbie saw the funny side, playing the fugitive with a dramatic emphasis which would have shamed many a film actor. But it did not take long for the joke to turn sour.

It was a cold, crisp evening, and many of the guests were in the lounge after dinner, sipping their drinks and listening to a trio of musicians playing selections from the musical comedies. Mercy happened to be walking through the corridor, looking for Peter, when through the open door of the writing-room, she heard a female voice.

'Darling, I knew you'd come,' Margo Hetherington was saying, in the low husky purr she affected when she was out to seduce. 'I knew you'd come. That's why I waited!'

The writing-room was usually deserted at this time of night, and Mercy grinned to herself. Some poor lamb had gone to the slaughter. It was not Dobbie, she was thankful to note, because she had just seen him enjoying a brandy and soda with some friends. Wondering if Peter might have gone back to the flat, she climbed the stairs. As she did so she happened to glance down towards the room where Margo Hetherington was ensconced with her latest victim. She wished she had not. From her new vantage point she had a clear view inside, of Margo with a tall dinner jacketed figure. She had found Peter!

An all too familiar misery settled inside her, a spiralling sense of impending disaster. Not again! she pleaded silently. We've been so happy together lately. Don't let this happen to us again!

Peter's affair with Tilly had ended before the war, and the Hewsons had left Torquay years ago. Since then Mercy would have sworn Peter had been faithful to her. At last she had felt secure in his love, even complacent, so certain that no other woman could come between them now. What a fool she had been not to see the danger signs! Margo Hetherington's attractions were very obvious and all too available, a terrible temptation for a man with Peter's fondness for women. It was no use trying to tell herself that the other woman's attraction were *too* obvious, and their availability *too* blatant. Her husband was susceptible to female charms, and she knew it.

Misery settled on her like a great weight, turning the pleasant evening dark with gloom. Then anger began to spark amidst her unhappiness. How could he? How could he betray her again? And with the Hetherington creature. Furiously she turned on her heel. She would go back and confront the pair of them! Yet even as she was mentally concocting the stream of acid comments which would have been a credit to Blanche, she stopped. There were guests about, and she could not disturb them by creating a scene. She would have to hug her hurt to herself until another, more suitable occasion arose. She felt sick with the familiarity of it all.

But the confrontation never materialized. Whether this was because an appropriate opportunity never emerged, or because, at heart, she was reluctant to risk shattering her marriage again, she was not sure. Peter was so loving and affectionate to her these days, she began to wonder if she had been mistaken about the scene in the writing-room. But she also wondered if it was cowardly complacency that was preventing her voicing her outrage. There was no denying that whenever she encountered the Hetherington woman he seemed to be in the vicinity. She devised a strategy whereby whenever she saw them together she immediately intervened, joining in their conversation with a false smile on her face, polite words on her lips. She had no proof that they were having an affair, only a dreadful suspicion which she did not know how to resolve.

Then came a crisis which drove even her misgivings into the background. The alarm clock had just woken them one morning when the internal telephone rang. Sleepily Mercy answered it.

'Mrs Lisbume, please will you come to Room Eight urgently,' said the night porter's voice. He sounded anxious. 'It's Admiral and Mrs Howard, they've been taken ill.'

'What, both of them?' Mercy was wide awake immediately. 'Very well, I'm on my way.'

'What the matter?' asked Peter.

'The Howards are ill. I'd better go and see what's the matter.' Mercy pulled a hasty brush through her hair and hurried off.

The hall porter was hovering outside Room Eight when she arrived.

'Am I glad to see you, Mrs Lisburne,' he said, with evident relief. 'They called me about twenty minutes ago. Fortunately one of the maids came on duty early, she's in there with them. They sound pretty bad.'

Mercy tapped on the door and entered. One look at the couple lying in the bed told her matters were serious.

'They'm both in agony, Mrs Lisburne,' said the maid quietly. 'And sick as dogs, the pair of them. The admiral's the worst, he'm almost unconscious, poor soul.'

'We'd better call the doctor, at once,' Mercy said, with concern.

The doctor was equally worried. 'Mrs Howard may stay here, if you can manage,' he said. 'But I think we'd best get the admiral to hospital straight away.'

'What's causing it?' Mercy asked.

'My guess is it's something they've eaten, though it's a bit early to say. Can I phone for the ambulance from your office, please?'

'Certainly.' Mercy went downstairs with him. As they approached the office Peter emerged, his face grave.

'If you can spare a moment, Doctor, I'm afraid we've got some other patients for you.'

'More?' Mercy was aghast.

'Yes. Captain Albright, his wife, and one of their children, and Sir Henry Harrison. Come, I'll show you the way.'

'No,' said Mercy numbly. 'You carry on here. I'll go with the doctor.'

There was no denying it, the symptoms were all the same.

'The little boy and the admiral are definitely hospital cases,' said the doctor. 'The others are less critical. Can they stay here?'

'Yes, don't worry about them. I'll see they're properly cared for.'

'Ah yes, I had forgotten you have nursing experience.' The doctor was looking at her sympathetically.

'You may as well say it, Doctor,' she said. 'The sooner we face it the better.'

'I'm afraid you're right. It looks as though you've got an outbreak of food poisoning on your hands. It's something that occurs more frequently in the hot weather than at this time of year. I'm afraid you may have been unlucky. I'm sorry.'

Mercy was too distressed to do more than nod in acknowledgement. While the doctor made arrangements to transport the more serious patients to hospital, she went downstairs to give the grave news to Peter.

'This is terrible! Those poor people, to be taken so ill so suddenly,' he said. 'It's not very good news for us, either, is it?' he added, as an afterthought.

'I'm afraid not. It could ruin us. We must ring Joey at once. Will you do it? I'd better make arrangements for a couple of nurses to come and look after those who are staying here.'

It took her some time to organize care for the sick guests. By the time she had achieved it Joey had arrived. And one more guest, a retired judge, had reported sick. Again the symptoms were the same.

'How can it have happened? That's what I want to know?' demanded Joey angrily.

'It is not my fault!' Alphonse, the chef, was voluble in his own defence. 'I 'ave a clean kitchen. The food it is fresh! I see to it most carefully myself!'

'I'm sure you do,' said Mercy consolingly. 'Nevertheless, we must try to discover the cause. Let's go through the menus for the last two days again and see if we can spot anything there. Then we'd better look at the kitchens.'

Although they were diligent, taking their searches far beyond the kitchens, to the storage rooms, the service areas, the drains and the dustbins, no obvious culprit emerged.

It was unrealistic to expect that the arrival of an ambulance and public health inspectors would go unnoticed by the guests. Although Mercy, Peter, Joey and the whole staff battled to keep things as calm and normal as possible an air of nervous excitement spread through the hotel. When the news arrived that Admiral Howard's condition was critical the nervousness came close to panic. Most of the guests had booked for the entire winter. Several ended their stay abuptly, two middle-aged matrons declaring hysterically that they had never felt well since entering the Villa Dorata.

'That wasn't the food, it was the drink!' said Joey bitterly. 'I've never seen anyone consume gin the way those two did. Try telling that to the press, though.'

'It won't get into the newspapers, will it?' asked Mercy in alarm.

'There's no way we can keep it out,' Joey said. 'We've a pair of reporters camped at the front gate. Haven't you noticed?'

'I have,' said Peter gloomily. 'I tried giving them a diplomatic statement. But I was too late, they'd got to those silly women first.'

'What can we do about it?' Mercy asked.

'Not much. Just be doubly careful about everything, and wait for the health inspector's report.'

Margo Hetherington had been one of the first guests to leave the hotel after the outbreak of food poisoning. Mercy was relieved to see her go, but at the same time she felt that nothing had been resolved. Her faith in Peter remained shaken, she feared he had betrayed her yet again. Only the seriousness of the present situation prevented her from tackling him on the subject. What did her hurt matter when people were dangerously ill? How could she play the aggrieved wife when the future of the hotel could be in ruins?

The health inspector's report, when it came, was painfully inconclusive. After saying some complimentary things about the food preparation at the Villa Dorata the concluding statement read: 'We can find no definite source of contamination, or cause for the outbreak.'

'That's no good to us!' Joey exploded. 'Word has already got round. It's bad enough the hotel being half empty, but have you seen how many cancellations have been coming in from non-residents?'

'Yes,' replied Mercy. 'I've just taken another one. The twenty-first birthday dinner for next week. They were very kind and regretful but "In the circumstances…"'

'In the circumstances we can't blame them,' said Peter gloomily. 'The doctor told me there were another five cases in the town, four of whom had eaten here recently. No wonder we're getting cancellations. You can't expect people to risk food poisoning.'

'And what of the fifth?' asked Mercy hopefully. 'Surely it proves that we weren't to blame?'

'I'm afraid not. I asked the doctor the same question,' Peter replied. 'He pointed out that eleven to one are pretty steep odds. The single case could have picked up the poisoning anywhere. One isolated incident doesn't help us at all. But, at least, here's one of our stalwart guests who hasn't deserted us. What can we do for you, Dobbie?'

'Desert you? I should think not!' Dobbie was indignant at the idea. 'I just came to ask what news there is of the admiral and the Albright boy.'

'I've just rung the hospital,' said Mercy. 'Young Tony's beginning to pull through; it looks as though he's over the worst. They're still very concerned about the admiral, though. He already had a weak heart, and to have this on top...'

'Such a shame!' Dobbie shook his head sympathetically. 'I like the old admiral. I was so glad when he came for the whole winter. You can depend on some interesting yarns after dinner when he's about! Poor fellow! There he was, enjoying the excursion only a few days ago along with Mrs Howard, laughing and joking as if he hadn't a care in the world, and now this!'

'I didn't know you'd been on an excursion with the admiral and his wife,' said Mercy.

'There was quite a party of us. Over twenty. It was a charity affair in aid of one of the seamen's funds. You must have seen the notice, Lisbume. There was one pinned up in the Yacht Club.'

'I vaguely remember something. Wasn't it to go to look round the dockyard at Devonport?'

'That's it. The admiral had organized it, and a friend of his showed us round. We went over a frigate, too. It was a most interesting day. Afterwards we had a splendid tea in Plymouth. Young Albright over-indulged in the cream buns and felt seedy on the way back...' Dobbie's voice tailed away as the other three stared at him intently.

'The Albrights were there?' asked Mercy in a tense voice.

'Yes, and the Judge, and Sir Henry. Mrs Howard was selling the tickets, you see.'

'Then surely this clears our name!' cried Mercy. 'Everyone who was taken ill had been on that excursion and...'

'And Dobbie here!' broke in Peter. 'Don't forget him. I'm sorry to dash your hopes, darling, but Dobbie hasn't ailed a thing, have you?'

'I've been absolutely top-hole all week, I'm afraid.'

'Please don't apologize for being well.' Mercy managed a smile. 'I was forgetting the other victims, too. The ones in the town.'

'Look, I don't want to start your hopes up again, but perhaps it would be as well to get in touch with the doctor or the public health chappies once more,' said Dobbie cautiously. 'Don't forget, tickets for the picnic weren't restricted to hotel guests, they were pretty freely available.'

'So those other victims might also have been at the excursion?' asked Peter. 'But that doesn't explain how you avoided being ill.'

'Not just me,' Dobbie pointed out. 'The two younger Albright children weren't affected either, were they? It could be that we've got particularly strong digestions, or it could be that we didn't eat the same as everyone else…'

He paused thoughtfully.

'Crab!' he exclaimed suddenly. 'There were crab sandwiches! I never touch the stuff, it brings me out in a rash. Nor did the two littlest Albrights, of course. Young Tony did, though! I saw him eating crab sandwiches with great gusto.'

'Oh Dobbie, I think you've solved the puzzle!' Mercy gave a gasp of relief. 'I could kiss you, I really could!'

'Please go ahead,' grinned Dobbie delightedly. 'Don't let the presence of your husband put you off. Though upon second thoughts, it might be better to wait until the picnic theory is proved.'

'The doctor will be here any minute now. We can hear what he thinks of all this,' said Peter.

'At least, the other patients seem to be on the mend,' said Dobbie. 'I popped in to see how Sir Henry was feeling, and he was on his feet. A bit wobbly, but upright.' He gave a chuckle. 'There is one bright spot in this terrible business. It did get rid of that awful Hetherington woman!' He clapped Peter heartily on the shoulder. 'I owe you a huge debt of gratitude, old man! I won't forget it.'

Mercy stiffened at the mention of Margo Hetherington but before she could inquire further the doctor arrived. He listened carefully to the new theory.

'I'll look into it,' he promised. 'Mrs Howard was selling the tickets, you say? Then if she has a list of names it would make the task much easier. I'll ask her when I go up to see her.'

When he returned after checking on his patients he was holding a sheet of paper.

'A list of participants in the excursion!' he said. 'Now comes the hard part for you. The waiting.'

He was right. For the rest of that day, and all the next the three of them – four, including Dobbie – were on tenterhooks. The vital phone call finally came just at the end of dinner. When Peter put down the receiver he looked quite pale.

'It's bad news?' asked Mercy, her heart plummeting.

'No, good! Very good! Very, very good!' He suddenly leapt to his feet and seized her in a bear-hug. 'The Villa Dorata has been cleared! Everyone of the victims was on that wretched picnic. While they were checking they even discovered two more cases who had not been affected severely enough to call in the doctor!'

'Thank goodness!' Mercy was grateful for his arms about her, she felt so weak with relief. 'I'd better phone Joey, to let him know right away.'

'Tell him an official notification has already been sent in to the local papers, exonerating us completely. If that doesn't cheer him up I don't know what will!'

'Where are you going?' Mercy asked, as releasing her, he headed for the door.

'To tell the guests and the staff. They'll be as relieved as we are!'

They were! The cheering from the dining room was so loud Mercy could scarcely hear Joey's jubilant exclamation at the end of the line. Peter did more than merely inform everyone, he ordered champagne all round. The week which had begun so disastrously ended in joyous celebration. Nevertheless, they were not out of the wood yet. Although it had only taken a few days to damage the Villa Dorata's reputation, Mercy knew it would take much much longer to restore the public's faith in the hotel.

'We're going to have to do something definite to bring the Villa Dorata back favourably into the limelight,' she said, at their next managerial meeting.

'The local papers have been very good, and given us an excellent coverage,' Peter pointed out.

'That's still not enough,' said Joey. 'A black mark like this will take a long, long time to be forgotten, even if it was a mistake. Mercy's right, we've got to do something positive. The alternative is to let memories of the food poisoning scare fade. Quite frankly I don't think we can afford to wait. I've looked at the bookings for the next few months.'

'Very well, we're all agreed on that point. The next questions are what shall we do and how much will it cost?' said Peter.

'We need something to catch the public's eye,' Joey said thoughtfully.

'How about a week of listening to music?' suggested Mercy. 'We could do a sort of festival whereby people could come to stay *and* hear good musicians.'

'Not a bad idea,' agreed Joey. 'It might do for the winter.'

'We could try one, and if it proved popular we could make them a regular thing,' said Peter.

'It's still rather a short-term solution.' Joey said. 'We need something to attract people for this coming summer. Folks won't want to stay indoors day after day if the weather's good, no matter how many top-notch musicians we hire.'

'So we need something in the open air,' mused Peter. 'Something like riding or—'

'Sailing!' exclaimed Mercy. 'That's it! We've already made provision for those who want to ride. But what if we could offer people the chance of some decent yachting included in their stay here? It would appeal to the good-weather sailors who don't have yachts of their own but who would enjoy a spot of sailing, or those who come from up-country and don't want the bother of bringing their own craft all the way here. What do you think?'

'It has possibilities! Distinct possibilities!' said Joey, 'I can see it being a real attraction. Goodness knows, we get enough sailing enthusiasts here already! It would only be going one step further. The only thing is it would put a lot of extra work on Peter because he's the obvious man to have charge.'

Peter had been sitting quietly so far, neither showing any emotion nor offering an opinion.

'Well?' demanded Mercy. 'Do you think it's a good idea?'

'I do!' he said simply. 'Of course I do! I think it's a marvellous idea, one that's right up my street. You know I'd be totally biased in favour of anything connected with boats, so you two had better make the decisions.'

'Could you cope with the extra work?' asked Mercy. 'Naturally it would mean taking on someone to help. I dare say you could find someone suitable.'

'Boyer!' said Peter. 'You remember? The man who sold me *Tango*? He'd be glad of the job. He's having rather a hard time of it, I'm afraid. He'd be ideal – an excellent fellow and a first-rate seaman.'

'Then can we leave it to you to see what sort of craft you think suitable, and work out the costs and so on?' asked Joey.

'Indeed you can!' Peter was beginning to beam. Then his smile faded. 'Can we afford it, though?' he asked. 'It will be pricey to get anything decent.'

'I don't think we can afford *not* to do it!' said Mercy.

They tried the idea out on Dobbie later that evening.

'All the comforts of the Villa Dorata with the joys of sailing thrown in? It sounds like Paradise to me,' he said heartily.

'Good, so we've got at least one totally impartial view on the matter,' chuckled Peter.

'You have!' agreed Dobbie with a grin. 'Now if I may change the subject; I'm glad to have caught you, Lisburne, old man. I want to give you these as a small token of appreciation.' He held out a rectangular package.

When Peter opened the parcel it proved to be a large box of Corona cigars.

'There was no need! I did nothing!' protested Peter, rather over-come.

'Nothing? I don't consider it nothing! I consider it bravery well over and above the call of friendship! He deliberately stepped into the firing line, putting himself between that Hetherington creature and me, drawing her fire,' Dobbie explained to Mercy.

'Peter did what?' she demanded.

'Sacrificed himself so I could escape from the vampire's clutches.'

'Don't you mean vamp, not vampire?' asked Mercy, though she was in no mood to joke.

'I know what I mean!' Dobbie said darkly. 'Which is why I'm so impressed by your husband's selfless bravery.'

'You don't need to overdo it!' laughed Peter. 'Nor do you need to explain to Mercy. She knew what I was up to. That was why I was in no danger! You should have seen the sterling way she would come to the rescue whenever La Hetherington got too predatory! I could always rely on her to turn up in the nick of time, like the relief of Mafeking. You should get married, Dobbie! It's a marvellous protection. But choose someone with plenty of spark in her background. Mercy gets hers from her grandmother. Now there's someone I'd love to have seen confronting the Hetherington woman!'

So Peter had not been having an affair with Margo Hetherington after all! He had been taking part in some charade to help Dobbie. Mercy struggled to maintain her calm expression. She felt so foolish – and so relieved! What astonished her was the way in which Peter calmly assumed that she had been a willing partner in his deception. Remembering the rougher passages of their marriage did he never stop to think she might misconstrue what he was doing? No, she decided, that was not Peter's way. He would be too intent on helping Dobbie out of trouble. On those occasions when she had thought herself interrupting his assignations with Mrs Hetherington he had actually been grateful for her intervention. She did not know whether to laugh or to cry. Upon consideration she decided simply to remain silent. His faith in their marriage had been stronger than hers. He had trusted her to understand what he was doing. He must never know what suspicions she had been harbouring.

–

Business was slow to pick up again. Although a few erstwhile regulars, who had dined elsewhere during the food-poisoning episode, gradually returned to the Villa Dorata, bookings remained poor. A blackened reputation, it seemed, was an extremely hard thing to live down, no matter how ill-deserved it was.

'It's so unfair,' protested Mercy, gazing around the almost empty dining-room. 'We had nothing to do with the food-poisoning outbreak. Why should we suffer?'

'Because it's a hard world,' stated Joey. 'Haven't you worked that out yet? We've just got to sit it out until people forget about it.'

Could they afford to wait for memories to fade? Mercy doubted it. Their running expenses remained high, no matter how few guests there were.

Their regular managerial meetings became more and more grim, concerned with how to make economies without compromising the high standards they had set for the hotel. Massive cuts in salaries for all three of them were among the first of their money-saving measures. Reductions in staff followed, along with turning off the heating on the topmost floor, where all the rooms were unoccupied.

The yachting project was something they debated for a long time. Finally they were in agreement – they could not afford to turn down the idea. It took more scrimping and saving, but Peter bought two yachts: an elegant eight-metre craft for the really serious sailors and a modest cutter for those who liked their sailing to be more sedate.

'Now we can offer a choice of experience,' he pointed out. 'Along with the dinghies we already own and maybe with the addition of a motor launch later, we will be able to cater for most tastes.'

The problem was that advertising their attractions proved to be a slow business. There was interest, but only for the future, and they needed guests immediately.

Nightly Mercy was tormented by anguished dreams in which the Villa Dorata was sold about their ears and the three of them were left standing on the beach at Meadfoot, penniless, with nothing to show for their hard work.

Business at the hotel *had* to improve. She was determined on it. She was not going back to being poor again! She was not! Every time she went back to visit her family she was reminded of what it had been like. Things were far, far better at Fernicombe now, but the memory of poverty still hung about the place despite the Seatons' present affluence.

A growing concern for Joey was another cause for anxiety. He was continuing to see a great deal of Angie Bolton; while their liaison remained beyond the boundaries of the Villa Dorata Mercy felt she had no right to comment. Unfortunately Angie was becoming a frequent visitor to the hotel these days, calling to see Joey on all sorts of trivial pretexts. Mercy did drop a few heavy hints about the convenience of the modern telephone system, without results. Angie continued to come.

Then one day, Mercy was coming downstairs as Angie happened to emerge from the office. The young woman looked flushed and happy, and rather rumpled. A couple of waiters, crossing the hall at that moment, saw her too, and Mercy caught the knowing winks that passed between the men. This, she decided, was too much! She marched into the office, confident she would find her brother there. Joey looked up from the pile of wages sheets in front of him.

'Is anything the matter?' he asked. 'You've got your disapproving look on your face.'

'And with good reason.' She closed the door firmly behind her. 'It's no use looking at me innocently, pretending you've been slaving at the books all morning. I've just seen Angie leave.'

'Oh!' Joey put down his pen, and leaned back in his chair.

'You'll have to be more careful. What you do in your own time is your affair, but she's coming here too often, and the staff are beginning to notice. For heaven's sake, can't you be discreet?'

Discreet! That had been the watchword during her own affair with Gunther! Immediately the bitter-sweet memories of those days came flooding back.

'Please take care, Joey,' she said softly, the anger going from her voice. 'It's a treacherous path you're treading, and you could get terribly hurt. I don't blame you for being tempted. Angie's a very pretty girl. But please, I beg of you, think what you're doing.'

She steeled herself for Joey's violent reaction as he told her to mind her own business. The explosion did not come.

'It's too late, I'm afraid,' he said very quietly. 'We love each other, you see.' And he buried his head in his hands.

The complete hopelessness in his voice tore at her. She put her arms about him, hugging him to her as she used to do when he was a little boy.

'I'm sorry,' she whispered. 'So very sorry.'

'So am I! What an awful mess I'm in!'

'Is there any way I can help?' she asked tentatively.

He shook his head.

'It's my mess. I'll have to find a way out by myself.' There was one question she had to ask.

'Queenie…? You aren't considering leaving…?'

He looked up at her, utter misery in his eyes.

'I couldn't do that to poor Queenie,' he said, 'it isn't her fault.'

'What do you propose doing, then?'

'I don't know and that's the truth. Carry on as usual, I suppose.' He straightened up suddenly, 'I'll have a word with Angie about coming here, though. It won't do, not if the staff are beginning to snigger.'

'Joey, I wish I hadn't spoken…'

'No, you were right to mention it. Now, while you're here will you check these figures of mine, if you can spare a moment.'

From his tone she knew the subject of his private life was firmly closed. Inside she felt such pain. He was so unhappy, and there was nothing she could do to ease his hurt. That was the hardest part of all.

373

Without another word she pulled up a chair and reached for the accounts book.

The next few weeks were hard financially, forcing them to take a further cut in salaries.

'You do realize the senior staff are earning more money than we are, don't you?' Joey pointed out.

'Yes, but they haven't all the fun of owning an hotel.' Mercy retorted. 'Just as long as I still get more than the boot-boy, I won't complain.'

She worried, though, no matter how optimistic she was in public, and the reservations book gave little comfort. It looked dismally empty at times.

The Villa Dorata Hotel's new 'Ashore and Afloat' holidays were now advertised widely in yachting and boating magazines as well as in the national periodicals. At last the response began to be encouraging. Bookings increased, slowly at first, then in a steady stream until, by Regatta-time, they were absolutely full.

'The winter prospects look very rosy, too', Joey remarked. 'Far better than last year.'

'Weren't the sacrifices worth it?' commented Mercy, her anxiety slowly melting away. 'Even though we'll still have to watch the pennies for a while, things are beginning to go right for us at last. We're getting closer to our goal!'

'And what is our goal?' asked Joey.

'I'm surprised that you need to ask. It's having four stars against our name.'

'Do you think we'll get them?'

'Certainlyl' There was no doubt in Mercy's voice. 'Next year, you'll see! That's when we'll know the Villa Dorata Hotel really is a success!'

Chapter Twenty One

'Mrs Lisburne, can you spare a moment?'

'Certainly, Lady Agnew. How can I help you?' Mercy stopped and smiled at her guest.

'Where's the best place to buy silk stockings, please? I'm looking for fully-fashioned ones, of course, in this new light colour.'

Lady Agnew raised her skirt above her knees, displaying legs that were still slim and shapely.

'Jane!' Her companion was shocked. 'What are you thinking of? Supposing Mr Seaton or Captain Lisburne came along at this moment!'

'Don't make such a fuss, Elsie. I doubt if it would be much of a thrill for either of them. I'm sure they've both seen female legs before.'

Slowly and deliberately Jane Agnew let her skirt fall.

Mercy had to bite back a smile. At times she found it difficult to believe that this elderly pair were sisters. They were both slight of figure, it was true. There was a definite facial resemblance, too, if one looked closely enough. There similarity ended, for Elsie was a retiring, demure little woman, prone to wear shapeless clothes in nondescript colours, while her sister, Jane Agnew, was the exact opposite.

'I may have missed the boat for being a bright young thing,' she had announced on her arrival at the Villa Dorata, 'so I'll have to make do with being a bright old thing instead.'

She certainly did her best to live up to her statement. Her clothes were in the latest style, dropped waistline, raised hem and all. Her make-up would have done credit to Vilma Banky or Gloria Swanson, while her silver-grey hair was worn short, in an up-to-the minute shingle.

'I usually find Bobby's, on the Strand, very good for stockings,' Mercy said. 'If not, you could try Williams and Cox, a little further on.'

'Thank you, my dear. I was certain you would know where to go.'
Lady Agnew scrutinized her for a moment, then said, 'Doesn't Mrs
Lisburne's hair look attractive, Elsie? Why don't you have your hair
cut in a similar style? It would suit you – not too short. And see how
prettily it frames her face! Yes, why don't you try it?'

'Oh I couldn't. I mean, I wouldn't feel comfortable.'

'You can't honestly say you feel comfortable going about looking
as if mice were nesting at the back of your head, can you?'

'That was not a nice thing to say!' Mrs Hastings put a hand up and
patted her wispy bun.

'It's true though,' said her sister, unrepentant. 'And why do you
continue to wear your skirts down round your ankles? You always
behave as though you are joined at the knees. How poor old Herbert
managed, being married to you all those years, I don't know.'

'Oh!' Elsie Hastings's face went crimson. 'You go too far, Jane, you
really do! To say such a thing in front of dear Mrs Lisburne!'

'I don't suppose Mrs Lisburne's learning anything new from me,
not when she's married to such a gorgeous man. Where is the lovely
captain, by the way? We haven't seen him this morning.'

'I'm keeping him hidden, away from the competition.' Mercy
replied.

'Spoilsport!' Jane Agnew's long jade earrings shook appreciatively.
'Perhaps you're wise, though. At my age I don't think I can be bothered
to break in another man; I've already had three husbands of my own.
It would be much easier to go for someone else's, for a change. I did
have my eye on yours, but I don't think I fancy the competition.'

'They do say that discretion is the better part of valour!' smiled
Mercy.

'They do indeed!' Lady Agnew chuckled, and patted her on the
arm. 'I enjoy talking to you, my dear! You give as good as you get,
and that's fun. Not like Elsie here, who just keeps going red and saying
"Oh Jane" in a shocked voice.'

'Oh Jane!' wailed Mrs Hastings.

'There, what did I say? Oh, all right, I'll be nice to you for the rest
of the day if you'll let me buy you some decent stockings instead of
those awful lisle things?'

Lady Agnew paused, her gaze riveted on something through the
window. 'Just look at that!' she exclaimed.

The object of her interest was Miss Manning. At eleven in the morning she was crossing the lawn wearing an elaborately beaded dinner gown, a woolly tam o'shanter, and furry bedroom slippers.

'Batty!' declared Jane Agnew. 'The woman's completely batty! If you'll pardon me for saying so, my dear, someone is foisting their responsibilities on to you in that department.'

Mercy merely smiled, though secretly she agreed with Lady Agnew. For some time she had been suggesting to the Mannings that their aunt needed greater care than she was able to offer. As yet there had been no response.

'Ah well, come along, Elsie. Get your hat, then we'll go shopping.'

Mercy shook her head in amusement as she watched them go upstairs to their rooms. It was typical that Mrs Hastings should be clutching a bulging canvas bag from which protruded knitting needles, while her sister carried only a copy of *Vogue*. Such diverse characters, yet underneath the sharp remarks and the bickering she suspected they were extremely fond of each other.

'Have I missed something funny? You're grinning all over your face,' remarked Peter, as he came in.

'Only the Terrible Twins. They do make me laugh.'

'And me. It's meeting people like Lady Agnew that makes hotel-keeping worthwhile.'

'She's certainly taken a fancy to you. I'm going to have to watch out.' She smiled, rejoicing quietly inside that she could joke about such things now.

'In that case, so am I. I don't think I could cope with a passionate affair with her, she's got far too much energy. I'd be worn out in no time.'

'Maybe you should get yourself into shape.'

'Don't be cheeky!' He slapped her playfully on the bottom, 'I'm too busy arranging moonlight cruises for our guests.'

'So you've managed to arrange it? That's wonderful.'

'Yes, the boat's booked. I've looked over her and she's nicely fitted out. The skipper says our people can go aboard a couple of hours earlier to lay out the supper. There's a bit of space for dancing, provided no one does too energetic a charleston. If this proves popular I can see us enlarging our fleet to include a small cruise-liner.'

'The hotel certainly seems to be acquiring a nautical bias,' smiled Mercy, 'so why not? A liner would fit into the scheme of things very nicely, though, I'd rather we didn't take on anything more until our four stars are well and truly secure. Now that we've applied to the AA we don't want anything to go wrong.'

'You're right.' Peter was suddenly serious. 'It's been a hard year, but when I compare how things were after the food-poisoning business...'

'It's incredible, isn't it?' Mercy agreed quietly.

'Business has improved dramatically, thanks to your hard work with the yachting.'

'No, the yachting's only the top-dressing. It's everyone's hard work that's brought about our miracle. There was a time when I thought we might go under.'

'Me too.' She slid her arms about him, the memory of those dark weeks causing her to seek solace. 'Not any more, though. We're a success.'

'So we are! How clever I was to marry you all those years ago. I knew you had potential, even then. That was the only reason I pursued you.'

'Wretch!' She pretended to pull away from him, but as she had hoped he merely tightened his hold, drawing her closer until their lips touched.

'Yer, you'm idn't supposed to be canoodling, you'm married!' broke in Dolly's voice. 'Besides, what'd the guests think? Us'll be getting a reputation as one of they naughty 'ouses next, the sort the police raid.'

'Now what sort of houses would they be, Dolly? I've no idea what you mean,' said Peter innocently.

'I'll bet!' Dolly gave a chuckle, and dug him in the ribs. 'Any road, I've come to break up your sweet'earting. The man from the linen supplier's 'as arrived with they samples you wanted.'

'In that case I'd better come up and see him.' Mercy followed Dolly up the staff stairs.

'I near enough bumped into that Lady Agnew on my way down,' remarked Dolly.

'What, coming down these stairs?'

'Yes. 'Er said, "Just taking a short cut, my dear!" as breezy as you like. 'Er's a proper scream; idn't 'er?'

'Life's never dull when she's around, certainly.'

'You know who 'er minds me of? Your grandma!'

'Oh, surely not!'

'I means it. I'm surprised you 'aven't noticed. 'Er've got that same determined way about 'er. 'Er'm going to do as 'er pleases, and no one idn't going to shift 'er.'

'You know, you could be right… I think I agree with you. Now you've mentioned it I see the resemblance. She is like Blanche.'

'Mind you, I've got to admit 'er smells a deal better than your gran ever did,' Dolly grinned.

Mercy pulled a face at her, but before she could think of a suitably cutting reply they had reached the linen room. Later, after dinner, she was pinning a notice on the guests' bulletin board when Jane Agnew came along, looking suitably elegant for the evening in a vivid green chiffon dress, the skirt of which hung in fashionable handkerchief points.

'Now what have you thought up to keep us entertained, Mrs Lisburne?' she inquired. 'It's one thing I like about this hotel, quite apart from the handsome men. There's always something exciting to do. I like it for my sister's sake, you understand. She needs dragging away from her knitting. As for myself, I can always find something to amuse me.' She said it with a wicked twinkle in her eye.

Dolly's right, thought Mercy. She *is* like Blanche. How odd that I have not noticed it before. Aloud she said, 'I think you'll both enjoy this. We've organized an evening cruise round the bay for tomorrow. There'll be supper and dancing and a full moon.'

'Ah, I can see you've thought of all the essentials.' Jane Agnew scrutinized the notice, reading every word until she reached Mercy's signature. 'Goodness!' she exclaimed. 'You're called Mercy! How odd!'

'Yes, isn't it? I think I must be the only person burdened with such a Christian name.'

'Not so! I said "How odd!" because we had an Aunt Mercy, and we always thought she was unique. Her name was really Mercedes, but that was too much of a mouthful, she was always known as Mercy. Well I never!'

'Oh, really?' Mercy was genuinely surprised. 'So I'm not the only one. I do hope your aunt didn't suffer as I did. I was for ever being teased about my name.'

'The poor soul had an unhappy life, certainly, though I don't think her name had much to do with it. Now this cruise of yours. Can I have your assurance there will be plenty of men?'

'Absolutely guaranteed!'

379

'Then put my sister and myself at the top of the list, if you please.'

The evening cruise proved to be an unqualified success.

'Everyone's saying how grand it was and when's the next one,' reported Joey afterwards. 'It's the sort of thing we could follow up. Mind, I'm leaving the arrangements to Peter; he can get the blame if the sea gets choppy!'

'Coward!' said Mercy.

'You've got it in one. Well, if there's nothing more you need me for I'll be off. I've got to get back to Seaton's.'

'How's business there?'

'Very satisfactory at the moment. We're making a comfortable profit, thank goodness.'

'You deserve it, you work so hard.'

'Work's the easy bit,' he said. 'It's the rest of life which is hard. 'Bye, Mercy. See you tomorrow.'

The sad smile he gave stabbed at her heart. Poor Joey, there seemed no solution to his problems.

After he had gone, Mercy went to see how the lunches were progressing. The dining room was gratifyingly full on this bright sunny day, the murmur of pleasant chatter competing with the bees in the rambling roses outside the open windows. She paused to pass the time of day with the guests at one table. As she did so she was conscious of a sudden silence behind her, followed by smothered titters. Looking round she saw Miss Manning standing in the doorway, wearing a very smart hat, her inevitable furry slippers – and knee-length summer combinations.

Fortunately Dobbie was sitting close by. He leapt to his feet, and had wrapped Miss Manning in his jacket before Mercy could reach her.

'Hello, Miss Manning,' she said calmly. 'Isn't it a beautiful day? Shall we go and choose you something pretty to wear at lunch? Your lavender silk would look quite delightful with that hat?'

'Do you think so? I wasn't sure. You don't think my navy-blue *crepe de chine* might be better?' Dulcie Manning cheerfully allowed herself to be led away.

Mercy handed the old lady over to one of the maids, who soon had her dressed, and returned, suitably clad, to the dining-room.

'Bless you for coming to the rescue before she got right across the floor,' Mercy said to Dobbie, giving him back his jacket. 'You prevented quite an embarrassing incident.'

'More than you know, m'dear,' he chuckled. 'The poor old soul had forgotten to button her coal-house hatch!'

Miss Manning's latest escapade caused a lot of laughter; nevertheless, it proved the last straw.

'She can't go on like this,' Mercy said. 'This time it was amusing, but she's growing less and less responsible for her actions. Something must be done. If the Mannings want us to keep her here they must employ someone to be with her twenty-four hours a day. We can't cope.'

The letter, couched in friendly yet firm terms, was completed and sent off.

'I said she was batty, didn't I?' remarked Lady Agnew. 'Still, she's quite harmless, poor dear.'

Lady Agnew and her sister were taking tea on the terrace as Mercy passed beside their table. Below them, slicing through the blue-green water, they could see the *Wild Goose*, the hotel's yacht, being put through her paces by Peter.

'I must say being afloat really does something for a man,' observed Jane Agnew.

'Your eyesight must be better than mine, Jane,' said Mrs Hastings, 'I can't make out any of the gentlemen from here.'

'I'm speaking from experience not eyesight!' said her sister cuttingly. She turned to Mercy. 'I'm glad you've come by at this moment, Mrs Lisburne. Have you got time to join us for a cup of tea? There's something I'd like to show you.'

'Thank you, I'd love to.' Mercy settled herself at the table, and signalled for the waiter to bring more tea and another cup.

When he had done so Lady Agnew produced a large brown paper parcel, and placed it on the table, to the imminent peril of the crockery. She removed the wrapping to reveal a photograph album. A highly superior album, although it was old, for it was of expensively tooled Moroccan leather, much embellished with gold leaf. On the front was a highly ornate and impressive coat of arms.

'The old family crest!' said Jane Agnew somewhat derisively. 'I'm afraid we suffer from delusions of grandeur.'

'How can you say that?' protested her sister. 'We do come from very old stock. We can trace our ancestors right back to the thirteenth century.'

'Everyone's from old stock!' retorted Jane. 'Just because there's written proof of our ancestors doesn't make our family any older than anyone else's. It isn't our coat of arms I wanted to show Mrs Lisburne, it is one of the photographs. I thought you might like to see the other Mercy. Proof that you aren't the only one ever to have existed.'

'I would indeed,' said Mercy.

'We've just been to Exeter to fetch it,' Jane explained, opening the album. 'We've been having it repaired by a marvellous man who does work for the cathedral library. I don't suppose this is as rare or valuable as the other books he works on, but it is a family treasure, and we value it. Ah, here's the right place. I knew I'd marked it.'

The page she turned to was occupied by a single sepia photograph, faded with age. It was of a family group, a man and woman with their four children. They were certainly well-off, to judge by their clothes, which were in the style of the 1860s or 1870s Mercy guessed.

'There's our Aunt Mercedes, the other Mercy.' With a well-manicured finger Jane Agnew pointed to the woman.

'She was our father's sister,' explained Elsie Hastings. 'Such a sweet, gentle soul.'

Mercy gazed down at the picture. Even primitive photography and the blurring of age could not hide the fact that the other Mercy had been a lovely woman. Her well-shaped features and large dark eyes gave her a timeless beauty which went beyond mere fashion.

'She is beautiful,' Mercy said. 'And doesn't she look happy, surrounded by her children. I see her husband is a clergyman.'

'Yes, Uncle Ambrose was in the Church. Had ambitions to be Archbishop of Canterbury, or the Archangel Gabriel, or something, but never made it!'

'Jane, that's not true!'

'Well, he certainly had ambitions which were never fulfilled, as his temper proved. A very irritable man! If Aunt Mercy looked happy in that picture it must have been a temporary aberration.'

'You really do say some wicked things…'

The sisters went on bickering, but Mercy no longer heard them. She was too engrossed in looking at the eldest child in the group, a girl of about fifteen or sixteen.

It was the dress which attracted her attention, a plaid crinoline short enough to display a pair of neat white boots. She had seen a dress like that before, and similar white boots! She looked more closely at the young face. It was indistinct, faded by the passing years.

'And this is one of your cousins, I presume,' she said as evenly as she could manage.

The sisters paused in their verbal battle.

'It certainly is! That's Cousin Blanche!'

'Oh…!'

Tension gripped Mercy. Tension and an almost unbearable anticipation. She struggled to remain calm, to hold her curiosity in check. After all, she might be wrong! It might be no more than a coincidence! The figure in the photograph was too blurred to be identified positively as her grandmother.

'She's the skeleton in the family cupboard!' went on Lady Agnew in dramatic tones.

'Jane!'

Mercy's excitement almost overwhelmed her – yet still she held herself in check.

'Your cousin doesn't look a very dreadful skeleton in this picture,' she said with incredible calm. 'She can't have done anything too terrible.'

'Nothing that thousands of girls hadn't done before and will no doubt do again. She got in the family way, poor little devil! Not long after this photograph was taken, at a guess.'

'What – what happened to her?' Mercy's voice was no more than a whisper.

'Uncle Ambrose turned her out of the house,' Elsie Hastings said primly. 'He couldn't have done anything else, a man in his position.'

'He could have shown some Christian charity,' retorted her sister. 'He was supposed to be in that line of business, wasn't he?'

'I'm sure he did everything necessary,' said Elsie. 'Everything necessary not to wreck his career, you mean,' snapped Jane. 'And what do you know of it, anyway? You were too young at the time!'

'I'm only two years younger than you!' exclaimed Elsie. 'And I recall that Blanche made some wicked, wicked accusations. How someone so young could have thought of anything so shocking—'

'Exactly! She was only sixteen and as naive as they come. Far too naive to have thought them up.'

'But to have accused a senior churchman – a dean!'

'Well, why not? Just because a fellow preaches a sermon or two on Sundays doesn't make him different from the rest. He's made exactly the same way under his cassock, you know!'

'Jane!' Elsie's face flamed its habitual scarlet. 'But to accuse the dean! I remember him! He was charming!'

'A bit too charming! If your memory were better you'd recall he was a bit too fond of cuddling young girls on his lap. I remember, though. I always tried to avoid him, he was too active with his hands. I wasn't the trusting sort, like Blanche. My word, did he make a fuss of her, calling her his "special little friend" and similar muck! And she took it all in! She was a loving soul, was Blanche. Loving and trusting. That was her trouble!'

'And her parents, didn't they believe her?' asked Mercy, shaken by what she had heard.

The sisters turned to her in some surprise, they had been so absorbed in their arguing they had apparently forgotten her existence.

'Aunt Mercy did, I think,' said Jane. 'By all accounts she went down on her bended knees to Uncle Ambrose, begging him to help Blanche, instead of turning her out. Not that it did any good. He wouldn't relent, not him. I reckon he believed her, though. He must have known what sort of a man the dean was; they'd been friends for years.'

'And still he sent Blanche away?' Mercy could scarcely believe that anyone could be so hard-hearted.

'He was an ambitious man, as I've said,' replied Jane with a cynical smile. 'He was relying on the dean to help him on his way up the ecclesiastical ladder. He had three daughters, but only one career, so he sacrificed Blanche.'

'He was a clergyman!' Mercy was shocked.

'So was the dean!' observed Jane. 'I remember Father remarking that knowing those two particular churchmen made him wonder what sort of fellows the devil was employing. Our parents were so distressed when they heard about it, a young girl thrown out like that, especially when she was far more sinned against than sinning. We were spending a year abroad at the time, you see, otherwise our parents would have done something to help. By the time we got home it was all over and Blanche was long gone. No one ever found out where.'

'I'm sure Mrs Lisburne is quite bored with hearing our family history,' Elsie said.

How could Mercy tell them she was anything but bored, that every word they had said had been relevant to her own life? This was her grandmother they were talking about! Her family!

'My sister doesn't approve of this washing of dirty linen in public,' Jane remarked. 'As if it mattered. They're dead now. Blanche, too, most likely.'

'Yes, Uncle Ambrose died soon afterwards,' Elsie sighed. 'They said it was because of all this trouble.'

'Divine retribution, more likely,' put in Jane. 'He never did get the advancement he so longed for. Not that he would have gone far if he'd lived, in my opinion. The money, and the background came from Aunt Mercy's side – our side of the family. She married beneath her, and maybe that was what fired Uncle Ambrose's ambition. At any rate, he died knowing he was a failure, but even that wasn't sufficient punishment for what he did.'

'And the dean?' Mercy hardly dared to ask.

Jane gave a harsh chuckle.

'The devil looks after his own, sure enough. He was made a bishop – the Bishop of Seaton.'

Mercy had to bite back a harsh laugh. How like Blanche to have chosen such a name! A subtle revenge!

'Seaton! Why, that's your brother's name, Mrs Lisburne!' exclaimed Elsie. 'Oh, silly me! It must have been your name too, of course. What an extraordinary coincidence!'

It would have been the ideal moment to have revealed her relationship, but something held her back. She had heard so much, learned such a lot about her background and her family's that she felt she needed to wait. She needed to assimilate Blanche's story, to get to know her grandmother again. She became aware of Jane Agnew watching her intently.

'Yes, extraordinary coincidences do happen, don't they?' said Jane, her eyes, so keen and astute beneath their painted lids, never once leaving Mercy's face. 'Now I think we really have worn poor Mrs Lisburne out. You're looking quite tired, my dear. You work too hard. I suggest you go and have half an hour to yourself, somewhere where you won't be disturbed.'

'That sounds good advice. I think I'll take it.' Mercy rose. It was true, she felt exhausted, containing her emotion had drained her. 'Thank you for showing me your album. It was... fascinating.'

With this understatement she left them, conscious of Jane Agnew's gaze boring into her back as she went.

She lay on her bed, her eyes closed, but she did not sleep. The story she had just heard went round and round in her head. Poor Blanche, she kept thinking, poor Blanche – she was so young and there was no one she could turn to. Was it any wonder she was so bitter about the gentry? It did not require much effort to imagine her hurt in the early days, her bewilderment, her fear. How she had supported herself there was no knowing. How she survived at all was a testament to her spirit. Yet she had survived and raised her son.

Mercy thought of her father; he was such a cold, self-centred being, totally impervious to the needs or feelings of anyone else. Had these traits been inherited from the self-indulgent man who had seduced Blanche then deserted her? The hypocrite who had callously lied to save himself?

Suddenly, the idea of her grandmother struggling to bring up a child who was so unloving, so self-absorbed, was too much for Mercy, and she began to sob. Sixty years after the event, Blanche's granddaughter wept bitter tears at the tragedy of it.

Peter noticed she had been crying the moment he came in.

'What's wrong, darling?' he demanded full of concern. 'Has something happened to upset you?'

'I've found out the truth about my grandmother! Oh Peter, what she went through… it must have been unbearable.'

He held her in his arms until the new wave of weeping abated, then he said, 'Would it help to tell me about it?'

She nodded. 'Joey must hear it, also. Blanche was his grandmother too.'

Joey and Peter listened in silence until Mercy told all she had learned. Neither of them spoke for quite a time.

'I've heard some rotten stories in my time,' Joey said eventually, 'But this one takes the biscuit! Poor Old Un, no wonder she used to hit the bottle. Who could blame her?'

'Who indeed!' said Peter quietly. 'You said nothing to Lady Agnew or Mrs Hastings about being their cousin's granddaughter?'

'No. I'm not sure why. Hearing her story made me see Blanche in a new light, I think I needed time to get used to this different view of my grandmother. The Blanche I knew was often difficult, yes and drunk too. Yet we suspected there was something more, didn't we,

Joey? She sometimes told us stories of her childhood when everything was idyllic and prosperous. A lot of people thought it was the drink talking; but it wasn't. It was all true.'

'Lady Agnew and Mrs Hastings are very well connected, you know,' Peter pointed out. 'There's a fair smattering of titles in their family, not to mention rather a lot of "old" money. Do you want to claim your place among them? It might be difficult to prove anything legally, though I dare say it's not impossible.'

'I don't know!' said Mercy desperately. 'I'm not even sure we should even mention it to Lady Agnew and her sister, let alone take legal steps. Oh, I don't know what to do!'

'I do!' said Joey decisively. 'You can please yourself. I say let sleeping dogs lie. From what I've seen those with "old" money have had a lot of practice at hanging on to it, and I don't fancy risking all we've worked for in lawsuits over some doubtful inheritance. Just having a share in this place has given me what I want out of life, as close as I can manage. What I haven't got I can't have.' He paused, then went on. 'Finding relations who are entitled to wear coronets isn't going to make a ha'p'orth of difference.'

Mercy nearly asked him what it was he wanted so badly, then stopped herself just in time. She already knew. There was no flirtatiousness in the glances between him and Angie now, only love and a deep sadness. They were caught up in the oldest triangle of all. Joey could not help loving Angie, yet he was determined not to hurt Queenie, no matter what it cost. At least he seemed able to find relief from his private unhappiness in his work. She wondered what comfort there was for Angie.

'Perhaps you're right, it might be better to leave well alone,' she said quietly. 'I'll have to think about it.'

Mercy felt she had suffered enough shocks for the time being, she was quite unprepared for yet another. The next morning she was called to the reception desk where a departing guest was paying his bill.

'I hope you enjoyed your stay, Mr Griffiths,' she said.

'Very much, thank you,' he replied, pocketing his receipt. 'I think I should identify myself.' He handed her a card.

It took a moment for the neatly printed words on it to register.

'Oh!' she exclaimed. 'You're the inspector from the AA!' She had almost forgotten they had applied for entry in the Handbook.

'I am,' he smiled. 'It's the Association's policy for us to make ourselves known to the hotel management after we have settled our bill.'

A dozen questions hovered on the tip of her tongue, one more important than all the others. Oh, if only she could ask how many stars he was recommending. Instead, she had to content herself with inquiring, 'I hope you found everything satisfactory?' Then she gave a groan. 'Miss Manning! You were there!'

'I was indeed.' His eyes twinkled. 'Don't look so stricken, Mrs Lisburne. We appreciate that in the hotel business you are dealing with all the vagaries of humanity. How you cope is the important thing. You've nothing to worry about. In due course you will receive the official report.'

Nothing to worry about! What did he mean by that? She pondered over it long after Mr Griffiths had left.

'He must have been favourably impressed,' said Peter, when she told him.

'Not necessarily. He might have only meant that he would ignore the Miss Manning episode. It gives us no clue as to what he thought of the hotel.'

'There's no use worrying about it,' said Joey. 'What's done is done. We can't change anything now. We must wait for the report.'

Mercy found precious little time to brood on the matter. All of the high summer months were exceedingly busy. She was quite relieved to have one responsibility removed when the Mannings finally took their aunt to live with them. In what seemed no time at all it was August, and the Regatta was upon them again. The hotel was full, and they were all extremely busy. She was grateful for the hectic activity, in an odd way it gave her a breathing space, for not only was she anxious about the hotel's ratings, she still could not decide whether or not to make her background known to Lady Agnew and Mrs Hastings. Then the need for any immediate decision was taken out of her hands. The sisters announced that they were leaving.

'With such regret, dear Mrs Lisburne,' said Mrs Hastings warmly. 'If it wasn't an emergency we wouldn't go; and at Regatta-time too! We've enjoyed ourselves so very much here, haven't we, Jane?'

'For once we're in total agreement,' replied Jane Agnew. 'But go we must. An old friend has been taken ill, and she has no one else.' She held out her hand and took Mercy's in a firm grip. 'You have our address haven't you? One day, when you feel the time is right, perhaps you will write to us, or telephone? Having found a second Mercy I would hate us to lose touch.'

She released her hold and patted Mercy's arm.

'I'm very glad you came to stay here,' Mercy said urgently. 'Very glad indeed.'

'You've no idea what a pleasure it's been for us knowing you – oh, and your little girl. We had a lovely chat with her in the garden just now.' A mischievous smile spread across Jane's face. 'Such attractive names you chose for her,' she said. 'Jennifer Blanche...' And her smile grew even wider.

She hurried off, trailing her sister behind her. As she went out of the door, however, she turned and gave Mercy a knowing wink.

–

Regatta days always seemed to start earlier than any others and have more activity packed into every hour. This year was particularly frantic, for the hotel had entered the *Wild Goose* in several events, captained by Peter and crewed by enthusiastic guests. Not surprisingly, in the general pandemonium the post was neglected for once. It was late afternoon, when the crew of the *Wild Goose* had returned jubilant at having won their heat, before Mercy finally got round to dealing with the pile of letters on the desk. The one stamped with the badge of the AA was near the bottom. For a full minute she stared at it, her heart pounding. Then she told herself not to be so stupid, it was only a letter and it had to be opened. First, though, she sent messengers scurrying to find Peter and Joey.

'You can have the honour,' they told her, leaning over her shoulder to watch.

She wished her hands would stop shaking. Finally she managed to draw out two sheets of paper. The first was simply a formal letter, informing them that the inspector's report on the Villa Dorata Hotel was enclosed. Turning over the page her eyes scanned the printed words hungrily.

'Very high standard of comfort and cleanliness... staff most attentive and courteous... excellent amenities provided for convenience and pleasure of guests... surroundings and level of decor exemplary...' The phrases leapt off the page, then there, in the last paragraph was the vital information:

'It is unusual for us to award such a high accolade to an hotel as small as the Villa Dorata, but the general standards maintained by this establishment are exceptionally high. Our inspector particularly commended the warmth of the welcome extended to the guests by the management, and the happy, friendly atmosphere that pervaded throughout. We are happy, therefore to award the Villa Dorata Hotel four stars, and the hotel will be classified as such in the next edition of our Members' Handbook.'

The next few minutes were a total blur to Mercy. She found herself being hugged and kissed by her husband and brother at the same time, the tears pouring down her cheeks.

'Celebrate! We must celebrate!' declared Peter. 'We'll hold a party for the guests tonight.'

'On Regatta Night? Most of them will be out!' said Joey. 'No, let's have a personal celebration now, and a party for the guests and the staff at the end of the Regatta. You two go out this evening on your own, for once. I'll hold the fort.'

'What about you?' asked Peter.

'I'll take some time off tomorrow instead.'

It did not seem fair, him staying behind on such a night, but Mercy did not argue. He had a hopeful air about him, as if he had already made up his mind how to spend his leisure time. She guessed Angie was involved somewhere.

'That's a splendid suggestion,' she said. 'You're a dear, do you know that?'

'Naturally!' he grinned.

'It's all very well talking of taking nights off,' stated Peter. 'Some of us still have work to do. I must be off, I'll see you later.'

'We haven't decided where we're going to celebrate tonight!' exclaimed Mercy.

'Leave it to me! I've an idea. It's to be a surprise.' Peter kissed her on the cheek, aimed a mock blow at Joey, and left the office.

'You know who we have to thank for our four stars, don't you?' said Joey, after the door had closed. 'Your Old Man!'

'He certainly works hard, and the sailing—'

'I'm not talking about the yachting side of the business... What were the inspector's special comments? Something about warmth of welcome, and a happy, friendly atmosphere. They are the important parts of the report – things which lift the Villa Dorata Hotel out of the ordinary – it's all thanks to Peter.'

'I know what you mean,' said Mercy, understanding him at last. 'He thinks of the guests as friends who happen to be staying with us, and treats them accordingly.'

'Exactly! This is one long private house-party as far as he is concerned. I don't think it has quite sunk in yet that this is an hotel and no longer his private home.' Joey gave a chuckle. 'I hope it never does sink in, either. The paying customers lap it up, the more so because he is absolutely genuine.'

'Yes, he's genuine all right,' said Mercy half to herself. 'He cares about people and wants them to be happy. That's what makes him such a perfect host.'

'And that's what gained us four stars! You take care of that man, do you hear me?'

'I will,' said Mercy, and she meant it.

–

Peter was extremely mysterious when they drove away from the hotel, later that evening.

'Where are we going to dine?' Mercy asked.

'Wait and see!' was the only reply she got.

At first she did not recognize the little restaurant in Torwood Street. Only when they stepped inside did she know it for the place where she and Peter had eaten supper on the night they first met.

'It's exactly the same!' she exclaimed in delight.

'I fancy the lighting is electric now instead of gas, and I hope they've changed the tablecloths, otherwise I think I agree with you.'

'Fool!' she said fondly.

'You wouldn't have called me that then.'

'Oh no! I was far too shy of you! You seemed like a being from another world to me.' She smiled at the memory. 'I was so ashamed of my rough hands I kept my gloves on.'

'So you did! I'm glad you don't have to feel so conscious any more.' He reached across and covered her hand with his. 'I ordered our meal when I booked the table. Lamb cutlets, with a good Muscadel to drink. I hope you don't mind.'

'You remembered!'

'Of course I remember! I haven't forgotten a single detail about that night, and I never will!'

It was like stepping back in time. The years were pushed away, and all the emotion of their first meeting came flooding back as they ate the same food and sipped the same wine.

'This is ridiculous,' Mercy said softly. 'I've been married to you all these years, yet I feel just as I did then, unreal and excited and very happy.'

'Good,' said Peter. 'The evening isn't finished yet, there's more to come.'

When they had eaten, he drove her through such a warren of side streets that Mercy had no idea where she was. They left the car, turned a corner, and there were the lights of the seafront and the pier below them, reflected in the dark waters of the bay. Peter led her along a narrow path bordered by bushes. As soon as she set foot on it Mercy got her bearings.

'Rock Walk!' she exclaimed.

'Right! We're in good time for the fireworks.'

'The fireworks! Good heavens, I'd forgotten all about them!'

'I hadn't. For years I've wanted to bring you back to the exact spot where we met, just the two of us, but somehow with the children… Now, if we can only find where you were…'

'It's down a little, I think, and further over. Oh, it's still there! The bridge! That's where Dolly and I stood all those years ago to watch the Regatta fireworks.'

'And where you caught the eye of a couple of young mashers. My, didn't I think myself dashing in those days!'

'Well, you were very dashing! I was so impressed.'

'No, you weren't. You didn't want to have anything to do with me. If Dolly hadn't wandered off with Freddie Parkham you'd never have gone with me at all.'

'Perhaps I wouldn't.'

She said the words with wonder. A chance happening, choosing this one spot from which to watch the fireworks, had altered her whole life. Anywhere else and she would never have met Peter. Her entire future had depended upon such a slender thread; she had never realized it before. She clutched at the rough rail of the bridge, and drank in the cool leaf-scented air. Everything had altered so little! The ilex bushes and the palms and the tropical shrubs had grown in

392

the intervening years, shrouding the cliff face with greenery. Looking down, the lights along the pier and bordering the sea were brighter, there were more cars crawling at a snail's pace through the crush, the ladies' hats were smaller, less flower-like. These were the only changes. The atmosphere was still the same, even up here among the people who thronged the precipitous Rock Walk to get a better view. The feeling of light-hearted anticipation, the good-humoured excitement had not altered.

'They're still the same, and still so beautiful,' she breathed.

'What are?' asked Peter.

'The yachts. They could be a little town, out there on the water, with all their lights.' She gave a laugh. 'I remember looking at them when I was here with Dolly and thinking, if Blanche's stories were true I might have some grand relations out there on one of those yachts who would recognize me and rescue me from poverty, so that I could become a lady. Such silly dreams!'

'You always were a lady,' said Peter, putting his arm about her and drawing her close. 'Right from the first moment I met you.'

'But you were the one who rescued me from poverty. You've given me so much. And it all began through meeting you here.'

'Yes, that Regatta Night before the war has a lot to answer for. I've often wondered if you had any regrets.' His voice had suddenly grown serious.

'About meeting you? Never!'

'I've sometimes made you unhappy, and things haven't always been easy for you.'

'We made each other unhappy at times! And, anyway, things were far harder for me before I met you.'

'Yes, I suppose so. Anything would be better than the life you used to lead.'

'I didn't marry you to get away from being poor! Never think that!' she exclaimed, appalled at the thought.

'I wouldn't have blamed you...'

'I married you because I loved you. I still do!'

His sigh of relief was barely audible above the rustling of the wind in the leaves.

'Is that what you thought?' she was horrified. 'All these years you've thought I married you for your money?'

'Only in my darker moments,' he admitted. 'Which bothered me, for it turned out it was money I didn't always have!'

'Peter Lisburne, you're a fool!' she declared so vehemently that heads turned in their direction. 'But you are a man in a million, and I love you for it,' she added more quietly. 'I can't think of anyone else who would worry about not having the money his wife had married him for! I couldn't help loving you!'

'A very ungrammatical statement!' Peter said. 'But I thank you for it, because I fell in love with you the moment I saw you standing on this bridge looking out over the bay, and I've never stopped. No matter how things have looked, I promise you, I've never stopped loving you.'

His arms held her more tightly now, and she nestled against him, happy to feel his closeness, yet too moved to speak.

'Your other dreams have come true, too. You have met your grand relations,' he said. 'You can join the realms of the aristocracy, if you want.'

'No,' she said, without a hint of doubt in her voice. 'Being a lady and well-born and all that nonsense – it doesn't matter any more. I suppose that's what happens to dreams, they come true when they're no longer important. Oh, I shall keep in touch with Lady Agnew and her sister, not because I want a place in their family tree, but because I like them both, particularly Jane. She reminds me so much of Blanche I want to know her better.' From somewhere below the strains of a dance band rose above the hubbub of the crowd. The singer could just be heard. He was singing 'I Want to Be Happy!'

To Mercy the words of the song summed up her feelings exactly. Happiness for those she loved, and for herself, that was what she wanted. She knew at last what was truly important. She gave a contented sigh and put her hand into Peter's. It was Regatta Night, and life was far better than anything she could ever have imagined in her dreams.

With a bang a solitary rocket shot skywards, warning that the firework display was about to begin. As they watched it exploded in a shower of stars, turning their world to gold. It was a time for new dreams: for their children, for their future, for themselves. It was time for them to dream, again...